LEWIS

A. Barsell Carlyle

iUniverse, Inc.
New York   Bloomington

LEWIS

iUniverse books may be ordered through booksellers or by contacting:

iUniverse
1663 Liberty Drive
Bloomington, IN 47403
www.iuniverse.com
1-800-Authors (1-800-288-4677)

ISBN: 978-1-4401-7216-8 (sc)
ISBN: 978-1-4401-7211-3 (dj)
ISBN: 978-1-4401-7215-1 (ebk)

Library of Congress Control Number: 2009936530

Printed in the United States of America

iUniverse rev. date: 10/17/2009

Friday, Day 12

There was no question about the weather. The Caribbean sun was already so high and hot at 9 o'clock that sitting on the little porch in front of the bungalow for too long would bring sunburn of a hellish grade. A small black and khaki lizard, upside down on the ceiling, looked at Lewis, below, and bobbed its head repeatedly, then scooted off. Lewis looked dead-serious as he sat drinking strong French coffee and smoking, in sunglasses and shorts, here on holiday, a few days into an island stay that he hoped could give him some distance from, help him make some sense of, the acceptable wreck that passed for his life.

The fear was on him and in him as always, not on the surface, not in his eyes, but there just the same, and to be taken seriously. He was a serious man, and hoarded his fears and passing terrors, and often, especially when alone, showed it in the set of his mouth.

Lewis would be sixty years old next year, in 2003, and was confused, unable for some time now to establish a cosmic sense of right and certitude either to his life, the now of his life, or to what or where the life might be tomorrow or the next day, assuming a next day, as all men must.

His path was confused in looking back upon it, although, he thought he knew that he had made some sense of segments of it and so had come to live it in segments, all leading, he thought, to no point at all except to the point he currently occupied, several hundred miles south-southeast of Florida. He was happy for a moment at the thought the he was not in Florida, where the old people went and waited. He did not like to eat dinner at five o'clock, would never attend an Early-Bird special, old folks depressed him more each year.

He lit another Lucky Strike, as he did each ninety minutes unless prevented by evil circumstance, and as he had been doing for almost fifty years. He was unconvinced that cigarettes would kill him, and knew the odds were better than even that something else would get him first. Cigarettes didn't scare him, rather, they comforted him. So he smoked cigarettes and drank coffee and alcohol and thought about women and took the drugs he needed and

1

went to sleep, when he could, and got up, on a pretty stable schedule, and built a lot of his life around these actions and thoughts, plus others. This was all boringly normal, and he revered and needed this normalcy. Although he had to admit that the thoughts of women and of sex with women were just as frequent as always, but proportionately greater than the actual having of sex with women had become, and sort of assumed that this was pretty much his fault, but was grossly unprepared to do anything at all about it that would interfere with his repetitive but rudderless routine. And there was the fear.

The problem Lewis thought he faced this day, as he sat on his porch, not so far from the beach, was no longer merely his own confusion and perhaps sadness about how he had so unequivocally lost his way. He was pretty sure, from his observation of others, from his reading, from all of the millions of contacts with the ideas of other during his life so far, that most people, most men, lived a life of day-to-day mechanistic reaction to the world. But a problem had arisen for him, personally, in the course of the meaningless and safe nothingness of his reactions and inactions, had slipped into his consciousness and dour isolation like a dope fiend into an unlocked condo. He continued to hope that the problem would just snatch the TV set and laptop, check the medicine cabinet for Percodan, and leave to go get high, and not come back, at least not right away. This hadn't happened yet: the interloper was hanging around, making a light lunch, taking a nap, and perhaps, waiting for him to come home.

Monday, Day 1

When the telephone had bleeped at 2:28 in the morning at the Vermont house, Lewis had been in a rare deep sleep, and did not pick up the receiver until the beginning of the fourth and last tone before the message went to the recorder. He wasn't truly conscious when he first heard the voice at the other end, and had trouble later trusting his memory of the call. He wished, later, that it had been the machine, and not him, that had picked up.

"Lewis…Lewis Melton?"

"This is he."

"Hey, Man, you're alive….I knew you'd be there….I got your number from Janey. I'm a little fucked up — I don't drink much, now, but it really fucks me up — I've been drinking all day — say, sorry, what time is it there?"

"It's two in the fucking morning. Who is this?"

"Shit, man, I'm sorry, but I had to talk to somebody who's there, you know…to you, I mean."

"Who the hell is this? Do I know you?"

"This is Billy, Man, from the Island, but I'm on the coast, I've been out here a while."

"Billy, it's been, what, thirty years! No — more than that — shit, we're getting old….how are you? You sound the same — drunk. The last time I saw you, you were headed off-island, all fucked up on heroin."

"I'm clean, mostly, now. I got clean from the dope a few years back; it was a bitch. I'm okay now."

Lewis was becoming more awake, and less oriented to the now. He was moving back in time and space, was sitting in a booth at the Bucket on Main Street on the Island, watching Billy going out the door for the last time to catch the ferry to America, as they called the mainland.

"Well, Billy, it's great to hear from you. Can you call me some other time, when I'm awake, and when you're sober? We can catch up then. I don't like to talk to drunks."

"Sure, sure, but I called for a reason. I gotta tell you something, man, you need to know. Doc is alive. I saw him last week in San Francisco. I spoke to him, he's alive, and he wants to find you. He asked about you, didn't really want to talk about much else. I thought the fucker was dead! Kinda freaked me out when I saw him, 'cause he looks pretty much the same as ever. You know how we all thought he was dead after that rip-off, and we thought you were dead, too. I told him you were dead. He said no, said he knew you were alive, and had to talk to you."

Lewis listened to the voice coming from so far away, and began to feel the anxiety that slept in his brain uncoiling, also waking for the day. As he listened to Billy, he tried to picture Doc, looking just the same, but thirty or thirty-five years older, and had no trouble seeing him, hearing him insisting that Billy tell him what he needed to know. Doc had never been a shy man, and perhaps had been intimidating to some. There had always been an intensity to him that came off him like a smell, like the smell of melting insulation on hot wires, slow and predictive. The voice continued.

"That's how come I ended up talking to Janey — she lives in San Francisco — she made some calls, and brought you back to life. Oh, and I think Doc talked to her first, but she says no. So Doc may have your phone number, too. You can't always believe Janey, you know. She hasn't changed, and now she's real sick, and the medication fucks her up a lot. So I decided I better let you know that Doc's looking for you. That's all."

"Billy, Doc isn't alive. They blew his fucking head off, I think. He was buried a long time ago. You're drunk, Janey is nuts, and Doc is dead. Let's talk some time when you're sober. What's your number these days?"

At this point, Lewis was sitting naked on the edge of his bed, smoking, getting pretty cold. The wood stove had likely gone out hours ago, and the furnace, set for 60, hadn't kicked in. It may have been 50 degrees in the upstairs bedroom where he sat. He did not like the cold, and didn't like late phone calls from apparently drunken madmen much more. He hoped that he sounded a bit pissed off.

"Billy, I'm awful glad to hear from you. It's late. Call me tomorrow."

Lewis hung up the phone, then disconnected the wire from the base of the instrument. It would still ring downstairs, and he would hear it, but the machine would do his talking and listening. He walked to the bathroom, the cold pine floor a shock after the wool rug in the bedroom, and took the middle-of-the-night leak that would have gotten him up anyway. He tossed the end of his cigarette in the toilet, and, now fully awake, went back to the bedroom to grab a robe and the wool socks he kept near his bed for chilly nights.

4

The ability to sleep through the night had become increasingly elusive in the past ten years, and he was fairly sure he was up for the day. Never a good sleeper, he now rarely fell asleep easily unless medicated heavily, and once awakened, had great difficulty falling back to sleep. He was half convinced that he only kept the Vermont house — an expense he couldn't really afford and a house he didn't actually need — it was a constant reminder of his unsuccessful marriage — mostly because there, usually, he slept a full six or seven hours. Perhaps it was the total dark, or the total quiet, or the fortress-like feel of the house, a small post-and-beam framed structure perched on the side of a mountain a dozen miles from Brattleboro. The telephone here seldom rang, and when it did, he rarely answered, letting the answering device broadcast, or keep silent, the caller's identity and intentions. And now, he had started out of a sound sleep and answered the fucking thing, taken a nonsense call from a former friend, another goddamn acid-casualty who now had made him, Lewis, edgy and awake, and so he was justifiably upset as he crawled back into bed. He looked at his watch — he always slept with his watch on — and saw that it was still too early to admit failure and get up for the day. It was way too cold, and the bed was still warm, and he was asleep within seconds of his head meeting the pillow.

Tuesday, Day 2

When he awoke the next morning, Lewis was assailed with the sudden alertness that had always scared him a bit. Asleep, then awake. He had never dealt in long goodbyes, and moved from space to space in his life with the rapidity of action and consciousness that only the hyper-vigilant possess.

He rose from his barely-rumpled bed, hobbled down the cold stairs on painfully arthritic feet, and started the coffeepot. Then on to the wood stove: first, two sheets of newspaper, rolled in a crumpling motion, then, four sticks of kindling — pine or spruce — with a square of birch bark stuck underneath. One kitchen match would set it all off, if the draft was right. He left the stove door open to let the roar begin, then back with a cup of coffee, added two pieces of dry, quartered maple, and closed the door. He closed down the draft one quarter, and set the damper on the stovepipe half-way.

The stove now set for a bit, Lewis moved to the kitchen table, drank his coffee, and lit the first of the twenty cigarettes he would smoke that day. As he smoked (and thought, was there anything quite as good as the first cigarette of the day?) he began to plan the next several hours. He knew he needed to get some writing done: today was Tuesday, and he had promised a piece to the magazine by the end of the month, four or five days away. He wanted to get writing as soon as the room warmed up, and the fog of early morning lifted a bit. He did not think about the telephone call of the night before (actually only a little more than four hours ago) because it had not lodged in the compartment of his brain that dealt with today. And so he set about the day's ritual businesses.

Friday, Day 12

The sun was getting higher and hotter, and things would stay hot until the brief rain shower rolled through around two or three o'clock. By eleven o'clock, the beach would be so busy that a chair or umbrella would be difficult to obtain. Lewis slipped on a pair of relatively clean khaki shorts and an old but intact pink polo shirt, put on his sunglasses, and filled his pockets with money, cigarettes, a lighter, and a small plastic case containing a few pills that he might or might not need, but would probably take anyway. He grabbed his ratty old boat bag, already filled with a large towel, a book that he would not read, and a notebook, in which he hoped he would write. Setting out from his bungalow, he followed the path down past the hotel restaurant and office, and on to the beach. The short walk south, along the water's edge, brought him to his preferred location, about halfway up the beach from the ocean's edge, and fifty yards south of the tiny, open-sided beach bar where cold drinks, espresso, and a bathroom could be accessed.

He found a chair with the umbrella already set up (saving a two-dollar tip to the chair guy or girl), laid his towel out on the chair, took off his shorts and shirt and folded them into his boat bag, and gratefully reclined, full length in the strong sun. Later, he'd have to get under the umbrella. In fifteen or twenty minutes, he would apply sunscreen to every inch of his body, as all but the foolish first-day tourists knew to do. He knew that soon his bones, still aching from the cold of New England after three days here, would be miraculously cured by the dry and intense heat, and that by the time he got back on the plane to return to reality, he'd feel years younger, and walk without the slight limp he had developed in his right leg.

Lewis looked around. The bay, with very light surf, was the startling green-blue only seen in this part of the world, and not too busy yet, just a few jet-skis and banana boats. He recalled that jet skis were now being touted as "personal watercraft," a phrase that he thought sounded more like part of a Personal Ad in the Boston Phoenix. Mesmerized by the heat, he was startled to hear a voice next to him.

"Excuse me…Mr. Melton?"

Lewis rose on his right elbow, then sat up, looking to his right. Twenty inches away was a lightly tanned and freckled belly, and further up, smallish breasts with small, dark pink nipples. His gaze flicked down for an instant to take in a very pretty pussy, the light brown hair crew-cut, probably invisible from further away. To be polite, he quickly looked up into the face of a young woman, maybe thirty-five. He smiled minimally.

"That's me. And who might you be?"

"I thought I recognized you from a lecture you gave in Burlington last fall. I didn't want to disturb you, if it was you, but I'm a great fan of yours."

In the hope that a few minutes of polite conversation would make her go away, Lewis turned more fully toward the interloper.

"I'm flattered. Are you down here hiding from the cold, too?"

"I am, indeed. I love Vermont, but by this time of year, I hate the cold. I teach at the academy in Dunsler, so I have a week to pretend its summer already."

She threw her towel down on an unoccupied chair a few feet away, and sat. Lewis guessed that he had guessed wrong, had been too friendly, and now this annoying person would pester him until he came up with an excuse to leave. He didn't want to leave, and searched his brain for a strategy to ditch her.

"I hope you don't mind if I sit for a few minutes. I truly don't wish to disturb you — you looked so relaxed — but I just walked up the beach and back, and the heat has kind of gotten to me."

"No, no, not a problem, please, sit…."

Lewis thought, as the words left his mouth, that, first, it was an incredibly stupid thing to say, as the woman had already taken control, and had already sat, and, second, he had lost pretty much all hope of ditching the broad. He knew that he frequently made statements that he, at least, regarded as stupid. Unlike his writing, his essays, his opinion pieces, there could be no second, third, or final draft. He could not do anything else, so he lay back down, readjusted his sunglasses, and closed his eyes. He could hear the woman, whose name he did not know, rustling around in her beach bag for a moment, then shifting in her chair. He twisted his head to the right, carefully, as he had somehow acquired a painful neck, and opened his eyes.

About to ask her name, his sight caught up with his speech, and he remained mute. The mystery woman (as he had begun to think of her) sat facing him, legs wide apart, smoothing sunblock carefully between her legs, using a single finger to bring the lotion up to the edge of her cleft, then, with three fingers, back to her anus and then down the inside of her thighs. She looked up, straight at the eyes he hoped his sunglasses hid well, and smiled. So, then he said, "Forgive me, but I didn't catch your name."

"I learned last winter that this is absolutely the worst place to get a burn. I couldn't fuck — or for that matter, walk — right for a week. My name is Marian."

"I'm pleased to meet you, Marian."

He turned his head — carefully — back to a comfortable reclining position, closed his eyes, and worked at willing his erection away before it, too, took control. He thought of chain saws, ice, and other bad things, and felt the tumescence begin to fade. Fears, real or imagined, were a great antidote to the hard-wired urge for pussy. He relaxed enough to drowse, and drifted back in his head to the Tuesday almost two weeks ago.

Tuesday, Day 2

The writing had gone well for him. In the room where he sat at his computer, the February sunlight streamed through the south facing window, warming him, giving him a taste of the spring he longed for. By noon, the piece was done, eight pages of unassailably twisted logic, character assassination, obscure reference, and dark and savage humor that only the cognoscenti and those who pretended to that state would actually relish: others would read it because he was the guy you had to read to try to keep up with your presumed lifestyle and belief system, you had to know what he was up to, even though it was whispered in certain circles that he hadn't got it anymore, that he hadn't really been cutting edge for fifteen or more years, and that he was still read — and paid to write — more because he was a very minor institution, and bush-league *eminence grise*, a symbol of what was. If they stopped reading, or he stopped writing, everybody got old real fast.

But the writing had gone well, and he would be paid, and then his creditors would be paid. He would send some money to his child, even though she knew he was old, she was good at keeping the secret. He was pretty much okay with writing bullshit, and doing the odd lecture, whatever it took to pay the bills. His real reward for writing the bullshit was to be given the opportunity to continue to do so, forever — or at least until he died. He wondered, again, what he should do when he grew up.

Lewis looked out the window that faced the road that led down the mountain to town. The sand truck had been by, and he could just make out the tracks of another vehicle or two that had followed the sand truck, so the road was passable. On snowy or icy days, he had begun to get a little apprehensive about the road. The Road Agent for the past two years didn't plow too close to the tar, probably to save his plow. That was alright during a winter that stayed cold, as an inch or two of snow actually improved traction. But these past two winters had gone from cold to warm to cold, the snow had turned to ice on the road, and the goddamned Road Agent treated sand like gold dust. Last week the school bus route driver had refused to go up the hill, and had caused a minor ruckus at the Selectman's Meeting, including personal attacks directed toward the Road Agent, his relative sobriety (not much), his personal hygiene (even less), and so on. The upshot — at least for now — was a bit closer plowing, and a bit more sand. All of which cheered Lewis somewhat, although he doubted it would last.

He put the eight completed pages and a brief cover note in a manila envelope, grabbed his down coat and gloves, and headed out the door to his car. Once in the village, he would mail the envelope, and pick up a few essentials (cigarettes, the Boston Globe, The New York Times) and head back up the hill to kill a few hours until supper. Then, with the traffic thinning, he'd head to his place in Boston for a few days.

Guiding his old Audi down the first, and steepest, part of the road, Lewis felt a flash of anxiety, followed by fear, and could neither name the fear, or make it go away, as he sometimes could. He turned to the left, onto the second switchback of five, where the trees on the southeast side of the road prevented full sun from melting the ice and snow effectively. He felt, rather than saw, the patch of black ice, as the Audi's tail slid to the right banking; Lewis spun the wheel to the right and hit the gas pedal, precipitating a fish-tail until the studded snow tires finally found purchase, and the car straightened. He dropped the gearshift into second, and slowed, wondering idly, as he drove automatically, if the sudden rush of adrenalin to his heart was a good thing, or a bad thing. He'd have to ask his physician when he got back to Boston.

The village store was almost deserted. One old man — a Flatlander from the look of him — was scratching some lottery tickets. He had a string on one dollar tickets that stretched almost to the floor from the counter top. Lewis hoped the man would win. Behind the counter, Eddie, the store owner and generally the only clerk (as well as being the town Postmaster, Animal Control Officer, a Selectman, and the town's surliest resident) sat on a bar stool, smoking a cigarette and eating a package of fried pork rinds.

"Eddie, how goes it?"

"Life sucks, and then you die... other than that, not too bad. Some Connecticut asshole hit a moose out on Route 9 last night: he's up at the Hitchcock, and the moose is hanging in my barn. You want some chops?"

"Absolutely, when you get to it, but right now, I need a couple packs of Luckies. Make that three, actually. I can't find them in Boston anymore. Is the Post Office open?"

The store, in addition to selling milk, bread, beer, ammunition, fishing tackle, and an eclectic collection of startlingly overpriced groceries (of the can and box variety) was the local Post Office. Lewis maintained a box there, as well as his Post Office Box in Boston. He enjoyed the idea of, at least theoretically, living in two places at the same time. He felt much safer if no one, except for possibly his ex-wife, who had figured him out in about two weeks, knew exactly where he was at any given time.

"Sure, Lew, I'll be right over...."

"No rush, I need to pick up a couple things anyway."

"By the way, Lew, some guy was in here Sunday afternoon, asking about you, about where you live. Course, I told him I'd never heard the name. Looking at him, I didn't expect you'd be wanting to have him stop by for a visit. If I saw him in the woods during deer season, I'd probably shoot him, just on general principles."

"Did he give you a name?"

"Nope. No name. I don't think so anyway. I'll admit, I was a little toasted. Had a joint after breakfast, nice 'Ghani girl. I can tell you though, he was an older guy, but with long hair, black jeans...not a biker, though. Looked more like Satan, if Satan was a head-banger. I didn't like his looks one fucking bit."

Lewis shrugged the information off, for now. He would replay it many times over during that day. Left to his usual panic, he could tie the mysterious stranger Eddie had mentioned to the late-night phone call from Billy, but he didn't want to seem paranoid, or even interested, here in the store. If he did, everyone in town would know about it by tomorrow. Just something to remember, especially if more shoes dropped.

Eddie finally slid down from his stool, and stomped over to the Post Office side of the store. As he passed, he reached out for the envelope.

"Priority mail, right? Pay me now, or I'll forget, and put the money in the store register, and I'll never balance the fucking books."

Lewis chose his newspapers — only one Boston paper was left, and one *Times* — and walked over to the counter. He thought about who the hell had been looking for him, and why. He hoped it was the guy he had spoken to back in the fall about re-pointing his chimney. He had said that he'd swing by and look at it when he had time, although Lewis had not necessarily believed him. He'd been calling people about the chimney for years now, and nobody had ever come by to even give him an estimate..

Eddie was returning to his post behind the counter, having finished his Post Office business. He snatched a bag of barbecue potato chips from the rack on the way.

"Lunch, part two," he said with a grin.

"Eddie, this guy who was looking for me — did he have a truck? He might have been the mason I called."

"Didn't see one — this guy just kind of appeared. And he wasn't any mason I know, and I think I know every goddamn mason from here to Rutland."

"Oh. Well, I'd best be getting up the hill before it freezes solid again. I don't imagine he'll throw any more sand on it until suppertime."

Lewis found a less-aged liter of cola in the cooler, and, just to be on the safe side, added a big can of Aussie beer. He put his purchases up on the counter, waiting while Eddie rang up the bill. He paid, then headed out the door with a final caution to Eddie.

"You take care, and if that guy shows up again, get a name, if you can, and give me a call, even if you can't get a name, okay?"

"Yup, if I don't shoot him…"

As Lewis drove ever so carefully home for a late lunch, he speculated idly as to whether the skiers, leaf-peepers and summer people would continue to flock to his default home state — or to New Hampshire or Maine — if they had a glimmering of understanding regarding the depth and breadth of contempt in which they were held by the local folk. The joking about shooting strangers, he suspected, was more or less serious. He knew — had been told, in fact — that his living in this town, at least part-time, for going on forty years had moved him up only a notch or two in the estimation of the natives. His place was known as the "old Blood place," for the family that had owned and farmed the land for two hundred years before he had bought a small piece of it back in the late Sixties. Maybe when he died and the place was sold, or kept by his children or sold , it would become the "old Melton place." But for now, he was pretty sure that if things went very bad in Vermont, and the groceries and the deer ran out, he'd end up in the stew-pot once they ran out of New Yorkers.

His drive up to the house was uneventful except for the anxiety that came flooding back as soon as he reached the switchback that had caught him on the way down. This is what happened, he ruefully thought, when he forgot to take his morning Xanax. He found himself driving so slowly that he hoped no one was watching: he was starting to drive like a fucking Senior Citizen. His angry and methodical tearing-up of the cards and letters that the AARP seemed to be sending with increased frequency — almost weekly now — had not done much to slow the implacable advance of his decrepitude.

When he finally arrived home, Lewis brought his groceries in and opened the can of beer, took his forgotten medication, and set three eggs to boil. He would have a couple of egg salad sandwiches with the last warm half-can of beer, and then fart horribly for several hours as he split and stacked wood, his only exercise, and a mindless task that he did not well, but meditatively and steadily. He never had as much wood on hand as he thought he should, although he really needed none. The propane furnace in the cellar worked well. He preferred the wood stove, perhaps because he felt it bought him some points from the natives. And he needed the exercise, or he'd be even fatter, a great fear for him. At four o'clock, he put away the splitting maul, and dragged himself in to the couch in the warm and darkening living room for a nap. At five or so, he'd awaken, make a pot of strong coffee for the drive, and hit the road for the two-and-a-half-hour trip to Boston.

Friday, Day 12

Lewis emerged from his nod in the sun with a start of fear that he had been unaware, maybe even asleep, too long. Had he remembered to put sunblock on? The sun here would raise blisters in a little more than an hour on those unwary, seriously Caucasian fools who tempted fate. He checked his watch, and sat up, relieved that only twenty minutes had passed.

He saw that Marian, who had planned to sit down for a brief rest, was lying on her back on the chaise. She wore dark glasses, and had a baseball cap pulled down over her eyes. He could not tell if she were awake or asleep, but took the chance to inventory her features.

She seemed a bit less than average height, but he could not be certain. Her auburn hair was quite short, and showed small ears with small gold rings in the lobes. Her features were a bit too sharp to be called pretty, but the whole package was not unattractive, her nose and chin were more pointed than rounded, and matched her breasts in this regard. Her face and chest, abdomen, arms and legs were uniformly lightly tanned — a reddish tan, a new tan — and uniformly freckled. She wore a wristwatch with a cheap leather band, and a slim gold bracelet on the other wrist.

She was not fat. He could make out her ribs, and her legs were slim, at least from the knee down. Her thighs were full, and he'd bet that her ass was not small, and she had a rounded belly, even lying on her back. She did not appear to be a fitness freak. And, as he had noticed earlier, she possessed the only pubic crew-cut he could remember seeing, and surely the only one on this two-mile clothing-optional beach. The style tended to run to three extremes for women who went bottomless, which included almost all women at this, the south end of the beach. They were either fully furred, or shaved to a "racing stripe," or shaved smooth. The men fell in either the first or last category, with most not shaved. Lewis, himself, was not, although he still toyed with the idea. It would certainly be cooler, and might even make his cock look bigger.

As he catalogued her parts, as surreptitiously as he could in deference to nude beach PC, he began to consider that this young woman might be more than an annoyance. Maybe he could fuck her. He had not had sex with anyone other than his ex-wife in two or three years, and had become rather depressed about this state of affairs, which is to say, no affairs. Maybe he'd never get to screw anyone new ever again….perhaps he would go to his grave this way. The prospect was horrifying, and made him feel older and useless. He had to pursue this possibility. Marian seemed friendly enough, and even a little flirty, he guessed, although, like most men, he was terrible at picking up accurate signals from women. He had to hope for the best.

He decided she must be asleep. He stood, and as he began to diligently apply SPF 15 sunblock to every inch of his not inconsiderable carcass, he nonchalantly peered about to check out today's crowd. In the short time since he had staked out his spot, the beach had filled up. He was, as always, pleased to see that hundreds of other Americans and Europeans were as dumb and desperate as he, coming to lie out in the dangerous sun during the hours when the locals stayed in the shade, ate lunch, and napped, if possible. Lewis believed that the primary cause of skin cancer was not excessive sun, but excessive sun for only the short periods of a week or two or four that most denizens of the temperate climes could claim as theirs.

Lewis had preferred "clothing optional" beaches since the 'sixties. He still believed, and often acted upon the old maxim "If it feels good, do it," and sunning and swimming bare-ass felt great. He additionally knew from experience that a group of naked people is more honest, affable, and respectful of each other than a group of clothed people. When all of one's corporeal imperfections and shortcomings (or beauty, or perfection) are exposed, the playing field is more level.

Nude beaches had yet another benefit, to his way of thinking: he almost never thought about sex when surrounded by naked people. Whether this was due to simple sensory overload, or of the presence of so many seriously overweight, out-of-shape sun-worshipers — about thirty percent on any given day, he reckoned — the effect was the same. As was true with many of his species (human males) Lewis could only truly relax during those brief periods of time when thoughts about sex did not occupy a substantial part of his brain. He was, therefore, disturbed (although not unhappy) that Marian had so quickly turned his thoughts to prurient speculation.

As Lewis' brain began a slow retreat from carnal musings involving Marian, it became more aware of one of its many internal alarms flashing and buzzing in a paranoid tattoo. Thoughts about the telephone call from Billy began to link with questions prompted by Eddie's report from the general store. Lewis, having what could be most forgivingly diagnosed as a Generalized Anxiety

Disorder, did not much cotton to the idea of unidentified persons asking after him. His notoriety was not that great, not even in the tiny Vermont town where he lived. But the information was too limited to bloom into a workable paranoid fantasy at this stage, and the alarms began to fade, after prompting only the briefest of flutters in his chest, so he shut it down.

A different feeling — hunger — began to make itself felt in his gut, and Lewis grudgingly considered that he would have to get up and walk to the beach bar or the restaurant, a bit further away, soon, unless one of the beach waiters or waitresses wandered by first. He decided that he had better check with Marian to see if she, too, wanted something. He leaned and then reached across the two or three feet separating them, and touched her reddening shoulder lightly. She really was cute, if not downright pretty, he decided. Marian stirred, pushed her hat and sunglasses up, and looked at him.

"Hi."

"Hello again. Sorry to wake you. I'm thinking of getting some lunch. Can I get you anything?"

"Hold on, I'll go with you....are you just going up to the bar?"

Marian fished a small, colorfully beaded purse from her beach bag, and stood. Lewis revised his estimate: she was shorter than he had thought. Her boobs, when she stood, assumed an almost conical shape. She raised her arms above her head and stretched, and smiled.

"Let's go. I'm hungry, and terribly thirsty."

Lewis allowed the woman to walk slightly ahead of him, his intent of course to better observe her back, which he found as enchanting as her front. She did not have the high and rounded boyish ass that so many young women seemed to cultivate — or were they born that way? She was in good shape, but not the I-work-out-at-the-gym-five-times-a-week good shape that he found intimidating. He reached the bar a step behind her.

They ordered: a can of iced tea for him and a beer for her, and a Kosher, all-beef hot dog for each. The bartender, a young French man with the darkest tan that Lewis had ever seen, regarded them with mild scorn and a refusal to speak English. He presented the bill in francs, and grudgingly accepted twelve dollars American as payment. Lewis loved the French sense of reserved disgust for all non-French speaking people, and hoped that if he were ever reincarnated that, at least one time, he would come back as a French man. He would finally be allowed, and even expected, to treat most of the human race in the way that he felt toward them.

Having returned to their chairs on the beach, Lewis and Marian sat and devoured the hot dogs in a very few minutes and without conversation. Lewis thought that sitting naked on a beautiful beach in the Caribbean, and eating lunch with an equally naked, not unattractive young woman was pretty damn close to as good as life would ever get for him. He thought that this was not likely to happen many more times in what remained of his life. He was almost always aware of his age these days. He was no longer middle-aged, even by the most benign figuring, and the potential finality of all his actions and thoughts was more comfort than curse. He could control that which he could quantify, and the less of life that potentially remained, the easier the handicapping of the likely remainder. He was beginning to feel blissfully absolved of the need for long-term planning and performance. He was starting to feel the freedom that a self-aware condemned man might feel. He was having a very good day.

Tuesday, Day 2

When Lewis finally pulled his car into a parking space on Phillips Street, he was tired, angry, and relieved. The short walk to his apartment two streets away would be a piece of cake compared to the twenty-five minutes that he had just spent driving around Beacon Hill, looking for a more-or-less legal (as in possibly a ticket illegal if need be, but not tow-able or boot-able illegal) spot to leave the Audi. He had a resident parking sticker, which was of little help as many more were issued than there were existing spaces to park. The space he had finally settled on was, at best, sixteen inches longer than the car, and had required backing up over a snow bank onto the sidewalk and almost through some poor bastard's front door, before pulling forward into the slot. Even with power-assisted rack-and-pinion steering, he had had to wrench the wheel mightily while looking backward. The bursitis in his right shoulder was now shrieking and intense, and showed every intention of staying that way. He conjectured loudly and with foul curses that he was now truly falling apart, and that it was all the fault of these fucking goddamn assholes who did not know how to park, taking up spaces better reserved for old bastards like him. He wondered how he could finagle a handicapped plate, and if he could, whether it would help. Then he got out of his car with his ancient brown leather traveling bag/briefcase/pill stash/book bag, and silently began the slog up the icy sidewalk to his building.

As soon as he let himself in to his two-bedroom, first-floor city home, he went directly to the fridge and extracted a Carlsberg Elephant, opened the bottle expertly as he walked to the bathroom, and shook two 10 milligram hydrocodone and aspirin tablets from the bottle that held his shrinking supply. He washed these down with the beer. With any luck, the combination, on an empty stomach, would give him a couple of hours of respite from the intense pain in his shoulder. It might help with the pain of awareness, too.

He proceeded to the smaller bedroom that he used as an office, and checked his email: a brief message from his daughter at Dartmouth entreating him for a few hundred dollars needed for a weekend ski trip to Maine, a

19

message from his editor — two days old now — mentioning that his piece was due very soon (thank God he had sent it in) and the usual messages from those who fancied themselves his colleagues. He would tap out some replies in the morning. There was no way in hell he could use his right arm or hand tonight, not even to slide the mouse around. He was more concerned about his ability to remove his shirt by himself. He went through his mail, sorting out the bills by importance (Amex card on top, MGH on the bottom), discovering one check, and promptly discarding all circulars and catalogs, even the latest from his former haberdashery, no doubt another horrendous departure from reasonable clothing into whatever they were trying to flog to the Slackers these days. Lewis was appalled by some of the clothing they carried now, and had converted to a smaller, more traditional haberdasher in Cambridge a few years ago.

Finally, he checked his phone messages. There was one from his ex-wife Judy, inviting him to dinner at her condo the following evening, voicing her concern that he rarely got a good meal these days. He very much doubted that he would get one at her house, but would go anyway. He loved her still and he thought she loved him, but they could no longer live together, for reasons neither could agree on. They had, as happens, become very different people.

There were no more messages, but Lewis could see that the caller ID light was active. There had been a series of calls — four, spaced by about twenty minutes — from an "unavailable" number. He thought perhaps it was those vile people who had been trying, not very hard, for years, to sell him vinyl siding for his house. He wondered how his landlord would react to finding his two-hundred year old Beacon Hill town house covered in vinyl. Finally, he ceased to care, and fetched a plate of hard, sharp cheddar and dark bread, and wandered into the living room, tuned his stereo to the local NPR jazz station, and sank, too heavily, into his chair. He would eat before the pills ate a hole through his stomach lining, and would sit, and listen to jazz, until he thought he could sleep. He would avoid thinking about his great advanced age, and his historical fucking failure to do anything right. He knew he would have the opportunity, again, to think of that tomorrow.

Suddenly Lewis was awake, listening to the telephone shrill from the end table a few feet away. His watch told him that it was just past one in the morning. Still a bit asleep, a bit stunned, he could not rise before the ringing stopped. The answering machine did not kick in — the caller had hung up. He forced his stiff frame upright, consciousness ordering body up to a standing position, and then two steps to the phone. He looked down in the dim light at the caller ID gizmo, the red light blinked, the "unavailable" tell-tale showed again. Thinking, finally, Lewis scrolled back through the previous phantom calls, and saw that all had been made between eleven at night and three in the morning. These had not been telemarketing intrusions, not unless the vinyl-siding sellers of America had embarked on a bold new strategy that involved waking potential marks from a dead sleep, perhaps counting on the element of surprise. Maybe they thought that the groggy and disoriented would be more receptive to their amazing offers and substantial discounts, discounts that they were only permitted to extend to the select few who were willing to allow their "home," due to its prominent location, to be a "model home," attracting new customers like roaches to a dark kitchen, a phenomenon not unknown on Beacon Hill, exorbitant housing prices notwithstanding. But he didn't think so.

Now, he began to worry. The hydrocodone was fleeing from his opioid receptors, his last Xanax was down to a weak half-life presence, and his bursitis was aching with a new and serious intent. He felt worse than he had before he took the pills, and now, who the hell was calling him in the middle of the night? Wasn't his life fucked up enough without this infuriatingly anonymous assault? Was there someone that he had offended so sufficiently that they were now staying up half the night to affect their revenge, and, if so, how could he get the bastard? So many signs, so far, pointed to Doc. But Lewis believed, as strongly as he believed anything, that Doc was dead, dead a long time. Lewis had to believe his memory was correct, or he was left with perhaps less certainty than he could tolerate.

No answers, he knew, were forthcoming tonight. Right now, he needed to go to bed. The thing that Lewis liked the least about living alone — although he greatly preferred almost all else about it — was that, waking in the middle of the night, there was no one else there to accidentally awaken, giving him the cue to go back to sleep.

It was far too close to morning to take any serious medication without screwing up his day, so Lewis padded over cold floor to the bathroom and gulped three aspirin and fifty milligrams of Benadryl. Oddly, Benadryl affected him more strongly than almost any controlled substance, and aspirin, at times, was incredibly effective for pain, so he crawled back under the covers grateful in the knowledge that he would likely be asleep and out of pain — physical and metaphysical — in fifteen minutes, awakening only with the dreaded Benadryl headache. He was asleep by four A.M.

Wednesday, Day 3

It was likely the smoke detector that awakened him, he decided later, but may have been the biting acrid smell of his coffeepot melting — not melting like a candle, so much, but more combusting slowly from the inside out: exuding its own plastic sweat, expanding outward and shrinking inward at different points, and growing shorter, sinking toward the counter, busy dying an appliance death. The glass carafe had cracked, but not shattered, and the metal heating surface glowed cherry-red like a cheap sheet-metal woodstove full of dry pine.

Later, when he had told the story to his ex, he used those exact words. She reminded him, then, that the locals in Vermont, back in the Sixties when the Freaks had first started to try to live up there, had called those stoves "Hippie Killers," as no one with any sense would use one, but, at forty dollars each, hundreds were sold to the Back-To-The-Land Loonies. Many small cabins burned down. Lewis wished, when he heard her, that he had remembered the appellation. Lewis was jealous about words.

When the alarm — or smell — had awakened him, in near-freakout status, Lewis popped from the bed like a young man, ran to the small kitchen, yanked the coffee pot plug (it was hot; he was burned) from the wall. He grabbed a dish towel and with this as protection, swept the bubbling, reeking mechanism into the sink with one swipe. He grabbed the spray hose, and doused the now-contained disaster with cold water for a few minutes, causing the carafe to explode in a spray of cheap *faux*-Pyrex shards. Then, instantly moving a chair to help his reach, he ripped the batteries from the smoke detector to silence the shrill alarm before, he hoped, one of his goddamn neighbors heard it and dialed 911. He could imagine how much more fucked-up his day might be with the Fire Department bursting through his apartment door, hung-over and wild eyed, axes at the ready.

With the crisis under control, Lewis managed, with the help of a huge and ancient screwdriver, to jack one of the small windows open a few inches to air out the kitchen, then, lit a cigarette with a finely trembling hand. Only adrenalin overload, thank heaven, not anxiety. Today, he hoped, could only improve, but was not likely to do so without a cup of coffee, a few more cigarettes, and a hot, fifteen minute shower so that he could move his already stiffening joints.

Rummaged from the old painted-pine jelly cabinet that supplied extra storage in the cabinet-poor six by ten foot kitchen, the ancient Nescafe jar held about four teaspoons of hardened brown crystals, which he hoped was instant coffee. He managed to chip out two heaping teaspoonfuls into a mug, added milk and sugar to kill the taste, and set some water to boil in an old white enameled tea kettle. Lewis despised instant coffee, but would drink it. The coffee prepared, he sat in his favorite living room chair, smoking, wondering why he had no recollection of setting the timer on the now-dead coffee maker that had apparently had no water or coffee in it, and how it had managed to combust. He was pretty sure that the directions that had accompanied it had said that this could not happen. As he had promptly discarded the directions after reading them, he would never know. His reverie was interrupted by the shrilling sound, identified after a moment of panic, as the telephone.

He caught up the receiver on the second ring, simultaneously scanning the caller-ID screen, and saw that it was Judy, his ex-wife. Calmed instantly, he answered.

"Good morning. I got your message. How are you?"

"I'm good. It's still early. You don't sound very awake for eight-thirty in the morning. Another bad night? You know, you're still the only person I know that I'd dare to call at this hour. I called early to see if you plan to come to dinner tonight. It'll just be you and me. I'll be out all day. Anyway, are you willing to take the chance?"

Lewis believed that from time to time, he could understand the arcane code that women spoke in, probably even to themselves. Today was a day that he believed that he could. He thought that he was being invited to their regular, but not frequent, dinner-that-ends-up-in-the-bedroom evening, and he was all for it.

"Absolutely. What time, and what will you allow me to bring?"

Judy paused for six or seven beats, as she always did in conversation. Lewis had known her for more than thirty years, and had no idea why she did this, except a vague guess that it was a manipulation of some sort. Maybe to give the impression of thoughtfulness, although he suspected that to most listeners, it, combined with the slightly spaced affect that had been her hallmark even before she got into psychedelics, characterized a problem with scattered thinking, perhaps a difficulty with focus when discussing even the most mundane issues. He did know that, while he had initially found it (and everything else about Judy) cute, it now drove him batshit, and had for at least twenty years. One of many reasons, perhaps, that while love lived longer than tolerance, they were no longer together.

"Judy?"

"Oh, seven, seven-thirty, I guess. And would you bring some of that good bread from the little place on Charles Street?"

"Okay. I'll see you then….and thanks; it'll be good to sit down with another human being."

"Oh, Lew, that's bullshit, but I want to see you anyway."

He gently clicked the receiver into its cradle and headed for the shower, hopeful regarding the prospect of a decent meal and some comfortable sex to end a day that had not begun at all well.

Tuesday, Day 12

Lewis finished his hot dog about two seconds after Marian did hers. He knew he ate too fast, and was cheered to see someone else demonstrating the same character defect. Brushing crumbs from his chest and belly, he could not help brushing also the top of his recumbent cock, his exceptionally sensitive and alert old cock, which immediately began its drill. Lewis began his drill, thinking very hard about polar bears and ice and chain saws run amok, but to no avail. His penis continued to fill with blood as he gazed at Marian brushing crumbs (not as many) from her chest and belly, as she looked directly at his lap and its changing contour, a half-smile on her lips. Lewis neared panic, and considered reaching for his towel to throw over the offending member, then considering that this might be even worse than sitting there with a soon-to-be raging hard-on.

"I think we should go in the water — it's getting hotter than hell," Marian offered.

"Excellent."

Rising quickly, they traversed together the twenty feet or so to the edge of the warm sea, then walked twenty or so paces to chest-height on Marian, just above Lewis' belly, covering what Lewis knew was, by now, a hard-on of the first order, an erection that a thirty-year old man might sport, one that was unlikely to disappear for a time.

"Do hot dogs always do that to you?" Marian chortled. She moved a bit closer, and he could feel her small hand gently close around his cock. Still smiling, she began an expert caress of his penis, and continued to tease him verbally. "Because if they do, you must have a string of acolytes at your door, bearing hot dogs."

Lewis, for one of the few times in his memory, was incapable of response. Marian cupped the head of his cock in her hand, and began a gentle milking motion, and he came without warning — strongly enough that he shuddered. She smiled brightly.

"I hope you feel better now. No more hot dogs for you today — or at least not for a while."

She moved her hands to Lewis; waist, and stretched up to peck him on the lips, at the same time bestowing a wet, friendly brush of hard nipples across his chest. She spun to the right, and swam away from him, heading north, lateral to the shore. She did not seem to be a very good swimmer, a failing Lewis thought he could endure. He stood there, watched her swim away, and waited for the vestiges of his erection to pass and for his brain chemistry to normalize enough for him to figure out what to do next.

Within a few moments, spent gazing toward the throngs of sun-worshippers on the beach, he felt secure that Marian and his actions had not been noticed, but a scent of paranoia remained. He had come of age in the U.S. of A., worse yet, in a small town in the right part of the Northeast, where any public display of affection was frowned upon, let alone sex in public. What sort of disapproval and punishment might follow an underwater hand-job? He could only guess. And he didn't, really, give a rat's ass. He felt better than he had for a long time, and could not focus on consequences, but could, and did, swim and the walk to shore, and up past scores of naked, absolutely disinterested people, searching for his spot under the high, hot sun. He found his chair, and Marian's chair with her towel and beach bag. She had not yet abandoned him.

Intending after food and sex to sleep, Lewis adjusted his chair to be more or less under the umbrella and in a fully reclining position, gently shook out and smoothed his towel, and began to apply more sunscreen. He was not fully convinced of the waterproof capabilities it advertised, and could not take the chance of a burn. He was keenly aware of the nude beach protocol for sun-screen application by a male, so began the process with his arms and shoulders, moving his ministrations down as he absently regarded something far away, focusing closely only when squirting the lotion into his hand. He did not actually look at his body until he had moved to his legs and feet, and then directed all attention to the even and thorough covering of his thighs, knees, the critical back of the knees, calves, and feet, even the soles.

While absently regarding the horizon, and actively observing his legs and feet, Lewis mulled over the marked differences in the behaviors of men and women, even in the application of sun screen. In applying sunscreen to their own bodies, all women that he had observed took pains to closely observe their activity and their bodies. Turning, bending, craning their necks, women, as he saw them, seemed to enter a plane of self-absorption otherwise seen only on a visit to the dermatologist. If applying sun screen inside, prior to going out into the sun, and if a mirror was available, he had observed the lotioning of backs and bottoms, backs of thighs and calves with heads turned so far around that that he feared for their spinal health.

Was this behavior the result of fear of skin cancer, or worse, uneven tans or burn-streaks, or was it related more to their obsession with their bodies? Did they behave the same way when alone, or if they believed themselves unobserved? Was it the same simple exhibitionism that he truly suspected was the motive for those nude beachgoers who made a point of their daily walk two miles down the beach and back through areas that, while technically clothing optional, were really the province of those at least partially clad? This seemed, to Lewis, like the subject of a great essay, or even a short story, if only he could put some meaningful structure and point-of-view to it, and have it actually go somewhere. Perhaps he'd run it by his editor.

Lewis lay down and closed his eyes, but did not sleep. His brain began to wander, off by itself to places it should not go. His thoughts strayed to questions like: why would a reasonably attractive and relatively younger woman seek him out on the beach, and within an hour or two, sexually assault him in the ocean. He knew — and so did his wandering brain — that although he was in pretty good shape, and not noticeably ugly or deformed for an almost sixty year old man, he was certainly not the best looking, or wealthiest, or most well-known single man in two miles of beach. What was Marian's agenda? The warning light began to pulse, again, slowly. Lewis, in his daily efforts to overcome frequent bouts of anxiety, suspicion and fear, had learned to ignore the warning light a good part of the time. He did so this time, also, and after a few minutes, drifted into beach-sleep.

Wednesday, Day 3
Thursday, Day 4

Lewis eased the old Audi up Massachusetts Avenue in the evening gloom. Almost-freezing rain, when he had started out, had turned to freezing mist, and he thanked God, again, for whatever German engineer had developed the excellent windshield defrosting system and the heated side-view mirrors. He liked to imagine that German engineering schools had whole programs devoted to the necessary bells and whistles that made driving in truly shitty weather possible. It was a shame, he thought, that it took the Americans and Japanese to come up with a superior all-wheel drive, which he did not have — he depended on studded snow tires all the way around, and had not gone off the road anywhere near as much as he deserved. As he crossed the Charles River over to Cambridge, he wondered if MIT had a shitty-weather driving improvement department, and if not, why not. Boston, Cambridge, and points north had autumn, winter and spring weather that challenged the best driver and vehicle, as evidenced by the scores of vehicles simply abandoned on Storrow Drive every first serious snow of the year.

Judy, his ex-wife, lived in Arlington. Most people driving from Boston to Arlington would take Storrow Drive, as it was at least twice as fast as any other route. Lewis would do almost anything to avoid Storrow Drive, terrified of the curving, two or three or three and a half lane highway that followed the Charles from Boston to Brighton, and then continued under another name. The road was posted for 30 or 40 miles per hour, but the average speed was closer to sixty, with the odd madman (or madwoman) going ten or fifteen miles faster. This, combined with tunnels, free-for-all merges, and exits and entries on both sides of the road made Storrow Drive host to a minimum of two or three accidents per day, per side, in good weather. Given Boston's precarious weather eight months of the year, Lewis viewed driving on Storrow as an invitation to mayhem. Given sufficient medication, he could drive on it, but only because then he drove pretty much like everyone else, and generally ended up scaring the bejesus out of himself. So, he took Massachusetts Avenue all the way to Arlington, and put up with the traffic and the stop lights, and generally pissed off his ex-wife and others by taking forty minutes for what could be a fifteen minute drive.

Besides, he thoroughly enjoyed driving through Central and Harvard and Porter Squares. It brought back memories of the Sixties and early Seventies when he had lived for a while in Cambridge, and when Cambridge was one of the two or three most hip places to be in the U.S., and with good reason. He missed those days, although, he could not truthfully say that he remembered a lot of them, just the feelings he'd had.

When he got to Porter Square in North Cambridge, traffic eased up considerably, and he was only another ten minutes in getting to Judy's street, and, through some miracle, finding a parking space almost in front of her door. Remembering to grab the bread that he had brought, and a small bouquet of spring flowers that had undoubtedly been flown in from some third-world hell-hole that very morning, he emerged most carefully from the car onto the icy sidewalk, and slipped his way to her door. Transferring the bread to the crook of his bouquet-holding arm, he knocked.

The door opened almost instantly. Judy reached out to take his hand, or perhaps to take the bread as it slipped from his hold, and managed only to grab onto his jacket as he slid sideways and lurched through the door, somewhat startled by this speedy, grabbing greeting. Judy was definitely getting stranger with age.

It was at least seventy-five degrees in the foyer, and Judy was dressed in a pair of light denim bib overalls over an old tee shirt, and as usual when inside, barefoot. Lewis, in heavy wide-wale corduroy trousers, an old and soft blue button-down oxford cloth shirt, a heather-green and exceptionally ratty old wool sweater, and an even rattier dark brown Harris Tweed sport coat, broke into a sweat immediately. He hated to sweat — to the extent that he seldom did — and hated that he had not yet learned that Judy's house would be so warm. He hugged her and kissed her lightly on the cheek, always uncertain of his current relationship, or lack thereof, with her, and what her agenda was, and how that would play out in terms of her reception of him.

"God, it's warm in here, you idiot. You must be roasting. Give me your jacket….and that sweater too," she ordered.

Lewis gratefully did as he was told, and followed this familiar stranger into the living room, admiring her and her refusal to succumb to age. She was fifty-four, and looked at least ten years younger. She had never been a great beauty, but had, when he had first met her, possessed one of the most impressive bodies that he had ever seen. The first time he had seen her naked, which was about four hours after he had first met her, he had almost had a heart attack. She still was pretty breath-taking naked, and he hoped to remind himself of this visually, later on. In their past, Judy was likely to dress in an innocently provocative way, revealing enough of her body to secure her power in most situations. He recognized the overalls that she now wore, he thought, as the pair that she used to like to wear with no shirt underneath, leaving the sides — and sometimes more — of her breasts exposed. She seemed to have stopped doing that a few years back (at least around him), perhaps due to the ravages of gravity.

He sat down on her old couch. It used to be his new couch. He had bought it one day, fifteen years ago, when he had apparently had an excess of money, and had set out to Paine's alone to refurbish their living room. It was tasteful and expensive then, and he thought, still. Judy brought him a cup of strong coffee without her having offered or his having asked, and sat down across from him with her own cup. She looked at him expectantly, as if waiting for him to speak, and then began to speak herself.

"Cinth called. She said she asked you for some money for a ski trip, and hadn't heard back. Are you going to give her some?"

"I just got her email. She didn't call me. It just seems so fucking impersonal. I don't mind giving her the money, but I'd like to talk to her."

"Well, she's your only daughter....I think it would be nice if you transferred some money to her account, or mailed her a check, or whatever. By the way, an old friend of yours called here looking for you the other day. Did he get in touch with you? I gave him both your numbers."

A wave of fear started in Lewis' chest, and as it rose toward his consciousness, he fought the panic he felt coming. He took a slow breath, and managed to croak out a response.

"Who called?"

"He mentioned his name, I think he said Dog, maybe Dock, he said you were old friends. Isn't he one of the guys you told me you used to deal with?"

Lewis broke into a sweat and began, instantly, to feel the effects of the wash of adrenaline into his system. His heart began to pound, and there was not enough air in the room for him to take a breath. He was certain that he was about to die, as he had been certain the last five hundred times that this had happened. His panic attacks were all pretty similar, and all a simulation, a dress rehearsal, for the end, it seemed. But he knew that he would not die, probably, and was just in for a few minutes of hell, or longer, if he were unlucky and without enough medication. It seemed increasingly likely that Doc was stalking him, putting Lewis' belief in Doc's demise at ultimate risk. What else did he have wrong? He felt reality receding too fast.

"Do you have any tranks? Xanax, Valium, whatever? I'm having an attack."

Judy bounced to her feet and walked quickly to the bathroom just off the hall that led to her kitchen. Lewis heard the click of the medicine cabinet, a sound he often, with varying success, tried to hide as he mined the medicine chests of friends and acquaintances for goodies. He was of the "run the water and cough at the time of the click" school. Others had their own methods, not often successful. Lewis thought that perhaps that was why few of the people he knew ever kept the good stuff in their medicine cabinet. Sure, you might find half a bottle of six year old codeine cough syrup, but never the high-octane pills. He would bet that the good drugs were safely tucked away in the sock drawer, or in the pocket of an old suit in the back of the closet. You could almost never get the good stuff.

Judy appeared back at his side in less than a minute with a glass of water and a prescription bottle. She handed him both.

"Diazepam, I think, for my back. You can only have a couple. I need them."

Without responding, Lewis expertly popped the child-and-arthritic-older-person-proof cap off, and shook two blue, ten milligram tablets into his hand. He tossed them into his mouth and drank the entire glass of water, only stopping afterward to consider that ten or even fifteen milligrams probably would have been sufficient, and now he would have to really limit his drinking to avoid the dreaded diazepam and alcohol blackout. Full relief would not come for twenty minutes, at best, but the very act of taking the pills made him feel better, to start to calm down. The placebo effect, or the drug-addict effect, he wondered. It was rumored — sometimes by heroin addicts that he had known in his younger years — that withdrawal symptoms stopped the minute the drugs were in their hand, even if it would be thirty minutes before they could get the heroin into their system. He hoped he wasn't a drug addict, but knew that he was a relief addict, and was okay with that. Better than the alternative, which might be no relief at all.

"Thanks. Sorry. These fucking panic attacks come every once in a while. Maybe 'cause you said 'Doc.' I did know a guy by that name, thirty years ago. But he's been dead for at least twenty-five. Are you sure he said Doc, or maybe it was just something that sounded like that."

"Lew, I honestly don't remember. This was a thirty second phone call, if that. I thought he said 'Dock'....why is this a big thing? It was probably one of your drunken friends just fucking with you, or just so crazy they think they're this 'Dock'....this is not a big thing. You came for dinner, remember? I've made a great Portuguese fish stew. Come in and help me in the kitchen, and we'll eat."

Dinner was better than Lewis expected, a heavy seafood mix with a light tomato-based broth, perfectly complemented by the sweet Portuguese bread he had brought. They split — unequally — a bottle of cold Reisling. The combination of the wine and the Valium Lewis had taken gave him just enough of that odd taste in the back of his throat to let him know that with another drink (or less) he might well slam into the dreaded, and instant, blackout universe that alcohol and diazepam sometimes took him to. And it gave him just enough of the alternate universe of warm and fuzzy euphoria that freed him of the last bond to the free-floating lump of fear that roamed his head, especially malevolent since Judy's unexpected reference to Doc.

As he helped to clear away the dishes and load the dishwasher, Lewis moved in, close, behind his ex as she stood at the sink, and reaching over her shoulder to place a glass on the counter, pushed his pelvis up against her bottom. Judy responded by pushing back toward him, and he took her in an embrace from behind, nuzzling her neck. He kissed her ear, as he deftly unbuttoned the straps of her bib overalls that rested against her chest, then the side buttons, letting the top of her overalls drop to her waist. Judy turned in his arms, and as she turned, pulled her T-shirt up over her head. Lewis remarked again, to himself, that for a large-breasted woman, her boobs had not fallen substantially since she turned forty. Within moments, they had stumbled, mostly undressed now, down the hall to her bedroom. They made love slowly, as two half-drunk, well-fed middle-aged lovers will do so well, and before eleven o'clock, both were fast asleep.

When Lewis awakened and peered past Judy's sleeping form at the lighted clock-face at six o'clock, he noted that he did not feel particularly good or particularly bad, considering his chemical intake and carnal calisthenics of the past evening. He thanked the god of pharmaceuticals for the good, long half-life of diazepam and thanked himself for his unusually moderate alcohol intake of the previous evening. He said another brief prayer of gratitude for the fact that he could still screw, and that his ex would still feed and fuck him, from time to time.

He was unsure that either he or Judy had any better understanding, now, of why they had divorced, than they had ever had of why they had married after many years of living together. They had, almost from the first, truly liked and loved each other, and had had good sex with each other from the first time that they met. Perhaps, Lewis mused as he crept toward the bathroom to take a piss and steal another pill to have with his coffee, he should talk with Judy about getting back together. Nobody was getting any younger, and it might be nice to have a companion to fall apart with over the coming years of crumbling decrepitude.

After a perfunctory washing-up (he would shower at his own place — he did not care for her soap, or her shampoo, or the color of her towels) and a large mug of strong French Roast coffee, Lewis kissed the still-sleeping Judy on the forehead, whispered "Good-bye," and silently let himself out into the cold dark of six-thirty Arlington. At this hour on a Thursday morning, he would miss the commuter traffic that, by seven-thirty, would slow traffic between here and Back Bay to less than a walking pace. He should arrive at Beacon Hill just in time to steal a prime parking spot from some poor bastard heading off to work.

He slid into the unlocked Audi (no point in locking it, he knew — they'd just smash the window to get in to steal the radio), turned the key in the ignition, and heard nothing. No engine sound, not the click of an almost-dead battery. He tried several more times, with the same, silent outcome. Although he knew next to nothing about the mechanics of cars, Lewis followed the socially appropriate model of male behavior, and pulled the hood-release, clambered out of the car, and raised the hood. He didn't need to be a mechanic to immediately observe that the battery cable, and every other cable, hose and belt that he could see had been slashed in at least one spot. He was clearly not going to get that early-morning parking space.

Friday, Day 12

When Lewis awakened, he looked at the angle of the sun, and at his watch, and saw little change in either. At two o'clock, the beach was at its most crowded. In an hour or two, many of the sunbathers and swimmers would head back to their hotels or villas or condos for the obligatory nap, or, if short-timers, might head into town, over on the Dutch side half-an-hour away for some shopping, or a late lunch, or to the casinos, for some early gambling. The urge to gamble can come on early, Lewis knew, especially if the last gambling venture had been successful, or terribly not so. He had experienced more than a few episodes of the gambling fever in his life, and so now, carefully, limited his gambling as he limited his drinking and his drugs (all prescribed, sort of, thank you very much) so that what he already knew was certainly a problem, ready to bloom into a disaster, did not get away from him. He so loved the changes in his brain chemistry that gambling (and other things) prompted that he rationed the pleasure, and found it even more enjoyable when sometimes denied. He had been raised, at least nominally, as a Lutheran, and had not managed to clean all the stains that had been left on his soul.

He believed, and would have been supported in this belief by former friends and accomplices, that he had the talent, for as long as he could remember, of becoming almost instantly addicted to any drug he happened to try. The sole exception was DMT. He had expressed to his druggie compatriots that a DMT high was, for him, the total spiritual awareness of a foul and deadly universe, ruled by a god who manifested his glory in the form and smell and feeling of twenty acres of burning tires, nauseous and reeking, dizzying and endless. But he truly loved all the other drugs, and so avoided their conspicuous and frequent use.

The sun burned like a fiery god in its own right this afternoon, and only a few amateurs lay out in the blaze without the protection of an umbrella. They would regret this. Lewis knew that it is not just possible, but likely, that one will acquire a crippling, almost hospital-level sunburn by exposing white

American skin to the Caribbean sun even with an umbrella — the deadly reflective qualities of water and white sand saw to that. The prudent (those burned already) used quarts of sunblock and any available shade between eleven and three o'clock.

Lewis sat up and peered around. Ten feet away, an enormously fat, naked couple, heavily tanned, lay sleeping like contented sea lions on mammoth towels. They would surely have collapsed the beach chairs. Another seriously obese pair was just to the north of the sea lions, and eating a late, large lunch. A bit further away was a very attractive, fit looking couple: the man looked like he might be a successful attorney, or the CEO of a mid-sized company. He had short, gray hair, and the good looks of a male model. His companion, applying sun screen to his shoulders, appeared much younger, and well-kept, in excellent shape for what he guessed was her late-thirties age. Her boobs were preternaturally full and firm, with the tell-tale roundness and lift of a plastic job, but the rest of her body must have been the result of good luck, good genes, and lots of gym time. As she stood to adjust the towel on her chair, Lewis could see that she sported the *de rigeur* racing-stripe pubic hair, abbreviated so that the fur ended a good inch above a cleanly-shaved pussy. She was a real beauty. Lewis felt some jealousy along with his appreciation. Marian was cute enough, but paled in comparison to this woman. On the other hand, he had to admit that, on his best day, he never looked like a male model for anything except, possibly, anti-depressants.

Turning about another fifteen degrees to the north, he spied Marian, thirty feet away and walking toward him with a surprisingly purposeful gait. She held two bottles of a local beer by the necks in her right hand. Lewis hoped one was for him.

"Hi! I hope you were looking for me."

"I was," he lied. "I've been sending out strong psychic thirst signals for the last half hour. What took you so long?"

"I had to use the bathroom, and then I had to escape from two island women who wanted to braid my hair, or put beads in it, or possibly both. Then I decided that I wanted a beer, and figured I'd get the old guy one too, and then I had to find you before the beer got too warm. Have you ever noticed how similar people look when they're naked? I had to look for very specific identifying characteristics. I trust that is sufficient level of detail for you?"

Marian smiled in a more genuine than coy way, and laughed. Lewis laughed, too, and wished that she would sit down, rather than standing there, so close, her nipples twenty inches from his face. It hurt his neck to look up at her face, but looking straight ahead might be worse. Instead, Marian moved closer, handing him his beer, and almost smacking his forehead with her right breast.

"Please — have a seat, or step back, or I'll be in trouble again."

Laughing again, Marian stepped back a foot or two, and crossed behind him to get to her chair. She was still smiling and chuckling, obviously pleased with her sneak attack on his libido. She sat, the, and turned to Lewis, and said, "What's next?"

"I'm going to grab another hour of sun, and then a nap, and a shower, and head into town — I thought I might go gamble for a couple of hours before dinner, or maybe after dinner. Would you have any interest in accompanying me?"

As soon as the words had been spoken, Lewis regretted his tone, his choice of words, everything. Why the hell not just say "Do you want to come?" or "Come on along!" or almost anything that would make it sound like he was less than ninety fucking years old, and terrified of rejection, which, of course, he was. He was hearing her potential replies even before he made his query: "Gee, sorry, but I'm meeting some friends" or some other hackneyed brush-off. Jesus, he was so fucking neurotic, so fucking fearful, it pained him, sometimes, to speak. Never mind, he told himself, that this girl had been absolutely, without question, up-front sexually aggressive, and that any sane man would be certain, by now, that she would say yes....he was so goddamn fragile, so scared that he acted like an old goddamn man.

"Sounds great....where do you want to meet? I'm staying at the Planter's House."

Relieved so immensely that he was sure that it showed in his face, Lewis suggested that they get together at the bar at her hotel, at five or five-thirty.

"Any later, and we'll never get a cab — unless you have a car. No? Well, I don't either, I refuse to drive down here, it's worse than Boston."

Marian agreed, with a smile that reached her eyes. "Driving here is no vacation, and it's worse at night. We'll take a cab. I need a long nap, and a shower, and I need to get out of the sun right now, so I'll see you later in the bar."

Lewis watched, enraptured, way past any pretense of distant politeness, now, as she bent over, her back toward him, legs apart, to stuff her towel in her bag. She gave him a double wink. He had to take this as a good sign. He watched as she stood, and as she walked away, slowly, up the beach and toward her hotel, less than half a mile away. Perhaps, he thought, life was going to get good again.

Thursday, Day 4 (Continued)

Lewis' mechanic's son had come, and gone, with the Audi on a flatbed. He had looked into the engine compartment, whistled long and low, and said the patently obvious, with some relish. "Somebody doesn't like you very much, man."

Lewis had awakened Judy, going back in to use the phone. He had no key to her place, nor she to his. She made more coffee, then left for work, instructing Lewis to turn off the coffeepot before he left. After a night of closeness, she did not kiss him on the way out. The first thing that he did (after her car had pulled away) was steal another Valium, and wash it down with scalding coffee. He called his answering machines in Boston and Vermont, and found no message on either, which surprised and bothered him. Whoever had fucked up his car didn't seem to have anything else to say. No threat, no warning. A savagely disabled car, probably not a random act, but possibly a misdirected one. Did Judy have a violently jealous boyfriend who watched her house, and took revenge on the cars of other men who stayed the night? Lewis would rather believe that, if he could, than suspect that someone directed the attack at him, specifically. Someone who would know where he would be that night, which almost certainly meant that they were following him, or tapping his phone, or both. Was someone stalking him? Was that someone also the person who thought he was Doc (who was, of course, quite dead)? Perhaps a better question to ask himself was: what argument can I make that it isn't Doc? Every single lead, every clue, said "Doc".

Panic tried to spiral up to his brain, but hit the benzodiazepine wall, and boinged back down into his sub-conscious like the cartoon coyote hitting a brick wall that the roadrunner had erected. Lewis was not a stupid man, but he was a highly paranoid man under the right circumstances. He was a man who sometimes felt himself to be greatly at the mercy of the unpleasantness that life could direct at him. He was, therefore, given to ignoring realities that did not fit comfortably into his carefully tended world. The idea that someone who, as far as Lewis knew, was dead, was trying to reach him by

37

telephone, and that the same someone, possibly, had now directed a violent act against his property, was far more than he was prepared to accept. So he didn't. He dismissed it, for now, and called a taxi.

The cab delivered him to the nearest car rental agency. He was given a choice of a small, suicidally underpowered Japanese-American mini-sedan, a huge, also underpowered Lincoln, and an SUV. He rented the latter, and drove directly to Beacon Hill, after stopping at a nearby hardware store to buy a new coffee maker. He was, through great good luck, able to find a parking spot only a block away from his apartment, and wrote a note in big, block letters on the back of one of the rental forms that he was, in fact a resident, and should not be towed or booted, and placed it on the dash where, he hoped, it would be readable through the windshield.

Lewis walked to his place, let himself in, and put a pot of coffee on. After a shower, he settled at his desk, and began to write. It relaxed him to write — it was one of the very few things that he could do passably well — and hoped to be able to get five or six hours of writing done before heading for his Vermont house for the weekend. From the sound of the weather report he caught on the noon news, he would need to leave tonight or early Friday to avoid a possible major snow storm that was predicted to move up the coast on Friday afternoon or evening.

The writing went well, and by early afternoon, he had a thousand words — second draft — and an aching back and neck. His ass and legs were numb, and his ashtray was full, so it was time to stop. He could feel his age in his bones when he stopped writing, and had to wonder how much his increasing girth was contributing to the decline. Just less than six feet tall, he had pushed past two hundred pounds a few years back, with a waist that had gone from thirty four to thirty eight to forty, and didn't seem to be through expanding. He was highly concerned about his size, and was almost as afraid of getting fat as he was of dying. He had even switched to light beer for a week, once last year.

He was worried about his drinking, too. He had experienced some periods, in his thirties, when the drinking got so badly out of control that he had considered going to AA, although he had not, and had been able to slow down and pull himself together with the help of his wife, his need to write, and the judicious application of medication when he thought that he was going to shake apart. For more than twenty years now, he had been able to control his drinking, and used other drugs in a way he viewed as moderate and reasonable. He slowed down his use of all substances from time to time, but could not contemplate stopping entirely. He was worried about his drinking and drug use, but he was starkly terrified of the fear that he knew would explode in him without his taking something, or a few somethings, each day. His concern was his fear of fear, fear of just fucking freaking out, as they used to say, and not finding his way back. He was afraid of many things, and having his back stiffen up and his ass go numb (stroke of some sort?) was enough to set him off, staggering almost legless (did your legs go numb with a heart attack?) to the kitchen for lunch, but first a beer or two.

He had not gone to the market recently, in fact, he rarely went to the market, and when he did, it was the local market down on Charles Street, or the general store up in Vermont. Large grocery stores were out of the question, involving crowds, lines, and other panic triggers. So the larder was pretty bare, and lunch ended up being a sardine sandwich on some half-stale rye, and a strong Danish beer. He felt better as soon as the first beer hit his brain, and by the second, as good as he'd felt in days, and he sat at his tiny kitchen table and read the Boston paper. The politics invariably fascinated and repelled him, a real freak-show here in Beantown. The level of corruption, greed and ignorance apparent even in stories that were only peripherally concerned with politics was truly appalling. Here in one of the few truly civilized cities in the States, and in Massachusetts, certainly a birthplace of democracy, anything could be bought, and anything forgiven. It restored his faith in misanthropy, and made him proud to be a citizen of Vermont.

After finishing the paper, Lewis checked his e-mail: nothing of note, unless he wanted to take advantage of some upcoming concert dates that his Gold Card was pushing to its members. He did not. In his twenties and thirties, and to a lesser extent his forties, his love for music and spectacle would allow him to put up with the incredible hassle of attending half a dozen shows a year, mostly rock, some jazz, but he hadn't been out to hear live music in a decade. He preferred to attribute this to maturity, and to his great sound system. He could sit in his living room in Boston and hear music that sounded at least as good as it would in person, with the added bonus of having to walk only a few steps to take a leak or to get a drink. But he knew, for he was sometimes honest even with himself, that he just didn't want to be bothered. His world was much easier to control if he kept it small.

The telephone interrupted his reverie.

"Hello."

"Mr. Melton…?"

"This is Lew Melton."

"Eddie, at the Valley Store….I thought I should call you. That guy was here again about an hour ago. I would have called sooner — I tried your place up here right away….but it got real busy, a shitload of skiers from New York came in and wanted sandwiches….anyway, that guy, the guy I told you about, came in for smokes and a Coke. He was real quiet, so I asked him if he'd caught up with you yet. He gave me a real funny look, and said, no, but he had contacted you, and he'd catch up with you soon."

"Did you get a name? Did you ask his name?"

"I did, I asked him his name, so I could let you know if you came in later. He said his name was Doc, and he said you knew his name, and he'd see you soon enough."

"Somebody's fucking with me, Eddie. The only guy named Doc that I know — knew — died years ago. What did this guy look like?"

"Maybe six foot, thin, long hair — down to his shoulders — blondish with gray, oh, and a beard. Black jeans, a dark sweater. Real thin- no fat on that guy. Couldn't see his eyes, he had those tinted glasses. Seemed friendly enough, for around here. But like I told you last time, I didn't get a good feeling from him. I got this feeling that something bad could happen, anytime, anywhere this fellow might be. I'm not afraid of too much, but he puts the fear in me."

"Jesus. Eddie, do me a favor, would you? Has the Chief been in today?"

"No. Why involve him? You know he purely hates having to do any policing. And he may not be the quickest guy in the world."

"Yeah, but he's a good guy, basically, and it's not like he has a lot to do. Ask him, anyway. When he comes in — doesn't he come by at the beginning of his shift for coffee and butts? — anyway, ask him to cruise by my place, check it out. Tell him I called, and I thought I might have left the door open. Or make something else up, but find a way to get him to swing by there anyway, okay?"

"Okay. If I see this Doc guy again, do you want me to tell him anything?"

"No. No, don't say anything. Just let me know. And let me know if the Chief finds anything. You're a good man, Eddie. I owe you."

"You don't owe me shit. And don't tell people I'm a good guy."

Lewis hung up. He truly did not know what to think. Eddie had described the long-dead Doc perfectly, but that was not possible- was it? Lewis thought back to the last time he had seen Doc alive.

1964 – The Deal, Cambridge

It must have been back in 1964. Lewis, an intermittent graduate student and occasional struggling writer, subsisted in the burgeoning Boston-Cambridge counter-culture, a small and conservative shadow of the doings in the Haight. His income was spotty at best, and, from time to time, he, and a few of his friends and fellow-travelers, often including a sketchy post-art school barfly named Johnson Edwin Booth, AKA "Doc" (he seemed to always have access to the best pharmaceuticals) would get some money together — most of it speculatively pre-paid — to buy large amounts of grass. On this occasion, he remembered, it was fifty kilos, at two hundred dollars per kilo. It would be re-sold (or had already been) at four hundred per kilo. Lew and his friends would double their money, and the buyers would sell ounces at twenty dollars each, making about one hundred and fifty percent, and supplying themselves with enough pot to last them until the next deal. Cambridge and Boston, full of students, always had an unfilled demand for pot. They were just helping out, they reasoned, and making a few dollars in the process. Capitalism was never mentioned.

It was a sweet deal, if you didn't get caught, or ripped off. Success depended greatly on the effective coordination of multiple events, something most Freaks (only the press used the word "Hippie") were not so good at. It was key to be in possession of the kilo-weight bricks of marijuana for as short a time as possible. At that time in America, fifty kilos — or even one — of pot could earn you twenty years in prison. Ideally, delivery would be followed by pickup by your many customers within a few hours. And there was another risk: there were people in the counter-culture, or on the fringes of it, greedy and willing to violently take the pot or the money when it was all in one place. If they took the money, you were in trouble. If they took the drugs, you were in real trouble, as you would owe a lot of people a lot of money, and they could be willing to get nasty to recoup it, or to satisfy their need for revenge. So, while easy money if all went well, there was always a danger of disaster.

This time, the worst had happened. Whether due to incaution, stupidity, or just plain old bad luck, no one could say. They — Lew, Doc, and three other guys, had put together a quick deal in October. Ideal timing, as the harvest was a month past, and the students were all back in town for the winter, so the prices would be good and the product would move fast and easily. Their cartel hoped to make enough money to slide through the winter without having to work. Lewis had pretty much completed his graduate study but still owed his thesis, and three or four months survival-money would give him the time he needed. Otherwise, he'd be driving a cab at night. Doc, a former art student, now in possession of a virtually worthless baccalaureate, and a journeyman alcoholic, simply wanted the means to spend the winter in a nice, warm bar, preferably in the Keys. The others — Tim, Robert (never Bob) and another guy whose name Lewis couldn't remember then or now, had all their own good reasons, and all were in a hurry. Rather than arranging delivery and pickup at a desolate location — usually a cottage on Cape Cod or a cabin in southern Maine or New Hampshire — they had decided to do the deal at Doc's place in East Cambridge. They had all the money up front, had divided up the profit, and wanted the deal to be over.

Doc lived on a short side-street near the Somerville line, chosen, certainly, for the cheap rent. He lived downstairs from a quiet, childless Portuguese couple in their fifties who were probably born in the neighborhood, and probably related to half of the other people who lived on the street. It was that kind of neighborhood; it was that kind of street. No one seemed to mind the quiet young man who was rarely home, and paid his rent on time.

During the day, all of the men who lived in the area were, of course, away at work, and the women stayed indoors, venturing out from time to time to hang out the wash on their back yard clothes lines, or to walk to the local market, or to yell for their children, shrieking and running in after-school or Saturday play. Doc, Lewis and the others figured that if they took delivery late at night, they could safely string out the pickups through the early morning hours, before the men began to leave for work at around five o'clock. There would be a dozen pickups, none requiring more than the quick transfer of a laundry bag of kilo bricks, a five minute transaction. In the darkness, no one would be likely to notice the activity, or, if they did, to divine the intent.

The deal started to go sour from the beginning. Delivery, set for eleven at night, happened, finally, at two in the morning. The "weight" dealer arrived horribly and obviously twisted on methamphetamine, agitated and paranoid, and counted the money many times, with a different result each time. Once satisfied with the count, the dealer and the five conspirators quickly unloaded the van, but not as planned. The bricks were supposed to be packed in cardboard boxes, but were loose instead, so they all carried armloads of the paper-wrapped kilos, stacking them in the freezing, cat-shit scented pantry just off the tiny kitchen. The perfume of medium-grade marijuana filled the apartment before the first joint was lit.

When the dealer finally left with his money and his paranoia, it was nearly three o'clock. Doc, Lewis and the others sat down in the sparsely furnished living room. They sat on worn pillows, except for Doc, who sat back, looking tired and worried, in a ratty green easy chair that he had snagged from the street the year before. In celebration of a deal half-done, they passed a jug of cheap Zinfandel and a huge joint rolled in newspaper, as no one had the requisite Zig-Zags, or the usual stand-by, a Tampax wrapper. The burning newspaper mixed with the pot smoke filled the room with a noxious, burning-dump smell, but no one complained. They needed to relax, and they needed to wait for the first pickup, forty minutes away.

The first furtive knock came sooner than they expected, and turned out to be a very nervous, very geeky MIT student, looking for the three kilos he had ordered. He didn't want to try it; he just wanted to get it and go, more afraid of the possibility of getting busted than of getting burned. Within the next two hours, all of the buyers except two had arrived, stayed only briefly, and departed with their goods. Things had proceeded so smoothly, and by now Doc, Lewis and the others were so stoned from sampling the wares with most of the buyers, that events had taken on the kind of cartoonish, suspended-animation feel that many found characteristic of the last few hours of a good acid trip. So when the front door flew into the room and crashed against the wall, no one reacted for a few seconds. The door was quickly followed by three men with guns drawn, the lead man swinging a Savage-Stevens 16-gauge double barreled shotgun back and forth in an arc , aimed about two feet above the floor. His two compatriots held what looked like 9 millimeter automatic pistols. All three men looked pumped-up, nervous, and Italian. They could have been plain-clothes cops from the Narcotics squad, but probably weren't.

"Give it up, assholes, NOW!" demanded the lead man, moving into the room, toward Lewis and Doc, who sat on the far side of the space.

"What the fuck?" asked Lewis, still horribly spaced and stoned, and quite unsure what was happening. As he began to stand up, the lead man swung the shotgun hard, up, and into the side of Lewis' head, generating a satisfying crack. Lewis actually saw stars for the tenth of a second before he went down, and went out, cold.

When he came to, whatever had happened was over. He could not hear very well, and could feel a trickle of blood still issuing from his left ear. When he reached up to touch the spot, he was unprepared for the pain the touch provoked, and for the size his ear had grown to. It felt like it was swollen to at least twice the size it had been, and hurt like hell. His whole head ached, and his vision swam a bit as he stood. There was no one else around.

The apartment door swung open on a single hinge. The cold fall air rushing in encouraged Lewis to try to get moving, first to his knees, and then, slowly, to his feet. Dizzy as hell, he shuffled warily in the direction of the kitchen, and found nothing: no bodies, no blood, no pot, no money, no sign or trace of a struggle. The next room in the shotgun apartment was Doc's bedroom, and was similarly vacant. Only a dirty sleeping bag on a dirty mattress, a pile of filthy clothes, and the rank odor of sweat and cat shit. No people, no bodies, no signs. The freezing bathroom was next, then the back door. Nothing. Nothing and no one. This was good, if confusing.

Lewis fumbled for the inside pocket of his leather jacket in a startled panic. His fingers grazed, then grasped, the roll of bills. The size felt right for the twenty-four hundred dollar bills that were his share of the profit, and possibly the only profit left from this deal gone horribly bad. Feeling a bit better — at least he had money — but still woozy as hell, Lewis wandered out the back door, determined to put as much room as he could between himself and the rip-off. He cut through several back yards, across the back half of a schoolyard, and out to the main drag. He was about twenty minutes, at a wounded amble, from his own place on the other side of Central Square. He had cleaned enough of the blood from the side of his head with his shirt cuff to pass muster in this part of the world. No one was likely to call an ambulance, or the police. He'd get home, crash, make some calls later, and try to find out what the fuck had gone down. Right now, he had his money and his life, and didn't want to risk either again.

Friday, Day 12

After another hour of sun, Lewis gathered up his towel and bag and headed directly for his cottage. He was staying, as he always did, at a naturist resort, and was not required to pull his shorts — or anything else — on, as long as he stayed there. It was a true vacation in all ways, as nothing was required. No dressing for dinner, so to speak. There were, of course, the usual admonitions. No gawking, no cameras (which everyone ignored), and sit on your towel, or wear something on the bottom, when sitting at the bar or restaurant. But these were usual nudist behaviors, and would be followed, pretty much, by such a civilized group.

The nudists and naturists who frequented the place ranged from self-conscious newcomers and occasional nudists to the more militant variety, many of whom shaved everything except their heads in an effort to be more nude than others. Lewis fell somewhere in between. He was not at all ill-at-ease naked, and tried his best (and failed) to not gawk, but did not see nudism as a contest that was worthy of him shaving his balls. The very thought of something sharp, or something buzzing, so close to his genitals made him queasy.

His cottage, with a bedroom, a living room, a kitchenette and a small screened porch was only a few hundred steps from the bar and restaurant and another few hundred from his favorite spot on the beach. He found the place comfortable, if a bit Spartan, and convenient, and preferred it to the more luxurious resorts farther up the beach.

When he got to his digs, he saw that there was no time for his intended nap, and decided he could get by without. After a quick shower to remove the layers of sunscreen, sweat and sand, Lewis dressed in clean chinos and an old, faded, blue Brooks polo shirt. He found a fairly clean pair of socks, decided against them, and pulled his moccasins on. He counted out several hundred dollars from his poorly hidden stash, and put the roll in his front pants pocket, then his wallet in his back pocket. The wallet held nothing, but would distract a pickpocket from the good stuff, if need be. Crime was very low on the island, but Lewis was a careful man. He grabbed a fresh pack of cigarettes, his old Zippo, and he was pretty much set. No keys, no bullshit, and only the slightest anxiety. Just to be on the safe side, he swallowed .5 of Xanax with some bottled water, and headed out the door, down the path, and north, up the beach to Marian's hotel, a good half-mile away. It was four-thirty now, and though the beach was clearing out, hundreds of tourists still lay in their beach chairs or played in the surf, while others had retreated to the beachside bars to begin their evening drinking, or to continue their all-day drinking. It was that kind of a place. Most of them were amateurs, not alkies, so the bars were loud and happy places.

Lewis noticed, as he always did, that the number of naked people diminished as he made his way north. Although the entire two-mile beach was clothing-optional, he had now reached the primarily American section, his favorite, where the nudity was more likely to be partial and hesitant. Almost half of the women were topless, many for the first time, he guessed, with very white or very sunburned boobs. The bravest also sported thong bikini bottoms, and were wonderfully self-conscious. He found nothing could excite his prurient interests quite like half-naked, self-conscious American women in a public place, and he was glad that he had chosen loose-fitting, pleated chinos. He figured he could successfully hide a small, live animal in those pants, let alone his ancient erection.

The local folk — both black and white — had clever sport with the newly-topless tourists at the beach bars. Lewis had deduced, through careful observation over the years, that bar-height was set to approximately the level of the bottom of an average American woman's tits. And the barstools were also coordinated to this relative benchmark. To stand at the bar close enough to drink comfortably, most boobs would rest on, or just above, the bar. Most of the beach-side bars were square bars with the bartender or two in the center. When a bare-breasted woman stood or sat at the bar, she would necessarily present her boobs for perfect viewing to the patrons on the other three sides of the square. Of course, for those women who had begun to experience the vicissitudes of gravity, and still, bravely, went topless, this worked less well, and presented an interesting dilemma to the drinker. Should she lift her boobs — either by standing or sitting very straight and throwing her shoulders back and hoping for the best, or actually, manually lifting her boobs up on to the bar, or should she give up, and just let them depend below bar level. Would this signify an inability to compete? Lewis believed that he probably saw the whole issue with more humor than the participants.

Continuing up the beach — almost halfway there now, thank God — and really just strolling and surreptitiously peering at any particularly attractive or startlingly unattractive women, Lewis was not paying attention, and was almost run down by a phalanx of fully-clothed day-trippers from one of the tour boats. Their Spanish was rapid and clipped, and sounded Argentinian. They walked fast, for the Caribbean, and were embarrassed and fascinated by the nudity and semi-nudity that they saw. These walking gawkers, who had come on the side trip expressly to see the strange, naked people were averting their eyes, were bumping into each other, were talking high and fast and laughing, joking with each other about the hundreds of people that, literally, surrounded them. They would walk all the way to the end of the beach, and would be disappointed when the security men would not let them take snapshots. The sunbathers, nude mostly, would laugh and yell "Take off your clothes!" at the hapless walkers, Argentinians or Italians or Midwesterners in their hats, Hawaiian shirts, white socks with black sandals, and the clothed gawkers would look away and laugh nervously. It was great fun for all.

Lewis moved up from the shoreline, into softer sand. He looked ahead toward his goal, and felt his heart speed up. About 75 feet away, down toward the water, at the tail end of the gawker group, he saw a man who looked exactly like Doc, his old *compadre*, not much different from the last time he had seen him 35 years ago. Dressed in black jeans and a black tee shirt, with long hair, dark glasses, and that walk that Doc always had, sort of like floating along. Lewis changed course and aimed toward the Doc-figure, not knowing what else to do. His heart pounded, his moccasins filled with sand, he picked up his pace.

Within a minute- no more- Lewis was exactly at the spot where the Doc lookalike should have been, with the stragglers of the tour group. There was no one resembling the man he had sighted, not one person in dark clothing. His anxiety subsided as his confusion grew. What had he seen? Maybe too much sun or too many pills, or not enough, or maybe, he thought, his mind was finally going. He knew or thought he knew what he had seen. No evidence of what he had seen could be found. He must have made a mistake, or had perhaps hallucinated, just for an instant. God knows, Lewis thought, I've hallucinated before, and will probably do so again. He recalled an event, many years ago, that still gave him the night terrors.

He had been up on the flat roof of his Back Bay apartment building, soaking up a strong spring sun as he recovered from a ten day drunk, one of his worst. He had had nothing stronger than soda and bitters for the last twelve hours; he was still a young and stupid drunk, and didn't know enough to taper himself off. He had opened his eyes and was sitting up to light a cigarette when a hundred foot high face of an old girlfriend rose from behind an adjoining rooftop, and began to scream, wordlessly, at him. Absolutely freaked, he had made it down from the roof and to the nearest bar in less than five minutes, and quickly downed a triple vodka and a beer before his panic had subsided.

He felt a bit like that now but knew enough to not start drinking on top of the Xanax he had downed twenty minutes ago. He figured the fear would go away, just as the apparition had. He was on his way to what he hoped would be a very pleasant evening, and wanted to be with this woman, Marian, more than he wanted to give in to the constant beast of fear, especially this new fear, a seemingly irresolvable fear about a very dead man who seemed to be seeking him out.

Again changing direction, Lewis turned away from the shore and back toward the strip of beachfront hotels and bars and shops. Marian's hotel was three hotels north. He was through the doors and into the beach-side lobby within a few minutes.

It was relatively cooler in the tile-floored room. Fans, suspended from the high ceiling, provided a welcome breeze that dried the sweat on his neck and brow. A few guests were sitting around cocktail tables in padded cane chairs, chatting desultorily in English, French and German. They sipped iced drinks or coffee, and nibbled on little pastries that were set out on the tables. Everyone seemed to be smoking. The hotel was a mid-upper range place, and was reputed to have a decent kitchen, and a marginally less rude staff than the other French-run hotels. As he could not remember where the bar was, he wandered toward an entrance that let onto the main dining room, not yet set up for dinner. They would begin to feed the Americans at six o'clock, to get them out of the way. Others would dine much later, and take their time, and be less demanding.

Finding himself lost, Lewis turned to head back to the desk to ask directions, when he spotted Marian at the top of a wide stairway that led to the larger, land-side lobby. She spotted him, smiled, and began down the stairs. Marian looked even better in clothes, Lewis thought, and was almost as fully dressed as she had been undressed at the beach. She wore loose, off-white linen pants, tan espadrilles, and a dark blue camp shirt that looked like silk. She wore no jewelry, and carried no purse. Her attire indicated that she was an old island hand, and was smarter than to go into town half-dressed, sporting expensive jewelry and a handbag that could easily disappear from her side as she sat at dinner, or at a blackjack table. The town, and the whole island was very safe, far safer than most places in the States, but there was some poverty on the island, and while violent crime was almost unheard of, the odd theft was not.

Lewis kept walking, and met Marian at the bottom of the stairs. He felt the old awkwardness surface, and was unsure whether to just say hello, offer her his hand, or move in for a perfunctory embrace, which must have been the wrong choice. As he said "Hi," Marian kept moving toward him, put her hands on his shoulders, and pecked him on the cheek.

"Oh, I knew you'd be early, I meant to get down here sooner to wait for you, but they were just doing my room when I got back, so I had to wait to shower, then I got on the phone.…anyway, let's go have a drink before we go into town, okay?" He assented with a smile and a nod, thinking again that she was very cute, although a bit scattered, and walked with her holding his arm, to the bar, which he had apparently walked right past, twice.

They found a table on the outside patio overlooking the beach, and ordered drinks. He decided on a Beck's, she had a gin and tonic. Lewis lit a cigarette as soon as he sat down, delighted to be in a civilized country where smoking was regarded as normal. People could smoke anywhere, and did. After taking a swallow of his beer — and knowing that he had to limit his drinking tonight, so enjoying it more — he complimented Marian on her attire.

He asked if she had a preference as to where they would go to gamble, and to eat. After discussing the pros and cons of several places in town, all of them over on the Dutch side of the island, they settled on a new hotel just outside of the town. The hotel had a fairly good-sized casino, and was reported to have decent food. Their dilemma revolved around which side of the island had what one wanted at the time: the French side had the best beaches, and by far the best restaurants, while the Dutch side had gambling, but many more tourists. Fortunately, the border was nominal, and presented no bar to crossing back and forth as often as desired. No checkpoints, no Customs, and only a small sign, set back from the road, indicating that you were changing countries.

As they drank, and Lewis smoked, Marian asked Lewis about his life, casually, but talked about her own. She told him that she had been married, once, when she was in her late twenties, but only for a couple of years. Her husband had been a nice and good man, but something of a loony. Trained in business, and in a well-paid position as a district sales manager for a pharmaceutical company when they married, he had become increasingly involved with religion, first in a Men's Bible-Study Group that a co-worker had convinced him to attend, and then in a church that sponsored the Bible-study. Marian did not care much one way or the other about this new interest of her husband's, and, although she was not a church-goer herself, figured that it was better than having him at a bar, or screwing some floozy from work, so she let it go. Her husband, though, had become increasingly convinced that she should go to church with him, fearful that she would suffer the fate of all non-believers if she, too, did not accept Jesus as her personal Savior, et cetera, et cetera.

She had, at first, politely declined, and at his further insistence, pointedly refused, which only seemed to whet his appetite for her conversion. And, his work began to suffer, as he was increasingly drawn into church-related activities. Finally, when he announced that Jesus had come to him in a dream, and had told him to leave his job and attend a small Southern divinity school so that he could become a Minister, Marian had given him a choice: me, or Jesus. He took Jesus, and Marian took a small apartment in town near her job. Since then, she had enjoyed a few long-term lovers, but had avoided marriage, and was convinced that all men were insane, only wanting the things that they did not have.

Lewis concurred with her philosophy, and noted that he believed that all women, too, were insane, but that they generally smelled better than men, had boobs and pussies, and consequently, got away with a lot more. She laughed at this, and he thought it was one of the nicest laughs that he had heard in a long time.

The drinks and conversation lasted almost an hour — three cigarettes — and evening was approaching. Lewis suggested that they leave soon, and ambled up to the hotel reception desk, only getting lost once in the process, to request a taxi. When they left the table, Lewis left enough money to cover the drinks and whatever gratuity the surly bastard who had waited on them might think he deserved. He and Marian rose, and walked together, Marian slightly in the lead, up the stairs and out through the main lobby to wait at the main entrance. Within five minutes, a cab — a van — arrived, piloted by a cheerful and polite Rastafarian gentleman probably about thirty years of age. They asked to be taken to the Honors Hotel and Casino, and rolled away from the hotel, Lewis feeling oddly relaxed and happy, and without a hint of his usual anxieties. Marian smiled, and sat very close. Things were looking up.

1964-Aftermath-Cambridge

Lewis awakened at around two in the afternoon, his head throbbing with a hellish resonance, deep bass notes, from both the blow he had taken, and the codeine he had taken for the pain before triple-locking his door and falling instantly unconscious on top of his unmade bed. His girlfriend, Amy, was away — home to New Jersey on a parent-reassurance trip, and was not due back until Saturday, when he was due to meet her at the bus terminal in Park Square. Amy was an undergrad at B.U. and remarkable in that she was both the slimmest girl that Lewis had ever slept with, and also had the biggest boobs. Naked, she looked almost freakish, but in a heart-stopping way, and was very smart, and quite pretty, and took no shit from Lewis, or from anyone else. He had been compelled to fall in love with her within minutes of meeting her, and had moved in with her within two weeks. Things moved fast in those days. They had been together since June, and still seemed to click. He missed her now, but was glad that she was not here to ask questions, or to be in harm's way.

Walking carefully to the bathroom, Lewis switched on the overhead light, looked at his head, and almost fainted. Dried blood covered the left side of his head from just above his ear down to his stiff and crusted shirt collar. The side of his face seemed badly swollen, and Lewis thought he could see, through his matted hair, a wide, deep and glistening gash just above his ear. Not feeling well enough to get to the Emergency room, he staggered, scared, to the capacious old kitchen sink. It was a deep porcelain tub, with a single faucet set high above. There was plenty of room to stick his whole head under the faucet, which he did, and to run lukewarm water over it. The run-off was disturbingly red, provoking a new surge of panic, but after a few minutes began to run clear. Having shut off the tap, he waited for the excess water to drip off his head, and then straightened up and swept his long wet hair back, as well as he could without touching the laceration, his ear, or his swollen face. He gingerly patted his face dry with a towel — not as clean as he would have liked — grabbed from the back of a nearby kitchen chair.

He trod shakily back to the bathroom (which held the only mirror in the apartment that was near a source of light) and, steeling himself, inspected his damaged head. It was worse than he wanted, but better than he feared. The shotgun barrel had split open the skin above his ear, two inches long, about a quarter of an inch wide. The bleeding seemed to have stopped pretty much. He didn't know if he needed stitches, and doubted it could be stitched anyway: too wide. He also didn't think he could come up with a reasonable explanation of how it had happened: "Yeah, I ran into a telephone pole...." didn't sound right, and that was the best he could do on short notice. Instead, he grabbed Amy's bottle of peroxide (weren't women just great at keeping all this shit around, he thought) (he had no idea what she might use it for) from the shelf above the bathroom sink, put his head down over the sink, and poured a couple of shots of peroxide over the gash. It didn't sting, but made a god-awful fizzing sound that worried him for a moment. He then patted the gash — and his hair around it — dry with a piece of toilet paper, and looked in the mirror again as he carefully combed his hair back over the wound. Except for the swelling, and the huge new ear he had, and the purplish-green bruise setting in from his nose to his ear, he figured he could pass for human. Just one more strange looking freak, common as cats in Cambridge. He decided the best course of action was to swallow four more quarter-grain codeine tablets with a glass of cheap warm Chianti, and spend the rest of the day on the couch with an ice bag on his face. He had no ice, but found three frozen orange juice cans, and wrapped them in a wet face cloth.

Lewis didn't see much point in calling his partners right now. He'd have to walk out to a pay phone, and they were undoubtedly scattered, licking their own wounds. He spent the rest of the day and that night on the ratty sofa (it had looked better on the curb, where they had found it) in that not-quite-enjoyable high that codeine and alcohol supplied, occasionally re-freezing the orange juice cans. He wondered if the juice would still be okay after multiple thawings.

By the next morning, Lewis felt marginally better, and was able to eat some bread, dipped in coffee. He could not chew much without setting off a round of pain. He took three aspirin and a couple more codeine tablets, dressed in cleaner clothes, and at around nine o'clock on Friday morning set out for the pay phone at DeDominoco's Variety, a few blocks away. He called Steve — the only guy in on the deal who actually had a telephone at his place — and let the phone ring until Steve's girl friend, Linda, answered.

"Hi, Linda, its Lew, is Steve in?"

"*Who?*"

"Linda, it's me, Lewis, can I talk to Steve?"

"Listen, you motherfucker, stay away from us, stay away from Steve."

Her voice was angry and scared, and she broke the connection as her last word ended.

Lewis was a little taken aback, but unwilling, so far, to ascribe Linda's response to anything other than her inherent craziness…and her overly possessive relationship with Steve. Steve's friends, Lewis among them, did not understand why he stayed with her. As Jim, another common friend, had summed up to Steve recently in an alcohol-induced moment of truthfulness, "Steve, it's not just that she's ugly; her personality sucks, too." That, and the fact that Linda had, under the influence of way too much methamphetamine for way too long a few years back, had a large cross tattooed on her forehead, made her the object of little affection among Steve's friends. Lewis believed her to be quite insane.

Not bothering to call back, as he suspected he knew the outcome, Lewis bought a quart of Pale Ale, a bargain at thirty-five cents, and began the walk back to his place, sipping ale from the still-bagged jug. He was tired, his head hurt like hell again, and he knew that he was destined to be back on the couch soon. Then he would, if he could, go to the bar, where he was pretty sure his erstwhile partners would show up in the late afternoon. It was Friday, and the bar would be jammed with freaks, drunks and a few working stiffs who appreciated the scene.

When Lewis finally made it to his apartment door, it was a few inches shy of closed. He was pretty certain that he had shut it, had heard the cheap latch click, and had probably checked it once or twice, recognizing, even then, that he was a tad obsessive about such things. Not knowing what else to do, he went in. It took only twenty or thirty seconds to deduce that nothing was missing, as there was not much in the three rooms worth taking. Just the cheap stereo (Amy's cheap stereo — she'd had it since high school, at least) and some shitty Goodwill furniture. The warning signal in Lewis' brain began to sound, and continued as he tried to make some sense of the situation, not an easy task. Clearly, someone had slipped the lock on the front door, two seconds with a piece of plastic or thin metal would do it, and had come in, perhaps, but not to rip him off, as there was nothing missing. The place did not look as if it had been tossed: no upholstery had been slit open, none of the cardinal signs of a speed-freak sneak ripoff. If someone had slipped the lock on the door, and if they had come in, and if the purpose was not theft, that only left one possibility. Someone had come looking for him. And they hadn't knocked and then gone away, so the odds did not favor a social call. So, despite his still-throbbing skull and his need to lie down for a bit on the couch that sat just a few feet away, he knew, without question, that it was time to get the fuck out of Dodge.

Lewis went directly to the ancient refrigerator that had, he guessed, sat in the same spot in the ill-lit kitchen for thirty years or more. He opened the door, and then the door to the tiny freezer. Reaching back behind the two aluminum ice cube trays that took up almost all of the freezer space, he grasped a package wrapped in tin foil, extracted it, and ripped an end open, exposing frozen meat that might be baloney. Between the frozen slabs of mystery meat was another, slimmer foil-wrapped package. Quickly disengaging the smaller package from the larger, he found what he had been hoping the house-breaker hadn't: his emergency stash of currency, five hundred dollars in fifties and twenties. Combined with his profits from the deal, he had almost three thousand dollars, enough to disappear for many months, if he were careful.

He decided, as he quickly packed a duffel bag with his clothes, a few books, and his toothbrush, that he would call Amy from the bus terminal in Park Square and advise her of at least the outline of the situation. She was probably not in any danger, but he would tell her that she should strongly consider staying with a friend for a week or two. In any event, it was her apartment, and as far as he knew, he was free to come and go as he pleased. Right now, he needed to go. He doubted that she'd take it well.

Friday, Day 12

The biggest problem with the casinos on the island, Marian told him in the taxi, was that they were so small that they had to screw you over on a much greater and more frequent basis than a "real" casino did. She played only the slots, and was devout in her play, continuing to feed coins in long after she had given up any hope of winning. She reasoned, out loud, that this was the best approach, as winning, or even breaking even, always came as such a mood-altering shock for her that only then could she walk away. She had no respect for the players who, upon winning, fed it all back to the house. However, as she seldom won, or even mitigated her losses, she rarely had the chance to try. Lewis opined, in return, that he was of the latter persuasion, and hoped that the combination of their divergent philosophies would allow them to keep at least enough money for the taxi home, as it was one hell of a long walk.

As soon as they arrived at the place, about four long blocks from the center of town, they went straight to the dining room that was peopled primarily by American guests of the resort that housed the restaurant and casino. They ordered, and ate, an almost-fine dinner of grilled snapper, rice, and a local vegetable that was green, which neither could name but both ate, washed down with a white wine for Marian, two beers for Lewis. Finished in less than an hour, with coffee but no dessert, they ambulated slowly, as full people do, through the lobby and into the casino. Marian gave Lewis a one-armed hug around his no-longer slim middle, and turned left toward the dollar slots. Lewis walked further toward the far end of the room, and found a seat (it was still early) at a five dollar blackjack table.

Lewis lasted through about twenty minutes and three hundred dollars worth of bad hands before he gave up, and wandered off in search of either Marian or a two dollar table, whichever came first. It was a small casino by American standards, with a card room with eight tables, another high-stakes card, craps, and roulette room, and a much larger room with the slot machines — maybe one hundred — with a service bar and a cashier off to the side toward the street-facing door. As Lewis moved through the card room looking for a cheap table, a short, solidly built and very drunk, very black man with a shaved head and too much cologne stumbled into him, looked up into his face, and threw one beefy arm over Lewis' shoulder. Pulling Lewis into a miasma of rum fumes and the smell of old sweat that was breathtaking, the man said in slurred and accented English, "Get me outta here…. we mus' get away from dis place. Da man lookin' for you have me lookin' too, but I don't want no piece a him."

Lewis looked around for anyone resembling Security, as the man's grasp on him tightened and he pulled Lewis closer, now with both arms. The man, speaking now in Creole, was urgent and intense. Lewis spoke perhaps twenty words of French, and understood fewer. Panic blossomed for him then, bursting through the benzodiazepine and alcohol barrier to the part of his brain where true fear lived. His heart began to race, and the oxygen seemed to leave the room. His eyes brought him cinemascope images of his surroundings, too bright, too well-defined, with the surreal colors of a spaghetti Western or a bit too much mescaline. He believed he was about to die, insane.

The round black man, still clutching him, seeming to sense the reality shift, was still peering into Lewis' face as he whispered what may have been a last warning in Creole French. He let go slowly, then entirely, and moved off, sideways, fast enough to almost seem to vanish. Lewis struggled to keep from fainting. As a drinks girl passed, he grabbed a full drink from her tray and downed it in a long series of swallows. The girl, scared and angry, looked at him and said nothing as she watched the color begin to come back to his face. He reached into his pocket for his roll, and taking it out, peeled off a five, and placed it on her tray.

"Lewis, are you alright?"

Marian had appeared in front of him at some point in time as he stood frozen to the exact spot where he had been when the round man had accosted him, just scant minutes before.

"Lewis, I said, are you okay….can you answer? You look like you're stroking out…."

"Yeah, yeah. I just sometimes have these moments. I'm alright. I need to sit down. Let's sit and have a drink."

"What happened, Lewis? You look like you've seen a ghost. Your hands are vibrating, and your face is splotchy — red and white. Do you need a doctor? Are you having chest pain?"

They walked, slowly, through the symphony of slot machine music and the fog of two hundred cigarettes to a cheap plastic banquette set against the wall near the service bar.

Lewis had no intention of telling his new companion about his panic attack, or about the reason for it. Other than the obviously negative effect that kind of revelation might have on his chances of getting into Marian's pants at some point, he truly did not know, not yet, what to make of things, or of the short round man who had set him reeling. Other than professionally, he was not used to being accosted by lunatic doom-sayers. His hope, as always, was that everything would just go away if treated with the proper avoidance and neglect. Talking about these things...well, that would be truly insane, and give the odd happenstance (real or imagined) more power, not less.

They both ordered a local beer, and sat quietly drinking. After a few minutes, Marian began her tale of woe at the slots, first winning, then losing, then losing even more on the dollar machines. She announced her intention of going back to try again, but on the quarter slots, as she was down to a hundred dollars. A hundred dollars would not take one through even a short bad streak on the higher-stakes machines. She thanked God that the crummy little joint didn't have five-dollar bandits, or she'd have to walk home.

Lewis was not the utter fool some thought he was, and could not pretend that his recent visitation was a normal occurrence, or even the type of abnormal event that life could throw at you, like having a bear on your porch, which had, in fact, happened to Lewis a couple of times, and could be dealt with, and then pretty much forgotten until dredged back up in a desperate attempt at wit at some horrendous cocktail party, or worse, family gathering. What had happened was either a high-octane LSD-25 level hallucination, or was a bad and scary and inexplicable thing that could not be explained away, and would have to be revisited and puzzled over until a self-satisfying explanation could be cobbled together so that it could be put away, so that he could continue with his limited, but not uncomfortable, life. The weapons-grade denial mechanisms that had been a big part of his craziness for all of his life could be less effective in situations such as this. The fear that lodged in his soul was not diminishing, although the panic was down. He could not explain it or discuss it or ignore it, and did not feel much like gambling any more tonight or even like being where he was. But here he, indeed, was, and with Marian, and had to do something.

So, Lewis assented to another assault on the slots, with Marian, hoping to break her streak of bum luck. At his suggestion, they went the only two dollar machines that were open: there were six in the casino, this was not a place for the high-rollers, but for the day-trippers, the nickel or quarter players. The noise of the bells and the coins (not many) dumping into metal trays soothed him with its familiar and hypnotic rhythm, elicited a change in his brain chemistry, loosing that blessed dopamine, calming him and making him feel almost okay. As Marian did sitting next to him, he fell quickly into the programmed spell of pushing the button that commanded SPIN, and barely registering the outcome before pushing it again. Given sufficient time and money, he knew he would sit and push the button for hours, neglecting food and drink and sex, like the monkeys in the cocaine study who, as our true cousins, self administered cocaine until they collapsed with exhaustion, or died.

His movements — push, pause, push, pause — were so automatic, and he was so utterly and pleasantly spaced that he did not notice, for a few seconds, the three double-diamonds lined up on the third play-line (he tripled the bet every third time) that set off the very loud music and the flashing yellow light atop the automaton and the numbers beginning to roll up on the payout counter with no signs of stopping for a while. He began to notice, though, the growing hush around him, and certainly noticed the panic gripping his heart as the elation chemicals flooded his brain too quickly, the old brain, the crocodile brain that couldn't tell flight from fight from victory, and he began to drift back from himself and observe this thing happening to someone else, the colors vivid and outlined in black.

Marian was beside him, then, and a clutch of fellow gamblers had crowded about to watch the numbers roll up. His machine would be a favorite for the next day or two, although the players knew, on some level, that jackpots, like death, were random, if temporarily localized. The numbers kept running up, the loud music and flashing light went on for almost too long, but stopped, finally when the readout said $34,666. Lewis had perhaps not fully noticed when he sat down to play that the slot machine was a progressive, part of the six-slot group, with cumulative payouts (when they happened) that exceeded all other payouts in the room by far. The biggest payout had been almost $70,000. His was enough, almost three months average pay for him, enough to matter, enough to, as he realized his luck, back down the panic part of his freak-out and bring quiet elation to the fore.

A casino functionary arrived within a few minutes with a bank draft for the post-tax winnings and a handful of receipts and releases for Lewis to sign. Lewis would likely have signed almost anything to get the check and make his escape from the crowded scene. Marian steered the happy, anxious man through the small crazy room and out through the wide doorway to the quiet lobby, then through the front door to an idling minivan taxi in the circular drive. Lewis listened as she gave directions to the slim and smiling driver, a man with the almost purple-black skin that the purest African-descendent islanders had, so different from most of the black folk Lewis knew in the States. The driver was happy and chatty, talking non-stop about the island as he skillfully, speedily navigated the crowded streets of town — it was only about ten-thirty now — and the hilly blind curves of the narrow but two-way road that would take them from the Dutch half to the French half of the island, and to the strip of hotels and villas on the northeast shore.

During the twenty minute drive, Lewis emerged from his fog of fear and joy that had enveloped him so quickly, prompted by the round man, but maybe starting earlier, maybe when he saw and lost the Doc-wraith on the beach, or maybe when he got on the plane days before. Or perhaps much longer ago than that, back where things were just so murky that you didn't dive in there: you might not come out. The prophylactic Xanax and few drinks he'd had since afternoon had not been nearly enough to counter the eccentric mind-fucks of the night, he knew, but knew too that he was an old hand at coping with the jokers that he believed life dealt him, had always had pride in his ability to cope, to bounce back, to level out and get his shit together, as they used to say. He was not loath to cop to his own craziness, nor to his ability to handle it.

But, God, it made him fucking tired. And the intervals of composure were so brief these days. He often wondered what is was, that made him persevere.

1964- Running: Cambridge and Points South

Lewis caught the last bus that would get him to the final ferry of the day, stopping only to buy a half-pint of cheap vodka and a pack of smokes, and to make a call to Amy, who received his information with less than calm.

"You fucking paranoid fucking asshole! My name is on that lease....how the hell will I pay the rent with you gone?" She went on in pretty much the same vein for a few minutes, until Lewis finally, quietly hung up. His guess was that the relationship was pretty much over, and was not inordinately sad about it. He wished for the best for Amy, which he was most certainly not experiencing, at least right now. His horizons were clear. He needed a change of venue, and probably a change of name, too. One could lose a lot more than a girlfriend if proper caution were not exercised, in this dangerous world.

The bus ride to the ferry landing was slow and quiet, a good chance to rest. His seat was far enough forward that he couldn't smell the uni-sex restroom at the back, and far enough back that the driver couldn't clearly observe him sneaking sips from his bottle, just a bit of medicine for his pounding head. As cheap vodka does, it smelled like rubbing alcohol, and tasted worse. The alcohol did its magic, though, and he was infused with a feeling of warmth, of safety. Travel always made him feel pretty good, as he moved farther from trouble and closer to freedom, although the freedom never seemed to last. It had always turned to routine, and to entanglements. Perhaps he should travel more. No one could find him on a bus or a boat, no one knew he was headed for the Island, and no one would be expecting him in two and a half hours way the Christ out in the Atlantic. The Island was just beginning to attract Freaks from all over, and he'd just be one more, if he played his cards right. They pulled into town with almost forty minutes to spare. The last boat, the venerable, flat-bottomed Mohican rocked at its moorings as the crew unloaded the last of the freight from the trip over from the other island.

Lewis went directly to the tiny ferryboat company office and bought a one-way ticket for four dollars and fifty cents, slung his duffel over his shoulder, adjusted his watch-cap, and crossed the parking lot to the nearest bar. The joint was full, fishermen and scientists from the nearby Oceanographic Institute drinking together and smoking one cigarette after another. No one paid him the least notice as he found a stool as far from the blaring television as he could. He ordered a draft beer, two pickled eggs, and a Slim Jim: dinner for seventy-five cents. The Snack Bar on the boat might not be open, depending on how many of the crew showed up for the last run, and he might not have another opportunity to eat until the next day. It would be around seven-thirty (with favorable winds and not too much chop) when they got to the Island, and there wasn't likely to be much open. Maybe a bar or two, that might, or might not, serve food. He had only been to the Island once before, and had been heroically twisted on acid and wine for most of that time. His memories, as they existed, were not all that clear. But, he did remember that he had a few friends there, old Cambridge hands who had opted for more bucolic surroundings and a bit less stress, their stress often characterized by the untoward attentions of the Cambridge and Boston narcs. Lewis was confident that his friends would still be there, a just as sure that one of them would put him up if there was a couch or a bit of floor space not taken.

Once aboard the ferry (already rolling and pitching, even moored) Lewis staked out a spot on two facing, vinyl-upholstered seats that looked as if they had come from a bus, and probably had. He put his duffel and his feet up on the opposing seat, pulled a navy wool watchcap down over his eyes, and tried to nod off. The past few days had been pretty goddamn freaky, and he hadn't sorted things out yet, or tried. He wasn't going to try now. This was the time to act, not think. And to keep acting, he needed more rest. The boat was not crowded, thank heaven. Lewis had counted twenty people, not counting crew, boarding, and they were spread through the sixty inside seats, or were still in their cars down below. He could close his eyes and sleep without worry, he could put his anxiety and paranoia on the back burner. He slipped out of conscious thought before the boat left the wharf, and only heard the whistle in his sleep.

About an hour into the journey, Lewis was jolted awake by a simultaneous roll and pitch that almost flipped him out of his seat. Given the look of the seas in the harbor earlier, he wasn't surprised, just a bit pissed off that he was awake. He noticed that his bladder was painfully full — maybe that last quick beer at the bar in the Hole had been ill-advised — and decided to hit the Head. He coordinated his quick rise from his seat with the motion of the ferry, and made it to his feet. The Head was only five yards away, and he steadied himself by alternately grasping the backs of the seats that he passed as he made his way. As he was congratulating himself on his surefootedness, a wild yaw threw him forward, toward the stern and past the door to the Head, and fetched him up against a gray steel bulkhead, face-first. Quick, always, he was able to break the blow with his hands, and only smashed his nose and cheek a bit, no serious damage done, although he felt pretty stupid, as the other dozen passengers may have seen his clumsy lurch and lucky save, and if they did, were probably chuckling to themselves. Maybe, he mused, the last beer really and truly had not been a good idea, and maybe he was a bit drunk.

He carefully back-tracked between the next two pitches of the boat, compensated for the roll, and slipped through the door to the Head without damage. The urinal had a grab bar on the right, no doubt as a joke by some misanthropic ship-fitter. He had to hold on, and struggle through the complicated and slow process of unbuttoning his Levi's with his left hand, and extracting his dick , and keep from pissing down his pant leg as the deck beneath him continued to move to every position except level. Once he had freed the necessary equipment and had it aimed properly and was not in imminent danger of hurting or embarrassing himself further and the urine was flowing well, he took some time to check out the graffiti scratched into the beige-enameled steel wall in front of his face. His favorite — as it was absolutely inexplicable and clearly meant for a small, discerning audience, was "Save a Pony — Shoot Billy." The rest was pretty standard shithouse art: invitations (perhaps genuine) for quick, illicit sex; some pretty lousy comments about women both specific and general, and one incredibly bad rendering of male genitalia. Between the intense satisfaction of a good piss and the outlandish wall-art, Lewis's mood brightened considerably during the short time he was in the Head. He even managed to get himself tucked back into his pants with minimal leakage, and then turned around so that he could hold on with his left hand while re-buttoning his pants with his right. Moving out the door into the cabin, he found that he could walk with greater confidence and ease, as the boat had, apparently, shifted into an almost dead-south heading, and while the roll had, if anything, worsened, the pitching had stopped. The wind, coming from the northeast now, was hitting the port side at an oblique angle, so the rest of the voyage would be a lot smoother. Lewis imagined that if he ventured out onto the bow in thirty or forty minutes, he would be able to see the lights of the town.

Returning to his seat without mishap, he sat down, leaned back, and closed his eyes. An intense feeling of safety and security swaddled his addled brain, and with an electro-biochemical shove, pushed him over the edge, into the first real sleep that he had experienced in two days. The sleep was deep, but aware, and signaled through some primitive sensibility the turn of the boat around the Point and into the inner harbor. Lewis opened his eyes, feeling refreshed, and grabbed his bag to cross to the other side of the boat and down the stairs to the car deck. He was anxious to disembark, to get on with this last leg of his escape, and to find a friendly face or two and a place to stay for the night.

Friday, Day 12

Marian directed the taxi to her hotel, and then climbed out of the van, leaving Lewis to settle the bill. He added five dollars to the twenty-five dollar fare, thanked the still-chattering driver, and accepted the man's business card.

"You are sure to call for me, man, I'm always ready, and I'm the best driver on the island. Not all the time stoned, like some of them are. That's my cell phone number. You and your Missus be safe, now."

With a last broad smile and a wave, the taxi driver pulled away, leaving Lewis rooted at the spot. He was fully slowed down from the craziness of the night and the long day, and he had to stand and do nothing for a moment before his brain re-engaged, which it did with now pretty happy thoughts, thinking that he might be having what passed for a lucky day. The bad times, the fear, were gone, attributed finally to too much sun, and maybe too much or too little medication.

These things happened to him, he knew, these weird things that were almost always the same, or at least similar in their vivid, hallucinatory nature, crises that happened and then were in the past, almost forgotten, it was just his fucking weird brain chemistry. He could accept that. And here he was, standing here in the warm night with a whole lot of other people's money, and the distinct possibility of sex with an attractive young woman.

"Lewis — come in for a drink. You look like you could use one, and I know I do."

He turned, slowly it seemed to him, toward the voice. Was it an invitation or an order?

"I'm coming — just couldn't recall if I'd paid the guy right. I never really know how much to tip here, you know, how much do you add to a rip-off just because the guy's nice about it."

Marian waited at the doorway to the hotel foyer, and when he arrived, they walked through the door together, she taking his hand as they negotiated the rattan-infested lobby and passed into the small bar. She asked for two beers, bottles, and charged them to her room. Carrying both beers by the neck in one hand, she led Lewis out of the bar on the far side, through another smaller lobby, and outside to a lighted wooden walkway that trended slightly uphill. Not far, maybe a couple of hundred feet, she turned, with him in tow, into a side path that led to a small cabana that seemed to house two guest quarters. Lewis could still hear the surf from the beach down the hill, and faintly, reggae music and loud voices from the nearest beach bars. Marian opened the door with a key that appeared in her beer-holding hand, passed him the bottles, and looking over her shoulder, smiled him into her room.

"It's not too bad a room — big — but too near the beach. I'd rather be up on the hill a little further." Marian remarked, as she walked to the kitchenette in search of a bottle opener. Lewis closed the door behind him, walked a few steps into the room, and stood a bit awkwardly. He felt that he should respond, should at least say something.

"Why?" What a stupid question, he thought, as the words left his mouth.

"So I'd have further to walk, naked. I like to be naked, and I guess mostly because I just like the feel of it, but not just for the feeling of the air and the sun and everything else on my skin. I'm not a very pure-minded naturist, if there are any. I guess maybe I'm an exhibitionist, if you buy that diagnosis. I absolutely love to be naked around people who aren't naked. It excites me. If I didn't think it was a bit trashy, and if I could dance, I'd really like to be an exotic dancer. Except, I'm not exotic at all. And my tits are too small, and I have absolutely no coordination, so I'd be more of an exotic stumbler. I think that maybe half the people you see at nude beaches are exhibitionists, although they probably don't know it. But I know it. What I really like is to be standing a foot away from some salesman from Dubuque or Caracas, some guy sitting there, with his wife, wearing a bathing suit, and maybe he's convinced his wife to lose her bikini top, so she's freaking out anyway, and then I'm there with my pussy almost in his face, or her face, and totally ignoring the fact that I'm naked. And I'll talk to them, engage them in some long conversation, just to string it out. So they sit there, either craning their necks, to be polite, or talking to my cunt. I just love that. So, now you probably think I'm insane, right?"

Lewis didn't have a response ready. While he watched her slip out of her shoes, then her slacks and blouse, it came to him. She was not encumbered with a bra or panties.

"So, I'll stay dressed if you like," he said, hoping that he didn't sound as if he really did think she was nuts. He looked at her face. She smiled, so he decided to take it a little further.

"I think what you say is true for more women than will admit it. I know it's true for lots of men. It's not a huge thing for me, but it's there. But for me, I think it's just breaking the rules that counts. It isn't so much, if at all, a sexual turn-on, although of course being naked and seeing the right woman naked is, but for me, it's more of a 'fuck you' thing. I love to do fuck-you things. I probably should have been a Hell's Angel, but I'm way too paranoid to pull it off."

Lewis became more animated, happier, as he spoke. He rarely engaged in conversation that included a truthful disclosure of his feelings, and didn't really approve of those who did. Perhaps he could have had more success in psychotherapy, years ago, if he had sought out a naked, exhibitionistic female therapist.

Marian, meanwhile, had discovered a bottle opener screwed to the side of a kitchen cabinet, and had walked the six or seven feet toward him with an open beer held in each hand. He took one of the beers from her, and sat down on the edge of the nearest queen sized bed, just a few feet behind him. Marian walked closer, and leaned her head and shoulders back to take a long drink of beer, her hips moving forward. Lewis was eye level with her rib cage, but now knew the game, and looked up at the underside of her boobs. Her nipples were erect, and he could smell her musk. Leaning forward, he brought his mouth to her closely-shorn pussy, ducked his head, and licked her slit from about two inches down, moving his tongue up and in until he reached the salty taste of her urethra. He pushed in with the tip of his tongue, massaging the opening for a few seconds and then stopped. Settling his weight back on the couch, he took a drink of beer and looked up into her face. She was smiling slightly, and looking down into his eyes.

"Time to quit teasing, I guess...." she said, with a little catch in her voice. Then she put her hands on his shoulders and pushed him down on the bed.

Thursday, Day 4 – Boston to Vermont to Trouble

Lewis snapped out of his reverie — a bit of unpleasantness, he thought, long gone and forgotten by everybody. He was respectable now, and respected, at least in his own small universe. He was not a happy man, but he was content, and most importantly, in control of his life. Except for this fucking "Doc" thing. He wanted the strangeness to stop.

He washed up the dishes that he had used that day, then made a small pot of coffee in his new coffeepot, carefully measuring five heaping tablespoons of finely ground French Roast into the filter for the three cups of coffee he needed for his thermos. He would pour half into his travel cup before he started the drive, and refill the cup, if he felt sleepy, when he stopped to take a leak at the halfway point.

He put on a medium weight Scottish wool sweater, changed from his city shoes into his ancient, low cut Bean duck boots, and after checking the burners on the gas stove a few times, checking the lights, the answering machine, and his computer several times to make sure that they were either off or on, he left the apartment with a ratty tweed hacking jacket and an even rattier down vest under one arm, the other holding his travel bag with thermos, travel mug, a fresh pack of cigarettes and the rabbit-lined deerskin gloves he liked for driving.

After initially looking for, and failing to find his Audi, he remembered that he should be looking for the Explorer that he had passed twice. Within a few minutes, he had successfully escaped the Hill and was on 93 North, just ahead of the serious commuter rush. He tuned in to NPR, and listened to the classical music that he did not particularly care for until the news came on at four. He would listen to painstakingly understated stories of the current misadventures of his, and other, governments, and to business reports about stocks that he did not own, as far as he knew. At thirteen minutes past four, he would turn to the AM station that gave out traffic reports, often incorrect.

And finally, about ten miles north of the state line with New Hampshire, he would switch the dial to New Hampshire Public Radio, and he could then begin to relax.

Lewis made good time. After getting away from the bulk of the Massachusetts traffic — Spring skiers? — he found the Explorer's cruising speed at eighty, smooth and safe, barring the odd moose that might choose to run into his path, and end both of their horribly misunderstood lives. He stopped at a rest area near the tolls for a piss and a coffee refill. The men's room smelled incredibly bad, considering that no one was in it but him. Just before Concord, he picked up 89 North, a road with great long, straight runs and near-perfect banking, but unfortunate dips and some truly crazed drivers. He slowed to sixty-five, and waited for the turn at Exit 5 that would take him on to one of the state's damn few east-west roads, Route 9. Once on 9, he followed it almost across the state, turning north at Stoddard to catch Route 123 North, which would actually take him northwest to the Vermont border at Bellows Falls. It put him a bit north of where he wanted to be, but saved going through some slow towns with many lights, and was the route he took, unless it was snowing. At five minutes before seven, full of coffee and urine, he pulled up beside the general store at the bottom of his road, took out his penis, and peed with gratitude until the pain in his bladder stopped.

The lights over the gas pumps in front of the store flicked out just as Lewis went through the front door. The store always closed at seven, unless Eddie was especially stoned, in which case it might close much earlier, or not at all. Eddie thought the best of everyone, and assumed that, by seven in the evening, his customers had been prudent enough to put by sufficient beer, cigarettes, and ammunition to get them through until six o'clock the next morning. And if they hadn't, well, that wasn't his problem, and maybe they'd be smarter the next time. Eddie was coming out of the side door to the cooler as Lewis walked up to the counter.

"You almost missed me, Melton. There's a ham and bean dinner down to the Odd Fellow's that I'm already late for."

"Hi, Eddie. I just need to check my mail. And get some beer. I'll be quick. You didn't see that guy again, did you?"

"Yup, not twenty minute ago. Actually, he didn't mention you. Just bought a bottle of wine. Best stuff I sell, which means I don't sell much of it, so I notice who buys it. It was the same feller. I kind of figured he was going up to see you — it was the kind with a cork — tough to drink in your truck. Now, come on in and get your beer."

They walked to the side door, and Eddie led the way in.

"Did he *say* that? Did he say he was going to see me?" Lewis had dropped his adopted Vermont drawl, and was speaking as clearly as he could. "Did the guy say that he was going to my house, or that he was looking for me?"

"No, no, no, slow down there, buddy, you're getting pretty wound up. Is this guy after you or something? Did you run over his old lady or screw his dog?"

Lewis knew that he had to get himself under control, had to somehow undo the damage that his obvious sense of fear had caused. This was a small town, and everybody talked about everybody, and if they didn't know what was going on, they weren't averse to making up a story to explain things. Eddie was probably making something up this very minute, to take to the Ham and Bean Supper he was late for. This was going to be a tough sell, as Lewis had no real ideas about why he was "so worked up," so…afraid. But, it had to be a serious lie, a really good one, to support his behavior so far, at least without making him look like an irretrievably insane asshole.

An idea came glimmering up from the depths of his overly educated soul, and found its way to his mouth.

"Eddie, here's the real story. I know I can count on you not to talk it around. This guy — he's calling himself 'Doc' now, but that's not his real name — he's another writer. He's crazy as a shit-house rat, and thinks that I stole an idea from him a few years back. He's been pestering me for a couple of years now. I hadn't heard from him in a while: now I hear that he's telling people that he's going to kill me, that I ruined him. He's had a run of bad luck, I guess, and he prefers to blame it all on me. So, I'm a little worried. I don't think he'll really try to kill me, but I don't know just how crazy he is."

"Holy Shit, Lew — why the fuck didn't you tell me before? Threats like that, that's what they call assault, I think. You should call the cops and get this asshole locked up!"

"I can't. I don't have any proof. It's all second or third hand. And I don't know where he lives, anyway. Nobody that I've talked to does. I did speak to the cops down in Mass. They can't do anything even if I swear out a complaint, if they can't find him."

"Well, Jesus Christ, it ain't right! We don't go for that kind of shit around here. If he comes in again, I'll hold him here and call the Chief."

"Don't bother. I can't do anything. I don't have any proof that he threatened me. Just let me know if you see him. Please, Eddie, I don't want to complicate this. Odds are, he'll fade away as quick as he showed up."

"Well, alright. But if you're going up to your house, what if he's there? I'll grab a gun and come along with you."

"No, you need to get to your supper. I'm pretty sure he's not there, and if I see a vehicle in the yard, I'll just drive by. If this guy is there, he had to drive, right? I don't think he walked two miles up the hill."

"Suit yourself, Lew. Do you have a gun in the car?"

"No, my guns are all at the house. All I need is to get stopped in Mass and have them find a gun in my car. They frown on that down there."

"Well, I got a pocket gun I can let you have. It was my ex-wife's. She never asked for it, and I felt safer that way. It's only a .32, but it's better than nothing. Hold on a minute and I'll get it."

Eddie, with startling grace for a fat guy, hopped up on the counter, lifted a panel in the suspended ceiling, and reached in, extracting a small cloth bundle. He placed the bundle gently on the counter as he descended, hopping back down to the worn wooden floor.

"It's loaded, so I didn't want to chance jumping down with it," Eddie said, as he unwrapped a small automatic pistol, blue-black, clean, and clearly well-used. "The clip is full, and there's one in the chamber. I never saw much sense in keeping guns unloaded: by the time you get it ready, you're already dead. Anyway, the safety is on. Try not to blow your balls off. And it's never been registered anywhere, so far as I know, so if you use it, just wipe it down and chuck it off the bridge by the falls. It runs deep there, but fast, so there won't be any ice."

"Eddie, I don't think I'll need it, but thanks. I'm sure I'll bring it back with the same load."

Lewis checked the safety himself, and then slipped the pistol into his right vest pocket. It was not noticeable, as, over the years, a good part of the down in the vest had slipped down toward the bottom, giving the lower third a distinct bulge in addition to any bulge that he might be contributing. When he got to his car, Lewis planned to eject the round that was already chambered. He didn't plan to shoot anyone, and certainly not at his own house. He could only imagine the legal nightmare that might follow.

He drove the Ford as slowly as he dared to up the mountain road, keeping as far to the right as he could on the switchbacks. Odds were good that one of his drunken neighbors would come barrel-asking down the hill in a doomed attempt to lay in more beer before the store closed. God only knows, he thought, how many times he had made that run, only to be, finally, disappointed at Eddie's closed door, and then to have to make the decision of whether to give up and slink back up the hill, or to drive, certainly legally drunk, the eight miles to the nearest beer store that would be open. Always a risky proposition, as the local cops knew exactly when all the beer stores closed, too, and if sufficiently bored, were not above lying in wait at the halfway point. They could get you coming or going, as the malicious spirit moved them.

As he neared his house, he considered shutting his headlights off, parking several hundred yards away, and walking in. This would give him an edge, but the tension, he feared, would give him a panic attack. Or a heart attack. He opted, instead, for the opposite tactic, switching on his fog lamps, keeping his high beams on, and roaring into his driveway as noisily as possible. He wanted, really, to give anyone who might be around there plenty of notice, plenty of time to skedaddle. He did not want a confrontation of any sort.

It had snapped pretty cold, down to ten degrees or less, and the snow and ice crunched and squeaked under his tires as he pulled the SUV up into the dooryard. The driveway snaked by the front of the house and around toward the back door and the small attached barn. As Lewis came almost abreast of the house, headlights blazed on about fifty feet down the driveway, dead ahead of him. He stopped short, yanking the wheel to the right and running the right side of the car into the nearly frozen five-foot snow bank that the plow guy had been building all winter. He could hear the side-view mirror rip off. The headlights, high and blinding, were on him in an instant, then a screech of metal on metal as the vehicle — it was moving too fast and dark to identify — ripped along the left side of his Ford, and took more than just the mirror. He would find, later, that both door handles, the body trim, and a good deal of the paint were gone, too. He came close to pissing in his pants.

He sat, shaken, for a full minute, then turned his ignition key to off, kicked his door open, and started up the driveway, pulling the pistol from his pocket. He moved quietly, a silent, shaky, overweight man, toward the back door. He could not be certain that the crazed driver who had sideswiped him was the only person who had invaded his house. He eased the door open as quietly as he could, and stepped in, the gun leading the way. He was in the mud room/back porch/summer kitchen, where he stored a few weeks worth of wood, old snowshoes, a shovel, and the bags of trash that moved by degrees toward his car and then the dump. He reached for the wall switch just inside the doorway, and flicked it on, illuminating the same messy area that he expected to see. He could see the steps up to the door into the kitchen, which was closed. Now holding the .32 straight down by his right leg, he slowly advanced, not even thinking, just reacting now. He'd have his panic later, when he had the time.

Lewis eased the kitchen door open with his left arm, then, with the same hand, flicked the light switch on. After twenty or thirty seconds, he followed his left arm into the room, gun hand in front. Nothing, no one. When he got to the telephone on the wall above the varnished heart-pine counter, he dialed 911, and got the area dispatcher.

"This is Lewis Melton, about two miles up Old Shire Road. My house has been broken into. I think I surprised whoever it was that did it, and they sideswiped my car when they left in a hurry. Can you send somebody by to check things out?"

"Are you okay, Sir?" queried a very young sounding woman.

"I'm fine, but I don't know for sure if there's anybody still in the house. I don't want to look around alone. I need to make a report on the damage to my car, and anything that might be stolen here in the house. When can you send somebody up?"

"We'll get in touch with your local police, or the State Police, whoever's closer. Are you safe where you are?"

"I don't know." Lewis replied, deciding not to complicate matters by telling the girl that he had a borrowed pistol with him.

"I want you to go back out to your car, Sir; lock the doors, and put the lights on. If you can drive it, wait at the end of your driveway. We'll have an officer there soon."

"Thanks….I'll be waiting." Lewis hung up the phone, an, as he began to walk toward his car, decided that he should probably take something for his nerves so that he'd be able to make sense, if not too much, when the cops came. He knew that he had some Xanax and some painkillers in his traveling bag. The pain of awareness, the fear of vulnerability were beginning to bloom. Hyper-vigilant, he almost jumped out of his boots when the ancient fridge kicked on. Having an "aha" moment, he reached into the refrigerator for a beer to wash the pills down with, and then quickly left the kitchen and the house. When he got back to the Explorer, he locked the doors, as instructed, and backed all the way out to the end of the drive.

A few minutes of rummaging in his bag produced half a milligram of Xanax and a ten milligram hydrocodone tablet. He opened the beer — some strange off-brand that someone must have left — and washed both pills down. He lit a cigarette, and waited for the police.

1964-Thursday Night — Friday Morning - Welcome

Lewis found his way to the lower deck where passengers, cars and freight were being off-loaded (not much freight on the late boat), and joined the ragged queue that ambled, strode and staggered across the steel gangway to the Island.

He noticed immediately that the air was much warmer than it had been in Boston or on the Cape. He guessed that it was in the high fifties, still, although the sun was long gone. With his light Levi jacket, he was warm. The weight of his duffel on his shoulder and the walk caused him to break into a light sweat. He looked around to get his bearings, found nothing he remotely recognized, and decided to follow those in the small crowd who looked most like they needed a drink. Chances were better than fair that they'd show him the way to the bar. This time of year, he knew, only two bars were open in town, and he was headed for the Bucket on Main Street, as he knew he'd most probably find someone he knew there.

A police car sat idling about ten feet from the end of the wharf, the cop standing outside and in front of the car, his hip resting against the fender, looking over the passengers as they came down the wharf toward him. Lewis could sense that he had somehow attracted the officer's attention, and that the cop — a townie, not a Statie, thank God — was beginning to close the distance between them. The thirtyish, tall, oddly ungainly looking keeper of the peace did not look happy. Then again, how often do cops look happy, Lewis wondered?

"Hey, you — hold up a minute." The cop directed, moving faster toward him in a few unsyncopated strides.

"Yeah — what can I do for you?" asked Lewis, beginning to feel the creep of fear that all citizens seem to have of those who serve and protect.

"For starters, smartass, tell me who you are, why you're here, and where you're going. You don't look like a tourist, and I know you're not an Islander."

Lewis was having a hard time figuring out why this buffoon had singled him out to harass. Was it just the long hair and the beard, or had something happened in Cambridge that would cause the cops a hundred miles away to be checking people out if they met a certain general description, the general description that he alone of all the passengers he'd seen on the ferry seemed to fit. Or had he been followed? How the fuck could they follow him — he hadn't even been sure, until he got on the boat, whether he was going to this island or the other. Could they read his goddamn mind? And, even more important, was he holding? Was there a forgotten pill, or a roach, in one of his pockets? Or in his bag? He knew, unfortunately, that the answer was probably "Yes." So, he figured he'd stick with the best lies he could invent, and hope for luck.

"My name is Bill Stoddard. I'm a graduate student, and I'm here for a little break — a few days, maybe. Why?"

"Cause you look like trouble. I hope you're not. Where are you staying?"

"Well, I don't know. There must be a guest house or an inn. I need something that isn't too expensive."

"No. There's nothing here that's not expensive. And there's not much open after Labor Day. I suppose you could try Frannie's, up on Silman Street. She rents rooms. She might rent a room to you, but I doubt it. And there's no camping allowed on the Island. And camping is anything that isn't under a roof. Enjoy your stay, but don't stay long. And remember, this ain't America."

"Thanks....I'll keep that in mind." Lewis assessed that he was dismissed, and so began walking away, toward town, as far as he knew. The rest of the passengers had disappeared, so there was no one to follow.

What the fuck was up with that cop, he wondered? Could they just stop people at random down here, question and threaten them? It seemed to him that what had just transpired was at least illegal, and at worst, a tell-tale of things to come. After all this, he needed a drink, or more likely many drinks, and needed a place to stay, a place to lay low. He was pretty sure that if the cop saw him wandering aimlessly around town later in the evening, he'd be provided with a place to stay, a court date, and a ticket off-island.

A walk of less than five minutes brought him to Lower Main Street, with only one wrong turning. He could see the sign for the bar two blocks up the wide, cobblestone way. Nothing else on the street seemed to be open. He made his way, really dog-tired now, to and through the door. He needed to find a friendly face.

The place was, busy, smoky, noisy, and two or three time as long as it was wide. The smell of beer, old urine, and a million cigarettes was welcoming. This was no cocktail lounge- people came here to drink with serious intent. Every stool at the bar was taken, mostly guys in their thirties, with a few old drunks who looked sixty but probably weren't. Some of the thirsty crowd were obviously fishermen, still in their high rubber boots. The rest seemed to be carpenters, masons, laborers, and related tribes, some with crew cuts, and quite a few with long hair. Half a dozen large, round wicker tables filled the center of the room, between the bar on the left and six or seven booths on the right. The tables looked to be exclusively Freak territory, longhairs, bearded, strange rangers, a sprinkling of women. He recognized one of the women from where he stood, just inside the door. Her back was toward him, but he was pretty sure it was Janey.

He walked quietly over to the table, and touched the girl in the worn jeans and the tie-dyed T-shirt lightly on the shoulder.

"Janey, what's happening."

The smiling, stoned-looking brunette turned, jumped up, shrieked, laughed, and threw her arms around him. He looked into her dancing, glassy eyes.

"Lew — holy shit, Lew, what the fuck are you doing here!"

"Janey, Janey, I just came out for a little visit — you know, had to get out of the big city for a little bit. When I was here that weekend — or maybe it was a week — last summer, I kind of liked the place, so I thought I'd come and see what was happening."

"Far fucking out! You know some of the guys from Cambridge and Boston are here, and some folks from Mission Hill — you know them all — Casey, Winter, some others. They should be here soon — they're working late, trying to finish up a job at the other end of the island. These guys here are Jay and Peter." She motioned, vaguely, with a sweep of her hand toward the two other people at the table. One seemed almost too alert, the other, not alert at all.

" Dynamite! I've got to get a beer. Some Pig hassled me as soon as I got off the boat, I'm still freaked. And I need some food. Do they sell anything here besides Slim Jims?"

Janey giggled. She seemed pretty twisted, but then, Lewis didn't recall ever seeing her when she didn't appear stoned, so maybe it was just the way she was.

"They have some kind of an instant oven here, they make these horrible-looking burgers and sandwiches — I don't eat them but sometimes the guys will. You could try that. And, they have bottles of Bally ale — the draft is cheaper, but it tastes like water. Sit down: I'll get you a beer, I've got a tab. You want a burger, too?"

When the girl had left to get his ale, Lewis sat in the only other vacant chair, and introduced himself, a small nicety that Janey had blown right by. Jay and Peter both seemed well-fueled, maybe with something more than the ale that had once resided in the dozen empty bottles on the table. Jay, a small, muscular man with dark glasses and a short, full beard, grinned constantly, exposing what seemed like too many sharp and crooked teeth. There was something sharkish about him, but pleasantly sharkish. He insisted, in his first words of greeting, that he knew Lewis, had known him for years, in fact, and had just that week been wondering why Lewis wasn't on the Island yet.

"Fuck, Man, this is the only fucking place to be….what the fuck do you want to be on the Mainland for — that fucking scene is brutal, Man — has been for a year or two — it's all *over* there, Man — and this'll fall apart, soon, but right now, this is it, this is the place to be….say, didn't you live in the East Village a few years ago, Man? I'm sure I saw you when I was doing the lights at the Electric Circus…."

Jay went on to name several other people who he had know in several other places, "Tim," and others, some of them major, some minor luminaries in the Freak pantheon, and who, according to Jay, had either just been on the Island, or soon would be. Absolutely nothing that the man said seemed believable to Lewis, beginning with Jay's contention that they knew each other. But Jay rolled out his riff with such good humor and apparent honesty that it just couldn't cross that boundary to offensive. Lewis liked the guy right away.

Peter, across the table, said not a word. He didn't, actually, appear to be conscious, although he held a smoldering cigarette in one hand. His head lolled forward just a bit, and his breathing was almost undetectable. Lewis noticed, then, because now he was looking for it, a very small brown apothecary bottle hidden among the much bigger green ale bottles on the table. He reached over and picked it up, just an inch or two, so he could read the label. Paregoric. Empty. No wonder Peter looked so calm. And, Lewis thought, the man was unlikely to be troubled with diarrhea any time soon.

"He's kicking smack," said Janey, who had just appeared with four ale bottles and something hot and gray in a cellophane wrapper. The wrapper said it was a cheeseburger. It smelled like death. "He's tapering off with PG and booze. He had a wicked jones going down in the City, and came here to clean up. He's supposed to deliver somebody's boat in St. Bart's before November, and he won't sail when he's fucked up. Then when he delivers the boat and gets paid, he goes right back to New York, and gets strung out again.

Seems kind of pointless, to me, but it's his thing. Here's your burger — good luck."

Janey set two bottles in front of Lewis, one in front of Jay, and kept the fourth. Lewis tried to unwrap the burger, couldn't, and finally had to get his Buck knife out of his jeans and cut the wrapper off. The burger was almost, but not quite, inedible, so he ate it. It didn't taste like meat, or anything else, either, but it was hot, and food-like, and filled the hole in his gut. He continued to drink the ales that Janey continued to bring him, and talked with Janey, and listened to Jay, who had an endless supply of apocrypha, most of it at least amusing, and some hilarious. Janey filled Lewis in on who was around, and where, which did little good, as he did not know the Island at all.

It seemed, finally, that Janey was confident that there could be a place or two where he could stay, if he didn't mind kicking in toward the rent. And plenty of work was available, if he wanted to work. There was a major building boom beginning: the entire waterfront was being redone in the hope of attracting the moneyed boat crowd, and new, expensive houses were just starting to spring up all over the island. Lewis did want to work, as the alternative was to sit around the bar all day, which could not end well. He did not know much about building, but figured that he could learn. The idea of working, living here, being absorbed into this community of self-exiled Freaks two hours off the Mainland appealed to him more with each drink.

Casey and Winter, who Janey had expected hours ago, never showed up. The possibility existed that they had stopped to drink at the club at the Navy base on the way back, and had never left. Or they could still be working: there was no sense waiting, and Janey suggested that they take off. Lewis could stay at her place tonight, as the other woman she shared the apartment with was up in Boston for the night. Tomorrow, she promised, she'd help him find something a bit more permanent.

They rolled out of the bar, he with his ever-heavier duffel on his shoulder, and began the half-mile walk to Lookout Road. Peter still hadn't moved, although his cigarette had dropped from his hand at precisely the right moment to burn itself out with the others on the floor, and at some later point, another had appeared, as if by magic, in his hand. Jay had expressed his intention to stay until last call, still more than an hour away. He had been drinking steadily for at least the past six hours, according to Janey, but showed no sign of serious intoxication. He would have to start drinking shots of brandy with his ale to reach critical mass by closing time.

Saturday — Day 13

Lewis woke up with a nasty headache, a sore dick, and a slight tremor in his hands. Instantly aware of his surroundings, he knew that he was in Marian's bed, Marian's hotel. He remembered all of the previous night, a night that had been long and late for an old fool. He remembered, for example, that they had screwed four times, two of those in the first hour. He consciously remembered as much as he could, and filed it away. He knew he'd want to access it again.

From the quality of the light, it seemed later than the nine-fifteen that his wristwatch claimed. He had to piss desperately, and with a big man's stealth, rolled from the bed onto his feet, and crept to the bathroom. After a loud, long, leak, he bent over the sink and splashed some water on his face and head, combing back his hair as well as he could with his fingers. He didn't want to scare the girl.

He needed to find some aspirin right away, his headache had gotten worse since he stood up. He spotted a small zippered plastic case on the vanity, half open. He rummaged, and found no aspirin, not even any Tylenol. But at the bottom, he found something that might do, a half-full prescription bottle of Talwin, a fairly useless painkiller that he recognized as something that his wife had tried (without much success) for menstrual cramps, back when that was still an issue, back when he looted her drug supply so regularly that she had taken to hiding it. He struggled with his conscience for a few seconds, then took two of the small blue tablets, washed down with tap water. If he still had a Xanax in the pocket of his chinos, he'd be set for hours.

When he walked back into the bedroom, he found Marian awake, uncovered and smiling. She had raised herself up on one elbow, and regarded him with apparent good humor.

"So, you're not bad for an old coot. Want to try again?"

"Later, please...I'm not that old of a coot, but I need some coffee and a few cigarettes before I do anything at all."

"Okay. That sounds like a better idea, although I'll skip the cigarettes. I can't believe you still smoke. No one smokes anymore. Not that it's affected your stamina."

"It's way too early to argue about smoking, so I won't respond. You, by the way, are beautiful, and a fantastic lay. Now, where can we get some coffee?" As he spoke, Lewis located his chinos and began to pull them on.

"Out the door, back the way we came last night. There should be coffee and rolls in the little lobby. Bring me back a cup, please, or two cups. I need a shower. I reek of sex."

Lewis finished dressing, fished a comb from his pants pocket, and did what he could with his hair. The image in the mirror was not reassuring. He looked pretty old, pretty tired. Well, what the fuck, he thought, I can still get laid, and I have a sizeable check in my wallet from the casino. Things could be a lot worse.

There wasn't much activity and few people around him on his short walk to what he thought of as the "small lobby," and, except for the short, dark woman behind the registration desk, no one in the lobby at all. It was still fairly early — the guests were either still in their rooms, or had left for the beach, or, most likely, had gone to the airport at some ungodly hour to wait — and wait — for the plane back to reality. Saturday and Sunday were big turnover days, the days that a new crop of tourists came in to replace the tanned, the sun-struck, and the broke.

The coffee dispenser was imposing beyond any right. Huge, square and brown, it had three spigots, with signs in Franglish indicating type. As he had not asked Marian what she wanted, he drew two cups of "Coffee Americain" and two "Coffe au Lait." Stuffing a napkin-wrapped and slightly stale croissant in each front pocket, Lewis balanced the thick ceramic cups and saucers, two by two, and walked slowly back up the slight incline to Marian's door. He was sweating a bit when he arrived, whether from the heat, or from the Talwin kicking in, he did not know.

Having no free hand, and no convenient spot to set the cups down, Lewis rapped at the bottom of the door with his right foot. There was no response in the next sixty seconds, so he rapped again, louder. A passing housekeeper, scowling, pushing a housekeeper's cart with the proverbial rogue wheel, turned her scowl toward him, but said nothing. It dawned on him that Marian must still be in the shower, and could not hear his tattoo. He somehow set the cups and saucers down on the wooden deck at his feet without spilling a drop, and tried the doorknob. The door opened, and he picked up his burden once again, and entered, setting the cups down on the first flat surface, the top of the dresser nearest the door.

Within a few loud heartbeats — the result of a walk uphill in the heat with what was probably exhaustion plus a hangover plus et cetera — he became intensely aware of the absence of sound in the room. He could plainly hear the squeak of the rogue wheel on the housekeeper's cart several doors away, but nothing at all within thirty feet. No shower noises, no sound of movement, nothing but the lazy whir of the ceiling fan that they had turned on last night as they became sweaty, and had never turned off. Lewis walked to the bathroom door and knocked. Again, no response. Suddenly envisioning an unconscious Marian, head split open from slipping in the shower, he knew it happened all the time, he barged in, and found an absence of Marian, comatose or otherwise. Also, the absence of any sign of a recent shower.

Absent the slip-and-fall, blood everywhere scenario, his panic vanished. Perhaps, he thought, she had just gone out of the room. Perhaps he had been gone a bit longer than he thought. She could have left the room right after he had, gone to the vending machine for some Anacin. Who could know? He was worrying, he decided, without cause, about someone he had known less than a day. He decided that the only reasonable course of action was to sit down, light his first cigarette of the day, and drink some coffee. Then he could think more clearly. Before he sat, he fished about in his left front pants pocket, extracted the now-crushed croissant, and, at the very bottom of his pocket, covered in lint and tobacco flakes and dirt, he found a single Xanax tablet. He gulped it down with the bad, lukewarm "Coffe au Lait," and prayed that it would potentiate the effect of the two lousy Talwin, which were currently causing him to see everything with a vague, blue outline but hadn't touched his headache.

Sitting on the edge of the bed, glancing idly about, he noticed a folded sheet of hotel stationary right next to the coffee cups that still sat on the dresser. L.M. was written, in letters big enough for an old man to read, on the outside of the sheet. The note inside was almost as brief. "Forgot — have to go into town. Sorry — see you on the beach. M"

Lewis was surprised that Marian had left so quickly. He was certain that he hadn't been gone more than ten minutes. Although time on the island always ran a bit slower, or faster, than one thought, not at all like back in Boston. He guessed that her trip had been urgent, as she seemed to have left without a shower or a cup of coffee. Perhaps she had needed to get to the bank or the American Express office for something. He knew he could not worry about it without devoting his huge, state-of-the-art worrying machine to the project, an undertaking that, once set in motion, would take over his whole being. As he was, after all, on vacation, he chose to forego the project.

So he drank two more cups of coffee and had another cigarette with each, and scrawled a note to Marian in return, saying only that he planned to be at the beach, with any luck in exactly the same spot. Then he let himself out, and began the long trek back to his place. He would have a shower, then try to write until eleven or twelve. Then, to the beach.

Day 4- Thursday Night - Vermont

Just as the drugs began to wrap their comforting warmth around his body and soul, Lewis noted the lights coming up the road, reflected in the side windows of his porch. He couldn't tell, from where he sat, if the lights foretold cops, or robbers. He forced his door open with no small effort, stepped from the battered car, and swiftly moved to a safer spot behind the corner of the woodshed, directly back from the porch door he had exited just fifteen minutes ago.

Always cautious, some would say to a fault, he drew the pistol, and waited for a look at his visitor. Within a minute or two, it was apparent from the height and position of the headlights that it was a car, not a truck or an SUV. He put the gun back in his vest pocket and walked out of his place of concealment with all of the wounded prudence he judged appropriate to a citizen whose dwelling has been violently trespassed.

Cops made him nervous; they always had, even when it was he who had summoned them. He knew that history — or story, anyway — was rife with examples of those who had summoned helping spirits, only to have those spirits turn on the poor soul who had sought their help. Despite his decades of good citizenship, his largesse as a taxpayer in not one, but two states, not to mention the blood-money that those bastards at the IRS and the Massachusetts Department of Revenue extracted from him, despite all this, he could not regard the police, individually or severally, as his servant. Firemen, perhaps, were helpers. EMTs, sure. Cops, though, they trusted no one. They were like he was. They needed to be in control, and he would never willingly cede it. Consequently, he rarely broke the law, at least not in an antisocial way. So he acted defensive as hell around cops, and it generally backfired.

Before he was halfway down the driveway, the police car (he could see it was the local cops, it was not the Chief, but some part-timer) had pulled to a silent stop a few feet from him. The cop was out, walking and talking.

"Are you Melton? Did you request assistance? I'm Officer Grimes."

The question, the statement, really, hung in the cold air as business, that's all, although it sounded like a bit of menace, too. Lewis felt he had to answer soon, and well.

"Yes, I'm Lewis Melton, and I called. I'm pretty sure somebody was here, in my house. I know they were on the property, because they almost ran me down, pulling out of here in a hurry. Look at my car....I barely got enough out of the way to keep out of a head-on."

The cop — Officer Grimes — was now beaming his flashlight (if it was a flashlight, why did it look so much like a truncheon, Lewis wondered) brought the glare around to Lewis's face, momentarily blinding him.

"Did you recognize the vehicle or the alleged intruder? Could it have been someone you know?"

Holding his right hand up to shield his eyes from the fierce light, Lewis answered in the most polite and measured tones that he could muster.

"Look, would you mind very much not shining that fucking light in my eyes? I can't see, or think. Thanks, that's better. No, I didn't recognize the vehicle or the 'alleged intruder.' By alleged intruder, do you mean that the person driving the truck might have also been an intruder, but possibly not, or that I'm only alleging that someone was driving the truck? Never mind.... No, I didn't recognize anything or anyone. But I'm pretty sure it was a pickup truck, probably a half-ton or one-ton, maybe four-wheel drive, because it sat pretty high. And sure, it could have been someone I know....that's kind of an open-ended question, since I have no goddamn idea whatsoever who it was. It could have been the King of Sweden, for all I know. But whoever it was sideswiped me, in their hurry to get out of here. I don't know if they just got here, or had been here, and freaked out when they saw me pull up. I really need to know whether there's someone still in the house. Will you go check, please? And, I'll need an accident report from you. This is a rental, and I can't begin to imagine the grief they're going to give me for wrecking it."

The cop remained motionless — except for lowering his flashlight — throughout Lewis' barely sufficiently tempered reply to what the cop had thought was a reasonable question. Lewis had noted, over the years, that cops always thought that their questions were reasonable. He'd try to be nicer.

"Well, sure, Mr. Melton, we should go look in the house, first. Do you want to come with me, please? Or would you feel better if I went alone? And, by the way I don't care for bad language. I'm here to help you, but you seem to want to be disrespectful. I don't know why you would want to do that."

"Hey, Officer, I'm sorry if I sounded a little cranky," he backpedaled, now, "but someone almost just killed me, I think. Why don't you go in alone: I'll wait right here. I'm still a little shaky."

Lewis would have said more apology-wise, but couldn't guarantee that Nasty Lewis would stay in the background. Better to just shut his mouth, for now.

As he spoke, Lewis moved back toward the injured Ford, and, with great effort and the squeal and pop of metal, dragged the driver's side door open. The car was still running, with the heater cranking a steady flow of heated air that drew him toward the big, heated leather seat.

"Okay, Mr. Melton. I'm just going to go to my car and call in. They get nervous if we don't call in." The cop thought, but didn't say, he planned to have a check run on one Lewis Melton, just to find out if he was as crazy as he seemed. Ounce of prevention, you might say.

Officer Grimes did call in, as he had promised, and did have them run a check, as he hadn't said, and nothing unusual came back. No recent police business, no pending charges, just a speeding ticket a few years back. He'd mailed in the fine.

All of this took about six minutes, while Lewis sat in his fucked-up rental, calmer now, wondering what the hell the big dumb cop was up to. A light shone through the window on his face, snapping him out of his reverie. The policeman was standing by the car door. Lewis motioned him to step back, kicked the door open, and got out.

"If you're ready, Officer, I've decided to go in with you…as long as you go first."

"That's fine, Sir. I don't expect there's anyone in there, not after all this time. Have you been drinking, Mr. Melton?"

"What? No, I haven't been drinking. Not since a beer at lunch, anyway. Do you think I'm drunk? Do you think I hallucinated all of this?"

"No, Sir, but your eyes just look a little glassy, probably just shock. Let's go in, check the place out, then, I'll make out an accident report for you. If I was you, I'd ask me to write it up like your car was just parked on the road. If you get hit in your own driveway by an unidentified person or persons, you may not ever get the insurance straightened out. Now, follow me, but stay back at least one room."

They made for the door, with Lewis lagging back a good fifteen feet. As the cop moved purposefully but cautiously forward, Lewis called out to him, *sotto voce*, where the light switches were, until the cop hissed at him to be quiet. They had traversed the porch/mud-room and the kitchen, and were in the living room now. Even with the light on, it was a dark, cold, and long room, lined with bookcases, furnished with two old and ratty couches and not much else except for the woodstove. The house, a hundred years old or more, creaked and snapped in all its parts, especially in the fall and spring as the ground moved a bit with the freezing and thawing that accompanied those seasons. It snapped now, loudly, somewhere in the next room, and the cop stopped still, as he did with each new house-groan. When the refrigerator (Lewis had paid a hundred, used, ten years ago) cycled on, the cop's right hand went to his holstered pistol. He seemed, to Lewis, to be a bit on edge.

Lewis, now even with the cop, moved into the front hall and checked the front door by sight. It was unlocked, as always. They moved up the steep stairs to the second floor, with the cop as point. Both bedrooms were vacant and seemed untouched, not a thing out of place. Finally, to the bathroom. The medicine cabinet was open. At the officer's request, Lewis took a cursory inventory, and found nothing missing. He knew that none of the good drugs were there, anyway. Only a fool would leave his medicine in a medicine cabinet.

Once they had established that the house was vacant — they checked the cellar almost as an afterthought — they circled back through one more time, for a careful cataloguing of any and all valuables. The padlocked tool chest where he kept his two rifles, a cheap old .22 bolt-action and a newer AR-15, and an ancient 10-gauge double-barreled shotgun, was still padlocked, and the guns were still there. The few bottles of booze he kept in the pantry, mostly for guests, were in their rightful places. Nothing at all was missing. He'd check his secret stashes later.

What wasn't missing confused Officer Grimes: booze, guns, and an expensive sound system. Not missing, but the preferred booty for local house-breakers, usually kids from town (or the next town over), or sometimes the desperate rural junkie, the poor bastard who had to pay four to ten times the going city rate for dope but didn't have the gumption to move to where the dope was. No vandalism, either. No one had taken a beer-shit on the kitchen table. No one had spray-painted misspelled obscenities on the walls. The whole thing just didn't make sense to Officer Grimes, who was the cop equivalent, in some ways, of the rural junkie. He was used to things the way they were, and couldn't wrap his brain around what he saw as anomalies. In the city, he'd be dead in a month. To his credit, he salvaged one conclusion. He turned to Lewis.

"Well, Mr. Melton, I think that whoever was here was looking for you, and nothing else. Is anyone looking for you, anybody want to harm you? Had any threats made against you recently? Maybe a jealous husband (or jealous wife, he thought)?"

"Look, I told you before, I don't know enough people to have enemies. Hell, I barely have friends. I'm a writer. Sometimes I teach. I have an ex-wife, and a daughter. I have one or two friends who I see, rarely. No one even knows when I'm in a room. Period."

Lewis, as he spoke, set about making some coffee for both of them, clicked the furnace on, and then began a fire in the stove, pretty much ignoring the tired and unimaginative cop, talking as much to himself as to anyone.

"Could I have pissed somebody off, unintentionally? Sure. Maybe I cut someone off in traffic, except there's no traffic around here. I haven't fucked anyone's wife, I'm sorry to say. I don't post my land, I don't go to Town Meeting, and I don't write Letters to the Editor."

Finally, as he drank the coffee that he didn't really want, the cop made out an accident report that Lewis could show the car rental people. The details weren't far from the truth: just about fifty feet, and a lot of fear. Then Grimes left, after cautioning Lewis to lock his doors, and suggesting that he load his shotgun and keep it handy, just in case. He recommended that if Lewis had the occasion to shoot anyone outside the house, he would do well to drag them inside before he called the authorities.

Lewis did load his shotgun, after he found some shells, finally, in the cellar. They might actually fire. He went up to bed with his shotgun, the borrowed pistol, and three bottles of strong ale, and fell asleep about three hours later.

1964 – Fitting In

The sound of a big DeWalt radial arm saw somewhere close by woke him instantly from a sleep so deep and far away the entry into consciousness was like a fall.

Eyes open, instantly oriented, knowing that the hangover would attack very soon, now, Lewis thought about his status, his options, his plan. He had from time to time considered that he was indeed fortunate, being both reasonably clever and truly lucky, a regular fucking water-walker when it came avoiding disaster (however narrowly). He sometimes came close enough to whiff the carrion breath of desperately bad karma, but, somehow, stepped out of the path, letting the bad-news banshee scream on by, undoubtedly to nail some other poor bastard. He figured he had just done it again, and for this was thankful.

He was on an old and odiferous mattress on the floor of what seemed to be a tiny living room, Janey's living room. He couldn't remember much of what had happened when they got back from the bar the previous night, but was reasonably certain that nothing of note had transpired. He did recall that Janey had firmly and repeatedly refused to let him into her bed, which, he guessed, was why he was on the floor, fully dressed, and beginning to feel dreadful.

Getting up into a sitting position brought a jolt of queasy pain to his head, and brought also the memory of his encounter with a well-swung shotgun barrel. He gingerly palpated the area of the wound, and felt a new crust of blood in his hair and behind his ear. It wasn't still bleeding. He must have thrashed about during the night and opened it up again, but he could feel it knitting together, the slight itch of healing. His nausea increased, either from touching the wound, or from his hangover, or from his recalled fear.

He staggered to his feet, nearly falling over a rickety coffee table next to his pallet, and barking his shin on the thick driftwood top. Bottles on the table clinked emptily, but did not fall. Lewis walked with a young drunk's tread through the small kitchen to the bathroom, took an endless high-pressure piss, and moved to the washstand to clean up a bit. A big skylight set into the pitched ceiling illuminated enough of his visage in the mottled old mirror to convince him to shower, to shave, to find a comb or a brush, as soon as he felt ready for a procedure that traumatic. The side of his head didn't look so bad, except for the crusted blood, but his ear was half-again as big as it should have been, and the adjacent eye was encircled by a green and gray and purple bruise.

Both of his eyeballs were a little past bloodshot, and his hair, long enough to lay down flat, stuck up in tufts. He looked scary, and could not now fault Janey's refusal to fuck him. It was a goddamn miracle that she had even let him sleep on the floor.

He turned on the cold water spigot with a tremulous hand, and splashed a few cupped-hands full on his face and head, finger combed his hair, and dried his face and hands with the edge of a suspect towel draped over the bathtub edge. With someone's toothbrush and the dregs of a flattened tube of Ipana (Bucky Beaver!) he scrubbed his mouth out, then, swallowed two Midol from the medicine cabinet with a mouthful of water from the tap. When he bent his head to drink, his balance almost left him, so he straightened up slowly, took deep slow breaths. This was not the place to faint. A guy might be good enough to leave you in peace, on the floor, until you got it together, but a girl might call an ambulance, and with ambulances came police.

As he studied his now-less-frightening head in the mirror, he saw the bathroom door behind him open, and a naked Janey, mostly still asleep, walked in, saw him, began to cover her tits half-heartedly with an arm, thought better of it, given the circumstances, and sat down on the toilet and peed.

"I'm not awake." She mumbled, in explanation, then tore off a few squares of toilet paper to dry herself. She got up and left, just as quickly as she had entered. He watched her cute ass depart, and started to get hard. He couldn't help it. He had seen Janey naked dozens of times, and she him. She had a pretty okay body, and was an attractive girl, but was, it seemed, more like a sister than a possible bed-mate, although that had never stopped him from trying, given sufficient alcohol. She was his type: they all were. But he was not her type, he thought, not quite dissolute enough. He didn't have that smell of danger that all of her boyfriends emanated. Doc, for instance, who she had slept with on and off for as long as he had known her.

Lewis was the un-Doc. Doc, and his brothers among men, were superficially predictable, generally easy to find, easy to be with. But Doc was equally likely to show up at your place at two in the morning, bearing a stolen pie from the Portuguese bakery down the street, or arrive in the middle of a sunny afternoon with a flamboyantly homosexual black Canadian gun-runner in tow, who he would insist that you, and everyone else, befriend.

There was no absolute that governed Doc, no way to rule out what he might do or say or mean. Everyone, it seemed, knew what Lewis would do next, because he himself had to know what he would do next. That, alone, ruled out an entire universe of potential behaviors and friends, but there was no other way that he could be. He couldn't help it.

His trip to the Island was an anomaly. His planet had spun out of its orbit, and those who knew him would be vaguely uncomfortable around him now, for a while, until he drifted back into Lewis-like behavior. It made him uncomfortable, too, and with the head wound, and the hangover, and all that potentially waited for him back in the city, he had to think that some reefer or a beer or two had to be the next thing on his agenda.

He cinched his belt up a notch, turned, and left the bathroom. In the kitchen, the 'fridge yielded one cold Ballantine IPA. He popped the cap on a corner of the refrigerator door handle, and tipped back half the bottle, feeling the alcohol soothe his raw nerve endings in seconds. He set the bottle down on the dirty table, lit a flattened and bent cigarette from the squashed pack in his jeans pocket, and walked to Janey's bedroom door. Peeking in to determine if she was alone (she was), he stepped a few feet to her bed and gently touched her bare shoulder to awaken her.

"Janey — sorry — I just need some info. You said last night that I could probably get some work with the guys painting out in 'Sconset. How do I get there?"

Janey lifted her head perhaps half an inch from the pillow, turned toward him, and regarded him with a bloodshot blue eye.

"Go away. Go into town. Look for the signpost. Hitch. G'bye."

She pulled the covers up over her head and shoulders as she turned away, signaling an end to the conversation. Lewis got the hint, and left to finish his ale. With any luck (and he had luck, he had luck) he could find some work and a place to stay before nightfall, and then retire to the bar for the evening to medicate his many ills.

Saturday, Day 13

Back at his own cottage, Lewis stripped off his clothes and, tired, well-laid, and uneasy, stepped into his shower, standing under the driving lukewarm spray until he was pretty sure that the sex and cigarettes and fear-sweat had been dissolved. Panic attacks, and last night's had been in the top ten, could be counted on to produce many physical manifestations, none of them good. After an attack, he stank, and the smell got worse with age. He scrubbed, then, with the cheap French soap provided *gratis*, and wondered, still and again, what had happened to Marian.

He knew the question was important, the riddle some sort of flashing caution sign, and knew that he was capable of obsessing about it to the point that it would take him over, and he could not, ever, afford that. He could not remember if he had taken any Xanax today, and decided that he should take some more, anyway, why take the chance. Maybe, he thought, I should get out of the shower right now and take some.

Turning the shower off successfully after only one try (why was this so difficult?), he padded naked, large, and dripping, to his traveling bag. He traveled light, and never unpacked, for fear he would forget something. Drying his hands carefully on the bedspread, he extracted an ancient Dopp kit that held his shaving gear, toothbrush, the odd ancient Band-Aid, and, in a zipped side compartment, his medications. One for his allergies, which he never took; one for his chronic gingivitis, which he took religiously, but did no good; several for aches and pains and the pain of awareness, and two for his panic disorder.

He lived in fear of having his drugs confiscated by an overzealous cop or customs agent, and so, he carried everything in the original prescription bottle. This led to great bulk, a problem for a paranoid man. He had found, years ago, the biggest travel bag that Dopp made, and found it just barely sufficient. His euphemistically named "shaving kit" took up a full third of his travel bag. He could have done without the rest of the stuff. The zippered compartment bulged with bottles, a sight he found comforting. Sometimes when especially nervous, he would line the bottles up, and count the pills. He needed that solidity now.

He laid the bottles out on the bed, preparing for the full sacrament. Setting the antihistamines and antibiotics to one side, he uncapped and counted the remaining five bottles. Xanax, .5 mg., 11; Ativan, 1 mg., almost full (54); Oxycodone, 10 mg., only 7 left — how had he taken that many?; Vicodin ES, just 10 left; Percodan, 20, the same number prescribed. He felt more calm with each pill counted, these were his Rosary beads. Instead of ten Hail Marys, he chose an Ativan and 3 Percodan, figuring the aspirin would help his headache. He estimated that he had ten days of pills left, if he were prudent, and he vowed to not take more than he absolutely, positively needed. Of course, he could always see a Doctor on the island and get more, but they either wanted to speak French, or worse, they were Dutch, and thought he was an addict. They would give him a large prescription that he could neither finish there or chance taking back through American Customs. He had flushed fifty oxymorphone tablets at the airport once in a fit of fear, and had felt bad about it for weeks.

The tiny fridge under the sink yielded a bottle of Evian to wash the pills down after he had chewed then finely to speed the process. As he marveled at how good the combination tasted — it was the aspirin that added the real flavor — his telephone bleated with the universally annoying French ring-tone. Without thinking, he picked it up.

"Lewis Melton, please — it's Marian…."

He answered quickly. Ah, one less thing to worry about!

"Hi, this is Lew. What happened to you? Are you alright?"

"Something's come up. There was a message at the desk. My Aunt has died. We were close. I have to leave."

Lewis couldn't quite make out what was wrong with the voice he was hearing. It was brittle, fast. It sounded as if she were at the bottom of a well…. an echo, almost, but muffled. Just not right. It sounded like a bad cell phone connection more than anything else.

"Marian, where are you. Are you at the airport?"

"No, at the hotel. Packing. I have a cab waiting out front. I have an eleven o'clock flight."

"Do you want me to come up there, go to the airport with you?"

"No — no time, sorry. Thanks. Listen, I need to go. I'll call you in a few days."

"How will you call me? You don't know where I'll be. Let me give you my Boston number, I'll be there next week."

"Okay, sure. Just leave it with the desk here. I'll call you. Bye."

The phone went dead. This all seemed terribly odd. For starters, thought Lewis, it was almost impossible to get a flight out with short notice. His experience — from the one occasion he had needed to leave quickly — was that the best you could do was to bribe your way on to a twelve-seater to San Juan, and then catch the "cattle car" to New York, and then the shuttle to Boston. Getting a seat on a scheduled carrier in the time she had since he had last seen her was impossible, unless she had been preternaturally lucky, or had paid off a dozen different people, or unless she already had reservations. If the last were true, why didn't she just tell him that?

He couldn't overlook how wrong her voice had sounded. She could have been reading lines from a script. And he was certain that the call had been made from a cell phone. Did she have a cell phone that worked on the island? He knew that they could be rented at the airport, but had not seen her use one in the hours they had spent together. Why would she use a cell in her hotel room, when the land line was only a few feet away?

Lewis was becoming increasingly uncomfortable with the whole thing, and could feel his panic casing the joint, looking for a way past the chemical security systems in his brain. Soon, the panic patrol would forget stealth, and just charge the guards. In the right circumstances, they could always overpower the drugs, unless he stoned himself down to drooling idiot status.

Perhaps another milligram of Ativan was in order. He went back to the stash, still laid out for inventory. When he opened the bottle to shake a trank out, two tumbled into his palm. A sign! He took both. He would be very calm, perhaps too calm for the beach. The pool might be a better idea.

Still naked, but now dried by the warm Caribbean air, he went to his deck to find a smoke. He found only two left in the pack, so lit one, and went to the bedroom to check his discarded khaki's for more. No cigarettes, but a roll of currency, francs and dollars mixed together. And a large check, that he apparently had forgotten about, and would need to put in the hotel safe if he expected to take it home with him.

There was no way he was going all the way back into town to get a carton of cigarettes, where, on the Dutch side, he'd pay almost nothing. He would go, instead, to the small gift shop and grocery store that the resort operated, and pay half as much for a single, stale pack as he'd pay for a carton in the town. Addiction is a terrible thing, he thought: it's nice that I can afford it.

At least he didn't need to get dressed. As a nudist resort, clothing was not required anywhere or anytime within the compound. He was beginning to forget about the weird phone call, for now, and pondered, instead, the odd and wonderful experience of sanctioned nakedness. He would walk out his door, and down the well-tended path, passing other naked humans, who would, invariably, greet him pleasantly. He would go into the tiny store, always crowded, where everyone would be on their best behavior. And, if there was a line, no one would bump into him.

There was a line when he got there, and the no longer youthful but very attractive woman behind the counter wore only a tiny apron made up of strings of brightly colored glass beads. It was only a few inches square, and reached just below her pussy, but only when she stood still. Apparently there was some government regulation that required store clerks to cover their pudenda; if so, the swinging curtain of beaded strings met the letter, but not the intent, of the law. Lewis could see that she was shaved, and that the dark tan that showed elsewhere showed there, too. Her face was skillfully made up, and her breasts, that must have once been impressively firm and high, now swung in a lower arc. But she had a wonderful smile, and looked as if she truly enjoyed the life she had, and that the years she continued to add to that life were not a burden but an honor, and she could still be naked and enticing in her own lovely way. Lewis wished that he felt that way. Standing still and looking furtively down, he could see his stomach, but not his dick.

The beautiful clerk seemed to have trouble with Lewis' English, so, he switched to very bad French, and was able to walk away with two packs of American cigarettes of a brand he hadn't seen in years, and was only ten dollars poorer.

The second two milligrams of Ativan were coming on now, potentiating the narcotics in a nice way, but a way that told him he must soon be prone. He walked the fifty yards to the big, seldom used pool, walking by the Pool Attendant's table to secure a fresh clean towel. There was a vacant chaise under an umbrella at the far side of the area, a spot with no close neighbors. He spread his towel on the plastic lounge chair, sat, then lay back, and was off to a relaxing place that might have looked like sleep to an observer, but was much, much better.

Friday, Day 5 - Vermont

The light coming through his bedroom window told him that it was around seven or seven-thirty in the morning, and that it would soon be spring, or what passed for spring in southern Vermont. More of the ice on the roads and the mounds of snow in the woods would melt, running into rivulets and tiny streams and then bigger ones, running toward the brooks and rivers and lakes, warming the thick ice, and finally, with the vernal sun and winds, bringing ice-out.

Lewis could hear the slow drip of water from the southeast slope of his roof hitting the heavy blue plastic tarp that covered a cord of maple, still half-green, that had been bought and delivered last fall. The drip reminded him that he urgently needed to piss, and he swung his legs off the bed and hit the freezing floor with his aching feet. The stove must have burned out some hours ago, and the furnace had not kicked on yet.

Getting to his feet, he flashed with dizziness just long enough to get his attention. He thought, maybe, he had a hangover, but not a bad one. The twenty steps to the bathroom were almost too much for his bladder — he had his penis out in anticipation before he got to the toilet, but then, of course, couldn't start the stream for a few heartbeats, and when he did, couldn't keep the flow going, but peed in starts and stops for what seemed like a very long time. He wondered if his prostate was going south on him.

"That's what I fucking need to spice up my life," he announced to the empty bathroom, "Fucking prostate cancer. I can have some horribly painful surgery, maybe radiation and chemo, and then spend the rest of my fucking miserable life impotent and incontinent!"

The brief rant and long piss made him feel much better. He hobbled to, and down, the steep stairway, and turned the thermostat up to seventy-two, hearing the furnace roar into life as he turned the coffee maker on. Then back up the stairs to pull on some ratty cords and a heavy wool sweater — he'd shower later, if at all, and perhaps shave, too. Right now, he needed a few cups of coffee and two or three cigarettes, and his morning pills. One for his blood pressure, one for his cholesterol, one for his arthritis, and a few for the pain of awareness.

Halfway through his first mug of coffee and his pills — adding a couple of Vicodin to ward off any hangover that might be sneaking up on him — he began to turn the events of the previous night over in his head. He had, as he saw it, almost been killed. His shotgun, loaded with number six birdshot, still leaned up against the wall by his bed. A wave of cold fear surged up from his gut to his head, bringing an involuntary shudder. Not a religious man, despite (or perhaps because of) his terrifying Lutheran upbringing, he prayed silently that the Xanax he had just taken would take hold very soon. He feared that pills weren't going to be enough for the direction his life was heading toward. He needed to get away, preferably far away, and soon.

Lewis had planned to make his annual spring get-away to the islands in May, when the rates dropped in the Caribbean and the black-flies were so bad in Vermont that leaving the house was torture. He could call his travel agent and see if things could be moved up a bit, see if perhaps he could get a plane out very soon. He thought today might be good.

1964 – An Old Friend

After pouring the rest of the bottle of IPA down his throat, and taking a precautionary leak, Lewis left Janey's place and hiked into town looking for a cup of coffee, a doughnut, and the 'Sconset road. Main Street was busy for that early hour, with new pickup trucks and old, rusty cars parked in clusters on one side of the street. He found a small restaurant near the cars and trucks, and was glad to step inside to the warmth and the cigarette smoke mixed with the smell of bacon frying on the grill. It had gotten colder outside, maybe twenty degrees colder than the previous evening, and felt like it was in the low forties, with a raw, wet wind blowing in from the north and east. He remembered hearing that "Spring" on the Island was more of a statement of season than a climatic indicator, and that warm weather would not reliably arrive much before the summer people did in late June.

The counter was busy and full and exclusively male. The men were dressed in brown carpenter pants and heavy sweatshirts or bib overalls or blue jeans, and almost all wore knitted wool watchcaps. They ate steadily but not quickly, and stayed for another cup of coffee and a cigarette or two. Their talk was loud and broken often by laughter. Today was Saturday, a half-day for most, and they were looking forward to whatever the weekend might bring. Lewis guessed that Monday morning would look and sound different here, as the poor hung-over bastards faced a day of work with shaking hands and empty pockets.

Lewis found a stool near the middle of the long counter, between two short, wide fishermen in high yellow rubber boots and oilskin jackets. They had been talking to each other between forks-full of pancakes and eggs and sausage, and continued to talk across Lewis, as if he were not there. When the blowzy middle-aged waitress arrived, he ordered coffee and bacon, eggs, and home fries, not the doughnut he had intended. He was not much of a breakfast person, and often ate nothing until lunch, but something about the place — or maybe the Island — had given him appetite. His order arrived quickly, even before he had finished the cigarette he had lit when his coffee had been served.

Just as he was dredging up the last of his eggs with a piece of toasted Portuguese bread, a large hand fell on his left shoulder. He half-turned, and was met with the flushed, glassy-eyed and oddly distinguished visage of Billy Carter, an old drinking buddy from Boston. Billy was a legendary drunk by the time he was twenty, a certifiable madman, but a friendly drunk. He did not have a sober bone in his body, or a mean one.

"Lew, is that you, you old whore- dog? What the fuck are you doing here?"

"Billy, my man! Are you still sober….it's almost eight o'clock. Yeah, it's me, got in last night. I'm actually looking for work, and a place to stay. I'm going to hitch out to Sakonnet- wherever that is — some guys I know are working out there."

"Lew, Lewis, you'll never get work out there….you're still just an over-educated fool. They need real carpenters. I'll get you work right here in town. Just let me get a cup of coffee, then, I'll take you down to the jobsite. The boss said yesterday that we need more laborers. I got an extra hammer in the car, probably a hammer hoop and a tape, too. We'll go see the man in a few minutes. Then, we'll go to the bar, it opens by nine. No work today, I'd guess — there's some nasty weather coming in."

"Far fucking out! What kind of work is open?"

"We're building the new waterfront. Right now, we're doing the big wharf, nailing oak strips to the pilings. You have to do it from this little raft, and we won't be doing that in a storm. And there's a storm coming: you see those guys in oilskins? They're scallopers. If there wasn't a nasty blow coming in, they'd have been out there since sunup. They won't pass up a fishing day unless it's really bad. Anyway, if you can swing a three-pound sledge for eight hours, you'll have work come Monday."

Fifteen minutes later, one coffee had turned into two, and Lewis and Billy had just, finally, left the diner. Billy had stopped at a booth where three extremely hung-over looking guys were gagging down some breakfast. He spoke with them, briefly, to confirm plans for duck-hunting Sunday morning, extracting a vow from each to put by a pint of brandy and a couple of six-packs on Saturday, so they'd have something to drink in the duck blind. That done, they walked out the door at just past eight o'clock, already very late for work. Work or no work, the crew was expected to show up at 7:30 to get the word. Billy did not seem particularly concerned about his tardiness, and drove the ancient blue Nova at a crawl the entire quarter-mile to the jobsite. The old car rattled like a bucket of bolts on the cobblestone street.

"Why so slow, Billy?"

"Well, she only has second and reverse at this point, and if I lose second — which is inevitable, so, really, when I lose second, I'm basically fucked. I'll have to drive home from the bar backwards, and that will leave the cops no choice but to stop me. And I certainly can't walk home from the bar, as drunk as I get. I'd pass out by the side of the road, and I'd get arrested for that, too. Anyway, we're there, so stop your bitching."

Billy and Lew clambered out of the dying Chevy, and went around to the trunk. Twisting the handle of a large screwdriver that was semi-permanently jammed into the lock, Billy swung the trunk open, revealing what seemed to be several hundred tools, beer cans, and various articles of dirty clothing. He rooted around for a bit, extracted his tool belt, and found a hammer hoop, an old framing hammer, and a twelve-foot retractable tape measure, handing the last three items to Lewis. Lewis put the hammer hoop and tape on his belt, dropped the hammer into the hoop, and they were ready.

"Let's go find the boss, Mitch is his name. He can be a real pisser. I'll do the talking. If he asks, tell him you've worked as a framer in Boston."

The fog had turned to a heavy mist, and then to a fine, cold drizzle since Lewis had entered the restaurant. Now that they were out of the car, it had become heavier, and the wind had picked up. The workers that they passed paid no apparent attention to the rain, although the onshore breeze was driving the precipitation at them at about a 45 degree angle. Most seem to have come prepared with yellow or black rain jackets, wool caps, and oiled leather workboots.

"Mitch!" yelled Billy, at a squat, red-faced, middle-aged man who was standing at the very edge of a new-looking section of the wharf. The man appeared to be screaming at the Atlantic Ocean.

"Mitch!" Bill yelled, again, as he and Lewis walked closer. Billy either didn't notice, or didn't care, that he was yelling into the wind, and was unlikely to be successful at the current distance. They could now see, though, that the red-faced man was not screaming at the ocean, but at two sodden laborers twelve feet below him, doing their best to stand on a small, flat-bottomed raft that was rolling badly on the incoming swells.

"...and I'll tell you assholes when it's time to knock off! Shit, it's not hardly raining at all, yet — don't be such fucking pussies! Now get the rest of those goddamn strips on those goddamn pilings! We might need to knock off later, if it gets bad, and this section has to be done by Monday. Do it today, or you'll be working tomorrow!"

Day 5 — Friday – Vermont to Boston

Lewis had finally gathered the needed resolve to shower and shave, and to then scavenge a breakfast of an old, not yet moldy slice of apple pie. He thought that he recalled buying it at the Valley Store a week ago, give or take a few days. Some of the local women baked pies and breads from time to time, and sold them through the store. The bachelors, through logic, luck, or divorce, snapped them right up. They were almost always quite good, and always anonymous. It was only a matter of time, Lewis presumed, until some crazed housewife poisoned half the men in town in a fit of pique. Still, he almost always bought whatever was for sale. It was like high-calorie Russian Roulette.

The block of cheddar that he found to have with his pie was pretty moldy, and had to be shaved considerably before he got to a single, thick safe slice. The moldy scraps were carried outside to his small front deck, and from there they were chucked as far as possible into the nearby woods. With any luck, one of the goddamn trash-bears that kept raiding his bird feeders would get one hell of a stomach-ache, and leave for safer haunts. On the other hand, these bears were known to snack on discarded tires, so the cheese could be a real treat. The Summer People thought the bears were cute, but Lewis had lost his old cat to a bear, and noticed more bears with each passing year, and wanted them gone. He had no serious grudge with the bears, but he didn't want them in his door-yard. He felt the same about the Summer People.

After washing up the breakfast dishes, and feeling, now, sufficiently Xanaxed and Vicodined to do business, Lewis moved his chair, phone, coffee and ashtray to a sunny corner of his living room. The warm rays felt like spring, motivating him to call his travel agent to see how soon he could expect to get to some real sunshine, some tropical sunshine that would fry his skin and roast his aching bones. His favorite agent in the office, Mindy, answered on the second ring. He made his wishes known to her in detail in the time it took to smoke a cigarette. Her response was friendly, but not optimistic.

"Lew," she said, her New York accent seeping through the two decades of living in Boston, "this could be tough on such short notice. You know that most places do a Saturday to Saturday, or sometimes a Sunday to Sunday. Today is Friday, I'll bet, even in Vermont. I know you want the same place, on the French side, which is even tougher, because the folks who stay there usually make their reservations for the next year before they even leave the place....and you're looking for two weeks. And, then there's the plane. Let me see what I can do. How much do you want to spend?"

As desperate as he was to get away, Lewis was a frugal man. His Ex, Judy, preferred the word "cheap." He knew he was a bit of both, and gave Mindy a number that he figured was about twenty percent less than he'd end up paying: four thousand, and not a penny more. He told her that he'd bonus her ten percent for every hundred dollars that she came in under the four thousand. He bet that she'd do better if incentivized over and above the cut she'd be getting anyway.

He bade her good luck. She told him to relax, and that she'd call him back before lunch, and to pack his bag, because he might need to get to the airport — she didn't know which one yet — on very short notice. Lewis figured he had a couple of hours to kill. He always traveled light, and could pack his small bag in five minutes. He'd drive to the store and get the newspaper, check his mail, and be back long before she called.

It had turned out warmer than he had expected, probably nudging the freezing point, with a strong sun that made the air almost warm, if one were out of the wind. Lewis took his winter jacket, but threw it in the back seat of the half-wrecked car through the open window. He walked around the car as far as he could without wading into the snow bank, and could find no parts in imminent danger of falling off. He didn't want to lose a wheel going down the mountain. He slipped into the driver's seat through the twenty inches that the door would still open, and turned the key that he had left in the ignition. The beast would not start, not until he realized that he had turned it off in Drive, and it would only start in Park. He hated automatic transmissions, believing them to be so thoroughly idiot-proofed that only an idiot was capable of operating one.

The car, of course, was well-mired in snow and ice and frozen mud, after sitting all night where he had left it. Repeated rocking back and forth finally freed it, although the sounds that the transmission emitted during this process were painful to hear. He also lost the front bumper on his last acceleration rearward: a low stump that he had driven over easily the night before had wedged itself firmly behind the bumper as the SUV had settled, and now ripped off quite neatly. He squeezed out of the door, picked up the bumper, and tossed it in the rear cargo area. The rental people were not going to be pleased with him, but he felt it only proper to return the entire vehicle that he could, even if no longer attached. He hoped he could leave the car at the airport return lot with a copy of the accident report on the front seat, and deal with it upon his return. They might want to speak with him at some length, after they saw the damage.

Considering what the Ford had been through, it drove well, although it did pull to the right a bit. Lewis made it down the mountain to the store in just a few minutes, as the road, oddly, had been well sanded. When he arrived at the store, the morning rush, usually from six to nine o'clock, had passed, and only a couple of trucks were parked in front. He recognized the trucks as belonging to locals, retired or unemployed, or maybe taking the nice sunny day off to sit parked back in the woods, drinking beer. Eight eyes turned to him for a split second when he walked in, and then away, and back to whatever they had been looking at before. Eddie sat on a high stool behind the counter, smoking a cheap cigar, and sharpening an impressively large Bowie knife. Lewis took a *New York Times* from the short stack by the door, and brought it to the counter.

"Eddie, how's it going? Just the paper, I think."

"It's going, Mr. Melton, its going. That'll be ninety cents. Hear you had a little excitement up your way last night."

Lewis knew the drill, and spoke his lines.

"Well, not so much excitement. I guess some kids broke in, but they took off when I pulled up. Hit my car though. Had to get a cop to come up to do an accident report."

Who knew, Lewis thought, what crazy stories were around town by now. Best to minimize it, and trust Eddie to play along.

"Yup, those little fuckers...." said Eddie, right on cue, "...they get a few beers on board, all of a sudden, they turn into idiots. Well, who's to say that we didn't all get a little wild when we were young? Anyway, they left, huh?"

"Yessir took off like bats out of Hell. Sideswiped my rental. Good thing I got the extra insurance this time."

Lewis picked up his newspaper, and made as if to head out the door, but turned back toward Eddie.

"By the bye, Eddie, I think I may be out of town for a bit. This time, I'll lock the doors. Hate to do that. I'll see you when I get back."

"Okay, Melton, you take care now. When I see the Chief, maybe I'll suggest he swing by your place, once or twice, make sure those doors stay locked."

Lewis waved a half-assed salute, and left the store with his newspaper. He knew that half the town knew the story already, and the other half would know it by suppertime. There would be some idle chatter about just who had broken in to that writer fellow's place. It would be just another winter break-in of the dozen that happened each year. They were mostly blamed on cabin fever, no one was ever caught, and the natives were never, ever robbed. From time to time, if the Police Chief was both bored and motivated, he would call a few of the usual suspects down to his office next to the fire station, and ask a few questions. Then, things would quiet down for a while. Small town life is as predictable as the seasons, and no one would think of the break-in at the old Blood place — the writer's house, what was his name? — as anything out of the ordinary.

By the time Lewis had arrived back home, twenty minutes had passed, and he realized that he had neglected to pick up the mail. As he walked to the phone to call Eddie and ask him to hold his mail, he saw the green light on the answering machine blinking. He pushed the "PLAY" button, and heard Mindy's cheerful voice.

"Good news, Mr. Melton. We lucked out….got you two weeks at the Club for $1750 a week, starting tomorrow. And, a direct flight — an extra seat on a charter, but what the Hell — for $600, round-trip. If you were serious about the bonus, which, of course, I can't accept, so, you should slip it to me in cash, my math says it should be $190. Stop by the office today for your tickets and itinerary. We close at seven tonight, and you need to be at Logan at six ay em tomorrow. See you later."

Lewis listened to the message again, then, after he had fetched a cup of bitter, tepid coffee, once more, scrawling the important parts in his pocket agenda. With no one else around, he didn't bother to smile, or not smile, but gloated internally at his good luck and his pending successful escape. His usual morning aches (lately, afternoon and evening, too) began to fade in anticipation of the sun and anonymity that would soon be his.

It was creeping up on ten o'clock. He'd need to leave soon to avoid the traffic that would grow increasingly brutal around Boston as the afternoon rush kicked in. Better to leave now, swing by Newton to pick up his tickets, and then hide out at his place on the Hill. It took less than thirty minutes for him to pack (and re-pack, and re-pack) his small bag, find his passport (expired) and his birth certificate (scary). He shut off power to the well pump and the water heater, and set the thermostat to the noisy and effective propane furnace to forty-five. He ran all of the faucets dry: a half-assed way to drain the pipes, but, better than nothing. If the power went out for long, and, it could this time of year, every drop of liquid in the house could freeze — the toilets, the low-spots in the cheesy plastic pipes that he'd had put in ten years ago, when the copper pipes had all frozen and burst — it would be a major, expensive pain in the ass. So many things to worry about, so little time! He navigated the suicidally steep cellar stairs again, and found an old gallon jug of anti-freeze. A cup in each toilet tank and bowl would cover that problem. The other hazards would have to watch out for themselves. He might have tried to drain the water heater, but had begun to obsess, instead, about the half-wrecked SUV in his yard.

He was rightly concerned. Would the Explorer make it to Boston, and then out to Logan airport the next morning, without the wheels falling off? Would he get pulled over for having no front bumper and no driver's side headlight? He knew he'd be okay in Massachusetts, as the cops down there had better things to do, but, driving through Vermont and New Hampshire in a blatantly damaged car with Massachusetts plates was just asking for trouble. If they decided to search his car — highly unlikely, but possible — would they be understanding regarding what might be considered an unusual amount of controlled substances in his shaving kit. It was all legal, of course, but by the time things had been straightened out, it would be tomorrow, and his plane, and his reservations, would be long-gone.

Against his better judgment, he called the car rental office, told them he had been involved in a small accident, and wanted to drop the damaged vehicle off in Keene or Brattleboro, and rent another car. He spoke to three separate people of, he hoped, increasing authority, and was finally able to get assent to his request. He could drop the Ford at the Keene, New Hampshire office, and pick up a different car. The only car available, they told him, was a Lincoln, at the same high rate he was currently paying. There would, of course, be an additional charge for dropping the Explorer in Keene, and yet another additional charge for dropping the Lincoln off at the airport. He hoped that the good people at his auto insurance company had a sense of humor, as he planned to charge the second rental to them, along with any overages on the damage that his rental car insurance and credit card insurance might not cover.

Before eleven o'clock, he was backing out of his driveway. He would go through town, then pick up the river road north, to the bridge over to New Hampshire, then take a better road straight south to Keene. Not the most direct route, but probably the fastest, and with less chance of annoying any interested cops, especially State cops. If they saw his vehicle, he was certain they'd stop him. Hell, he'd stop himself. It was the front left fender waving in the wind that really made letting him drive on by an impossibility for any cop worth his salt, and the State Police were too sharp by half. They could smell fear miles away, and got a real kick out of stopping paranoids. The roads that Lewis chose were patrolled, if at all, mostly by town cops. He could talk to them without the tremor of fear in his voice.

The road was posted at 45 or 55 miles per hour, so, Lewis didn't get to the rental office until noon, and was stuck there, filling out reports, until almost

12:30. When he finally left, he was hungry, so he searched out the least-offensive fast food joint, and shortened his life a bit with a bacon cheeseburger, fries, and a large, dreadfully weak coffee....sufficient calories and caffeine to get him to Boston, with any luck.

The Lincoln was large, underpowered, and felt ungainly, of course, compared to his Audi, so, when Lewis walked into his apartment at four, tickets and itinerary in his pocket, only his violent fast-food heartburn prevented him from feeling very, very happy. He had a double shot of antacid, and began to relax. He'd need to get to the airport tomorrow with enough time to stand in various lines for an hour or two, and then sit in a poorly heated departure lounge until boarding. Part of the price for a ticket to paradise, even if you'd already paid in full.

As he planned to be in bed by nine, and had no food worth eating in the house, he walked down to a local bar on Cambridge Street at around six. They served food, as long as you wanted pizza or a burger. He took more antacid before he left, to treat the heartburn he had, and that yet to come.

The place was busy as hell, with standees two deep at the bar. There was one open booth, meant for three or four, but Lewis made a bee-line for it, and slid right in. He could see, but not hear, the TV above the bar. Thanks to the miracle of captioning, he could just make out the news-crawl at the bottom of the screen, including a weather report that hinted at a nasty storm forming off the coast of Georgia. Well, the plane could fly above the weather, or so he'd been told. Given his deep fear of flying, he always strove to accept any mollifying half-truths that might be thrown his way. He knew that "a little turbulence" could mean that the ice would rattle in your drink, or, on another day, your drink would fly up and hit you in the forehead. So, he now flew only when heavily self-medicated. It was often a challenge to remain conscious enough to board the plane and find his seat. If the boarding was late, they'd have to wake him up to board. If on time, he'd board, and be out of it by take-off.

Sometimes, he would awaken during the flight, but was always able to drift off again. The tough part was to swim back up to consciousness early enough to be alert by landing. He loved landing, despite having been told that it is the most dangerous part of the flight. All landings, even Caribbean landings that seemed to always include a precipitous drop, followed by a screech of brakes and reversed power to, one hoped, stop the plane before it hit the mountain that seemed to be at the end of all Caribbean runways, brought him joy. He loved to be back on the ground, and would kiss the earth after leaving the plane, if he thought he could get away with it.

Saturday, Day 6 – Fly High, Lay Low

So it was, with his flight to the island the next day, Saturday: he rose at four-thirty, although he had not really slept that much. He had over-estimated his narcotic intake needs by quite a bit, and had been so stoned, had felt so good, that sleep was out of the question. He did have a great six hour "nod," then hopped out of bed (well, almost hopped) and into the shower in time to hear his alarm go off once he was fully lathered up. He, uncharacteristically, let it go until he was out and dried off.

Breakfast was coffee, one milligram of a short-acting benzodiazepine, and a quarter milligram of a long acting one. He made it to the airport in twenty minutes, dropped off the Lincoln, and took an apparently unheated shuttle to the correct terminal. He had to circumnavigate the airport twice to get off at the correct terminal, but felt a little bit proud that he hadn't gotten off at the wrong terminal, despite the shuttle driver's urging. Once in the terminal, he was directed to stand n a very long line of sleepy, angry, excited fellow-travelers. He thought for a bit that this might be the wrong line, which was not that unusual. He frequently found, after an extended wait, that he was in the wrong line for whatever it was that he thought he was lined up for. Not many of the people in his line looked like they would be going to the island he was going to. They actually looked a lot more like a line of people — half of them children — waiting to go to Orlando, or some equally frightening place in Florida. Their vacation clothes were clearly just that, and smelled strongly of discount. Then, he remembered that his seat was on a charter flight, and, presumably, most of these good folks would be going to the other side of the island, not the side he was destined for, and, with any luck at all, he would not see them again until the return trip.

What the fuck, he thought, and dry-swallowed another half-milligram of the shorter-acting stuff. He would wait in a perfect trance state as they shuffled, oh so slowly, toward security. In the departure lounge, which he estimated was a good ten minutes away, at this pace, he could buy a cup of reasonably bad coffee and take a couple oxycodone tablets with it. They were the last pills in his pocket. Everything else was neatly put away in the original prescription bottles in his shaving kit. He wouldn't need any more pills until he got to the island around eleven o'clock, ten o'clock island time, after his four hour snooze in the middle of the air.

He had, almost an hour later, oozed successfully to the departure lounge, and was washing down the final pill with cold coffee when he heard his name on the overhead speakers — rarely a good omen.

"Doctor Melton, please report to the ticket desk."

What the hell? No one, except for his travel agent and the airline, and probably the government, knew he would be at this place at this time. He had planned to call Judy from the island; this was probably just a ticket thing. He rose, and went off to find the ticket desk. When he found it, it looked more like a lectern, but he supposed if they called it the ticket lectern, no one would ever figure it out. Anyway, there was a sign that said "Ticket Desk." It also said "Information." He figured he was about to get some.

The heavily made-up, not-so-young-up-close blonde behind the "desk" eyed him suspiciously as he approached, but, many people did. Perhaps he was a bit glassy-eyed.

"Yes, I'm Melton, you paged me?"

"Are you Doctor Melton?" the crumbling beauty asked, accenting the 'Doctor' part a bit dramatically.

"No, well, yes, but not the medical kind. No one calls me Doctor, although some people call me Professor. Anyway, what is it?"

"Well, someone called you Doctor; a Doctor Smith just called us to let you know he'll see you on the island. So maybe only other Doctors call you Doctor. Professor."

"I don't know any Doctor Smith," Lewis retorted, he hoped, more brusquely than peevishly.

"Here's a printout of the message." She handed him a six-inch long piece of flimsy with a torn bottom.

Lewis reached into his shirt pocket for his cheap reading glasses, did not find them, and instead, held the paper at arm's length. The sheet of light paper was clearly computer generated, tagged with today's date, an hour ago. The heading said "Dr. Lewis Melton, Flight 163A, from Dr. Smith."

An inch or two down, the brief message; "Lewis, see you on the island. Doc."

Lewis blanched, and all the air left his lungs just evaporated. He tried not to show it. Better to drop dead right here, right now.

"Did this come here? Did this call come to you?" he demanded, in a voice not his own.

"No, Doctor. Sorry, Sir. Messages come in at our main office, down at Terminal B. They just send it over by wire."

"So, this is just a transcript of a phone call?"

"Yes, Mr. Melton. Is that all?"

Melton wandered away without responding. He didn't know a Doctor Smith, but he sure as hell knew a Doc. But Doc was dead. And even if he were not dead, he would never, ever have a way to know where Lewis was. No one knew that was half the payoff of a journey: one disappeared into time and space, and then appeared somewhere else.

Thanks to the dangerous (for a mere mortal) concentration of anxiolytics and narcotic analgesics swimming around Lewis' brain, he was unable to focus on the problem for very long. In fact, he could not focus on anything for very long. It would be a miracle if he could get back to his chair in the departure lounge. Then, when he was almost back to the chair that held his traveling bag, which he should never, ever have left there, what with all his medications in it, he heard his boarding call. His travel agent had somehow gotten him the only empty seat, right behind the cockpit bulkhead. If the plane had a First Class section, which it did not, officially, have, he would be in it. Consequently, his row was among the first to load. He walked like an overweight old somnambulist through the boarding gate and down the tunnel to the plane. He imagined that something very much like this might happen when one died, if anything at all happened.

He must have said hello to the flight crew as they lurked at the doorway, but did not remember it later. Nor did he remember settling into his narrow seat and buckling himself in. He did, consciously, stuff his carry-on under his seat, and was pretty sure he said a short prayer for a safe flight and no obese or juvenile neighbors. He was asleep before the plane left the ground.

Then he was in a dream. He was lecturing about something, seemingly obtuse but actually quite simple and clear, to a classroom full of disinterested hippies, and he was not one of them. He wore a very nice three-piece suit (the vest was too tight) in a muted moss green Donegal wool, and he was older, by much, than the students. They all looked to be about nineteen or twenty, at their peak, never to be like this again, but ignorant of that verity and all others except the verity of the rut. They had beads, long hair, leather headbands. They looked like a *Life* magazine photo of a classroom full of "Hippies." Some of the young men and young women were naked to the waist, but not in a way that looked out of place, or regrettably, in any way prurient. One of the topless young ladies had painted her torso in bright colors and designs. She might have been wearing a really tight T-shirt, except for the way that her mismatched breasts moved when she moved. The students were ignoring the lecture, passing joints around, and he could see a half-gallon of cheap red wine circulating. Occasionally, one or two would look attentive, but just for a second or two. He knew that they were not paying attention because he had nothing to tell them. As he walked to the edge of the dais from which he spoke, he lost his footing (the shoes were brand new, and he had not sanded the slick leather soles as he should have) and began a slo-mo fall into the crowd of Freaks.

He fell awake, and felt the plane dropping down from under his seat. He hoped that they were landing, not dropping out of the sky into the evening news. But, either way, he really had to piss. Looking out of his window, he saw only blue sky. Across the aisle, the windows showed the green and brown of the island, very different greens and browns than those of Vermont or Boston. The plane was dropping fast, and banking steeply for perhaps fifty seconds, then regained its equilibrium and within a few seconds, the tires hit the runway for the first bounce. The jet engines did a frantic reverse, and the plane, hesitantly, began to slow. He knew that the pilot could see the mountain dead ahead.

As the plane slowed rapidly to a stop, the passenger cabin began to sussurate with polite, golf-game applause. So happy to be on the ground, intact rather than scattered over fifty square miles....but, still, not all was perfect. God, thought Lewis, do I ever need to piss. It was, of course, the fault of the fear that did not allow him to get up and walk to the rest room in flight. Silly, really. He undid his seatbelt and rummaged his bag out from under the seat, although the doors were not yet open, and the crew had not indicated any imminent de-planing. He cracked heads, but softly, with a remarkably ugly woman next to him, who was rummaging for her bag at the same time, and he apologized to her shy smile, a tremor running through him at that smile, afraid she would start to talk to him, the man who had remained successfully, unapproachably comatose for almost four hours. He "sorry"'d again, and turned away.

He was one of the first off the plane. The drugs had mostly worn off, at least down to the maintenance levels, and he was able to navigate the steep metal stairs that had been pushed up to the plane. No tunnel to the afterlife here, but real stairs in the blinding and hot sun, a shock after the cold stale air in the airplane. Down the stairs, across the tarmac. He was happy that he had taken off his tweed jacket and stuffed it in his bag; it must be eighty degrees in the shade. God, did he have to whiz. Up to the tiny customs booths, where he chose the slowest line, the reason he avoided supermarkets (well, that and the crowds in those places. Too many people!). He showed his birth certificate and his expired passport to a seriously disinterested, heavy-faced black woman, who gave him two little cards, which he promptly stuffed in a back pocket and would later discard. He knew that they meant nothing, although on his first few trips down here, he had hoarded them like gold (or drugs), and was ultimately disappointed that they were never called for. He signed a paper for her, without reading it, and was given permission with a nod of the head to walk away.

He made a bee-line for the men's room, pretty much open-air, with a deep urinal mounted on the floor. The place was crowded, as it was only a few steps from a bar. When his turn came, he dutifully hauled out his pecker, and stood there, waiting for results. He counted backward, hoping to blast off, and was rewarded with only a small squirt. He counted again, and finally peed, painfully, then less so, standing there until drained. It worried him that there was no velocity to his pissing these days. Well, actually, for a few years. It had been not at all gradual: he was doing fine, pissing a stream that generated a fierce blow-back if he were too close to whatever it was that he was peeing against. Then, the water pressure was gone. He peed like an old man, he thought, and was so embarrassed by it that he could rarely piss in public anymore, not that there was much call for that.

On the island! Hot damn! He started to peer about for a cab, and saw the van for the Club just pulling up in front of the passenger terminal. He walked over, arriving as the door swung open and the driver stepped out, only to learn that there would be (of course) a wait. Six more guests were expected, due in on the American flight that should land in twenty or thirty minutes. He decided to go get a beer, and then call Judy.

The airport, as diminutive as it was, had a number of venues where one could buy beer or food or soft drinks, not to mention T-shirts, hats, cigarettes, and booze. Lewis favored the most bar-like, open to the outside on both ends, but dark and bar-like inside with rattan furniture and a slowly turning ceiling fan. He found a seat at the bar (several were open). The bartender was at the other end of the bar, looking surly as she put together some ridiculous tourist drink. She was a dark-haired young woman, and looked American, but could as easily be French or Canadian. She was pretty, even with a sour look on her face. She might be twenty-five, or thirty, probably not older than thirty-five. It was hard to tell. It was easy to see, though, that a forty-foot long bar of fast and nervous drinkers was keeping her too busy to fill orders for the waitress who worked the tables, and who now stood at the service bar, looking furious and bored at the same time.

Lewis had little hope of getting his beer anytime soon, but didn't much care, if he could ogle the bartender as he waited. She wore a sleeveless thin cotton blouse with capacious armholes, and the way she was standing, he could clearly see most of the side of her firm, small left breast. The nipple was just out of sight, until she turned a bit toward him. The blouse was unbuttoned almost half way. Depending on her stance in relation to the viewer (or ogler, in Lewis' case), she was peekaboo-topless in a most fetching way. Clearly intentional, of course. She didn't need to smile to fill her tip-jar, which was full of ones, fives and tens. When, a few minutes later, she worked her way down to Lewis' end of the bar he ogled dutifully, as she bent over to fish a frosty bottle from the ice-chest. She had world-class boobs, blessedly unmarred by nipple rings, cute tattoos, or breastfeeding. He gave her a five, and told her to keep the change.

He took the icy bottle with him to a pay telephone in the corner of the bar. With a few moments study, he was able to decipher the instructions for dialing the States, and using his telephone credit card, reached a phone — possibly Judy's — that rang with a U.S. ring-type. When the message machine kicked on, he heard Judy's voice, and left a brief message indicating who and where he was, how long he planned to be there, and how to reach him in an emergency. He didn't want to drop dead in the Caribbean (or anywhere) and have his rapidly putrefying cadaver sitting around for weeks while the authorities tried to figure out what to do with it. Assuming that they would even do that, rather than making him shark-chum. In his wallet, he carried a laminated card listing Judy and his daughter as the people to notify, as the card put it, "In Case of Emergency."

Hanging up the phone, Lewis wandered, beer in hand, back toward the van that would transport him and his comically inadequate luggage (one very old canvas overnight bag, stained and ratty, that would seem to fit only a very large Dopp kit, a clean pair of khakis, shorts, one pair of cotton socks in a horrid Nantucket red, two superannuated polo shirts, and a sport coat) to the Club. He didn't expect to need much in the way of clothing, as he was staying at a nudist resort.

The smell of a different world was in his head, beginning to overpower the beer-old urine-tobacco smoke aura of the bar. He could smell the ocean, but not the harsh crisp sea-smell he had grown up and older with in New England, but a warmer sea smell, with undertones of wet clay and sand. He could smell the low sparse vegetation, and the ubiquitous dogs and sheep and goats that roamed a part of the island's hills. He could smell sweat of a thousand different flavors with hints of sunblock and good old-fashioned coconut oil. It smelled like his last visit here, and all of his visits before that one.

Lewis had been to this particular island a dozen times in the past ten years, and felt absolutely anonymous, and therefore safe, here. He had, from time to time, chanced upon travelers from Boston or Cambridge or other cities he knew well, some of whom he even knew casually. But those were consensual contacts. He had said hello, on occasion, to the person or couple sitting next to him at the bar or on the beach, or had responded when said hello to, and had even engaged in conversation. He need not have done so, and on those days that he did not crave conversation, which was more days than not, he could avoid it. He relished that level of control, so available to him here.

The van was exactly where he has last seen it. There were four passengers on board: he could see through the windows, when he got closer, that two were older men (younger than he), who seemed to be together, although under what auspices, he could not yet presume. In the back of the van, sitting close to each other, was a younger couple who looked excessively Middle American. He'd bet that they were dressed in shorts and tank tops and sneakers or sandals, hopefully not matching. He looked straight at them for a few moments, but they did not notice or return his gaze. They had to be first-timers, he thought, flirting with the sinful world of nudity. They would be disappointed, probably, when they found that after the first half hour, nudity seemed the norm, and was about as naughty as bowling, but less entertaining. He made a mental note to seek them out and stare at their genitals. It might be a real downer for him, but someone had to do it.

He took the seat behind the driver, and promptly opened his window, despite the air conditioner that whirred away in the roof of the van. He lit a cigarette before the driver boarded, hoping to finish it before he was asked to not smoke, please. He could hear the couple in the back stir and mutter at his effrontery.

Within a few more minutes, the final two passengers climbed the two metal steps and found seats directly opposite Lewis. In their early forties, perhaps, they were smiling, tanned, and half-drunk. He pegged them as all-day beach drinkers, then evening beachside bar drinkers. They were fortunate to have found each other. They both favored silver jewelry. He would avoid them like the plague.

The driver, a slim, black man with a pinched face and startling blue-green eyes, swung himself into the van and the driver's seat with a single fluid motion. He adjusted the rear-view mirror, and counted the passengers. He smiled, and welcomed them to the island.

"Hello, hello. You are all here now, so we can go to the Club. It's a beautiful, sunny day, and we will be there in fifteen minutes, but it doesn't matter, because you are now on Island Time!" The tanned drunks cheered, the older guys clapped their hands, and the younger couple smiled, uncertainly. Lewis thought he should say "About time!" but didn't think anyone would get the joke.

Lewis watched carefully, as he always did, for the sign that declaimed the border between the two nations that owned the island. It was a small sign, set back a few feet from the road, and easy to miss. He relished the border crossing almost as much as he did arriving on the island. Once away from the Dutch side with its casinos and tourist traps, the presence of the Spandex-shorts types from the square states could be reliably expected to diminish significantly. It didn't keep all the assholes out, as evidenced by the crowds of loud, lame and boisterous South Americans found at one of the hotels on the two-mile beach that he was bound for. But they rarely left the hotel swimming pool or the beach in front of the resort, so were easy to avoid. They were actually pretty nice folks, but too noisy for Lewis, who preferred the sound of the surf to the sound of a hundred radios and CD players.

The driver was making good time, and after only ten or fifteen minutes, the van took a right off the main road and down a sandy dirt drive to the parking area directly behind the Club. When the driver swung the passenger door open, the tanned alkies hustled right out with impressive speed and grace, and Lewis was right behind them. He was, he thought, exactly where he wanted to be.

1964 – Tale Of A Dead Doc

Lewis had been headed to the Bucket for a drink or two, but was stopped at the entrance by Billy and Terry, who he knew slightly. It was Terry who had to blurt out the news first – Doc, who he surmised they all knew had been killed – well, had died, anyway- during or after a pot deal that went very bad. This was news to Lewis, who had been there, so he feigned shock, and went in to the bar with them. He ordered an ale, and sat down to hear the details of the story.

Terry claimed that a friend of his, an old Cambridge freak, had called him at the bar just the night before, and told him the story of the rip-off and of the kidnapping and the presumed death of Doc, who, as it turned out, knew almost everyone of a certain age and proclivity, said proclivity being the constant pursuit of drugs esoteric: yage, yohimbe bark, baby Hawaiian wood-rose seeds, acid, and even the much-maligned DMT. Not to mention MDA, STP and all of the other combinations of letters that might or might not be something, or maybe just a way to sell weak acid, heavily cut with methamphetamine. The friend had heard it from his old lady, who had heard it from a girl she knew, a girl who was the lover of, but not the old lady of, one of the guys who had been there, who was in on the deal. To Lewis, that didn't narrow the possibilities all that much. Most of his friends slept around on their women when they could, and so did their women. And that was pretty much the story, again: a drug deal, a rip-off at gunpoint, shots fired, Doc bundled off to maybe death (or maybe, Lewis thought, to split the take with the guys who did the rip-off: who knew? Freaks could be perfidious.).

But the story was wrong, simply did not sound right, so far, to Lewis. He had, after all, been there, and did remember a gun, but no gunshot, just a gun barrel against his still-tender head. Maybe the gunshot came after he was knocked unconscious. But he saw no body, no signs of struggle, no blood but his own. He hadn't done a thorough search; of course, he was in too much of a hurry to get the hell out of there. But he would have noticed a dead body. He had to ask a question or two.

"So, Terry, who did your friend say got shot? Did he hear a name?"

"I think the guy said Marlow. Or Miller. Something like that. Did you know him?"

Lewis had an epiphany, of sorts. "It wasn't Melton, was it?"

Terry thought for half a second, and answered vaguely. "Coulda been. Like I said, this is what my friend's lady told him, and she heard it from someone else, who heard it from her boyfriend. But I'm sure about the Doc part. I knew Doc, sort of. Bought a couple of keys from him, one time. Fucking ditch-weed, so I remembered the name. There's no question, she heard 'Doc.' Can't be that many dope dealers named Doc."

"Well, maybe so. But I don't think anybody killed anybody. I heard about it, too, from a guy who was there."

Lewis instantly regretted his statement. He had come all the way here to get as far as he reasonably could from the whole mess, and now he had just established a link, however tenuous, between himself and the alleged killing and kidnapping and rip-off. How stupid could he be? He imagined he could be infinitely more stupid, but didn't think this was the time to try it out. He had done enough damage. His only hope was that they would all get so drunk and stoned that nothing would be remembered.

Billy was on his second or third beer, and was good and sick of the topic. "Listen, you assholes. If this guy Miller got killed, we'll for sure hear about it. If Doc got taken or killed, we'll hear about that, too. We may not be on the mainland, but we do get the papers and TV. And, fuck it, anyway. From what I hear, Doc was a prick. Let's just get a buzz on, and then we'll go out to the Ritz or the Navy Base. At least they've got a pool table."

No one disagreed with the plan, so the topic changed and the beer and ale bottles began to collect steadily on the table. At eleven or so, they all shared a small pipe of hash in the Men's Room, and mellowed right out.

The bar had been half-full at ten-thirty, but an hour later, anyone who had begun the day at work had given up and drifted in, maybe due to the weather, or maybe because it was, after all, Saturday, and a day to drink in earnest. It was a hard-drinking place, the Island, and had been since whaling days. The normative level of drinking was pretty intense, by Off-Island standards. On the Island, a man (or woman) would have to work very hard, not only drinking daily, but drinking to spectacular excess almost every day, and acting-out, drunk, to the point of arrest, if not prosecution and conviction, to gain the title "alcoholic." "Drunk" had become a sort of honorific title: "Drunk Eddie" could be distinguished from any other Eddie. Fewer than half-a-dozen souls in the winter population of less than two thousand made the grade. At any given time, half that half-dozen were at the V.A. getting a tune-up or in Bridgewater State Hospital for excessive drunken crazinesses. Drinking as

Lewis, Billy and Terry (and everyone else in the Bucket) did was considered absolutely acceptable behavior for a Saturday. And everyone, almost, would show up for work bright and early Monday morning with a gray complexion and a very slight tremor. As long as they showed up for work, rarely a word was said.

Among the new arrivals, half were Freaks, and most of them knew, or were known by Billy and Terry. Even Lewis spotted the odd familiar face. As the three were debating the relative merits of certain trucks (in this case the Dodge Power Wagon 4x4 versus the Ford F-100) despite the fact that none of them had ever owned a truck, a very tall, thin, bearded, long-haired man of indeterminate age walked over to the table, hooked a chair out with his foot, and folded himself down into it. With his feet on the floor, his knees were almost up to his chin. It didn't seem to bother him, as he smiled around at the three half-drunk men sitting around the bottle-covered table. His very dark sunglasses hid his eyes, and his mustache and beard hid his mouth, so it came as a surprise when he spoke.

"Billy, who the fuck is this guy? Is he okay?" gesturing vaguely toward Lewis with an inclination of his curly brown beard.

"Hey, Cap, haven't seen you in months! Yeah, that's Lew, I know him. So, where the fuck have you been?"

"I just brought a boat up from St. Bart's. Me and two guys I signed on down there. Took us a month. You guys want some acid? It's powerful shit, but mellow. Orange barrels. Really head stuff. You can walk, but you wouldn't really want to."

Billy and Lewis looked at each other, while Terry looked at the tall man, and then spoke: "Sure! Fuckin' A! Thanks, Bob....how much?"

"No charge. I unloaded a few hundred in New York on the way up: I've made my money. The rest is just for fun." He reached in the left breast pocket of his beat-up Levi jacket, and pulled out a baggie with what looked like a few dozen cylindrical pills of a muted orange color, and tossed in onto the table.

"I took two a couple of hours ago. They're supposed to be 300 mikes, but I doubt it. One takes care of most people. Take what you want, and enjoy."

Terry picked up the bag and extracted six tablets. In his open hand, he held them out to Lewis and Bill, who each took one.

"Now, or should we go someplace else to trip?"

"If we take it now, we'll have time to go somewhere before it hits," said Billy, "...maybe the Bird Sanctuary?"

Terry considered for a few seconds, then popped a bill in his mouth and followed it with a swig of ale.

"We need to pick up some wine to keep us mellow. Let's go to the Midget's House, though. The Bird Sanctuary's going to be pretty wet: the shack out there leaks like hell."

Lewis had eaten his acid already, almost a reflexive action. If someone held out a pill, he took it, sometimes without knowing what it was. Now he spoke. "Cap, can we get a few more? We'll want to see if we can get some chicks to trip with us. I'll bet Janey's up for it, and Chris may be back."

The tall man finished lighting a cigarette that smelled, initially, like burning trash. Why, thought Lewis, did anyone smoke French cigarettes?

The sailor smiled almost imperceptibly, and said, "Take all you want. But you're on your own. I wouldn't trip in the Midget's House if you paid me."

Billy took three more from the baggie, and slid them into the watch pocket of his jeans. The three stood up — Captain Bob had already gotten to his feet and was walking toward the bar with a floating gait — and went up to pay their tab, thanking Bob again as they left the bar. They walked into a driving rain, a cold rain, and broke into a run for the twenty feet to Billy's dying Nova.

The trio were probably not yet legally drunk, but the first few beers of the day had loosened them up, and the acid they had all dropped could hit anytime in the next thirty or forty minutes, perhaps much sooner. They would have done well to proceed in a straightforward manner to check and see if Janey or Chris wanted to trip with them and then gotten the hell out of town. They needed to get to a place where they could become uninterruptedly weird for six or eight or twelve hours, but that was not how it was playing out. Terry wanted to pick up some cough syrup — the good kind — as the drug store was open, as he hadn't bought any for a couple of weeks. He got back out of the idling car, while Lewis walked a block and a half downstreet to the newspaper store to get cigarettes for them all. Billy sat in the car and fiddled with the radio, which sometimes would bring in a Boston rock station if the atmospherics were just right.

By the time Terry and Lewis had returned, Terry chugging his cough syrup as he crossed the broad, cobblestone street, almost twenty minutes had passed since they had dropped, and Billy was getting paranoid.

"C'mon, you assholes. I think I feel it coming on already. Let's get the fuck out of town. Put that fucking bottle away, Terry — Jesus Fucking Christ, you can't do that in public."

Lewis swung into the front seat, pushing ale bottles aside to make room for his feet.

"We still need to pick up the wine. Where's the nearest packy?"

Billy pointed down the street. "Down by the wharf. Across from the supermarket...they should just be opening up now."

At the package store (the Massachusetts euphemism for "liquor store," for reasons that few remembered), Lewis didn't browse. He snatched two gallons of the cheapest red wine available, and in less than five minutes, was back at the car. He, like Billy, was concerned that the acid would come on like gangbusters long before they were ready for it. They should have waited, he thought, but, hell, no one ever waited. Maybe best to just go with the flow. Odds were that at least one of them would be able to drive out of town.

Lewis saw that Billy and Terry were at a pay telephone about fifty feet away. The rain was now driving in from the water, and they were getting wet and cold. Lewis was suddenly aware of the taste in the back of his mouth that told him that the LSD was starting to scoot around his circulatory system. The very edge of his field of vision grew brighter, on this dark day. He could see clearly, though, that Bill and Terry were off the phone now, walking back, almost to the car.

"We called Chris. She's going to wake Janey up, then meet us out at the Midget's house. She thought you were at Janey's, 'cause you left the bar together. She said she doesn't know who you are, but wants to meet you, because all the guys on the Island are assholes! Do you suppose she meant us?" Billy laughed, cackled really, as he recounted the conversation. His cackle was one of his less endearing habits, although the general opinion was that he had many equally annoying quirks.

Lewis looked at Billy, stunned by the speed with which information circulated on this small island. How many other people, now, knew that he was here? How many knew he had left the bar with Janey, and had stayed at her place? It became clear that he would have to find a place by himself, and be circumspect in his comings and goings, if he were going to hide out here.

"So," Terry asked, "did you nail her?"

"No — too drunk. Besides, she's more like a sister.'"

"All the better! You could move to Maine, and raise a family!" Terry laughed, pleased with his wit.

Billy ignored them both, concentrating much too hard on coaxing the ailing Chevy into its only forward gear. It finally clunked appropriately, and began to roll. He made a right, off Main Street, then a series of confusing turns that constituted the back way out of town, leading them to the cross-island road that would carry them through the rolling Moors, and then to the other side of the Island, where the Midget's House sat, abandoned. He turned in his seat, and spoke, his voice accented with excitement. "Holy Shit, this stuff is coming on like a fucking freight train. I probably should have waited. I hope we can get there before the steering wheel turns into a snake or something….I can't drive when I'm peaking…."

"Billy," Lewis said, he hoped, reassuringly, "just shut up and drive. One of us can drive if you want. I drive fine on acid, as long as there's no traffic."

"Jesus, Lew, wait till you see this fucking place! Two midgets — I think they were married — had it custom-built maybe fifty or sixty years ago. Had it built just for them. Everything is tiny! Little doors, little windows, little stairs. The fireplace is only about two by three feet....then, I hear, after they lived there ten years or so, they disappeared, or maybe killed themselves, I don't know for sure. But it's been empty since. People pretty much stay away from it. It was locked up and taken care of until a few years ago....I heard there was a trust or something that kept it painted, kept the lawn mowed, all ready for them to come back. But, they never came back. The Island kids busted in, used to party there, but they stopped 'cause the cops would come out and hassle them. So now, hardly anyone ever goes out there. It's prime real estate, right on the water, but for some reason, it can't be sold. Anyway, you'd need to be a midget to live there. But it's really trippy...." Billy seemed to have run out of steam, and stopped his tale abruptly, focusing, now, on his driving. Lewis and Terry didn't know what Billy was seeing, but whatever had taken his attention and stopped the story was welcomed. They were dealing with their own heads. The acid was now in charge.

Lewis had tripped enough to know how to handle himself, and rarely had a bad time. He had learned, early on, that successful navigation of the psychedelic landscape required a certain passivity, a willingness, to let go and enjoy the ride. He looked at Terry, and at Bill, and grinned, and said nothing.

Billy seemed to come out of his trance, and without warning, took a very hard right off of the blacktop and onto a rutted dirt track that continued through the Moors for a quarter mile, then into a stunted grove of scrub oak and pine. If the windows had been open, and the rain had not been thrumming against the sheet metal that enclosed them they would have begun, now, to hear the surf crashing against the sand, less than a half-mile away. The car was now traveling so slowly that the engine kept trying to stall. Bill had to play with the clutch, and keep revving the engine, maintaining forward motion at the speed of a brisk walk, just a little faster than visibility — about ten feet through the rain and fog — would dictate. He braked every now and then, for no apparent cause, but they made way, and soon enough came to a bend in the road, and then a grown-over driveway on the left, inclining, finally, down to the shore. Billy cut the engine, and let the car roll silently through the fog, thicker now that they were almost at the water's edge.

The Midget's House sat in the fog, which, with the rain — and, of course, the LSD — made the edges indistinct, made the picture a bit blurry, but, otherwise, quite ordinary. It looked just like any other center-chimney Cape

Cod style house: cedar shingled, with six-over-six windows, et cetera. Except that it was small, that is, the house was a bit closer to them than it seemed, the perspective was skewed. The house, from the ground to the peak of the roof, could not have been more than twenty feet.

It seemed to be in decent repair, although some of the front windows were broken. A yellow, torn curtain flapped out of a broken pane in the bottom right window, next to the door. The door was peeling crimson enamel, the color of blood. Granite steps, just three, led up to the door, which was closed. It did not look strange at all. Nor did it look inviting.

The three stoned young men sat in silence in the Nova, the engine ticking as it cooled. They couldn't hear the engine, just the wind and rain slamming the car, coming in laterally, through the trees that surrounded the house, sluicing down the windshield and side windows in a fury of an October storm. Often, in October on the Island, it was beach weather. Warm days and nights that were merely chilly, not crisp or cold, as it would be in Boston. But October storms, if they weren't hurricanes, were gales. This one was a least gale force, and would continue for hours or longer.

Five minutes, or ten, passed. Then Billy gathered his senses from wherever they had been, found his head, and looked at Lewis, then at Terry. "This is it. Grab the wine. And Terry, grab that old blanket off the rear deck. Let's go in and get comfortable. We need to get the fireplace going, if we can, before the chicks get here. There was some driftwood and some dry spruce piled out back the last time I was out here, this summer.

They gathered their things. Billy went to the back of the war, popped the trunk with the screwdriver that was jammed in the latch mechanism, and rummaged out an old Army tarpaulin and a shingle hatchet. Lewis had the two jugs of wine in a death-grip against his chest. Terry had the old, not so clean olive drab blanket folded around his shoulders like a serape, and had pulled his watchcap down to just above his very stoned eyes.

Lewis was the first to the door. He thumbed the latch, with no result. Then he pushed down harder on the thumb-plate, and pushed in on the small, brass handle, tarnished green, and kicked at the bottom of the door (the kick-plate was greened brass, too), and the swollen door popped open.

Day 13

He awakened slowly to the sound of quiet laughter. Not the good kind, either. He was uncertain, as he often was upon waking, of his whereabouts, and tried to figure that out in the seconds before he opened his eyes. The answer came to him at the same instant that he became aware of the almost painfully excellent tumescence of his cock. Best, he thought, to keep the eyes closed for now, feign sleep, and will the hard-on away. He was pretty sure that he had committed, was committing, one of the acts that is not acceptable at a nudist resort or beach or pretty much any gathering of naked humans (or even one naked human with other clothed humans), except in porn films, and that infraction, of course, was sporting an erection. An erection, however uncontrollable in fact it had been, however much one and all knew, for a fact, that it was sometimes just a psychoneurobiological reaction to the sun, or a breeze, or a dream (as in his case), or perhaps a side-effect of medication, despite all of these rationales, there was still the main issue: an erection could be interpreted as sexual. Nudists (or naturists) were unified in the primary tenet of their faith, to wit: nudism and nudity, as practiced by them, the respectable nudists of the world, was not sexual. Or even sexually titillating. Ever. It just took one bad apple with a boner to make them all look like perverts, and they would cast a strongly disapproving glance, or worse, laugh. Women, in particular, looked, then laughed. That, alone, was often enough to wilt the offending member.

Lewis didn't know who was laughing (his eyes were closed in self-defense) but he was pretty sure it was more than one woman, and that it was directed at him. He knew that, having been asleep, he was, to some extent, off the hook. It wasn't like he had been roaming the beach, schlong in his hand, leering and drooling, seeking out the most exposed of the most exposed. But he was moderately mortified, nonetheless, and needed to lose the object of his shame.

He concentrated on those awful images that men relied on to kill unwanted erections, like chainsaws near the crotch, freezing winds, and after a few minutes he felt the woody begin to flag. It wasn't gone, but was down to the semi-tumescence that made him look the way he thought he should, but rarely did. He opened his eyes, slowly, behind his dark glasses. Directly across the swimming pool was the couple — he had presumed them Midwesterners when he saw them on the van from the airport — who must have been laughing. They both had nasty sunburns, he noted with quiet glee, and were peeling in a most unattractive way. The woman of the couple had small but sagging breasts, almost flat against her ribcage, and huge thighs. Her pubic hair grew almost to her navel: it looked like a small, dead animal in her lap. Thank God, Lewis thought, that such an ugly woman had laughed. If the laugher had been a young, tanned beauty, he'd probably just kill himself now.

Escape was necessary, but must be done smoothly. He manipulated his chaise into a less recumbent position, and reached for his cigarettes on the tiles next to his chair. He presumed that the laughing Midwesterner didn't approve of cigarettes, either, so he lit one and puffed clouds of smoke with great relish. Consulting his almost-cheap watch, he saw that it was past one o'clock. He had slept too long, but had needed it after being up half the night. He wasn't twenty anymore, or thirty, or forty, or fifty either. He felt hungry, but not stoned. The pills had worn off; he was down to maintenance level. It was time for some lunch, and maybe a beer or two. With Marian gone God knows where, he could fall back to his usual island routine of sunning, writing, sleeping, eating, drinking. As much as he had enjoyed the dalliance — and as good as the brazen approach of a pretty young woman had been — dealing with another person was, at the best, a great deal of trouble.

He rose abruptly, grabbed his smokes and towel, and walked away from the pool, only stopping to throw his towel — soaked with sleep-sweat — in the proper bin. It was a short walk to the open air restaurant that the Club operated, right off the beach. The place was cool and dark inside, out of the sun, and with huge ceiling fans circling lazily. He was able to secure a table near the entrance from the beach right away, spared a wait at the bar, a spooky sort of enclave, where the same people — mostly men, but a few women — sat all day long, naked, drinking, and very rarely venturing out to the beach. They had paid a lot of money to drink nude in a warm climate. They were an odd lot. Everyone else avoided them, and they did the same. His small table — a table for two, but small for two, was as far from the bar and the kitchen, visible through a large open doorway, as could be. He didn't see her coming, but a waitress appeared next to him, startling him. Of course, she was barefoot, and bare everything else, too, except for the tiniest thong he had ever seen. It covered the lower two-thirds of her pudendum, leaving remarkable pussy-cleavage. On top, she just wore perfect American boobs. Her English was without discernable accent: he guessed Florida, but was wrong. She was from North Carolina, and had come down two years ago on Spring Break, and had stayed.

He ordered a cheeseburger with bacon and tomato, medium, and a beer. He lit another smoke, and settled back in his chair. He sat, of course, on a towel that he had snagged at the door, in keeping with the Unwritten Rule, "Thou shalt not plant thy dirty asshole on any chair or stool or chaise directly, for others must also sit there."

The place was pretty full, as it usually was. Almost all of the diners and drinkers were nude, or almost nude, although a few wore shorts or bathing suits. One ancient woman sat at a long table full of half-naked younger folks: she was fully dressed in a long, flowered dress, complete with stockings and shoes, and a straw hat. The table was loud with conversation and laughter.

The bar staff and wait staff were mostly at least partially clothed, except for his, and another waitress he saw who wore only a gold chain around her waist. She wasn't as pretty as his waitress, but was stunning in her choice of work clothing, set against a flawless dark tan. It was difficult to look at her without feeling stirred. Perhaps she was the exception that proved the rule about nudity being non-sexual.

When his order came, Lewis ate slowly, looking mostly out toward the Caribbean Sea, and wondering if he really needed to ever leave, or, as his waitress had done, just decide to not act, to not go back to something that was less than this. Not go back, in his case, to Boston with its cold spring rain, not go back to Vermont where it would snow, again, before ice-out, and snow some more even after the trees had sprouted small leaves. The summers were so short there, and he had so few left — maybe ten or twenty, at best.

And then he thought again, because the pills had pretty well worn off now, about how quickly and oddly Marian had disappeared, and about how some dead man named Doc seemed to be looking for him, and about how much he needed his own Doc, who would write for him pretty much what he needed, and what was the story, anyway, why did he need all these pills? Was he moving that quickly toward decrepitude? He hurt pretty much all the time, except for the hour or two after he took the painkillers. With them, life was okay, and he could work, and enjoy music, and screw his ex-wife a few times a year. If he gave all that up, the job, and the medical care he needed, and the ties, still strong, to the ex, and to his daughter, who he rarely saw but loved nonetheless, if he gave all that up, what would he have here? He was wool-gathering, really not paying attention, and had let his head take him somewhere else. He snapped back to the here-and-now for a moment, drank down the dregs of his beer, and held his empty bottle up for his waitress to see. He wanted another beer or two, right away.

He could feel a very bad feeling coming over him, washing over him like a wave. He lit a cigarette, and his hand shook so much that he had difficulty holding the match steady. He thought that he heard the laughter, again, that he had heard by the pool, but when he looked around, he saw no possible source. His beer came while he was peering about. He had finished the last cigarette already, and lit another one, right away. His hands didn't shake, this time, but his shoulder hurt like hell when he raised his arm to strike the match. He was in dire need of a couple of Percodan, but would hold off a bit longer. He didn't want to get too stoned this early in the afternoon, and he didn't want another hung-over morning. He had come here to escape the craziness that was building around him at home, but also needed to take some time to do his writing. So far on this trip, he had written nothing except a few pages of ideas, not even an outline. The week after he was due to return to Boston, his Editor would be looking for some pages for the June issue, and if he didn't get started now, he'd have to work ten hours a day to make up for lost time. Lewis wasn't at all sure that he could still do ten hours of good work, and didn't want to find out. So, he decided that he would stay in this evening. He'd pick up some French bread and some cheese at the little store at the Club, brew a small pot of coffee, and write. That would keep his mind off his fears, his thoughts of strange appearances and disappearances, thoughts that made no sense in the bright sun of the beach twenty feet away from where he sat.

No wonder, Lewis thought, no wonder I'm such an anxious and unhappy man. These things happen to me. I need to keep this shit under control. I need to shut it down.

Internal dialogue stopped in an instant. His eyes, which had been seeing nothing at all as he argued with himself, focused now on the couple that had stopped at his table, the couple that was staring at him with alarm and concern. His civilized brain told his mouth to smile in a mildly reassuring way, but his face was already busy, locked onto looking angry and scared.

The couple, he was able to register with some higher, alternative function, must have just come in from the beach, looking for a table, or perhaps on their way to the bar for a drink. Something had caused them to stop short a few feet from his table. He stared at them.

They were an average, not unhandsome couple, maybe twenty years younger than he: just enough to be threatening and/or disregarded. The woman was a short blonde with too much silver jewelry, although it looked pretty good, against her dark tan. She wore a towel for a skirt, and the wrong shade of red nail polish on all four paws. The man, who looked as if he really wanted to be elsewhere, could be a year, or five, or more, older than his petite blond partner. He was hairy, almost furry, all over, except for his head. He might have been a Yeti. When he shuffled off his mortal coil, he could be skinned, and serve as an excellent fireside rug. It was he who broke the spell of silence.

"I'm sorry…are you alright? You seemed to be trying to make noises, to say something, and your hands were waving about. Are you epileptic? I had a friend, growing up, who sometimes had seizures like that."

The words came at him in a way that should have been clear, but were so divorced from his momentary reality that there was a delay. He had to hear, to translate, and to make sense. Still, the stranger's speech didn't make sense, didn't fit in with Lewis's world. He felt that he should answer, but didn't know the language. Angry and confused, he had to choose the sounds that he should make.

"I'm okay. I'm a writer. I was trying to figure out some dialogue." It was the best he could come up with. "I don't have epilepsy. I'm not having a seizure. I don't need any help."

The couple looked at him, doubtfully now, not as concerned as they were confused. Lewis had to wonder what they had seen. He wanted them to go away. He stared back at them, now. The woman had exceptionally cute tits, and brown eyes that didn't go with her hair or eyebrows. She had no freckles. He didn't think that she was a real blonde, but could not tell, unless she dropped her towel. And, maybe not then. She started to move away, saying, as she pulled at her boyfriend's hairy paw, "Okay. Glad you're okay. Sorry that we intruded."

They left, slowly at first, picking up the pace when they were a few feet away. They took a seat at the only free table, the one, of course, by the open kitchen door. Lewis kept them in his sight, afraid they might return, or have the manager (how would they pick the manager from all the nearly-naked staff?) call an ambulance, or maybe the cops. The couple were now in hushed conversation; the man, who faced him, looked in his direction from time to time.

Jesus Fucking Christ, Lewis said (he hoped) to himself, am I losing it? Am I blacking out, and saying everything I'm thinking? Have I finally gone over the edge?

He knew, from his own experience, and from hearing others speak of it, that Xanax and alcohol sometimes caused blackouts, even at a really low dose, let alone at the doses he, sometimes, worked up to. How much he had taken today was unclear to him. And how many beers had he drunk? It must have been the beer. He'd lay off alcohol for a few days: none at all. And he'd keep better track of the pills, write down what he took, and when. He did that, sometimes, when he was getting low on meds, and he knew that it was too soon to get more. He'd devise a schedule, and parse out the pills stingily, so he'd avoid any nasty withdrawal, but also not run out. On a few occasions, when he had taken far too many, and the number left until refill time was frighteningly low, he'd cut back drastically. Those were tough periods. His anxiety would rage without limits. He couldn't sleep. He would feel as if his chest was full of moths, fluttering blindly, banging into walls.

He hadn't noticed any of the other diners or wait staff looking at him oddly: whatever had happened to him had been brief and taken hold the instant that the strangers had been near enough to notice, and had ended quickly. He wasn't convinced that a second episode would be as benign. He signaled for the check, and tipped handsomely, over and above the gratuity built into the bill. It was time to get out of here, out of the public eye, and back to his bungalow to count his pills, to try to figure out how many he had taken, and devise a dosing schedule for the rest of his stay. Perhaps he could forget the strange happenings, and get some writing done.

1964 — The Midget's House

The smell of sea-damp and mouldering fabric was not quite strong enough to stop them in their tracks as they ducked through the small doorway and into the cramped foyer, then the living room. Terry, the tallest, had to stoop to avoid slamming his forehead on the top of the doorway, less than six feet from the warped oak floor. The ceilings were only a few inches higher, but must have looked just right to the midgets who had the house custom built. No furniture, which was said to have all been also custom-built, remained, except for a very short footstool, situated next to a fireplace that was small even by Cape Cod standards.

"Holy Fuck, this place is even trippier than I remembered! And cold! I'll go see if there's any dry wood left out back," Billy commented, walking through the living room and through another short doorway that probably led in the direction of the kitchen and the ocean side of the house. "If I'm not back soon, come find me. I'm rushing like hell, and I could get sidetracked."

Lewis and Terry looked at each other with dilated pupils and stupid grins. The acid had hit them all at roughly the same time; now waves of rushes surged through their brains and bodies. If they had been a little drunk earlier, they weren't now. They were, or thought they were, hyper-aware of themselves, each other, and everything around them, and felt good and powerful, removed from the cold, damp house as a god is removed from the daily sensations that man must endure. Terry took one of the jugs of cheap zinfandel from Lewis' death-grip (Lewis hadn't ever put them down), unscrewed the metal cap in one smooth motion that sent the top frisbeeing across the room, and hoisted it to his mouth for one long swallow. Still without a word, he set the bottle down gently on the floor, and crouched before the cold, blackened fireplace. He reached up and grabbed the flue door lever, yanked it, and jumped backward as a deluge of soot, rain-soaked creosote, and the desiccated corpse of a bird fell into the fireplace and out, onto the hearth.

"Fuck a Sheep!" Terry laughed, and then reached back into the hole and wiggled the lever again — only a few ounces of soot, this time, mixed in with brown pine needles. He stuck his head cautiously into the fireplace, looking up the chimney. "Clean enough, now, for our purposes....I'll go find a shingle or something to scoop this shit up with."

Lewis watched in stoned silence as Terry turned, still crouching, and rose slowly to his feet, arms and fingers extended, as if he were on the high wire. He really didn't look capable of getting anything at all, and Lewis knew that he, himself, was way too wasted to help. He was afraid that if Terry wandered off in search of a shingle, he would not find his way back for hours. On the other hand, time was growing increasingly relative, so it probably didn't matter. Lewis planned to stay exactly where he was until reality ceased shifting around him, however long that might take.

Terry walked, unsteadily, out of the room, through the same door that Billy had taken. Despite his heavy workboots, his footfalls were barely perceptible through the white noise generated by the rain and wind, both of which sounded like they were beating the bejesus out of the back of the house and the surrounding trees. The wind and rain eased up for forty seconds, as if planned, and Lewis heard the sound of a car splashing down the muddy, puddled drive, the slam of car doors (two), and the tattoo of frantic knocks on the front door.

"Let us fucking in, you idiots....it's fucking pouring!"

Rising slowly, Lewis turned and made for the door, ten feet away. His senses were as acute as a coyote's, he thought, and could almost see the girls through the door.

"Coming! Coming!" he yelled, at least inside his head. Perhaps he only spoke it, or said nothing. He couldn't tell. Things moved so slowly that his voice had not come back to him yet. He could hear and smell the girls on the other side of the warped door — Chris and Janey — and thought that he could sense Terry, or maybe Bill, coming from behind him, somewhere.

"Hurry up, you assholes, we're soaked," yelled Chrissie, he thought, her voice without the Boston accent that Janey had and gloried in. Chris was not from New England. He thought, maybe Florida? Didn't she go to school in Gainesville? He was at the door, now, searching for the handle. It didn't seem to be where he thought it should. He thought he saw an eye. He closed his own eyes, tightly, and reached out and clamped his hand on the door handle, just where it should be, turned it hard, and yanked, and the two women, cold and wet, fell into him. They stank of patchouli and French tobacco and pussy, wet hair and wet wool.

"Wow, are you fucked up!" said Chrissie, standing now a foot away, dripping on the dirty floor. He stared at her: she was devastatingly cute. Blonde short hair, wet black Levi's, too-new Bean boots, an oiled-wool sweater beaded with water like diamonds where her good breasts pushed out.

"Give us some of that acid, Pal. We need to catch up. It's fucking freezing in here. You need to get a fire going."

Lewis paused for what seemed an hour; he needed to form the words in his head, first, before he could force them out. He gave up, and just smiled, grinned like the Cheshire cat at the girls who still stood there, looking at him and around the gloomed, strange room.

Billy and Terry appeared. An armload of wet broken lengths of scrub pine, oak leaves, some strips of ancient tarpaper, and a rusted beach pail and shovel, painted whales in faded white on a pitted blue background. They greeted the girls, curtly, sounding scared and relieved. Bill said, "Hi...." looking confused, but glad to be with other humans. Lewis guessed that wherever he had gone had not been a friendly place. Terry walked over to the girls very directly, brushing past Lewis to kiss Jane's neck, grab a little bit of Chrissie's ass, until they both smiled and slapped at him.

The girls gobbled up the acid that was offered, and started with the bottle of wine that they had brought, an over-rated Spanish light red, costing far too much because of the nice ceramic bottle. Everyone lit a cigarette and stood around drinking fast while Billy cleaned out the fireplace with his pail and shovel, and then while he got a roaring spitting snapping pine-and-tarpaper blaze going, too big for the small fireplace, flames licking up and out to scorch the mantle fascia. The trim around the fireplace was so damp from the air that it could not burn, but the paint blistered, and sent out tendrils of oily acrid smoke.

One of the girls — Janey — went back out to her car once the fire was going well, a borrowed denim jacket over her head and shoulders, and came back with another blanket, this one much cleaner than Billy's, and a baggie full of pot. The blankets were both spread in front of the fire, and the five passed joints and jugs of wine around, waiting for something to happen, or not. The acid started to hit the latecomers in less than half an hour: Lewis could tell when their silence took on a different tone. He then found that he could form words and get them to come out of his mouth, once again, and broke the silence.

"Boy, this is really pretty good. It's hot here, now, like summer. Shit, am I twisted. Look at the flames...."

They may have taken his speech for what it was worth, but did not reply. He looked around at them all, mesmerized by the heat and the dance of the fire and the sound of the driving rain and wind outside, which had picked up now: it sounded like maybe it was blowing a gale. He was starting to sweat, and pulled his ancient green sweater and soggy black tee-shirt over his head. Chris, sitting next to him, looked at him, and did the same, but carefully, shaking the sweater out, and folding it carefully before laying it next to her on the blanket. When she pulled the sweater off, her tee-shirt rode up to show her belly and the bottoms of her rounded boobs. Lewis, as stoned as he was, had turned to watch, and was disappointed when the shirt fell back into place.

"Chrissie, take your shirt off. I really need to see your breasts," he said, he thought, reasonably and politely. Chris looked at him, the pupils of her blue eyes huge, leaving just a rim of color. She smiled a little bit, and pulled her shirt very slowly up and off, and turned and looked across the semi-circle at Janey, who was rolling another joint.

Janey caught the look, saw Chrissie with her shirt off, and stood, unbuckled her belt (she had long ago shed her boots, and wore just heavy gray ragg socks on her feet), and, with some effort, slithered her jeans down to her knees, then sat cross-legged and extracted each foot, socks still on, from her pants. She threw them behind her. Sitting cross-legged, it was apparent she had no panties to deal with. She never wore underwear, unless she was menstruating. Janey smiled back at Chris, and went back to rolling joints.

Terry watched the performance, showing the mildest of interest. He leaned toward the fireplace, and threw another stick of pine on the now-modest fire. The pitch, dried and hardened in the wood, began to pop and spit. Billy, who had been sitting with eyes closed, snapped them open, and they locked on Chris's breasts. Billy took a long swallow of wine, and then crawled across the bright space in the center of the semi-circle to Chrissie, and without a word, started licking and sucking on her nipples. After a minute or two, she pushed him away, as if he, not she, had now had enough.

After that moment, things became hazy for all of them, as far as anyone would say, although they never discussed that evening again. They had been so immensely stoned, and were so isolated in that strange house in the storm that it was clear from the beginning (before anyone had arrived, or had even thought of going) that all rules were to be suspended. It was hours before they finally crashed and fell asleep, next to and on each other, curled up for warmth, intertwined to continue their companionship. When they woke up in the early morning, long before dawn, cold and naked, everyone dressed quickly and silently shivering, crashing from the acid and everything else. Except for Lewis, who decided that he would stay and hitch into town later (he ended up walking most of the way), everyone went home to sleep off the rest of the crash. They planned to meet up at the bar later on Sunday. The other four were at the door, ready to leave. Lewis walked up to stand next to Chrissie, who he guessed he had been with most of the night. Janey and Terry had paired off, mostly, too. Billy had passed out early, to dream of all the sex he had seen, but not actually been involved in, despite his best efforts.

Chrissie still smelled pretty good, through the acid-sweat and wine and all the cigarette smoke, now with an overlay of wet burning pine and the ancient must of the Midget's poor, abandoned house, all imbued in her heavy sweater and thick blonde hair. Lewis was close enough to see her pulse beating beneath the skin of her pretty neck.

"You're fun, Lewis….you're a good guy, I think. Are you staying on the Island long?"

He felt the exhalation of breath she made with each word, and wanted to breathe it in. He moved closer yet, and put his hands on her hips, and looked right into her stoned eyes, now showing more arctic blue around the edges of the black pupil.

"I don't know — I think so. I picked up a job: now, I just need a place to live. This is okay for tonight, or I could stay at Janey's again, I guess, but I'll need something a little more permanent if I'm actually going to make it to work every day. Yeah, I guess I must be staying, at least for the winter, if I'm making plans like that."

Chris smiled a very small smile, and snuggled up against him.

"I'll see you at the bar, tomorrow. I'll sleep late, then, I need to go to the laundromat, but I should be at the bar by five or so, have a drink or two. If I'm not there, you know where I'm staying, right?" She gave him a nuzzle and a quick lick where his neck met his shoulder, burrowing into his open collar. The she turned and walked to the car, where Janey waited, smoking what could be her fortieth or maybe sixtieth cigarette since arriving the afternoon before.

Janey rarely smoked when she was straight, but smoked compulsively when drinking or stoned. Later, after a few hours sleep in her own bed, she'd feel like her mouth had been sanded on the inside. She'd brush her teeth and tongue until her mouth bled, then rinse with powerful mouthwash. Now, she watched Chris and Lewis from her seat in the car. The rain had stopped, but the windshield was still a filigree of raindrops and pine needles blown down by the gale. She knew that they couldn't see her, but they knew she was there.

What the hell was it with Lewis, she wondered? He didn't have Terry's dark, dangerous good looks, didn't have that smell of an outlaw that she could pick up from fifty yards off. She had been balling Terry, on and off, for the past year, and always found him attractive and sexy and great in bed, if a little rough. He could be a bastard, and an unapologetic son of a bitch. Lewis she had known since his days at B.U., had hung out with him, gotten high with him, had even slept with him, but he had passed out, and nothing happened, although he had said he wanted to fuck her. He didn't try again, and she didn't encourage him to. She thought she should screw him, but just couldn't work up enough interest. He wasn't particularly good looking, or even bad-looking. He just looked — ordinary. Right now he barely had a job, had no place to stay, and didn't seem to have any money, either. But she had watched him before, and watched him now, ending up with a good-looking chick, almost by accident. So Janey was jealous, and was starting to think about how she should punish him for being who he was.

Janey knew Lewis' current old lady, who, as far as Janey knew, still thought Lewis was with her. Janey could call her tomorrow, and let slip that Lewis was fooling around with Chrissie. That would be a start. And she could tell Chrissie that Lewis already had a woman, but that would just get Chris mad at her, and wouldn't stop her, anyway. She decided to do nothing, for now, at least until she got her head straight, and could think it through.

Day 13 – Ripped Off! Freaked Out!

"The Spastic Pervert," as he half expected he was now being called, had progressed to his bungalow without further incident, stopping to buy a small, fresh baguette, some mild French cheese, and a bottle of mineral water. It felt hotter inside than outside. He hadn't used the air conditioner, an antique that did little other than making a sad, grating whir, and wasn't about to try it now, but did switch on the ceiling fan, and then busied himself making coffee with the cheap French press he had found in the cabinet below the tiny sink. The coffee, once made, was not hot for long, but was strong, and except for the grounds suspended in the liquid, drinkable. The three spoons of sugar helped, giving it the syrupy consistency of Tussionex, his favorite cough medicine. Unfortunately, the coffee didn't merely energize him, but pushed him quickly into a new spiral of anxiety about the vanished Marian.

He fretted, and paced, and twitched a bit more with each passing moment. What the hell had happened to her? How had she found him on the beach after seeing him only once, at a distance, many months ago, and fully clothed? It was sometimes damn hard to recognize naked people the first time you see them that way. Could this have all been some kind of a set-up, some plot, some subterfuge to put him off his guard and…and…and then, what? Why bother? He was almost a nobody, and became more of a nobody with each passing day.

None of his thoughts, he knew, were rational. He was just doing his usual freak-out, and it would all go away with the correct pill, or pills. Perhaps he had better count them right now, and see what sort of rationing, if any, must be imposed.…given that he must, must take a certain number of pills tonight, right now, so all this fear would disappear. So that he could sit and write a few pages, or just sit and read a bit, or just be able to sit still. And most of all, not think about all the now seemingly clear and nefarious connections between the late night phone call from the West Coast (hey, how did he know it actually came from the West Coast? It could have come from the bar down on Charles Street..), not so many days away now, and the man who was, seemingly, looking for him (the man he pretty much knew to be dead, thank you very much), and the truck at his own, hidden house, said truck screaming away down the mountain after almost killing him, and, then, the miracle: a cute young thing picks him up (and this looked ever more ridiculous) on the beach, they go gambling, he wins a jackpot, and he gets laid! and then, poof!, she's gone in a heartbeat, tells him by phone (From where? The room next to his?) that she has to leave immediately, that she managed to just get a seat that very minute. And can he get a seat that quickly, should the need arise? He would not bet on it.

It was all so absolutely shriekingly and thoroughly unreal, so bizarre, that the section of his enfeebled consciousness in charge of fear and loathing just had to run with this baby. And tell him that the next step, of course, just had to be that Doc, not so dead after all (or worse, dead after all) must come tap, tap, tapping at his door, almost certainly with a message Lewis didn't want to receive.

Frowning at no particular thing, he crossed the eight steps to the bedroom/sleeping alcove, knelt on creaking, popping knees (one creaked, one popped, generally) and felt around under the bed for his poorly hidden giant Dopp kit, hoping that no neighborhood scorpion was napping on top of it. It was exactly where he left it, to the extent that objects stuffed under beds are stuffed with any exactitude. Lewis placed the bag on his bedspread, and tugged the cranky zipper open. Brown plastic bottles with child-proof tops peeked out, looking for their owner. Extracting the largest bottle, the oxycodone tablets, he didn't like the heft of it. He liked it a great deal less when, having struggled to get the cap off, he dumped the meager contents on the bed. What the fuck? Six white tablets lay there, looking entirely inadequate. He couldn't possibly have taken 21 pills since he last looked, could he? He knew there should be 27, or, allowing for error, and maybe an occasion he didn't remember, at least 20. This was all wrong, all of it some mistake. Maybe I took them out to count, and then put them back in the wrong jar, Lewis desperately hypothesized. He snatched up the other big bottle, the lorazepam, sure that when he dumped it, way too many would roll out because, surprise, he had put the wrong pills in! All a mistake!

But, the tranquilizer bottle didn't feel heavy enough, either. He was sweating, now, his hands were wet, and so he dried them carefully on the bedcovers. If he touched the pills with wet hands, they would swell up and crumble apart, and he'd end up having to lick the bedspread, and he'd destroy half of the pills. Hands dry, now, he unscrewed the top, and upended the jar. Six more pills rolled out, almost exactly like the six oxycodone a few inches away, maybe just a little more flat. Just like the oxycodone, too, in that there were way too few. He had arrived on the island with almost 60. He could not have taken 50, not in a few days, not by mistake, or on purpose, not in a fucking coma. The serrated knife edge of abject fear began to rip upwards through his guts.

He dumped the other bottles, in a haze, no longer connected to what he was doing. A thought was trying to worm its way into his consciousness, so he shut his consciousness down. In a fog, he watched the 6 pills roll out of each bottle, except, of course, the ones he needed, but didn't care about. Plenty of blood-pressure meds. Well, they'd help ward off the stroke he was going to have if he let that thought, the awful thought, in. He finally turned out the little plastic side-pockets inside the kit, and shook the whole damn thing, hard, repeatedly, over the bed. Band-Aids. An ancient condom, lubricated for his pleasure. Flakes of soap. Hair. He had no choice: the thought came clear and fast, evading his blocks. He has been ripped off. He had been left just about enough to get off the island and back to Boston. And, he had been ripped off by someone who knew him, knew his needs and habits. A junkie would have taken all of the pills. Someone, some evil motherfucker, had left a day's worth, maybe two days. This was no happenstance. They were still after him.

He'd have to leave the island. Oh, he might get a local doc to write him 10 or 12 pills, maybe even 10 or 12 of each. Hell, on a bad day, he'd take half that many. On a real bad day, he'd take more than 10.

Maybe the maid took them. Maybe that's all it was. But he could never prove it. He'd go to the Front Desk: they'd just shake their heads, sympathetically, and tell him how sorry they were, and had he read the notice, perhaps, in his room, that suggested that he have his valuables locked up in the hotel safe? Did Mr. Melton know that many guests would lock up medication in the hotel safe? After all, even on a safe island such as this one, there was sometimes petty theft.

He walked over to the annoying French telephone on the small desk, the desk he had planned to be sitting at in an hour, writing productively. He tried to decipher the instructions for dialing, but the print was too small. He found his sand-scratched drugstore reading glasses in his beach bag, and balanced them on his nose. Now, the words clear, they made little sense. To dial the Dutch side of the island required more numbers than he could fathom. Well, he had no choice. He had to call the airlines.

The telephone book, only half an inch thick, yielded the numbers of all airlines serving the island. American had the biggest ad, so he dialed them first. He knew it could be expensive, and would undoubtedly, take him via San Juan, a city he did not care for. But, he was the picture of a desperate man. He'd try any and all escape routes. He punched in what seemed to be the correct number and sequence of digits, but got only a strange, melodic electronic chorus of beeps and burps for his efforts. He tried again, a few times: on the final try, the switchboard at the Club picked up, clearly having had enough of his foolishness.

They were polite and silent as he explained his problem. Something had come up, he said, an emergency, and he must fly out tomorrow, if not today. Yes, it was indeed a shame, and yes, he understood that they could not refund the money he had paid for the rest of his stay, but, they would be glad to help him. They would call him back just as soon as they were able to find him a seat on a plane to Boston or New York, or even Washington, DC. Perhaps a seat for tomorrow, or the next day.

Feeling marginally less immediately panicked after their soothing offers of help, Lewis decided to strike while the iron was hot, insert another plea into the conversation before they could finish the brush-off. Was there, he inquired, a doctor, a physician, who they could recommend? He had, unfortunately, a chronic condition for which he must take certain medications, and he had, foolishly, brought an insufficient supply.

But of course, the desk clerk replied, they had an excellent Doctor who would see their guests, usually on very short notice. But, today was Saturday, and tomorrow, Sunday, so he could not be seen until Monday, unless it was an emergency. For that, he would have to go to the Clinic, which was always open. Should they call him a taxi to the Clinic?

Lewis declined, politely. A long wait in a crowded waiting room with all sorts, coughing, puking, bleeding. Then, an interview with a doctor who was there to deal with urgent problems. They'd be unimpressed with Lewis's issues. They'd ask their sneaky questions, pegging him as an addict in the first few minutes. "So, Monsieur Melton, you come here to vacation, to relax, but have such pain, such anxiety, that you must have ten or twenty pills each day?"

They'd send him away with nothing but a stern talking-to, or, if he were lucky, a few codeine tablets, and instructions to follow up with his own physician. Not worth the hassle; not if he could fly out tomorrow. If the desk couldn't get him a flight, of course, he might have to go to the clinic…for now, though, he had enough pills. If he could get to Boston tomorrow, Sunday, he'd see his doc first thing Monday, and be home with full prescriptions by noon.

He went, now, to what was left of his stash, and selected one Vicodin, one oxycodone, one Zanax, and one Ativan. He dumped them into his mouth with a sip of water, and chewed carefully. He washed the fully masticated pulp down with another swig of water, and then swished a third sip around his mouth to capture any fragments lurking in his teeth. Instantly calm, he knew that he'd be fine in twenty minutes. For two or three hours, no random fear or thought of harm would trouble him. Although he might argue that he was not addicted to drugs, he could not argue that he was addicted to relief.

Day Six, Laying Low (Continued)

Lewis remembered where the check-in desk was at the Club, but asked the huge security guard at the gate anyway. An imposing black man, he did not sweat in his dark blue trousers or light blue short-sleeved shirt, nor did he smile. Lewis wondered for a moment what he thought, what all the black islanders thought, about the crazy naked white folks who came here to be improper. He was well paid, for the island, to keep out the gawkers and the hawkers, to warn off those with cameras, to keep the riff-raff away from the paying guests. He was paid to interact, if need be, with crazy nude Europeans and Americans (or worse, Canadians) as if he thought what they were doing was perfectly normal and acceptable. He could not be a gawker, and the odds are, thought Lewis, after the first few weeks, gawking was the farthest thing from his mind. What did he talk about when he got home? Did he talk with his wife about all the strange things he had seen? Maybe he kept a tally of strange cases, unusual sightings, particularly large or small or curved or surgically enhanced appurtenances. He'd really have to ask, once he got settled. There was the chance of a good story there.

He spied the registration desk, vacant now. It occupied almost one quarter of the small, airy building that was set to the side of the walkway from the parking lot to the cluster of bungalows and utility buildings further from the beach. More bungalows — the better ones — and the restaurant/bar were closer to the shore, with the swimming pool, the tennis courts, and the community building in between.

Seeing no one at the desk, Lewis looked around for a chair to ease his wait. After traveling for the last eight hours, he was feeling every day of his age. As he glanced about, a striking young woman — well, young compared to him — materialized behind the desk. With short, jet-black hair and icy gray eyes, she looked as French as Lewis imagined he looked American. He could not see what she wore below her waist, but whatever it was, it was likely more than the choker of colored sea-glass gracing her slim neck. She was elegantly topless, topless being the most ill-used and inaccurate descriptor

137

in the current American lexicon. This woman, thought the ancient scribbler, was exquisitely "topped." And pleasant, polite, and possibly prescient, as she demonstrated with her first verbalization.

"Mr. Lewis Melton, I think, yes? Welcome to the Club. We have missed you since your visit last winter. You are all registered. I just need your signature here. Your bungalow is all ready. May I offer you a glass of wine after your long journey?"

A sweating bottle of decent chardonnay sat, with two glasses, on a varnished teak board. Lewis was not a wine drinker, certainly not if something else could be had, but accepted, primarily, he admitted to himself, to watch her pour. She was as graceful and informal as could be wished for.

A good swallow made him glad he had accepted. The wine was cool, not bad, and filled his head with an expanding taste. Then, the alcohol hit him, and he took another swallow to sustain the reach of the warm glow in his chest.

"Merci....for wine like that, I'll sign anything. I'm delighted to be here again."

The woman, without a name tag or a place to put one, laughed politely, just enough to send a tremor through her breasts. She reached below the desk, and came up with a key with a stamped-metal fob, imprinted with the number "64." She dropped the key and fob into Lewis' outstretched hand, and smiled with her very small, not startlingly white teeth.

"I hope you enjoy your stay. If you require anything, please, just stop by, or dial 6 on your phone."

Lewis thanked her, slipped the key into his right front pocket, and, bag still suspended from his left hand, by now entirely numb, and walked back outside. Number 64, he guessed, must be to the north, on the other side of the pool. The walkway of crushed stone and seashells led him past the first of the older bungalows. They were bigger than the new ones, and closer to the parking lot than to the beach. About forty feet further on, a small wooden sign indicated that to the left he would find numbers 55 to 65.

He passed the pool, deserted except for a small cluster of unfortunate and surly teens. Their parents, not understanding them at all, had brought them to a place that scared, mystified, and excited them, a place where the rituals were outside of their ability to appreciate or even tolerate for very long. They shunned the beach (too many naked adults — eww, gross) and huddled together for safety, the two girls and the boy, in their conservative bathing suits, whispering together, planning a cigarette and liquor heist from someone's parents, perhaps.

Other adults passed Lewis on the path, and by the time the fifth nude vacationer said hello, he could no longer register their nakedness. By tomorrow, he knew from experience, he'd only note the clothed ones, or those somehow oddly formed or otherwise remarkable, the Freaks of Nature. He kept a running count of the percentage of his fellow humans who should be by law prohibited from nudity, as well as those who should be required to be naked at all times, so perfect were they in all respects. There were a hell of a lot fewer in the second camp. He had not rated himself.

Cottage 64 appeared in front of him sooner than he expected. He had not even begun to sweat, despite the eighty degree heat. There was no humidity, and a breeze (or just as often, a good wind) blew in off the sea. The climate was hard not to like, and made it all the more difficult to justify living where he did, with temperatures, at least in Vermont, that could vary one hundred and forty degrees in six months.

Before putting the key in the lock, Lewis turned the door handle, and as he expected, the door swung open. The key was symbolic, not necessary. He had one of the newer cottages, very much like the older ones where he usually stayed. There were two to each small building, with porches and entrances on opposing sides. His smelled of garlic and beer, not as bad as it might be. The turnover was constant, and the cottages were only vacant long enough for a cleaning and a changing of linens. Last year, his cottage had somehow smelled of tom-cat pee, and he could neither get the smell to leave nor get a different cottage. He had tried splashing cheap cologne on the floor, a method that not only did not mask the original smell, but combined with and expanded it to a nausea-causing level. It became necessary to enter the cottage only when extremely drunk, and to spend the rest of his time elsewhere. Fellow guests began to regard him as a social animal, always around the bar or the common rooms. The resentment still festered in his soul. But this cottage, this year, had a smell he could coexist with. He might even grow to like it.

He shed his clothes, gratefully, lit a cigarette, put his sunglasses back on, and left for the bar for a gin and tonic to celebrate his safe arrival, and the disappearance of his clothing for the duration of his visit. Drink in hand, he did not tarry in the dark bar, but wandered out to a vacant beach chair and plopped down on his towel.

The sea was a magical fluorescent blue-green, white-capped by the moderate breeze coming out of the south. He watched the ever-changing pattern of the water, and drank his drink in swallows, not sips. When it was almost empty, he dumped the sliver of lime into his mouth, and chewed on it until he could no longer tolerate the tart bite.

The beach was beginning to clear out for the day. There was only a scattering of bodies. Many were dark-brown, some lighter, with white patches (boobs and asses, he had to guess, without his glasses), and some a dangerous pink. But now, in the late afternoon, the sun's rays were no longer lethal: the damage for the day had been done, and the badly burned were pouring alcohol down their throats to ease the pain they'd feel later, or when they sobered up. In the morning, they'd have sun blisters to go with their hangovers. Lewis looked forward to the rest of the day, every minute of it, and to the next several days, and to every hour that he would be here, removed, safe from everything except his own stupidity, and, of course, the random acts of a Jokester God.

Exiled for now from the day-to-day rituals and peregrinations that constituted what he imagined was his winding-down of life, the Old Bastard, as he was beginning to call himself, was left with only the calming expectation of doing a few different sorts of nothing. The needs of all those who continued to play some part in his life were, each year, becoming more of a hassle to meet. It seemed to him that he spent a good part of his hours doing those things that he no longer felt were important or enjoyable, and still had to cope with his own personal demons, none of which seemed to be losing interest in him.

He was losing the ability to differentiate between the warning signs of a looming anxiety attack and some type of normal agitation, the kind that he guessed other people experienced from time to time. So, he treated any symptoms heroically, with ever increasing doses of tranquilizers, doses that became less and less effective. It had become more of a holding action than a battle.

He hoped, believed that he could feel better here. The anxiety would be less, and the horrible fucking constant aches and pains that could and would suddenly occur somewhere in his body — his bones, his muscles. His doctor told him that it was probably just a bit of arthritis, or a result of his "anxiety problem." Lewis didn't believe that, and told the Doc that he didn't believe it. He thought it was fibromyalgia, or possibly bone cancer. Wherever it was, it always got worse, except here on the island, where it got better. Whatever it was, his doctor gave him plenty of pain meds, and he took all he obtained, and they seemed to help. But not as much as a week in the sun, not as much as a change in venue, because, he could go on and on with his litany of ills. Physical ills, and the other kind, the regrets, the remorse, the confusion, so bad these past couple of years. It was all about the miss-steps he had made, had made but could neither change nor think about too often. They were like landmines from an old war, unexploded ordnance buried along the pathway. Would it be his boot that came down in exactly the wrong spot — or someone else's?

Distance, though, distance was the great protection. Here on this island he was safer from the things that pursued him. Almost safe enough to think back to a different island, and to consider what might have happened there.

Lewis drank off the remainder of his gin and tonic, lit a fresh cigarette, and looked off toward the sea, out past Green Cay, to the north.

1964 — The Temporary Empire

The fall, and then the winter days on the Island were all pretty much of a sort. Cold, but not very. Rainy and damp and windy, or just windy. You could almost always feel or hear the wind. It snowed one time, a few inches, just enough to send a few drunks with bald tires hurtling off of the flat roads in their rust-buckets. Anyone who had lived there for very long had forgotten how to drive in the snow. Then, again, there wasn't much to hit, once you left town. You could leave the road at fifty miles an hour and just bump along the moors, or hit a scrub pine that didn't have the mass to bend your bumper.

Lewis had steady work, more than he wanted, and had not been forced to spend his escape money. He kept the stash, wrapped in plastic and duct tape, sewn (poorly) into the hem of his only warm jacket, so the money was always with him.

After the night at the Midget's house, things fell together for him. He had seen Chrissie at the bar the following afternoon, after work. He was cold and wet. The rain had come back, intermittently, but not enough to stop work. The job boss had his own ideas about what constituted unworkable weather conditions, and they were extreme. He expected his crew to have the sense to show up in foul-weather gear, so work could progress. If it rained so hard that he could not see his hammer at the end of his arm, he might send everyone home. By December, they would have inside work for about half of the crew: the rest, if they wanted to work, would be cold and wet until June.

Lewis was so cold and wet that two double Metaxas with coffee did not stop his shaking, so Chrissie took him home for a hot bath. It was a big old-fashioned bathtub, so she climbed in, too, with room to spare. They sat facing each other in the steaming water, legs in Vees, his over hers. She rested her blonde head against the rim of the tub, and looked beautiful to him. They passed a joint back and forth. Stoned, they talked, just beginning to learn about the other. Chrissie started in.

"I came down last spring, last May, before the weather turned. It was supposed to be for a month or two, to help a friend's sister get her new shop set up for the season. 'Judith,' it's called, over by the police station. You've seen it. She has a shop in New York, and thought it might work here. The place really took off. She sells beachwear, casual stuff, expensive. It's nice stuff, but lame. Nothing I'd wear for real. I had been living in the East Village, with a guy. He was turning into a real asshole. Smart guy, but he got into smack, which wasn't so smart, 'cause he got a habit in a couple of months, started stealing from me — and everyone else, I'm sure. He tried to get me to start turning tricks to support us — support his habit, is more like it.

"I wouldn't hook, but I did some other stuff I'm not proud of. I was doing meth crystal, doing cocaine when I could afford it. I think I weighed about ninety pounds. So, I shouldn't tell you, but I ended up doing some films — soft-core stuff, mostly. It was kind of exciting, to be so bad. Doing stuff with guys I'd just met five minutes before. My mother would absolutely die if she ever found out. And that bothered me. And the guy I lived with bothered me, so I got out. I got the chance to come down here, and I was on a plane the next day. I came with one bag, left everything else that hadn't been stolen yet.

"I was crashing from the meth and the coke for the first week — all I wanted to do was sleep, or kill myself. I just kept smoking reefer and drinking coffee to stay awake, and by the end of two weeks, I wouldn't start crying until noontime. I started eating like a pig, and by July, I was up to the gorgeous one hundred and four pounds you see before you!" She smiled at him, and spread her arms dramatically. "So, now you know I was a speed-freak porn-star. Sort of. Do you still like me?"

Lewis looked at her (he hadn't stopped looking at her) and saw a cute little blond with a nose a little too big for her face, great tits rising up through the bath water, a darker patch of pubic hair barely visible through the suds. A great smile, lovely eyes, and maybe a little too much honesty.

"Yeah, I still like you. I like you a lot. I like you so much that I really hope it's mutual. But, I won't tell you all the things I've done, good, or not so good. I really haven't done shit since undergrad. I was in grad school — actually, I probably still am, technically — but I got sidetracked. A lot. I smoke way too much: cigarettes, pot, you name it. Sometimes, I drink too much. Until a few days ago, I was living in Cambridge with a very nice girl, who now has no idea where I am. I won't be going back there for a long time.

"I will tell you that I got involved in a grass deal — for real weight — that went bad, really bad. I don't know all the details, and if I did, I wouldn't tell you, 'cause then you could be in some danger. Maybe you'll hear some stories about what went down, but not from me. Anyway, I'm here for a while — at least for the winter. Right now, I think we should get out of the tub, dry off,

and go fuck our brains out, then sleep. I need to go to work in the morning.
I just hope my boots dry out."

Some days and weeks went by, and they ended up being together. They
found a cheap, tiny, drafty cottage out at the very far end of the Island. The
rent was two hundred dollars a month in the off-season, and they paid it
gladly, and had enough money to get by, and to enjoy their life as it was.
Lewis forgot about Boston and Cambridge and the deal as if none of it had
ever happened.

Sometimes, friends and acquaintances would go up to Boston for a day
or a week on various errands, not always legal. When they came back, they
would sometimes have stories. Doc, it seemed, was gone, whether alive or
dead. He just disappeared. Someone heard that someone else had seen him
down in the Tenderloin in San Francisco. He was said to be working with a
wizard, turning out barrels of crystal as white and fluffy as the first snowfall
in Maine, and making huge money, and living as he liked. But there were
stories, too, that he was dead, that he had been set up, that his dealing was
cutting in to the interests of some guys from Revere, and maybe a Cambridge
cop or two, and he had been taken out to the sandpits, not willingly. It was
said sometimes, in bars, late at night and not too loud, that when you went
out to the sandpits, not willingly, you didn't come back. These stories were
sometimes told at the Bucket, swirled in with the stories about fishing, about
storms that took men away from fishing, and about other topics of interest to
those who had been drinking now since afternoon, and slurred out tales they
hadn't intended to tell.

If they talked about Doc, then they talked about Mel the egomaniac,
about Owsley and his pink helicopter, about Tim up on the Farm in New
York and how he had the habit of getting piss-himself drunk while preaching
enlightenment, so the stories had no singularity of importance. They were part
of the alcohol-soaked fabric of the lives on hold for the winter that populated
the bar. It was its own civilization, one not meant to exist for longer than each
soon- forgotten day.

The temporary empire was thick with peace and love, now, with the
hippies taking over, the working stiffs and VA alkies making room for this
new batch of losers. New Bedford scallopers washed up to wait out the storms,
and ended up spending their time and money with some little lady, late of
New Canaan, vague from too much of a good thing. Dropouts and draft-
dodgers, long-haired and tie-dyed, bought shotguns so they could go duck
hunting with the crew-cut ex-Marine builder they worked for now. Lines
were crossed. Crossed lines tangle, and sometimes must be cut...but not yet.

Lewis and Chrissie were oblivious to the whole show, and at the bar less
and less. They were as in-love and lust and as happy as any two people ever had

the chance to be. They stayed home most evenings, reading, fucking, smoking reefer, and eating ice cream. Chrissie insisted that they get a telephone, and began to have conversations with her mother (she called each week or more often). Chrissie's mother asked if she would please come home for a few days at Christmas, it had been so long since they had seen her. Chrissie said yes, if….if she could bring her boyfriend, a really nice guy, a (she lied just a bit) graduate student taking a semester or two away from his studies. And, they had to be nice to him.

Her mother said yes, he could of course come; he could stay in the Guest Room. They — Chrissie's mother and sister — had a huge apartment in Manhattan, some of the spoils of the divorce a few years back. Dad had moved his practice to Albany, along with a new wife who had been his office manager, and was younger than the old one, but a bit older than Chrissie. He would not be in attendance for the holiday celebration.

Lewis wasn't so crazy about the idea, and was having some trouble getting the time off. The inside crew was sheetrocking and painting the new shops on the wharf, and Lewis had turned instant pro at taping sheetrock, an arcane skill that generally called for the expensive and troublesome importation of French Canadians, the best and fastest sheet rockers, drunk or sober. His boss, understandably, didn't want to import help if he had Lewis, and finally, would only give him the weekend and a day on either side.

More than almost anything, Lewis wanted to make Chrissie happy. So, he took the time he could get, and dug into his stash of get-away money, and at the bar after work one night, talked a charter pilot that he knew into flying them down to La Guardia, and then coming down again to pick them up — all for the price of fuel, an ounce of weed, and a couple hundred dollars. When he got home, he found Chrissie sitting in front of the fireplace, stoned, patching a pair of his jeans that were, by now, more patch than jeans. He said "Hi!" grabbed an ale from the fridge, and laid out the plan in a very few words. Chrissie jumped up and wrapped herself around him.

"Lewis, you are so great! Wait till I tell Mom. She'll freak. She's still tied up in all that materialistic shit, so she'll really dig the chartered plane. And I know you'll like Mom. She's not too much of an asshole most of the time."

"Yeah, well….I really did it for you, Chrissie, but I also did it to make sure we got there and back without getting hung-up….you know, a broken-down car, a missed bus — 'cause I absolutely have to be back to work on the Tuesday after Christmas. I've got to keep that job, for now….we're going to need a lot of bread, if we plan to go back to Boston next year, so I can finish my degree, and you can get your last two years of college in. So, we can't have any complications, right?"

"I know. Things will go fine. I mailed that box of presents today to your family, but I still think we should stop in to see them; we'll be in Boston anyway. I've never even talked to your mother."

"No, I can't go — don't want to go — to Boston, yet. I want things to cool down a little more; maybe in the summer."

Lewis found a spot to sit on the floor next to Chrissie, and they fell into a discussion of what they could have for supper, considering the paucity of the ingredients on hand, and the fact that the only grocery store on the Island had closed an hour ago. Chrissie got up to go into the kitchen — just a different part of the room they were in — to check the cupboards once more, but came back with two glasses of cheap Mountain Red, and half of a smoldering joint. They smoked, they drank. Chrissie moved to a chair behind Lewis, and began to rub his shoulders. Within moments, they were on the floor, naked, mauling each other like small mammals in heat. They'd get to supper a little later.

Day 13 — 1998 (Night)

The four tablets that Lewis had taken thirty minutes ago had the effect that his reeling psyche required: an envelopment of his anxiety in a soft, warm blanket of feel-good brain chemicals. The rogue neurons had stopped firing wildly. Lewis was compelled to survive in his constant battle with himself. The odds were heavy that he could get back to Boston by Monday, at the latest, so the worst-case scenario involved one or two achy, anxious days. The rest could be sorted out, or simply forgotten, later. He knew that the Doc haunting, the Marian incident, all the related craziness would become indistinct with time. His plan of coming here, for not just escape, but introspection, was farcical. He had proven to himself, once again, the accuracy of the adage, "Wherever you go, there you are." The island was no more secure for him than Vermont or Boston, because he was there. The same cosmic baggage that had, one time, led him to another island, had led him to many more, and now again to this one.

One of his contemporaries had written something about the need to turn pro when things got weird: he wasn't far wrong. Lewis needed, badly, to turn pro right now. He had the means — a retirement stash of a few hundreds of thousands of dollars. He could take steps to ensure his material and physical security, as he slid toward death or dotage. He just had to get back to America to plan and execute those steps.

Much calmer, now, Lewis moved from the hard, straight-backed chair by the telephone to the small, worn love seat on his miniscule screened porch. The love seat was upholstered in a floral print most often seen on very "big" women in parts of the South, and southern Mid-Maine. Huge, colorful flowers, blessedly faded from the sun and salt-air. He reclined his bulk as comfortably as he could on the too-short pallet, and closed his eyes, hoping for a twenty minute nap. With some rest, he might be able to write.

Lewis has dropped off instantly, and awoke just as rapidly to a polite, insistent rapping on the screened-porch door. It was now past dusk, but the security lights that had clicked on throughout the compound gave sufficient illumination for Lewis to make out two uniformed policemen, one dark, the other one white, standing patiently at the door, watching him most unpolitely as he came awake. The man closest to the door — the black cop — kept knocking, steadily, moderately, the cadence interrupted each six knocks for two beats, then back to the knock. It seemed a rote behavior, something designed to keep the rousted from slipping back under, passing the visitation off as a normal night-terror, a simple hallucination. Lew was under no such impression.

"Okay, okay, I hear you, hold on. I'll be right there."

He then did the opposite, and walked away from the cops, into the next room to retrieve his wrinkled shorts from the floor, and stepped into them quickly. Answering the door and talking to cops bare-ass was a point not yet reached in his personal development. Now dressed for the occasion, he ran his fingers back through his tousled hair as he walked slowly to the door.

"Yes, gentlemen, what can I do for you?" he said politely, but not deferentially, as he opened the screen door. "Come in, come in."

The officers exchanged a fleeting glance that Lewis couldn't decipher. The, the darker one, who appeared to be in charge, dropped the verbal burning bag of shit. "We are inquiring as to the whereabouts of one Miss Linda L'Ange. A number of people who we have interviewed today report seeing her in your company. Is she here?"

"I don't know anyone by that name," said Lewis, hoping for, but not expecting, relief. "I'm sorry (like Hell, he thought). There isn't anyone here except me."

"Perhaps," said the black cop, "you would look at a picture that we have of this Miss L'Ange. It was wired to us, so it is not a very good picture, but maybe sufficient."

The policeman passed a letter-sized sheet of paper to Lewis. There, in black and gray and white, was a picture of a youngish woman who could be Marian. The woman looked very serious in the picture, and had longer hair, but it could, it could, maybe, be Marian. Lewis — fleetingly — considered asking if they had a picture of her genitals, so he could make a positive I.D., but decided against humor in this situation. He decided to play it straight.

"I think I may know this woman. It's hard to tell, from this picture. But if it's the same woman, I don't know her by that name. I know her as Marian. We spent several hours together yesterday, and I stayed the night at her place. I haven't seen her since this morning....she kind of, disappeared, I guess you could say. I went out to get some coffee for us, and when I returned, she was gone. She called me later, and said that she was at the airport, ready to hop a flight to the States. May I ask why you are looking for her?"

"Mister Melton, you say you know her as Marian. What last name did she give? Perhaps, if she did take a flight, she used that name."

Lewis was stumped….had she mentioned a last name? And if she hadn't, had he really slept with someone without knowing her last name? Hell, he hadn't done that since the Sixties….or Seventies. So much for "safe sex."

"I don't recall her last name….I'm sure she told me….we had a drink or two, so it's all a bit fuzzy. You didn't tell me why you were looking for her. Can you tell me?"

"She has been reported missing. By her husband. She was due home several days ago, so he became a bit concerned, understandably, no? Now, we must ask you if we can look around your bungalow. You can say no, and we will note that, but we are permitted to look around anyway, as we have the permission of the Club management."

"Husband? She has a husband?" Lewis sounded stupid to himself, and, he was sure, to the policemen. "Yeah, sure, look around all you want. It won't take long. And, she was never here. We….I don't know…was she missing when I was down helping you try to I.D. that character Billy?"

Lewis stopped himself. Why was he running his mouth? He was, he reminded himself, in a foreign country, being questioned by two policemen who seemed mightily suspicious of him, and they were not bothering to hide their suspicion. No more information, he told himself. Cooperate, but don't answer questions that haven't been asked. In all the times he'd been to various vacation spots – of the warm, palm-tree variety, at least- he'd never spoken to a cop, not even to ask directions. Something was amiss.

The policemen didn't seem to have noticed his abortive "we," or if they had, they made no comment. They immediately began to wander very slowly around the small cottage, touching nothing, but visually inspecting everything: the living room, which was also the bedroom, and the much smaller bathroom, and then back to the screened porch, where they had begun. They made no notes, although each carried a small black notebook — the notebooks looked like government issue, so perhaps anything written in them was instantly transmogrified into official writ. That thought was not as reassuring as Lewis had hoped. He was, as always, looking for some sign that his current disaster would flow away, could be forgotten, with the rest. The harbingers of nothing good indicated that they were through with the search by returning to where Lewis still stood, flat-footed, in his dirty, wrinkled khaki shorts and his trembling brain, trying as hard as he could to appear neither nervous nor guilty.

"Well, Mr. Melton, as you said, the L'Ange woman is not here. We shall take our leave, for now, and continue to search the area. Her husband, a Mr. MacDougal — she did not take his name, apparently — is quite anxious to hear from her. I believe that he is flying in, today or tomorrow, from California in the States. If you should hear from the woman, please call me immediately."

The cop passed a business card to Lewis.

"We may need to speak with you again, as you could have been one of the last people to speak with her. I hope you do not plan to leave the island soon."

One of the skills that Lewis had developed early in life was the ability to appear to be paying rapt attention to the person speaking to him, while, in fact, tuning them out, but unconsciously filtering their speech for critical information. He was in that mode now, and did not change expression as his sensors picked up the last seven words that the policeman uttered. Then, the full import of the words slammed him in the chest with enough force to elicit an audible "Ooooff!"

"Pardon?" said the white officer.

"I said 'Ooof.' You surprised me. I'm afraid that I'll be flying out tomorrow, or the next day. Medical problem, I'm afraid…have to get back to see my Doctor. No way around it, you see."

"Well, Mr. Melton, then you had best hope that Madame L'Ange turns up, or calls her husband soon. We cannot allow anyone connected to the investigation to leave the island until we are satisfied that Miss L'Ange is alright. I am not at liberty, at this time, to go into any detail, but we have some reason to believe that she may have met with some foul plays, as they like to say in the States."

Lewis could not answer. His punch-drunk mind was still at "Ooooff," and he couldn't muster a word. The meds he had consumed not so long ago were doing their job very well, fending off the shrieking harpy of panic, of doom, of disaster. Yet the fear and doom and disaster were visible, just now letting themselves out the screen door, calmly, reeking of implacable officialdom, impervious, finally, to all defenses but one. And the experience had left him, he hoped only temporarily, speechless. A rapidly aging, increasingly fatter American, standing in the middle of the room, his crumpled shorts in danger of slipping down from what used to be his waist. Had he been able to see himself, expressionless, eyes glazed with drugs and shock and disbelief, he might have, on a better day, laughed.

But he couldn't see himself, and he couldn't, right then, see any way out. Habit kicked in, motivating him to walk to the kitchen(ette) counter where a pack of cigarettes lay, and to the fridge, where, behind the bottled water and the butter, a lone bottle of Dutch beer stood. He lit the cigarette, lifted the beer bottle out of its hole, and, not thinking, tried to spin the cap off with his hand. As it was not a spin-off cap, he managed, instead, to rip a nasty gash in the meaty mid-forefinger of his left hand. Blood welled and then began dripping to the floor almost instantly. Ignoring the wound and the mess, the speechless man found a bottle opener screwed, very reasonably, to the edge of the countertop, and pried the cap from the bottle. He hoisted the cold malt to his mouth, and drank off a third of the bottle in one swallow.

The rest of the bottle took four or five swallows. Then, calmly, he turned on the not very cold water tap in the sink, and watched his blood leave his hand and swirl, diluted, down the drain. He began the search for a bandage of some sort. The alcohol — or maybe the thought of the alcohol — was starting to mix nicely, maybe a little dangerously, with his meds. His brain rebooted, along with his power of speech, beginning, now, softly, pensively.

"Holy fucking *shit*! *Holy* fucking *shit*!"

With no audience, he kept it brief, and to the point. In a classroom, or a cocktail party, he would have droned on, pontificated, some would say, regarding how his plight, here and now, reflected, in microcosm, the human plight that so often looked like this: the tendency of things in our lives that have gone badly awry to precipitate the going-badly-awry of other things, related or not-so, and how this shows up, again and again, in stories and tales that we all love, because, perhaps, they are so fucking *familiar* to us. And how this, or variations of this, are the warp and weave of pretty much all real stories: how the hero discovers himself to be, so to speak, screwed, and employs his intellect and/or physical strength to triumph over these serially worse disasters, these off-color jokes of the gods and goddesses, and is, finally, able to win out, and return home (although, somehow, home has changed, too) a changed and better man, a man returning not with the boon he sought, but with a prize of much greater value.

He could almost imagine the yawns and not polite smiles, but imagined, too, that he would feel better about things in general, had he another human to declaim to, or at....but, hero or no, audience or not, he figured it was time to pull up his imaginary socks, and using what was left of his once-almost-legendary intellect to *make things come out right*. Which really meant, go home, get some drugs, and continue a comfortable (and now, no longer quite so meaningless) existence until he dropped quite meaningfully dead.

Prepared to do the right and only thing, he vowed to ignore the day, so far, and take some more meds. He had put together a dosing schedule, mentally, anyway (he was afraid to write it down) and knew that, worst case, even if he couldn't get a plane until Monday, he could have four pills, twice a day. If, however, the new potential worst-case became reality, and if his actual departure date could be fucking never, then, it really didn't matter if he took one pill a day, or took all twenty-four, right now. All twenty-four, unfortunately, probably wouldn't kill him, but it would hospitalize him, and then, they would have to either give him drugs, or watch him fall apart in front of them.

It was a thorny question. He took one more of each pill, to help him think. And then, the telephone rang.

Day Six, (Continued, Still)

His sense of time and place was twisted, so badly, when he swam up, out of the reverie that had swallowed him whole, that he was initially inclined to blame the gin and tonic — "I drank that like it was water!" he thought — but a study of his watch told the tale, only seven or eight minutes. When he thought about it for another few seconds, he decided that it was more like road-amnesia, his own appellation. It happened to everyone he had asked about it, after the first time he noticed the effect. One is driving, maybe tired, maybe thoughtless, down a long stretch of road that one has driven before, more than a few times. Suddenly, nothing is familiar. You don't remember passing through that little town, what was it called? Nothing looks right, then, just before the panic hits, it is all okay, all familiar again, one knows *exactly* where one is. Almost like a mini-blackout. Maybe a TIA? Scary shit. But he was, instantly, okay.

The walk to his cottage was brief, but each step was more careful and desperate, the way a man (or woman) walks when they know that, any second now, they might soil their pants. The airline food had caught up to him at the same time that a couple of week's worth of anxiety-induced constipation was relaxing its grip. All other thoughts retreated, paled, compared to his need to get to the toilet before his exquisite stomach cramps became something else.

When he emerged from his miniscule bathroom twenty minutes later, he was, literally, drained and exhausted. The idea of walking to the restaurant at the resort for some sort of dinner didn't have much appeal, although he knew, as un-hungry as he might be, that he'd be ravenous at ten that night. But it was early now, not even seven. He could have a few pain pills to quiet his stomach, and then take a little nap. Dinner might sound better to him when he woke up, took a shower, and felt through with his traveling for the day. It wouldn't yet be dark, and closer to the time that he had become used to having his evening meal. On the island, he liked to stay up until one or two, and then sleep until nine in the morning, sometimes later. It was a change from his usual schedule, and seemed to help relax him.

He hadn't unpacked, and probably wouldn't. He extricated his gigantic shaving kit, the biggest one Dopp made. Unzipped, it gaped open to expose a half-dozen brown plastic pharmacy jars, and he easily found the bottle of oxycodone, 5 milligram immediate release tablets. He pried the lid off, and let three roll out into his cupped hand. Selecting another bottle, he took out one Xanax tablet, then threw all four pills into his mouth, and started to chew them up while he searched for something to wash them down with.

The kitchenette boasted a tiny stainless steel sink (which made an excellent urinal, Lewis discovered), and a little under-the-counter 'fridge, of the dorm-room variety. In the 'fridge, as he had expected, was a bottle of cold mineral water. He drank it halfway down to get the meds into his system as quickly as he could, and not incidentally, to replace some of the fluids that he had lost to the runs.

He could feel the icy water hitting his jittery stomach, and at the same time, a nice cool breeze coming off the ocean and into his cottage, chilly enough, compared to the heat of the day, to raise goose bumps on his arms. He wandered out onto his screened porch, a small one, perhaps four feet deep and ten feet long, and stood, holding the cool bottle at water, waiting for the drugs to announce themselves to his brain. His gut was still jumping around a bit, recovering from the spasms that had emptied him out. He looked down at his belly — not difficult at all to see, unfortunately, he thought — and wondered when it had gotten so big. Not too long ago, he could see his dick. Now, he could just see the tips of his toes, if he leaned forward a few degrees. His gut had slowed it's jumping to once every fifty or sixty seconds, and soon, with the help of modern pharmaceuticals, it would cease entirely.

When he grew bored watching his gut twitch, he looked up, and out through the screen. There was a woman on the porch of the cottage across the way. He didn't have his bifocals on, or even with him. They were probably on his nightstand in Vermont, where he had placed them so he'd remember to bring them. He had, of course, brought his drugstore reading glasses, useless to a Peeping Tom, unless one were peeping at insects. Too bad, really, as even blurry, the woman looked to be worth watching. She was of Rubenesque proportions, in shadow, through two screens, twenty-five feet away. God damn it, no glasses, no binoculars, a perfect opportunity spoiled. He might as well head for his nap before he got a hard-on from imagining that which he could not see.

The drugs were beginning to work. The spasms had stopped while he thought about what he couldn't see, and he began to relax. His bed, so far unused by him, was calling. One full hour of sleep then, or even less, a decent half-hour doze, and all would be right with the world. He recapped the bottle of water, and put it back in the 'fridge. The bedroom was only a few paces, then, he tore the spread off — he had it on good authority from a friend in the hotel trade that they were seldom, if ever, washed — fluffed up the not very fluffable pillow (without thinking how many sweaty heads had lain on it), and rolled onto the bed carefully, the way a man with some seriously deteriorated disks should. Just as he closed his eyes, the telephone bleated.

It was out of reach, of course, a few feet away on a small desk. The noise the phone made was quintessentially French, and rude and annoying, as it should be. He wondered if the telephones on the Dutch side of the island made the same insufferable sound. He was not capable of ignoring a ringing phone, and so, hauled himself upright as he rolled to the edge of the bed.

"Hello?" he said, he hoped sounding far more awake and oriented than he felt.

"Lew — it's Judy....I called to see if you were okay....I just had this really gruesome flash, you, and blood all over the place. Everywhere. Are you alright?"

"I'm fine. You and your psychic powers — you've not been right one time since I've known you. You should have been right at least once or twice, just coincidentally, but nope, never. Anyway, I'm good, just really beat from traveling. I was just thinking of taking a little nap, before dinner. Hell, I may skip dinner, just sleep until morning."

"You should. You need to relax more. You think you're, I don't know, thirty-five or something, but you're not. I worry about you all the time. I didn't bring it up the other night … didn't get a chance to, you lewd old bastard…but have you thought at all about living together again? Not getting married again — just living together: we're both getting kind of older, and it would make sense to have someone else there, you know, in case anything happened. What if you had a stroke, chopping wood up at the Vermont house? What if I had a stroke in the shower or while I was sleeping?"

"Well, if I had a stroke chopping wood, and it was winter, which would be likely, seeing as there's about ten months of that, and only two of summer, then, I'd probably freeze to death, quite peacefully. Of course, if it were summer, I'd probably lie there, paralyzed, for hours before some stupid fucking Flatlander drove by, and asked me directions. If I didn't answer, then they'd drive away, and I'd die with a wicked good sunburn!"

"Lewis, I'm serious!" She sounded more like she was seriously trying not to laugh, Lewis thought. "We can talk about this when you get back....just try to relax some when you're down there, and don't drink too much."

"Judy, I'm still crazy about you, of course, but you just demonstrated in a few sentences why we can't ever live together. You'd *give* me a fucking stroke, with all your worrying, all the disaster scenarios that you run through your head. Tell you what — I'll give you a call every couple of days, if I can figure out how to use these goddamn phones."

"Okay, I get your point — but I'm not through with the issue. Oh, you got another phone call — I'm sure it was "Doc" this time. Not Doug, or Dog. Doc. Same as the last time. He said he really needed to catch up with you. I asked for his phone number, so you could call him. Do you want it?"

"Whoa, stop. I don't even have pants, let alone a pen. Give me a minute."

He rummaged through his traveling bag, his sport coat pockets, his pants, and finally, the tiny desk drawer, where he found an ancient Bic that looked capable of writing, perhaps, one more word. The worn inscription on the barrel indicated that it was from an insurance agent in Iowa, and must have had an interesting journey.

"Okay, you still there?" asked Lewis, picking up the handset again. He heard an ominous thud, and then a crackling sound, but then Judy came back on.

"Yes — sorry — I dropped the phone when I was looking around for the number. I thought I had written it on the newspaper, but I actually wrote it on a pizza box, I found it in the kitchen."

Judy read the number, slowly, twice. Lewis didn't recognize the area code, but that happened all the time since they had started adding new ones. It could be anywhere.

"I'll call him, and find out what the hell this is all about. Thanks. And, I'll call you in a day or two."

After Judy cautioned him again about his drinking, and reminded him, once more, that he was not thirty-five years old, she said good bye, and he gently placed the handset in its cradle. He stood in the same spot for a bit, silent, thinking. A phone number… a ghost with a phone number? He didn't know how he could do the simple, innocuous thing of dialing the number. And, he knew for sure that he couldn't do it sober. Possibly not even drunk, but definitely not sober.

His fear of the phantom Doc had continued to grow as he had continued to ignore it, and he feared that, by now, it had grown out of any proportion that he could deal with. So, he decided, it was time to go get pleasantly hammered. He undid his belt and waistband button, let his horribly wrinkled and not so clean shorts drop to the floor, and stepped out of them. If he was going to drink, he certainly didn't need to be dressed. He picked up his cigarettes, lighter, and room key (so he could charge his bar tab to his room) and walked out of the bungalow, letting the wooden screen door slap shut behind him with the summer sound of his youth.

Day 13, (Night)

The phone had rung seven times before Lewis realized that there was no answering machine, and he would have to answer it himself, unscreened. He didn't like that at all: who knew what fucking disaster lurked on the other end of the line? On the other hand, it could be some form of salvation… it could be Marian, or whatever her real name was, calling to explain the mix-up, laughing sheepishly, saying she was sorry, telling him that she had explained everything to the cops, saying, finally, good-bye. So, without his brain making a conscious decision, his hand reached out and picked up the phone on what could have been its final ring.

"Hello?"

"Lew, Lew, Lew. It's Doc, man! I've been looking all over hell for you, you paranoid old motherfucker! Listen, I'm over on the Dutch side of the island, maybe twenty minutes away. It was the only place I could get a room, on such short notice. So, I'm over here with all the lame-ass Americans, at a place called the Coral Inn. Except it's not an inn, it's more like a Caribbean Motel 6. I've been here a couple of days, just kicking back, although, I was sure I saw you on Orient Beach the other day, but then I lost you in the crowd. Anyway, I have to see you. It's been a really long time. Actually, I thought you were dead, until about a year ago, when I came east. It's a really long story: too long for the phone, man. You should, for sure, come over here… we'll talk."

Lewis felt his brain start its panic drill, and the rest of his body began to respond. His heart first skipped a few times, and then kicked into high gear. He forgot to breathe, and then couldn't seem to get started breathing again. And he knew this was only the pre-show warm-up for a full-blown, ER-grade panic attack, if he couldn't shut it down right away. He began to force his heart rate down, and then, when perhaps twenty seconds had passed, he felt that he had better answer Doc.

"Look, I don't know if you're Doc, or not. I'm pretty certain Doc is dead. So, maybe I'm hallucinating all of this. Or, maybe I'm dead, too: I just don't fucking know. But, I do know that I'm not going anywhere right now. Things are too fucked up. A woman I was with has gone missing, somehow, just fucking vanished, and the cops have come to see me about it. So, I'm really fucked up, not to mention tired, not to mention old. I think somebody, maybe you, is trying to fuck me up, or maybe even kill me. So, no, whoever you are, I'm not going anywhere tonight."

"Lew, you don't sound so good, not good at all. Everybody is worried about you. I really do need to see you…I can answer all of your questions, I think, if you'll just come over here. Or, do you want me to come over there?"

"Give me your phone number — I'll call you tomorrow. I have to sleep — I'm just not feeling well." Lewis hoped, hoped like hell that Doc would agree, would stop insisting. Lewis was as frightened as he'd ever been in his life, although, if you asked him why, he couldn't have given a reasonable answer.

There ensued what seemed like at least one full minute of silence from the other end of the telephone line. Lewis was staring at himself in a very small, oval mirror with a wicker frame, mounted on the off-white sheetrock wall behind the little telephone table. He saw that his face, looking old, was a fiery red, and that tears were rolling down his cheeks, coursing more slowly through the days-growth of stubble that he must have forgotten to shave. He wondered why he was crying. He wondered how many decades it had been since the last time he had cried.

Finally, the voice on the telephone spoke, very deliberately, not at all conversationally. To Lewis, the change in tone and cadence, the slowing and enunciation, sounded a lot like a no-longer-patient teacher reciting, for the tenth time, a set of very simple directions to a not-so-bright student.

"No," said the teacher-voice, "no phone number. The room doesn't have a phone. I'm calling from the lobby. You should come over, and if it has to be tomorrow, then tomorrow is fine. Tomorrow is very soon. Not that it matters much, now." (Lewis thought: Now? It doesn't matter much NOW?) The voice/Doc went on, "I'm in the last room on the right. The place is laid out like a horseshoe, around a small pool. The rooms don't have numbers, they have names. I'm in *Sunset*. Come over tomorrow, or say no, and I'll come over there right now."

Lewis had to conclude the conversation, if only so he could stop crying, light a cigarette, have a drink, have a little something for his head. So, he did the easy thing.

"Okay, I'll come over tomorrow, around noon. The Coral Inn, Sunset Room, got it. I'm going to leave word here, at the desk, about where I'm going."

The conversational voice was back. "Finest kind! Can't wait to see you... I'll have a cold beer waiting for you. I'm afraid I can't drink with you — liver's shot to hell. Oh, and come alone, needless to say. Don't bring Marian."

The line went dead, and, after a few beats, Lewis hung up on his end. Marian? Don't bring Marian? Had *he* said anything about her, or used her name? Or, had the Doc-voice said it at all...Lewis knew that his brain had become, to put it mildly, "unreliable." So, the Marian thing may have been "manufactured" by his own staggering psyche. Or, maybe the entire conversation — but, no, the conversation was at least as real as the rest of his life. It actually made sense, in a bizarro fashion. He could almost have written the story himself. If he had written it, Doc *would* know about Marian, because Doc and Marian would both be part of the conspiracy against him. Or, Doc would know about Marian, because the cops had paid him a visit, also — the Doc Lewis remembered was the kind of guy the cops would always question: he simply looked guilty. But Lewis stopped himself before he conjectured a straightjacket for himself, too. There were, perhaps, a hundred variations on the plot of his story, so far, but he didn't think that it was a story. He didn't think it made sense, on any level, to believe that all of this was his creation — too many other people were involved. He'd need a cast of hundreds. So, he thought, the best and only thing to do right now, short of suicide was to make a list. To write down each and every thing that had happened to, for, or because of him and this "Doc" phantasm.

Lewis pulled his notebook — he always used a cheap "Composition" notebook to draft his essays and his stories — from his traveling bag, along with his favorite pen. He very carefully tore a sheet of paper out, and began to outline his saga, thus far:

WEIRD SHIT

1. Calls from Doc, who I think, no, thought, was dead!
2. Man reported by trustworthy friend to have been at general store at least twice, asking about me — man fits what I remember Doc to look like, adding a few years (like twenty or thirty)
3. Audi wires/hoses slashed at Judy's place
4. Someone at the Vermont place doing god knows what — runs me off road making getaway
5. I get picked up on beach by "Marian," followed by sex — why? Younger, pretty woman picks up older, not so pretty man, then goes out with him and fucks him — Kissinger effect?
6. Cops show up about Marian/Linda after she disappears in a strange way

7. Pill stash plundered, but thief leaves exactly 6 of each

8. Call now from "Doc," intimidating, "don't bring Marian," has level of information no one would have, unless…

When Lewis finished writing down number eight, he just sat, staring at the list, reading and re-reading, and understanding no better, except for one point that logic demanded he recognize: if this was a plot of some sort, no one was trying to kill him. It would have been relatively easy to kill him on a number of occasions, but that had not happened — and it was only once, really, that he had been in fear of his life: when the truck came barreling down his driveway, forcing him off the road. What had happened, what was happening, was that someone — or some ones were going to a hell of a lot of trouble to raise his anxiety almost — but not quite — to the snapping point. They could have taken all of his drugs, but that would have pushed him into the hospital or onto a plane right away, and then, Game Over! So — what was the point? There was, probably, an intricate and expensive plot against him, but, to what end?

Lewis was pretty well numbed out by events and drugs, and the numbed-out state was a very good thing, perhaps the only thing keeping him from running, shrieking and naked, from his cottage to careen wild-eyed and bawling down the beach, scaring naturally nervous naturists.

He knew that he could not stay where he was, physically or mentally, staring at the Weird Shit list, mulling it over, seeing it still make no fucking sense whatsoever. He needed to get out and walk, see some humans, maybe eat something. He couldn't remember when he had last eaten, or had even felt hungry, except for more pills. If he could just straighten out a bit, then perhaps, the Weird Shit list would make some sense, and he would know what his next move must be.

It was night time now, eight-thirty by his watch. The beach bars would be filling up, but he'd still be able to find a seat, get a beer and a really lousy cheeseburger accompanied by wilted iceberg lettuce and too many fries. His wrinkled and dirty shorts were still on, so he struggled into a clean polo shirt. It seemed oddly tight around the middle: he thought it had fit pretty well last summer. Maybe his gut was growing again. Or the shirt had shrunk. He discovered a few twenties in his pocket, so needed only to grab his cigarettes and lighter, and he was good to travel.

As he left, he thought that he should, really, be more careful. Halfway out the door, he ducked back in and found his key, then left, locking the door behind him. It wouldn't keep anyone out who was at all determined, but it made him feel a bit smarter. Better late than later, and so forth.

The path to the beach took him through the north side of the compound, and past the pool, which, still apparently open, reinforced that the night, by island standards, was yet young. He heard a piercing shriek, laughter, a splash, and more laughter — a man's laugh, this time. The low-wattage lights spaced too far apart by the edge of the path guided him, poorly, downhill, the downhill very relative here, measured in tiny increments from the horizontal. Just enough to throw his gait off, enough to catch the toe of his moccasin on something that was barely there. He felt his balance going as he was already falling forward, kicking himself in his right heel with his left foot, arms wind-milling, as he tried to grasp enough air to stop the plunge.

Lewis knew he was going down, knew that he couldn't possibly recover in time, even though time, for him, had slowed almost to a dead stop. Before the realization was complete, his pain center told him that his almost-sixty-year-old right arm had hit something unforgiving. The other two-hundred pounds of superannuated hipness kissed the sandy earth, and his instantaneous epiphany screamed that this was not going to be pretty.

When his forearm hit, he heard a cracking sound and a bellow of pain at the same instant. He sounded, to himself, more angry than hurt, although the bolt of pain that lit up his crocodile brain burst like ball-lightning. He bellowed again, and heard running flip-flop footsteps coming in his direction.

"Are you okay, mister?" An obese teenaged boy in dripping swim trunks stood over him, blessing Lewis' head with warm, slightly chlorinated water. "Should I call someone for help?" the boy inquired, already sounding less interested as he noticed a lack of blood or protruding bone splinters.

Lewis struggled into a sitting position slowly, his head spinning still with vertigo. He looked around cursorily for whatever it was that had tripped him, but spotted no obvious suspects. He gingerly felt along his right arm with his left hand, and found no obvious breakage, only extreme sensitivity and a growing lump. He could not touch the area with more force than a bare brushing with his fingertips, for fear that he would scream or worse, cry. He shakily got to his feet as soon as he could. The fat boy still stood a few feet away, wide-eyed, and spoke again.

"You really took a header. It almost looked like you tripped on something, but there isn't anything you could have tripped over. Can you walk okay?"

The boy — fourteen, maybe older, Lewis guessed — seemed not so much concerned, but, rather, happy to have someone to talk to, or at least to talk at. Lewis had not responded, yet, to the boy's comments, and feeling a small twinge that could have been empathy, spoke.

"Yeah, it sure felt like I tripped, but I guess I just tripped over my own feet. Now, actually, my arm hurts like hell. I don't think it's broken, though, so you don't need to get me any help."

As he had now done his part by responding, Lewis decided he might as well hike the rest of the way to the nearest bar and treat his throbbing arm to a drink. It was difficult to imagine that anything he did now would make him feel worse, and some alcohol might improve his foul and increasingly paranoid mood. Perhaps he should get drooling, passed out in the wrong place, terminally, stupidly hammered. He would not do so, but enjoyed believing he still had that kind of freedom. After years on much better drugs, alcohol had lost most of its charm for him. If he drank with any regularity, he found that it interfered with the relief he had found in other sedatives and in narcotics. But, still, for medicinal purposes, he'd have a few tonight.

He said good-bye, dismissed the Fat Boy with a wave of his hand, a "thanks anyway, but forget about it, I'm fine, and who the hell are you to interfere, anyway?" wave, and began to step along as smartly as he could while peering about for any more invisible objects in his path. The going was slow, even slower once he figured he was out of Fat Boy's sight. He had only made it a couple of dozen steps when he heard Fat Boy's lament, as his prey escaped.

"You be careful, mister. A guy your age could break a hip, end up in the hospital." That little motherfucker, thought Lewis. Not as nice as he pretended to be...must have that Fat-Boy rage in him, probably pulls the wings off flies.

It was another ten minutes before the five steps up to the nearest, loudest, and most interesting beachfront bar confronted him. This year, it was called "Conchita's": it had been something else, also Mexican sounding, last year. Kind of odd, really, as they were not very close to Mexico, and no one on the island, other than tourists and a few imported workers, spoke Spanish. The bar was in the No-Man's Land between the unofficial "Topless" part of the beach, and the unofficial "Bottomless, too" section. Technically, the whole beach was topless, bottomless, and everything — else-less, if one so desired, but there had been a truce of sorts, established to bring as many tourists as possible to the area, regardless of their level of prudery, or lack thereof, so the bar drew all sorts, and was more entertaining for it. Lewis, a Yankee and a prude, of sorts, in the deep dark well of his psyche, would never consider going there bare-ass in the evening.

As fate would have it, the odd couple who had witnessed his "attack" (or whatever it had been) in the restaurant were there, both of them well past drunk, and sitting, stunned, in the high chairs that ringed the bar. The man (the very hairy man) sat facing the bar, with his elbows on the bar to hold his arms, then hands, then head, up. If his elbows slipped, his head would certainly hit the bar with an interesting sound.

His blond companion (with a very large ass) perched with her back leaning against the bar, elbows on the bar, behind her, while ahead of her was the doorway, the ocean, and the passers-by, and now, Lewis, just clearing the final step. Her beach-towel skirt, was on the chair, but not on her. She sat, knees akimbo, seemingly airing out her vagina. Her open-legged position had spread her nether lips enough to show the next, pinker set. She smiled a drunken, not un-lewd smile at Lewis. He winked, as lewdly as he could.

Lewis had to walk almost entirely around the squared bar to find a vacant stool. Fearful of using his injured arm to hoist himself up, he attempted, and almost failed at, a maneuver that must have looked like a cross between levitation and a leap, gaining his seat more through luck than skill. The bartender, a thirty-something brunette who looked half-pretty in the low light, must have been impressed, as she glided right over and gave him a tip-me smile, but no words.

"A Cape Codder — vodka, cranberry juice, a splash of Rose's lime juice, if you have it. A twist of lime, if you don't," he smiled and said. She smiled back, and, wordlessly, moved away at island speed — a glide, a saunter that spoke to no urgency of purpose.

By the time, though, that Lewis had dredged up his cigarettes, his lighter, and a crumpled twenty from his grungy shorts, the barmaid was back with his drink. Lewis laid the twenty on the bar, but she made no move to pick it up. She could sense that her new customer was far too sober, and would drink through the money in short order. She, finally, spoke.

"Careful, there, Professor...I may have dumped too much booze in that. You don't want to end up like our new greeter, over by the stairs." She jerked her thumb in the general direction of the pudenda-flashing blonde.

The first drink was strong, but not as strong as Lewis had hoped for. He drank it off in just a few minutes, as much for thirst and nerves, as for pain relief. He managed, then, to hop down from his perch with less clumsiness than he had shown mounting it, and walked to the men's room to take a leak, and to, more importantly, examine his arm in the mirror: most of the damage felt as if it was on the side he couldn't easily see.

The mirror was small and none too clean, and the feeble light from what seemed to be a forty-watt bulb in the high ceiling was inadequate; still, Lewis could see enough to frighten him. Four or five inches up from his wrist, a lump about half the size of a large Idaho potato rose, and didn't slope fully back down until it almost reached his elbow. Merely looking at it was painful to him...and he began to smile. He was pretty sure that he had hit an ER jackpot, in a twisted sort of way. The (still growing) lump on his arm was going to qualify him for that thing he now wanted most — a large supply of drugs.

He'd have one, maybe two more drinks...not enough to in any way appear inebriated...then, he'd have the barmaid call him a taxi, proceed directly to the island's Urgent Care Center, and legitimately acquire some, hopefully sufficient, drugs. He had passed the Urgent Care Center dozens of times, and was certain that they operated The Center for the tourists, for the ex-pats (a growing population — French, Dutch, American, and others), and for government functionaries of the higher grades.

Lewis knew a score of people who had used the Center for the kind of urgent problem which could not wait for them to get back home for treatment: brutal sunburns, scorpion stings, broken arms, and the like. They reported that the Center was open around-the-clock, and that the young, efficient Docs spoke English, and accepted most insurance plans from the States. And, that they were remarkably free with the antibiotics, pain meds, blood-pressure pills, and so forth, that were so often needed. The islanders — the natives, and those, not native, who had lived and worked there so long that they had become indistinguishable from the natives — went to the Clinic at the island Infirmary. The waits were long, but the services were without charge, and the care was good. Tourists, though, would be charged, after waiting for hours with sick children, with minor trauma victims bleeding into basins. So, the tourists didn't go there, at least not intentionally.

Lewis was confident that the injury to his arm, still swelling, and now turning some lovely pastel purples and greens, would warrant an x-ray, probably an air-cast, and certainly 60 or 90 pain pills, oxycodone or hydrocodone, sufficient, if he was prudent, to get him through the four or five days until he could get back to his doctor in Boston.

He caught himself in mid-rejoicing that he had been hurt badly enough to require serious treatment, and had a capital-letter PANIC EPIPHANY — how addicted was he to these pills that he was gleefully measuring the degree of his injury by the quantity of narcotics it rated? How far was he, he questioned, from slamming his hand in a car door to get a few Percocet? Would he, back home, start doctor-shopping, perhaps start calling unknown dentists for emergency appointments, and, of course, palliatives for the terrible pain?

Hell, No, he argued, determinedly, back at himself, he wasn't an addict, not really — he just took what he needed for the pain. If the pain ever stopped — and his Doc didn't hold out much hope for that — then he could certainly taper himself off. But, right now sure wasn't the time. What with all the stress, the arthritis, the ruptured disks, and now, a badly fucked-up arm, he needed all the drugs he could get. And so, he dismissed the stupid panicked thought, and came back to the now.

He had been lost in the men's room for what seemed too long, so, quickly pissed, dampened his hands in the trickle of tap water the single faucet gave up, and dried them on his shorts. The trudge back to his seat revealed no curiosity about him from the other drinkers; there was no reason he should have expected any, other than a decent helping of paranoia. His fresh drink dripped condensation into the soaked napkin it sat upon, and sent tendrils of tumbler-sweat south, down the less than level bar. A man always ready to rescue a dangerously warming drink, Lewis hoisted the glass before he sat, and drank it half off, then leapt almost perfectly, but not gracefully, onto his stool.

The barmaid came back, with a fairly clean rag and a dry napkin to sop up the flood. She seemed to have undone a few buttons on the front of her black, sleeveless blouse, as Lewis was now able to glimpse a full-boob view, only hinted at, previously. The boob he could see was not so enticing, and he took her estimated age up a few years, and simultaneously calculated the percentage that the tip was expected to increase for this unrequested peep. After all, it was the thought, not the imperfect breast, that counted.

This seemed to be the perfect time to settle the bill, tip more than generously, and get the bar-wench to call him a cab. He did, she smiled, he asked politely, she called. And then, she said, "The taxi will be a few minutes. He'll come to the parking lot out in back. And, don't worry — they'll take good care of you at Urgent Care. I had to go there to get a coral-cut stitched up, and they were great."

Lewis knew that the cab would be on island time, and would take much longer than a few minutes, so, he lit another cigarette from the almost empty pack, sipped at the watery remains of his drink, and began to surreptitiously check out his bar-mates.

They were almost exclusively white, although many were so deeply tanned that "white" was an iffy descriptor: better to conclude that they seemed to be mostly European and American. The chatter was a mix of languages, with English and French most common, but with an occasional word in German — and Swedish or Norwegian-breaking through the polyglot hum and rant.

The six-lipped greeter by the stairs had, thank heaven, turned around to face the bar. Whether this was due to her becoming less drunk, or more, was difficult to determine. He eyes were mostly open, still, but as glassy as those of a cheap stuffed animal. Her husband, if that was what he was, had disappeared. Maybe, thought Lewis, he had just had enough, and was wandering, somewhere, looking for their hotel. It was not unlikely that he'd end up sleeping it off on the beach, hopefully above the tide-line.

The woman, though, she could be more of a problem for the bar. She wasn't doing anything, except staring straight ahead, and, presumably, breathing. And the puddle that had formed at the base of her chair seemed to indicate her continued ability to urinate, which was probably a good sign: at least she wasn't dead. The bartenders would very likely have to walk (or carry) her down the five stairs and sit her in the sand. As with her male companion, she might sober up and find her way home, or awaken with a hangover of exceptional nastiness when the sun, and the crazed naked joggers brought the beach to life, early the next day.

Lewis hadn't been paying attention, because it was the barmaid's third, and loudest announcement that got his attention.

"Mister, your taxi is here, right out back. You should go. Do you need a hand?"

"No," he answered, back to reality, "no, I'm fine. Thanks so much for all your assistance." He looked down at the change from the twenty: a five, two singles, and some coins. He left it, jumped down to the floor, and began a slow walk to the stairs, the parking lot, the taxi, the Doctor, the drugs. He rubbed the Greeter's head for luck as he passed.

1964/1965 – Family Visit, Making Plans

The Christmas visit to Chrissie's Mom's place went about as well as could be expected, or maybe even better, or so Lewis told those very few who later inquired; the siblings liked Lewis better than their mother did, par for the course. She would like Lewis a lot less if, and when, she noticed that her prescription cough syrup that she kept in the master bathroom medicine cabinet had gone from nearly full to almost empty in just a few days. If she ever noticed, though, Lewis wasn't the only suspect. Chrissie herself had been caught using drugs (just pot, but her mother did not differentiate between types of drugs) in high school, and would be almost as suspect as the well-mannered, but long-haired beau she had brought home as if he were some sort of trophy.

It might have been better, actually, for Chrissie's mother, and for everyone else, if she had discovered, and made an issue of the amazing disappearing Hycodan, had it prevented the near-stroke-material shock she inadvertently brought upon herself by walking into Chrissie's room without knocking late on Christmas Eve, there discovering her oldest, prettiest, smartest daughter cheerfully fellating a long-haired, bearded pervert, surrounded by the huge, fluffy stuffed animals of her not-that-long-ago little-girl-hood. Always polite, she had closed the door as quickly as she had opened it, but not before getting far too good a look at the action, and getting full eye contact and a sleepy grin from the dreadful young man.

Other than those potentially problematic instances, the visit went well, just long enough, and just short enough, to avoid really ugly happenings. Everyone was clever enough to avoid discussing politics, religion, personal grooming choices, morals (or the presumed lack thereof), and the dozens of other ugly things that tended to flog two generations of exceptionally stubborn Americans into a furious, sometimes violent, frenzy.

The day that Chrissie and Lewis planned to leave, the weather was starting a turn for the worse, with a Nor'easter fulminating off the coast of Jersey, threatening to slam into New York the following day, and from there, right up the coast. Their friend and pilot, Rocco, phoned Lewis just before taking off from the Island airport. The couple left for LaGuardia by cab ten minutes later, and arrived at the airport only a few minutes after Rocco did. They refueled and took right off, into a stiff east wind and pewter-colored skies. They couldn't get above the weather for most of the short trip, and had the kind bumpy and terrifying ride that can turn a hangover into a major mental illness, but with vomiting. As Rocco was still drunk, he fared better than Lewis and Chrissie. Lewis was too stubborn to throw up, so Chrissie did it for him. And, on him.

The approach to the Island was so dark and murky that they had to drop down and in on instruments only, not seeing the landing lights until they were almost on them. Lewis and the pilot were in a cold sweat when the wheels made their first bone-rattling, scrotum-tightening bounce on the strip. Chrissie had fallen into a foul-breathed sleep right after barfing, and woke to find the plane on the ground safely, with Rocco and Lewis standing outside, retching, shaking, and sharing a joint.

After the Christmas trip, Lewis and Chrissie didn't venture off-Island again for months, but consciously let their lives fall back into the comforting routine of work, sleep, sex, and just enough drugs and booze to knit it all together. Friends complained, friends said that the two of them were acting just like an old married couple, not going out to the bar, not leaving their little house at night. It was true, and perhaps not a bad thing at all. They had done their share of partying, they knew how to get staggering drunk every night, and could do it again, anytime they chose. They chose not to.

Winter turned to the Island's version of spring. The only noticeable difference was that it became, slowly, a few degrees warmer, and a lot rainier. The seasonal hotels and restaurants and stores began to gear up for the season, and some uneducated tourists began to arrive, perhaps thinking the weather would be like Bermuda, not Nova Scotia. They didn't even stay long enough to spend all their money.

Chrissie and Lewis began to suggest, hesitantly at first, that they should, perhaps, start to make plans to move to Boston at the end of the summer, and get back to the business of finishing school. The discussions occurred with increasing frequency, as it morphed from an aside to a topic, from a topic to the bud of a plan.

They spoke of the possibility (now a probability, possibly, probably) at the bar one night, and were jointly and separately horrified when Janey picked right up on the thread as if she had been an originator, including herself, thereby, in the plan. Janey took it so far so fast that she asked Terry if he wanted to go, too. Had Chrissie and Lewis not been as cool (and sedated from an earlier pipe of hashish) as they were, their jaws might have dropped.

Chrissie, for once the less stoned, jumped in with a kibosh that she hoped seemed more like a clarification. She said, as sweetly and nonchalantly as she could, "Oh, Janey — we'd love to have you with us, but we're going up there to go back to school. Lewis has to get back to his grad program or they'll drop him — all the time and money he's put into it will be gone! And I need to find a school that will accept my credits so I can get my bachelors. We're going to be pretty fucking boring for a couple of years. No partying. School, work, sleep maybe, more school, more work; it's gonna suck. We just want to get it done. No distractions. You wouldn't enjoy it."

As Chrissie's monologue progressed, Janey started to look angry, then angrier. Lewis could almost hear her brain bubbling and grinding away as it manufactured a response that wouldn't sound as pissed-off and uncool as it was certainly going to be. She could be having trouble finding the right words for a few seconds, but she must have snapped back on course, as she had a working version within ten or twelve seconds of Chrissie's conclusion. She smiled an unfriendly smile, and lurched into speech.

"Oh, hey, I'm cool with that — I'm hip — I'm kind of looking for the same thing. I've wanted to pick up a few courses on the side so I can get some college to admit me without my diploma. You know, I was way too far into acid to bother with my senior year (or my junior year either, she didn't say) in high school. But I always got good grades; I'm not as stupid as you seem to think. I want something besides getting fucked up all the time, and waitressing, and sleeping with losers — sorry, Terry, I didn't mean you — and, if there were three or four of us, it would be cheaper…so, that's why I thought it might be good to go with you."

As her defensive-sounding interjection unfolded, Terry stared at her with a mixture of disbelief, disapproval, and increasing disinterest. Chrissie listened with poorly-feigned interest, while Lewis had fired up a fresh cigarette, and appeared to be acting as if none of the verbal drama was happening. He watched the television on the wall at the far end of the forty-foot bar, which he, pretty obviously, could not see well, even if the reception had afforded a clear picture — which it did not.

As the set was tuned to a rerun of one of the more boring episodes of "Flipper," the favorite show of some wet-brain customers at the bar — who spoke the dialogue of all of the characters, including the dolphin, a split-second before their mouths (or beaks) moved, lending a sense of English-and- dolphin badly dubbed into English-and-dolphin unreality to the performance, it was pretty clear to all that Lewis simply had no intention of dealing with, or even acknowledging the reality of, any interaction occurring between Chrissie and Janey.

Counting Janey as more-or-less of a friend, Chrissie decided that she needed to respond somehow with a statement that drew a bright line that left no question of her intentions, or of the order of importance of the people and things currently in her life. Lewis amped-up his non-acknowledgement a level, knowing Chrissie well enough to predict that her decision in this would be horribly incorrect.

"Janey, nobody thinks that you're stupid. I think it's great that you want to go back to school. But, if Lewis and I go to Boston, it's something just the two of us are doing. We're not looking for any roommates. If he can get his T.A. gig back, we can live in grad student housing for almost nothing. I can live there because we'll say we're married. They allow other people to visit, but not to live there."

Terry, always impressed with a good scheme, smiled at the beauty of the plan.

"That's fan-fucking-tastic guys — what a cool idea! I can see why you wouldn't want to fuck it up by having Janey there. And if I move back to Boston, and take Janey, I have plenty of places I can stay. I'm tight with the people at the commune up on Mission Hill — the one on Fort Hill, too, although they're a little too fucking lame for me. And we can always get together when you guys take some time off from playing student. Right, Janey?"

It had to be evident to anyone unlucky enough to be within 50 feet of Janey that she was furious, and getting more so. The vibes emanating from her small frame were unmistakably angry, nasty, and verging on violence. But, she said only, "Sure, Terry, that sounds cool. I must have misunderstood. I thought that this ignorant, one-way cunt was my friend." Then, she pushed her big wicker chair back with her legs as she stood up, drained her half-glass of beer, picked up her pack of cigarettes, and walked, stiffly, out of the bar, and into the thinning crowds on an almost-dark Main Street.

Terry widened his normally sleepy eyes, and laughed. "Well, sorry about that. That chick has a pretty good temper on her — she'll get over it. I'll go talk to her, after I get drunk enough to deal. Her problem — well, one of them — is deciding what she wants to do. When she does decide what she wants to do, then she goes ahead and makes plans that include other people, but she never lets the other people know, she just kind of expects them to know, and to do what she wants, so she can get what she wants, when she wants it. Then she gets all pissy when they disagree."

Chrissie and Lewis exchanged a look, and stood up at the same moment. Lewis, having just switched from draft beer to ale, brought the bottle to his mouth and tipped it up, opened his throat, and poured the remaining 9 or

10 ounces into his system. Within several seconds, he opened his mouth and coaxed an impressive belch out into the atmosphere.

Chrissie said in a kindly voice, "You fucking pig!" she turned to Terry.

"Thanks for your explanation, but I don't really give a rat's ass. You'd better talk to her. You tell her I expect an apology, so I don't have to tear her face off. Now, we gotta go. Lewis needs to work tomorrow, preferably without a hangover."

Lewis smiled at Terry, and slapped him on the shoulder as he, and his very pissed-off girlfriend, left the table. They walked out to Main Street, where Chrissie's car was parked, nosed in, diagonally, to the curb. The Jeep and the pickup truck that had bracketed her sedan hours earlier were gone, as were most of the other vehicles on the broad, cobbled street. She got in on the driver's side, before Lewis could make a play for that spot. He would want to drive, but she had seen him have 8 or 9 beers, 2 shots of Hudson's Bay rum, and a bottle of ale, all in 3 hours — and knew he wouldn't pass any kind of sobriety test, if they were stopped anytime on their ride to the far end of the Island.

There weren't many cops on the Island in the off-season, but the few that might be working had a high level of suspicion of anyone they thought might have spent time at The Bucket, especially is they happened to be of the long-haired Hippie persuasion. They kept an eye out for those types, and made quite a few "random" stops. They had stopped Lewis a couple of times already, but he had been reasonably sober both times, which had made the officers less than pleased. They would, therefore, continue to pull him over when it was convenient for them: they knew it was only a matter of time until they caught him drunk, or with a roach in the ashtray, or with a burned-out tail-light. They truly believed — probably correctly — that only dedicated harassment would keep the Freak population of the Island under control.

Lewis knew all this, drunk or sober, and reckoned that tonight, he was drunk enough to make the cops happy. He, resignedly, swung himself in through the passenger-side window (the door hadn't worked in months), and promptly pulled his brass hash-pipe out of his pocket, loaded it, and held it out to Chrissie, holding his lighter over the tiny bowl while she took a big toke, and gave him her sexiest smile as she exhaled a fragrant blue cloud back at him.

As they tooled down the two-lane road that would carry them directly to their cottage, Lewis thought about the increasing number of nights now when he woke up in a cold sweat. He'd be the first (well, perhaps the second) to recognize that his alcohol and drug consumption had soared on the Island, that everyone he knew drank or drugged even more than he, that alcoholism seemed to be the norm here. It worried him more than a bit, but worse yet, it made him dream. He would awaken, drenched and shaken, the sheets sopping wet. He'd get up, and so as not to disturb Chrissie, he'd lay a big beach towel over the cold wet sheets, and crawl back into bed. For a few minutes, he could remember parts of the dream — always pretty much the same one. The dream featured a life played out in some bleak upscale suburb, and starred Lewis, and Chrissie, and an inconstant number of children. And, an asphyxiating fucking job for Lewis, usually a life sentence teaching at a no-name state college. And then, just before he killed himself, (usually with a rope), he'd awaken, in the frozen pool of sweat.

When he awakened from these dreams, he would sometimes be too freaked out to go back to sleep right away. He'd go sit in the dark living room, smoke a few cigarettes, and drink a beer. If it was close to the time he needed to start thinking about going to work, Lewis would switch from beer to coffee, and perhaps some breakfast, and then, off to work. The beer(s) would wear off by seven or eight o'clock, and he'd feel shaky for the rest of the day — or at least until lunchtime, when, generally, most of the crew would go to the bar for lunch, lunch being 2 or 3 beers, a pickled egg, and a pickled sausage. He, and a few of the other heavy drinkers, would not feel much like going back to work, but generally did. The days after he had the Dream were ruined days, to him. He began to fear the Dream, and the more he feared dreaming, the more he'd dream.

Chrissie could often tell when he had experienced a bad night, as he'd already be at the bar, drinking heroically, when she arrived to meet him there at four o'clock. Lewis rode in to work each morning with another Freak who lived nearby — a single guy, 22 years old, and a full-blown alky already. His ride wouldn't leave the bar until Last Call, so Chrissie would meet him, and get him out of there by 5 or 6, and drive him home for supper. She'd ask him about the dreams, and ask him if she could help. But, of course, he couldn't talk to her about it — she'd misinterpret the problem horribly, and feel hurt. Things would get worse, not better. So, he'd tell her he was fine, maybe they'd just been on the Island too long.

More and more often, he, and then Chrissie, too, started to believe that the Island was the source of any problems between them. They took steps to lock themselves into leaving in August, going back to school, the whole deal. Lewis flew up in mid-August to straighten things out with the school, giving them a large check to seal the deal. He confirmed his TA status, and notified the school of his married condition, securing one of the last married grad-student apartments.

He submitted an application for a student loan, knowing that if Chrissie and he couldn't find exceptionally good part-time jobs, he'd need some help to pay for the last two semesters. He didn't want to have to deal pot again, not after that last horrendous deal. While Lewis accomplished all of these tasks, he maintained a state of almost-unbearable paranoia. He avoided all of his old haunts, including entire sections of Boston, and all of Cambridge. He even shelled out a hundred dollars for a decent hotel room downtown, registering under another name. No one who knew him would ever think to look for him in such a lame setting.

The die was truly cast. In a few weeks, he and Chrissie would pack her car with all of their possessions, filling only the trunk, and half of the back seat. Their dump-found kitchen table and two chairs would be lashed to the roof with half-inch line, enough, they hoped, to keep it from ending up in the front seat of the car driving behind them.

Lewis's fear level increased daily. Soon, he could not tolerate it without drinking around the clock. Anxious to avoid a monumental bender and all the nasty fallout that those things tended to bring, he purchased 50 Librium from an older, end-stage alky he knew from the bar. The VA sent the alky 90 capsules by mail each month so that he wouldn't drink: he sold them promptly, so that he could.

They said very few good-byes. They told each person who knew that they were leaving a slightly different story, especially concerning their destination. Lewis's boss was very pissed-off, and fired Lewis before he could resign. Then he called Lewis at the bar the night before the day of departure, and told him that if "things didn't work out," Lewis could come back and work for him anytime. The Island was full of people who had left, had not had things work out, and had returned so quickly that their bar-stool hadn't even cooled off.

Chrissie didn't speak to Janey again, after that night in the bar. Lewis did speak to Terry, and got the names and numbers of a couple of high-end dealers that he hoped he wouldn't need, but might.

And they said good-bye to the Island at 7 o'clock in the morning on August 21, 1965, a morning so foggy that by the time the ferry has rounded the point, the Island had disappeared.

Day 7 –Vacation/Hiding Out Mode

Lewis was so fucking hung-over that his hair — each individual hair, and all of his hair together — hurt. He had awakened at least four times since the first morning light, the Blessed Caribbean but-not-quite-right-for-a-Yankee light, had begun to infiltrate his cottage. The first three awakenings had come, and gone, without any progress to speak of, except, twice, for the nine shaky steps to the sink that had made him feel a bit faint, but were necessary to both take on, and drain off, water.

The second of the three awakenings had, indeed, moved him as far as the sink. He knew he should not, ever, drink the tap water, and knew why. But he had no bottled water. He ran the "cold" water until it was less than warm, and drank down three cups slowly as he concomitantly pissed into the sink. He enjoyed the conceit that he was keeping the water in motion, and flushing the poisons from his beleaguered old corpus.

The third awakening, at least two hours later, full light now, and almost warm enough to sweat, brought him to a warm bottle of beer that sat waiting for him on the bathroom floor. He didn't know where he had gotten it, and did not know why it was on the bathroom floor. He took the beer back to bed, where he pried the cap off with his belt buckle. A few expeditionary sips, while still reclining, and then without moving more than necessary, grabbed his shaving kit and accessed his stash of pills. He shook out and chewed up a few painkillers (an action that he wished they were actually capable of), a few tranquilizers, a few aspirin, and washed it down with the beer. The beer tasted pretty good, for warm beer. At least it didn't have a cigarette butt floating in it. In his younger years — and now, all of his years were his younger years — he had cheerfully imbibed more than one post-party wake-up beer with a cigarette butt or two suspended in the murky liquid. It seemed like an economical way to get his nicotine and his alcohol together, first thing on a hangover morning.

As soon as the alcohol, then the benzodiazepines, then the narcotics broke through to his brain, he felt so much better that he fell into a restful and soft sleep for more than an hour. When he awakened, for the fourth time, from his rest, he was able to get out of bed shake-free. He made some coffee, drinking two cups, a cigarette with each. He barely gagged. Awake and stable, Lewis took a long shower, shaved his stubble off, and pulled a pair of shorts and a tee shirt on to combat the chill he felt, strangely, in the seventy-five degree air.

The nicotine that Lewis had taken in — nicotine being a gift from the gods, and from the Indians, of course, who had given it to the White Man before they realized that they had, quite unexpectedly, met Pure Evil, allowed his brain to begin to function acceptably. Once he had determined that he could remember absolutely nothing since a few minutes after he had checked in the previous day, he had to wonder just how much he had drunk the night before. He rarely drank more than one or two drinks at a sitting, these days. He knew, from his drinking history, that he was probably an alcoholic. On those now-rare occasions when he drank enough to cause a blackout, he felt scared, felt out of control. The questions that came after "How much did I drink?" were the truly bad ones: "where did I drink, who did I drink with, and what did I do?"

A search through the pockets of his wet shorts yielded a few soggy, crumpled twenties. He was sure he had gone out with almost two hundred dollars in his pocket, and the pocket had been in a pair of khakis, not the shorts. He must have come back to the cottage at some point, and left again after changing clothes. And he must have been drinking with other folks, or at least buying drinks for others, to have gone through that much cash. Or, perhaps he had been rolled. It didn't matter so much which. What mattered was that he had no ideas at all about the where, the what, the who, of the missing chunk of his life.

Lewis determined that, of the choices he had at this point in time, the best choice was to forget that anything had happened. If things had gone really badly awry, he would be dead, or injured, or in the hospital, or in jail. So, fuck it. He needed to go to the beach and let the sun bake the poisons out of him.

Still not without the other-worldly tremulousness that followed a bad drunk, the gathering up of his beach supplies and accoutrements — towel, cigarettes and lighter, notebook and pens, sunscreen, money and pills — took what seemed like a very long time. He had to go back and forth, checking what he had, due to a serious spell of forgetfulness. When everything was accounted for, and stashed in his beach bag, Lewis took a final trip to the bathroom for a piss. He looked in the mirror above the sink, and quickly looked away from the haunted old man that he saw.

He was running late, the sun was high, and the beach chairs, if not all taken yet, soon would be. He inventoried the contents of his bag one last, obsessive time, and trod, a naked shaky man, out of his door, and down the little path to his cottage, and then onto the broader path that would carry him to the beach.

As he walked along, he could hear snatches of conversation from some of the other cottages. Maybe they, too, were running late. Or maybe they had opted out of the ritualistic broiling for a day, and were putting on their tourist costumes to go shopping with the mobs of cruise-ship losers across the island. The giant ships disgorged their captives on the Dutch side, where the shops, restaurants and casinos were. There was even a McDonald's, for those in need of a desperate fix of Pennsylvania or Indiana or whatever middle-America hellhole they hailed from.

No other guests passed Lewis on the path. He only saw a few black islanders, the housekeepers and maintenance guys, some looking heavily dressed, wearing slightly more than all the clothes that they could survive the heat in, wearing unneeded layers of clothing to, somehow, balance out the sinful nakedness of the guests, the crazy Americans, crazier Germans and Swedes, and craziest of all, the French. The disapproval that the islanders felt toward the tourists was never verbalized in public, but only the truly obtuse could fail to notice it.

The walk to the beach, and to the section of beach Lewis favored, could seem as if it took no time at all, some days. Today was not one of those days. It seemed more of a trek than a stroll, and he was sweating freely by the time he got there. The chair-and-umbrella guy spotted Lewis coming. Remembering his preference, he had already placed the beach chair in exactly the right spot, and was driving the point of the umbrella pole into the sand with a finesse that came from a thousand repetitions. He'd expect, and get, a fiver for his efforts. He made very good money. He had been a chair and umbrella guy at the Club for almost a year, after coming for a month-long escape from the icy winter rains of France.

He wore few clothes, had no expenses, and had many friends among the other young staff at the Club. He got laid far more than he deserved, and often collected two-hundred dollars American in the four hours he chose to work each day. Lewis would probably have tipped him less generously had he known how delighted the chair-guy was with his life, or might even have resented the young man his good fortune.

But, Lewis didn't know, never even gave it a thought, and was grateful to have the lounge-chair and umbrella placed well, so all parties prospered, in their own ways. After carefully arranging his towel on the lounge-chair, he less carefully arranged himself on the towel. Adjusting his dark glasses on his sunburned nose, Lewis began his usual observation of the local fauna; a type of relaxation exercise preparatory to the nap that he sensed was creeping up on him.

His vantage point was twenty-five or thirty feet back from the warm and gentle surf, far enough so that the sand that was picked up occasionally from a brisk on-shore wind couldn't reach him. Newcomers, he had observed, invariably picked a spot close to the water. Not long thereafter, they would move back five or six yards, picking sand from their tongues, their ears, their other parts.

The Club restaurant and bar was about twice as far back from the water as Lewis' redoubt was, and, for him, less than a minute's walk. His chair, when placed as he liked, afforded him a panorama of sunbathers, swimmers, and the ever-present obsessive beach-walkers. Today, at least, his view was populated with "normals" — those with a cross-section of fairly normal body types. No four-hundred-pounders, no anorexics, no grotesques. This was as good as it could get.

Lewis was soon hypnotized by the sea, the sun, the scores of nude humans enjoying themselves and each other, and felt that his eyes were starting to close. As he was considering fighting the nap, he fell fast asleep. When he awakened, he was cold and shivering, fully clothed, on a dirty wood floor that reeked of cat shit, urine, stale beer, and the lingering scent of sandalwood incense.

From floor level, his eyes open just to slits; he could see two sets of cheap, black brogans, white cotton socks, and the stiff new denim that could only be the bottom ends of two brand-new pair of dungarees. Sensing bad and current danger, he closed his slitted eyes, and listened intently with the ear that was not pressed against the floor.

"….come the money isn't all here, motherfucker? You trying to fuck us over, too? I…"

(A different voice) "Shut up, Mikey, shut the fuck up! You almost fucking killed him; you hit him too fucking hard!" (and the first voice, again), "shit, just grab him, let's go, let's get the fuck out of here…take him with us. We'll get the real story!"

And then, a familiar voice. The accent, he recognized the accent (but there seemed to be a pounding his head, making it hard to hear clearly: "…told him there'd be more — how much we…" and then, the drumbeat was way too loud, it took over, it took him over. He passed out, the smell of blood, now, and cordite, along with the cat shit and the cold wood under his loudly pounding head.

His body soaked in hot sweat, his eyes opened behind dark glasses. He was awake, he was on the beach, and he could see an exceptionally tall man with an exceptionally long, thin penis walking slowly by him. He felt more than disoriented — he was in a time-slip, a place — slip, a shift in his reality that was far from his understanding. He thought, for just an instant, that he might be dead. He reminded himself to breathe.

What the hell was that all about, he wondered, when his usual Now returned enough for him to question the other Now that he had fallen into? He posited that the dream was most likely a memory, or a fragment of a memory, and he could place it — it was surely a re-run of that rip-off in Cambridge, lifetimes ago. That smell at floor-level was the smell of the apartment where the madness had taken place. But he had not remembered any voices at the time, so, why would he now?

What were the two guys talking about? They — the way he had seen them in his dream — they had to have been "under-cover" cops. No one else wore heavy, spit-shined black shoes with white socks. No one else wore jeans so new that they were stiff with sizing. Except people who want to look like under-cover cops.

He gave himself a good few minutes thought, about the length of time that it took for the sweat to dry on his body. He could see the beach waitress with the perfect tits coming toward him. Today, she wore a thong bikini bottom, no top. She had such a perfect body that looking at her was like staring into the sun.

"Can I get you something?" she asked, bending very slightly toward him. Her boobs moved with her, no independent jiggle there. They were very firm indeed. She smiled at him so nicely that Lewis felt compelled to order a beer. She knew that a fat tip was already hers, as she turned away to point her unnervingly excellent breasts at the beach bar. Her equally perfect ass demanded that he follow its exit with his eyes until she was so far away that he could no longer see, and consider, how the thin cord of the thong back disappeared into her butt, certainly snug against some other piece of perfection. The Lord works in mysterious ways, he thought, and so, too, do women. Then, his brain snapped back to the horrific dream recall that he had awakened from just moments ago.

As frightened as he was of the whole scene, the unreal sense of being — *being* — in that place again, in Doc's old shotgun flat in East Cambridge, thirty years before the Yuppies decided that East Cambridge was cool, as scared as he was, he felt strongly that he had to do it once more. The previous trips back through space and time had been thrust upon him — was there a way to make it happen? If he could feel the dirty wooden floor against his cheek, maybe he would hear a few more words, enough to clear some questions from his mind about what had really happened, perhaps enough to find out why Doc was reaching out to him, chasing him through his settled life all these years later.

Lewis closed his eyes, began to breathe in through his nose, out through his mouth, the way he had learned to do it years ago, when he thought meditation might give him some answers. He could feel himself relaxing into a calm place within a few minutes. He thought about the rabbit hole he saw, in his mind's eye, as the path back to that night. The sun, reflecting up from the sand, beat against his red eyelids in syncope, then began to be felt, then heard, the faint background thrumming of the war-drum of throbbing pain where the ungiving steel of a shotgun barrel had creased the side of his skull back when he was only a dumb hippie, too smart for his own good.

The mix of dirt, patchouli oil, rank bong-water, catpiss, and blood smoked coldly into his brain. He heard a thump that could be someone's head bouncing off a worn threshold if that someone were being dragged by their feet, dragged along a dirty wooden floor of a dirty shit-hole apartment, dragged and carried and dropped in to the trunk of a waiting car.

The one good eye that Lewis, decades and distance removed, could force partway open (the dried blood on his eyelid didn't help) saw nothing that he didn't already recollect. The cheap hollow-core front door, shattered at the deadbolt and the top hinge was swung three-quarters open. Very cold, very damp air rushed in through the gap. He could see no people, no bodies, and no blood. His one good eye twitched closed, and everything went, instantly, away. Even the hollow bass beat in his skull vanished. Warmth flooded his current incarnation, on a beach chair, on a beach, at his appointed place in the sun.

"Sir...?" a query with a sexy female flavor — Jittering Jesus — she had somehow gotten her voice to sound as naked as the rest of her — Lewis really had to be here, now.

"Yeah — yup — yes, great, my beer..."

Sounding awake, he thought: I was only resting my eyes. Good God, she had to have the absolute best tits in creation. She was smiling at him with what seemed like too many very white teeth. "Here...." the waitress handed him his beer, and a paper napkin. He passed back a five and two ones, far too large a tip, as expected, and probably the same sized tip that every other straight male, and not a few lesbians, would give her that day. The beach waitress would be able to go back to grad school without a single student loan. Everyone got what they wanted.

But not everyone got everything they wanted all of the time. Here, on the beach, in the sun, with a cold beer warming quickly in his hand, Lewis should be a very, very happy man. Except that he, he who lived an exemplary, boring, and ultimately trite life, was having odd things happen. Anxiety-provoking things, things that second (or third?) rate academics and writers should not be expected to countenance.

He had paid the price, in full, demanded to buy a life of predictable safety. When, way back at a major fork in the road, he had walked away from a woman whom he loved like no other, before or since, and walked away, too, from other people and places, he had chosen the better lit, better paved road. And now, someone was shooting out the streetlights.

Lewis poured the last two inches of beer down his throat before it became too warm to drink. He guessed that he'd just have to hang on until these disturbances to his equilibrium passed, as he had no doubt they would. Just ignore the phantom complications, until they dissolved in the toxically boring atmosphere that was his life.

Except that he was either hopeful, or fearful, that he was verging on the memory of something that he had forced himself to forget. He could feel the presence of a nagging, elusive flash of something vile, something about that long-ago pot deal rip-off. Something to do with him. Something to do with Doc.

If he were back in the States, he could find one, maybe two of the guys from the old pot cabal. One lived down on the Cape, where he had made a good life for himself. He had married a Portagee girl, and become a fisherman, instead of finishing college. He owned three boats now, and half the revenue of each trip was his. Tim, that was his name. Irish kid from the North Shore, from Beverly. Tim would talk to him, might even be willing to sit down over beers with Lewis, and process the whole ugly event. It had been so fucking long ago that the statute of limitations must be exceeded, so there was no real reason why Tim wouldn't discuss it, even if it was pretty bad.

Unless, of course, Tim had been the one who had set them all up. Somehow, Tim had come into enough money in a short period of time to quit school, get married to a very nice but very poor girl, and buy a controlling share in his first boat.

There was another guy, although not so close, probably. One who would take some digging to find. Robert — Bob — had been a full-blown alky by the time he was a junior, and never stopped drinking, even as his old drinking buddies were dropping dead from various diseases. He had, so far, outlived two wives, and a number of girlfriends, and the last Lewis had heard, was living in Taos with a new wife of less than half his age. And, it was said, drinking more than ever. He could be tracked down with good luck and enough phone calls, but, would it be worth it? The man had been drunk since 1963, and must have some degree of squash-rot by now. Lewis would have to go to Taos to talk to him, and the sight of all those superannuated hippies would depress him beyond words.

But the arguments for, and against, talking with Tim, or Bob, or anyone else were meaningless, for now. Lewis was on his favorite Caribbean island, and should be focusing on relaxation, tanning, eating well, and drinking just enough — but no more — than needed to keep him in vacation mode.

What he remembered — or, more accurately, what he had been moved to remember by dreams, or trance-states, or dyspepsia — told him that it was at least possible that the deal and rip-off had not gone at all as he remembered. There had perhaps been some skullduggery to blame for the loss of the pot, the loss of some money, and maybe the loss of someone's life — but not Doc's life. Doc — or some Doc impersonator — could have real reasons to be looking for Lewis. And he, Lewis, might not be without some blame, somehow, in the whole fiasco.

So. Tiring shit, this thinking, he mused, as he set free an unnecessarily loud beer-belch. He closed his eyes, and drifted into drowse.

Day 13, Day 14 – Medically Necessary

The taxi ride to the Urgent Care Center was fast and scary. The island had no mountains of the Vermont genre, just very steep hills — but the roads were definitely mountain roads. Steep, with sharp turns, and two lanes compressed into one-and-a-half lanes of width. The roads didn't get any wider in the daylight, but everyone drove faster, probably in an effort to get where they were going before they were flattened against a sheer wall by a truck, or knocked over the drop on the other side of the road by a van loaded with tourists. It was a contest of will and bravery, and the passengers had to participate once the ride had begun.

Fortunately for him, Lewis had enough alcohol and other drugs on board that the terrifying ride appeared to him as an exceptionally good 3D movie. He became lost in the defensive construct he had created that he really had to focus on a new reality when the taxi pulled up in front of the Center. He peeled a soggy twenty and a drier ten from the roll in his pocket to pay his fare and tip, and got the driver's business card, so he could call for a pick-up when he was through at the clinic. It was never safe to assume that any taxi he called would show up, so more options were better.

Once Lewis passed through the automatic glass doors into the clean, brightly-lighted lobby, he felt dirty, and under-dressed. The place was one hell of a lot quieter, cleaner, and better-smelling than the Emergency Room at the huge, world-famous hospital just down the street from his Beacon Hill place — he had been there a couple of years back for either chest-pain or rampaging paranoia, depending on one's P.O.V.

He walked, hesitantly, to a counter at the other end of the room, passing what looked like comfortable furnishings: good-quality padded plastic chairs, solid-looking wooden coffee tables, and the requisite piles of tattered, ancient magazines in a number of languages. There was no sign or notice posted at the counter that indicated purpose, but it seemed evident that it served as a registration/triage desk. Maybe it was an I.Q. test: if you couldn't figure out what the counter was for, you were too stupid to treat. Peering about, Lewis saw no one — then a white door in a white wall behind the counter opened, and an extremely Black — bluish, anthracite-black — nurse, or aide emerged, with a broad smile just for him.

"Forgive me, please — I was having my tea. As you can see, things are a bit slow at the moment. I was just putting my cup away when I looked up at the monitor and saw you come in, looking lost."

"That's okay," Lewis said, smiling as well, and thinking himself a bit dense for having missed the TV camera mounted high on the back wall. "I'm just glad that someone is here — I seem to have hurt my arm, probably badly, when I slipped and fell a few hours ago. It seems to still be swelling up, so I figured I should see a doctor." He held his damaged arm up in front of him during his soliloquy, but the nurse didn't seem particularly interested.

"May I have your name, Sir?" she inquired.

"Melton. Lewis Melton."

"Mr. Melton, I'll need you to complete some forms while you're waiting to see the doctor…unless, or course, you think you will pass out, or bleed to death, or die, in which case he can see you right away."

Lewis took the several-page form from the nurse's hand, assuring her that he didn't expect to drop dead right away, although, one never really knows, does one? He took the sheaf of paper and the proffered pen to a chair, sat, and started scrawling as neatly as he could, which was not very. His very best penmanship had been denigrated by his ex, Judy, during their marriage. More than once, she had compared his efforts to those expected from a profoundly retarded chimpanzee with a seizure disorder. He breezed — illegibly — through the usual demographics. When he came to the health history, and the ever-present list of current medications, he was undecided as to how forthright he should be. He knew that, considering all of his problems, his list of meds was reasonable, but the amounts he took might cause some doctors to see him as over-medicated, or even a manipulative drug-seeker. This, objectively, was true — he was manipulative, and did seek drugs. On the other hand, he sought drugs because he legitimately needed them. So, just to be on the safe side, he halved the amount of benzodiazepines that he took, and added twenty percent to the pain-killers.

In describing "the nature of the health problem that brought you here today," he was more than honest, perhaps even embellishing the violence of his fall, and included a murky reference to the effect that some of his medications had gone missing, or maybe hadn't been brought along, so he had cut his dosages in half, and was distracted by the pain that he was feeling when he tripped and fell-leaving the door open, of course, to another interpretation. Not that it would matter: he knew that doctors rarely, if ever, read every word, or even any word, written by the patient. It seemed to interfere with their omnipotence level.

Finally, he came to the section that would be read, headed "How Do You Plan to Pay for Your Visit Today?" He listed his health insurance data, and wrote, in the appropriate place, that he would pay for today's visit with a major credit card. He passed the completed packet across the counter to the nurse, who glanced briefly at the forms, snapped them on to a clipboard, and asked him to follow her into the examination room.

"I'd ask you to put a johnny on, but the problem seems to be just your arm, so I fear you won't have that pleasure today. I just need to get your weight and your blood pressure, and then I'll go see if I can scare up the doctor. It's Doctor Nolan today — you'll like him. Everyone likes him, even me."

As Lewis cooperated by climbing on the scale, climbing off, and letting her get his blood pressure, he tried to place her accent. It wasn't the Black islander accent, wasn't French, wasn't Spanish, and wasn't Dutch. It sounded very much like middle-American English, but some words were almost unintelligible. He had to ask.

"Excuse me, Nurse, but I have to ask: I don't recognize your accent, which is very slight. Where are you from?" He was watching her face, carefully, as he posed his question, so that he could quickly back-pedal if he had offended her. He saw her begin to break into a broad smile.

"I'm from the States. I was born in Calais, Maine, lived there till I was about six or seven. Then my family moved to Jersey — just outside Bayonne. So, I ended up with a Down East, Jersey accent, and no one — absolutely no one — has been able to figure it out. I've been down here for a couple of years, so, I'm starting to pick up some of that accent, too. Sounds weird, eye?" She chuckled as she explained, and Lewis had to join her. She was right — no one would ever be able to figure out that accent.

When the nurse left him alone to go and find the doctor who everyone liked, Lewis hoisted himself up to sit on the exam table — there were no other options, except for a very narrow Formica-topped counter that ran around the perimeter of the room, and was cluttered with supplies and trays of forms. He was about to jump back down to grab a dog-eared copy of *Match* to keep himself amused when the door opened, and a sun-burned, perhaps hung-over, and generally raffish looking younger blond man walked in. He seemed a bit apprehensive or anxious, and had the clip-board with Lewis' paperwork clutched in one sweaty hand. He looked up at Lewis, sitting on the exam table, poised to jump, and forced a pleasant smile. Then, he spoke.

"Well, well, Mr. Melton! What seems to be going on with you today? Busted-up arm, I gather?"

Lewis guessed that the Doc hadn't had time — or hadn't taken the time — to look at any of the paperwork except for the name, and knew all that he knew from speaking with the nurse for twenty seconds. That was a plus — now, Lewis could explain, in colorful detail, what had happened, and make a pitch for some decent meds, although he was sure that an x-ray would intrude on the play and slow things down.

The Doc — looking both younger, and more hung-over as he drew closer, gently and carefully examined the now very badly swollen forearm. He then looked closely at Lewis' eyes, ears, nose and throat, and took his temp with what seemed to be an electronic thermometer of some sort — Lewis had not seen anything like it before this. The Doc spent a minute or two searching the capacious pockets of his hip-long white coat for something, and then discovered that something — his stethoscope — draped around his neck. He listened to Lewis' heart and lungs. And then, to the eventual delight of his first — and the doctor fervently hoped only — patient of the day, he walked to a stout cabinet mounted on the wall above a small sink, and unlocked it with a key he chose from a ring of keys that he pulled from his pocket.

Lewis watched, mesmerized to the degree that he didn't know the doctor was speaking to him until he turned from the cabinet to face his patient, clearly well-launched into a standard speech. "...don't really want to have you fill a prescription here in town, as someone will surely notice, or suspect, what you have gotten, and maybe try to get it away from you....so, I'm going to give you a small supply of meperidine — Demerol — you're not allergic?... good...in these foil strips. That should help with the pain. No point doing an x-ray, your arm isn't broken. Or, if it is, it's a tiny, hairline fracture that casting won't help. The nurse will bandage you up, and give you a sling, which you probably will not use. But, back to the pain medication. Just take one or two every three or four hours, and take a couple aspirin at the same time. No booze. Rest. Ice wouldn't hurt. And, of course see your own doctor when you get back to the States."

The doctor had ended the last sentence with a finality that indicated that he was through, but he was not. He was merely engaged in tearing two long strips of pills encased in foil from a large roll, folding the smaller strips, putting the result in small manila envelopes, and then scratching something — Lewis hoped directions — onto the envelopes with a red pen he had fished from his trouser pocket.

"Thank you, Doctor," Lewis intoned in the expected solemn, grateful manner. He figured that his greatest problem now would be to go through the bandage-and-sling business with the nurse without smiling, and without taking the envelopes of pills from his pocket to admire them, check their strength, and count them. He guessed that there were about sixty tablets and that they were 50 milligram doses — but, they could be 100 milligram. He knew that he was set for at least 3 or 4 days, even if he got piggish. Things of a pharmaceutical nature were definitely looking up for Lewis. Almost enough for him to forget that tomorrow, he had a meeting with a dead man.

He began, once more to examine — from whatever shreds of memory he had — the occurrences in Boston and Cambridge back in 1964, the bases of his belief that Doc was gone, disappeared, dead. He didn't get far when the Blue-Black nurse from Jersey was, all of a sudden, standing next to him, her hand on his good arm, speaking loudly.

"Mr. Melton — can you hear me? Are you with us?"

He answered quickly, trying to seem alert, although it might be a bit late for that act.

"I think you might be in a bit of shock, Mr. Melton. I spoke to you several times before you responded. And your eyes don't look so good — we need to examine you just a bit more, before we let you go. Sometimes, with older patients, a fall can have other consequences, or may have happened for other reasons. Have you ever had a stroke? Or any heart problems?"

Fuck, thought Lewis, if I'm not careful, they could end up keeping me all day or even admitting me to the hospital. I need to play this one just right...

"No — no strokes, no heart problems. I just had a very complete physical (he lied) a month ago — my Doctor gave me a clean bill of health in those areas."

"Well, still, Mr. Melton, we need an EKG before we let you get away. The doctor insists. It will only take fifteen minutes — and it must be done. You stay right here on the exam table — there, put your feet up. I'll go get the EKG cart, and be right back." She strode purposefully from the room, as fast as Lewis had seen her move in the brief time that he'd been at the Clinic.

Shit, shit, fuck, shit, goddamn! he swore silently....I need to play along, I need to get out of here. They're afraid I'm some old bastard who'll walk out the door, and crump on them. If I just take off, they'll really be scared. They'll at least chase me, or more likely, have the cops chase me, because they'll think I'm off my rocker. So, I'll be the model patient. No more wool-gathering, no jokes, no resistance — unless they try to send me to the hospital.

The nurse was back within minutes, pushing an EKG machine on a metal cart, and trailed by a very large man in scrubs. He didn't have a stethoscope around his neck, so he probably wasn't a doctor. Could be the EKG tech. Or, just some muscle, in case Lewis wasn't so cooperative.

Lewis, now, was instructed to change into a johnny, and he did so without a complaint. Then, he lay back on the exam table, and let the nurse and the unidentified man attach the leads to his sunburned body. The test was over in less than five minutes, but it took another twenty to find the doctor and have him read the results. All was as it should be, according to the young physician.

"Mr. Melton, the EKG looks fine, especially for a man of your years. I think you may have just had a bit of a shock from the fall, but, you seem fine now. You can go — we can call a taxi for you, although there is often one right across the road, by the new hotel. And just to help you relax and get some sleep tonight, I'm going to give you a few tablets of a very mild sedative."

He extracted a foil and paper packet from his pocket. "These are Xanax — a very low dose. Just take one at bedtime, and another when you get up in the morning. And, absolutely no alcohol with these — it could be very dangerous."

Lewis couldn't believe his luck. He had been upset about the delay, but it had gotten him a dozen tranks. This injury had been profitable, in a way. He was effusive in his thanks.

"Doctor, you've been a great help. You really have a wonderful Urgent Care Center here — as good, or better than anything I've seen in the States."

The young physician smiled. "Well, we try to keep up, you know, but, very kind of you to notice. I hope you enjoy the rest of your stay on the island."

Lewis shook everyone's hands, then got dressed with dignified alacrity, and was out of the door, and into a taxi, in less than five minutes. He was on his way back to his cottage, with a pocketful of drugs for the pain of awareness.

Much of the awareness that was causing pain for him now was a new awareness of hospitals and clinics. He hadn't been in a hospital in years, except for some diagnostics that are best done there, the endoscopies and colonoscopies and other unpleasant procedures — but, everyone did that, after a certain age. His concern was more focused on the fact that he had fallen, for no apparent reason, and then had gone to what was, essentially, a hospital, for treatment. He had seen his parents, and the parents of friends, go through the drill: fall — hospital, fall — hospital, fall — hospital — nursing home — pneumonia — hospital — death. It seemed way too common, and he sure hoped that he wasn't starting his own version. Because, he was getting awfully close to that age. He didn't spend a lot of time thinking about his age, but was aware of it, every minute of every day.

This was, ultimately, a really scary subject. If a writer wanted to pen a real horror story, he wouldn't write a slasher, or a zombie tale, or a Kingsian morality play, but a real screamer — a book that the reader wanted to put down, and was afraid to pick up again, a book about the race to debility and death, with all the gory stops along the way. That was a book that Lewis didn't want to write, and wouldn't ever read.

Except — except that now, maybe he had started to read it, just when he thought that he was going to relax, and have some fun. Here, in one of his favorite places, surrounded by (mostly) younger flesh, parading around naked, showing off all of their unwrinkled health. It had occurred to him that one reason that he liked beaches — especially nude beaches — was that there were almost no old people there. It was rare to see anyone older than 55 or 60, and those were the healthy 60-year-olds. Islands, in general, were that way, too. Damn few old people. They went off-island where they'd be closer to a real hospital, or to stay in assisted living, or, worse yet, a nursing home.

Up at home, in New England, life was difficult in the winter, especially on the islands. If the harbor froze, you couldn't get a boat out to see your specialists. They were no place for an old geezer to be. He had lived on the Island long enough to know some "old" guys in the bar: they were in their fifties, and went off-island to the V.A. hospital for the winter. In the spring, if they were still alive, they'd come back to the bar, to drink some more.

So, he was, he guessed, old, finally. He had just been treated for a fall that could have happened a few years ago, or a few years hence, but was bound to happen. Maybe the Fat Kid had been right. Watch out, mister — you could break a hip. Very scary words.

Day 8 – Flashbacks, Memories, Nightmares?

Lewis woke up to the sunlight coming in through the window to illuminate his rumpled hair, most of which he still, quite proudly, had. Groggily, he intuited that he had left the curtains open — something that he never did — and must have been exceptionally relaxed when he turned in. Judging by how his head, his body felt, he had gone to be relatively sober, and sufficiently sunburned.

The day before this one had been exactly as he wished each Caribbean day to be for him. He had dozed, he had drunk a few (or perhaps several) beers on the beach, he had remembered to slather SPF 40 on his cock. He had enjoyed a light dinner early in the evening — a bouillabaisse and half of a heavily buttered baguette. The, he had found his way back to his cottage well before the raucous bands in the beach-bars had cranked their amps up to "Stun." He had still been sober, evidenced by his having read for two hours, and was in bed, snoring and farting (he presumed) by a bit after ten o'clock. And now he was awake, and not hung-over.

He lurched out of bed, and padded on painful arthritic feet to the tiny sink for a piss that wouldn't wait. Having had the remarkable foresight to buy some good, ground coffee at the Club's tiny store, he put some tap-water on the gas ring to boil. He brushed his teeth (many of them his actual teeth) at the sink/urinal, and stared into the mirror, as if seeking its opinion on whether he should have to shave today. He settled for splashing water on his face and head, and combed his hair — getting a little too long — straight back, part of his I'm-not-from-the-States disguise. He admired his gray-stubbled visage in the clouded mirror (still a bit ugly, but tending more toward distinguished, he thought). He sniffed one armpit — not so bad. With all the Frenchmen around, he'd blend into the general miasma. The teakettle began to whistle at him, and he set to preparing the coffee. After half filling the pot with boiling water, he dumped what looked like a reasonable amount of ground bean into the poor-quality press, then pushed the plunger and screen down, until the cap lodged where it should be. With any luck, he'd have drinkable, strong coffee in a few minutes.

Extracting a brown plastic prescription pill vial from his shaving kit, Lewis opened it and shook out two blue Valium tablets, and tossed them into his mouth. He repeated the procedure to secure four yellow (not a yellow that was found anywhere else in the world) Percodans, adding them to his mouth. The coffee must be done — it looked like tar — so he poured a bit in his cup, sipped a bit, and swallowed, then took a bigger gulp of the hot, bitter brew. He couldn't tell if the aspirin in the percs made the coffee more bitter, or less. He had loved the taste of aspirin since he was a child, and he'd been given vaguely orange-flavored children's aspirin for almost every malady.

Lewis settled his awakening bulk on the love seat to sip coffee, smoke cigarettes, and wait for the magical concoction he'd just imbibed to take effect. It wouldn't be long, not on an empty stomach. He was content, just waiting for the warmth and the soft calm to spread throughout his body, removing all of the little aches and pains — and the bigger ones, too — that his decades on the planet had tattooed on his body, his brain, his soul.

The sun and salt-bleached rattan love-seat on the small screened porch was a fine place to sit, and the only truly comfortable place in the cottage. It was one of those magical locations where one could just sit, and hours could pass as minutes. Lewis had such a location in both of his houses, but had not expected to find one in a rented cottage.

The love-seat provided a view on three sides, the screening opaque only when it caught the sun directly. He could watch his neighbors come and go, and observe all who used the walkway. The situation of the porch kept it fairly cool, as the Trade Winds, warm but not hot, blew through from east to west.

He settled in comfortably after spreading a towel on the cushions — he was a good citizen of the Naturist Nation, and didn't want to rub his ancient ass around on a seat that others would use. Not entirely altruistic, he also didn't know what sort of creatures the last twenty — or two hundred — renters had been, and wasn't anxious to share whatever they might have been afflicted with, even if it was unlikely that such things could be transmitted via couch.

He lit another cigarette, sipped some more of the thick, black coffee. He could feel the caffeine already, long before the other drugs would announce their presence. The tobacco smoke tasted wonderful as he brought a toke in through his mouth, expelling it through his nose. Lewis loved to smoke, and couldn't imagine quitting. He'd have to be heavily sedated, shackled, and locked up, on suicide watch.

The actions his body performed to smoke a cigarette were automatic, independent of all other mental and physical acts. He smoked as he breathed. He told people, sometimes, that he smoked while swimming or skiing, even while taking a shower. He'd tried to smoke while screwing, but his partner invariably objected. He thought about all of this, as he choked and hacked on the inhaled coffee and swallowed smoke that a system error in his automatic smoking had caused. The error was a direct result of his sudden and unobstructed view of an exquisitely lovely woman who had, just at that instant, emerged from the front door of the cottage directly to his west.

She moved with the regal stride of a princess, or a top model. Her perfectly straight back didn't detract from all of the curves that had caught his attention. His eyes were locked on her as she glided forward purposefully, making headway while almost seeming to stand still. Her straight, long neck supported a small and perfect head, crowned with a very short, European style haircut. The strong nose and chin, the high cheekbones, and the small and delicate ears set close to her head could look severe, even intimidating. They were in contrast to her warm dark eyes and gently smiling lips that were turned his way — to see, of course, what the horrible coughing and choking noises were all about. Was she looking at him with concern and care, or laughing at him, he wondered?

Now, as she drew closer, he could better make out the details of her body. Small, perfectly shaped breasts — the left noticeably larger — with tiny buds of nipples, above a torso slim enough to show her ribs. The distance from her boobs to her small waist was no more than fourteen inches, and her flat stomach contrasted with the classic curves of her butt. Please, turn my way just a little, Lewis silently prayed, desperate to see the convergence of her long and perfect legs. His God must have been listening. The woman turned on small, high-arched feet, and floated a few feet closer to Lewis. She was less than ten feet away, close enough, now, for him to make out a lightly furred pussy, the plump outer lips of which were slightly parted as she moved to a better stance, shielded her eyes with her right hand, and asked in mildly accented English if he was alright.

He felt as if his heart had dropped into his scrotum, the better to pump blood into his cock. He hadn't been this immediately and completely aroused since Junior High School, when he had convinced his fourteen-year-old girlfriend to take her bra off. If he had another ten seconds, he could fall helplessly in love with this woman who he had never met. But, the vision of loveliness, aware now that the older man on the screened porch had a boner, and was, therefore, probably not in much danger, turned her perfect head back toward her destination, and began to glide away.

One big plus to the Nudist scene was that awareness of beauty and of all that which was not beauty, was maintained, and over time, balanced. It did not play out evenly, and days could pass without noticing anyone who was either gut-wrenchingly ugly or ethereally beautiful. But then, in a half mile of beach, there could be a cluster of either, or both. And they were all worthy of note, if only for their courage.

Fully awake now, Lewis was ready to get his things together, and head for the beach. His erection had disappeared as quickly as it had arrived, and he was thoroughly medicated and fit for duty. He checked his beach bag to make certain he had the essentials, including some SPF 40, for his sensitive parts, and his writing supplies: a couple of good ballpoint pens, and a fresh Composition Book — the cheap drugstore-variety notebook with the familiar black and white mottled cover, and 200 pages of 9 ¾ by 7 ½-inch ruled paper. He must get some writing done, and his first draft was always longhand, always in a Composition Book. And he kept them, kept half of a closet-full. Forty years of scrawl.

A fast rummage through his traveling bag brought to light an unstained, but badly wrinkled pair of faded Nantucket Red shorts. Some days — today was one of them — Lewis chose to wear shorts, even a T-shirt to the beach. The sun was already set at "brutal-burn," and if he was going to spend the whole day exposed to it, he'd need to spend some time covered up.

Stuffing a thin money-clip in his right front pocket, he felt ready, even anxious, to get going. Any day that had begun as well as this one had could hold infinite promise, especially for a man of low expectations. He just wanted to laze in the sun, immerse himself in the ocean to cool down, and not be hassled by tourists or by the obese, middle-aged island women who had the racket of braiding beads into one's hair.

His only other expectation — his responsibility, probably — was to write one thousand very good words in the next few days, only about 7 pages in a Composition book. Perhaps not exactly the right words, as that could come with the re-write. But, at least good words. It was the only talent he had, other than misanthropy, and, on those days when he voted for an ordered Universe, the only reason that he had been allowed to survive.

Less than five minutes after he had let the screen door slam behind him, he was comfortably ensconced in a beach chair, in a spot very close to his favorite spot. Only 9:30, the south end of the beach was busy, full of naked vacationers, lying down or sitting or standing, conversing quietly, if at all. The breeze was brisk off the ocean, making it chilly enough, if one were wet, to raise goose-bumps. Dry skin, reclining out of the wind, felt the breeze as a balmy comfort, preventing sweating, precluding any accurate assessment of just how hot and dangerous the sun was, although high noon was hours away.

It is considered bad form, on a nude beach, to stare at another sunbather. Almost everyone does it, but very surreptitiously, and Lewis was no exception. Sunglasses helped a great deal, as did a cap pulled low over the eyes.

He could spot lots of newcomers today. They gave themselves away with snowy white butts, or boobs, or worse — painfully burned parts that should have been slathered with the highest SPF, but had not been. They were a group worth observing, the source of pithy social commentary, and a veritable group-behavior lab. Each of them had found a reason to (or no reason to not) enter a new tribe, one with customs that were the polar opposite of what their tribe-of-origin practiced.

They had believed, been taught, that nakedness was sexuality, and the more skin that one exposed, the greater one's interest in sexual behavior — usually unacceptable to the group. But here, what was going on here? All these naked people, many of them unattractive, some of them very old, or even young — children! — and none of them seemed to be very sexually oriented. Not an erection to be seen. Very odd.

Poor Herb, poor Betty (from a very nice little township in the "nice part" of New Jersey) were walking into Lewis's view, just entering the Club's end of the long shoreline, he in baggy Polo swim trunks, she in a very daring bikini... so daring that, when Herb first saw it on her no-longer-buxom thirty-eight-year-old body, he developed an almost-instant boner. Betty didn't do that to him anymore. It was fortunate that she had modeled it for him in the hotel room, as he wanted sex, right away.

But the daring bikini, for which she had, inexpertly trimmed her pubic hair, wasn't going to cut it here. She had, to her husband's surprise, removed her top a half-mile back, had carried it for a moment, and then had stuffed it into her bag. Herb was trying valiantly to stifle a burgeoning erection, and was successful to a point — he had only a soft-on. They decided to sit, and were in the act of spreading their mammoth L.L. Bean towels on a vacant plot of sand, when the beach-chair guy materialized next to them. He had two lounges set up, and an umbrella stuck in the sand before Herb could object.

Herb quickly over-tipped him, happy for the cover, happy to have a place to hide the partially-engorged pecker that had crept out of his bathing suit next to his thigh. He sat down, then reclined, casually, he thought, opening the latest terribly written, best-selling crime novel, and tenting it over his crotch. He concentrated on not staring at the naked folk surrounding him.

Betty, sitting in her beach chair, felt wonderful with that too-tight, too-small, push-up top in her bag instead of on her chest. She looked meaningfully through her sunglasses at Herbs sunglasses, and said, in a stage-whisper, for some reason, "Herb, I feel silly — I'm taking the bottom of this goddamn suit off, too."

Before Herb could say, "Well, honey, I don't know it that's a good idea," she had already slipped the miniscule bikini-bottom off, and was applying sunscreen to the newly exposed skin.

She turned to Herb, and said, not-so-softly, "You should take your swimsuit off. No one here has one on, so you just look silly." She had intended to sound cajoling, but it came out more like a criticism, to Herb's ears.

"Maybe you're right, honey....I can't, right now. I'm hard...." he muttered, *sotto voce*.

"Oooh, what a waste," Betty retorted, a little coquettishly, she hoped. "Well, lose the woody, pal — we're going to try to blend in, and I don't see any other guy with a boner. Exercise some control — think about Lorena Bobbitt!"

Herb, unwilling to take any extended ribbing, slipped quickly out of the trunks, and in the same motion, flipped over onto his front, thereby squashing the offending member between his belly and the rough canvas of the beach chair. It was sufficiently painful that any aspirations that his normally quite modest dick may have had for growth would soon be forgotten.

Lewis, a scant fifteen or twenty feet away, had heard, and seen, enough of the drama to fully appreciate it. He thought that others might, too, and had been scribbling as quickly as he could in his notebook. He might never use any of it, but, if he did, he wouldn't have to change much. It stood, by itself, as a telling vignette that reeked of real life, and of the societal insanity that he liked to speak to. It had, at first, almost awed him that seemingly sane, intelligent humans could be relied upon to act out these plays in public, although probably not for the amusement of others. Maybe they didn't think that other people found them interesting enough to steal their stories and their souls for laughs.

He had to wonder, with only vaguely empathetic curiosity, if Betty, and her less adventurous husband, wondered at all about the large, sunburned naked man fifteen feet away, . What was he writing about? If I were he, what would I be writing about? Holy shit — you don't suppose he's writing about us, do you?

Lewis had grown weary of his speculations about Betty and Herb, and any empathetic projection of them toward him, or vice versa. And, he was just plain tired anyway, in a mid-morning, chemically altered way. He had enough writing done to stop the guilt for now. He tucked his Composition Book in his beach bag, lit a cigarette, and settled back in his chair to simply gaze out over the blue-green-light blue luminescent Bay.

When his cigarette was gone, he buried it, head first, in the sand. The sun was as high and as hot as it would get: he could feel the heat all the way to his bones. Behind his Ray-Bans, his eyes fluttered shut as he fell into beach-sleep. If the waitress with the marvelous tits came around, he knew that he would sense her, and awaken enough to order a cold beer. Otherwise, he'd snooze.

The day went timeless. Hunger woke him around two o'clock, prompting a walk to the tiniest beachside bar around, and an empty stool within. Lewis ordered a roast-beef sandwich and a beer. The sandwich tasted exquisite, so good that he ate it slowly, not drinking his beer until the sandwich was gone. It was his fourth beer of the day, and didn't taste as good as the first three.

He believed that he could accurately gauge just how much sun was enough for his Caucasian hide, and assessed that he had reached that point. He planned to return to his chair only long enough to smoke a cigarette and to let his lunch settle, as he regarded the inimitable vista of beach, water, and sky.

As he looked out at the water, he saw that the sea, flat earlier, had kicked up, with some waves close in, and whitecaps a hundred feet out. A plastic "Banana Boat" full of drunken tourists was having serious trouble getting back to shore, about a quarter-mile to the north, and a worker from the boat-rental place was high-tailing it toward them on powerful jet-ski. He'd attach a line to the bow and tow them in, before some half-wit took on a lung-full of the Caribbean.

Lewis knew from the look of the water, from the time of day, and from the slightly cooler breeze that had just sprung up, that soon it would rain, but only for 3 or 4 minutes. The temperature would drop ten degrees in less than a minute, causing the less alert to wonder what the hell was going on. He pulled on the shorts he had with him for the walk, and swung his towel, serape-like, around his shoulders. He'd ride out the mini-storm under his umbrella, rather than chance the walk to his cottage, as there probably wasn't time. He didn't like being soaked with a cold rain, despite the likelihood that he'd dry in minutes when the sun burned through.

As soon as the rain and wind had gone, Lewis gathered up his things, stuffed them into his bag, and began the trek to his temporary home, for what he hoped would be a temporary nap. He wanted to sleep for an hour or two, and then walk to the pool for a cooling dip before he sat down to write for a few hours. Then, at six o'clock, he hoped, he'd be rested, and ready for a drink or two.

When he did awaken, he knew almost instantly that his hopes hadn't entirely come true. He was certainly ready for a drink or two, but, assuredly, not rested. He had chosen to nap on the bed, rather than the Love Seat, as it was just an inch or two too short to completely stretch out. The air in the bedroom was hot and still, after many hours of the tropical sun beating on the roof. Lewis hadn't turned the air conditioner on since he had shut it down upon arrival. He liked heat more than he liked A/C. But even for a tired, naked man, the heat in the cottage today was a bit much…even the bed sheets and pillow were hot to the touch.

He had a nasty headache coming on, perhaps the product of hours in the sun with only a few beers for his thirst. It felt as if he had a touch of sun-sickness, more pronounced each minute that he spent in the stifling hotbox of his bedroom. He turned on the ancient, 4000 BTU air conditioner, knowing that it could take hours to have any real effect. Feeling worse by the minute, Lewis drank down two glasses of tepid tap water, and reclined on his bed. He broke into a cold sweat, and began to feel very shaky, more internally than externally.

Perhaps, he thought, he was having some withdrawal: he'd had no meds since morning, having felt so good on the beach that taking any pills hadn't occurred to him. He rose from the bed to find his beach bag and the pill case inside, and promptly took the meds it contained. He lay back down, dropped his hot, cold sweaty head on the equally hot pillows, and closed his eyes.

He felt relief within minutes. It actually felt cold all around him — and smelled cold, like a late October day in Vermont, with the dead-leaves and dirt smell that the woods produced after the Summer has died. He began to understand, or to hope, that he was in a dream. He didn't want to feel the fear that could be coming at him, but had to open his dreaming eyes. He looked down his extended arm, and saw in his hand what seemed to be a very real, very ugly chromed .357, aimed pretty accurately at a crying man, a long-haired Freak kneeling in the dirt. The man was blubbering, trying to talk through his terror, but Lewis couldn't understand a single word.

They seemed to be in a new growth forest, mostly hardwoods, with a monolithic hill of granite, earth and vegetation about twenty yards behind the crying freak. Lewis knew that he had to aim low, and not chance a ricochet from the rocks. He knew, too, that a shot from the ridiculously flashy revolver that he held would sound like a fucking Howitzer in this setting.

He was as surprised as he could be when he squeezed the trigger, heard no report, and threw himself off the edge of his bed, vomiting chunks of roast beef, bread, and a couple of un-dissolved pills across several feet of his living room and bedroom.

In his dream, he hadn't been scared. Awake now, he was terrified. This wasn't the first time he's had this dream, or a similar dream, in the past few months. But this time, instead of watching the Freak's head blow apart in a red mist, he had only blown lunch. The dream seemed less dream-like, and more like a memory, each time. And this time, unlike the others, he, Lewis, was holding the gun.

He felt shaky, but much better than — than whenever — it must have been hours ago: it was dusk, now — he had fallen asleep. And now, he suspected food poisoning, not sun poisoning. Maybe the mayonnaise — not a good idea on a hot beach, as his mother used to say. Whatever it had been, it didn't matter much; being sick didn't scare him. And it wasn't just that, this time, he felt his fingers exert the surprising force that it took to squeeze the trigger while holding the goddamn uselessly heavy gun steady. It was, really, that this time, he thought he could recognize the blubbering Freak. He had looked an awful lot like Doc.

It was growing pretty dark outside his cottage. The lights that lined the paths between the cottages and the path down to the restaurant and the beach had all clicked on. Lewis was mentally engaged in dismissing his recent and horrific dream as his just come-uppance for being dumb enough to get food-poisoning, along with a bit too much sun, and heat. Then his telephone made a loud, annoying noise, and he had to force himself to become more focused before answering it. He hadn't expected Judy to call, but it was Judy, and she was completely freaked out.

"Lewis, thank God you're in — I thought you might be out at dinner. Things have happened here, today — my place was broken into, while I was at work. I don't think they took anything....I called the cops, of course, and we went through every room. Nothing was even moved. The cops didn't really understand it — they figure that whoever did it got scared off by something."

"Judy, are you okay? You seem pretty freaked. I can try to get a flight out tomorrow, if you need me there"

"No, no, I'll be okay...I called a friend, and he came right over. He'll stay the night, just in case whoever broke in decides to come back. But, Lewis, I haven't told you the whole story. Nothing was taken, but something may have been left — unless it's something you left out the last time you were here. You're in it, standing in front of some building — in front of that bar on the Island that you told me about, maybe. Your face and maybe one or two others I recognize. Do you remember having it out to look at, or something? I've never seen it before."

"Judy, I haven't seen that picture in years. I remember when one of them was taken, when I was still around there....but I haven't seen it. I didn't leave it there. There are lots of copies, though — most of us had a few made up."

"Lew, why would someone else leave that? Is it a joke? Is somebody fucking with you, through me?"

Lewis knew it was no joke. He knew, too, that many of the people in the picture were dead, but that didn't seem like the best thing to tell Judy, so, he lied.

"I think it may be some sort of elaborate joke. I can think of half a dozen people who are in that picture who wouldn't hesitate to do something like that. If they were drunk, or stoned, they may not have even had a reason. Say, do you suppose you could fax me a copy of that picture? I know you still have that ancient fax machine....just call the desk here at the club, and get their fax number."

Judy didn't respond right away. He could picture her as she tried to make sense of his request. Then, she must have reached some level of acceptance, if not understanding, as she came back, verbally.

"Sure, Lew, I'll fax it tonight. Can you transfer me to the desk?"

"I think I can. I'll try. And, Judy, I really appreciate this. I wouldn't worry too much about anyone coming back — they're not interested in you — as you said, they're going through you to fuck with me. I'm sure it'll be okay. You'll have to find other uses for your friend. I'll try to transfer you to the desk, now, so you can fax it soon."

Judy responded with the expected promise to send the fax, then with the expected "you know, you should move in with me...you're going to get in trouble...."

Before he pushed the "Transfer" button, Lewis said: "Judy, one more thing. My grasp of geography isn't so great, as you know....so, can you tell me if there are any fairly remote, wooded, hilly areas of land within 30 or 40 minutes of Boston? I think they'd have to be less than half an hour, by car. Mixed growth forest, and at least some big granite cliffs or outcroppings. It would have to be far enough out that a gunshot wouldn't alarm anyone who shouldn't be alarmed."

"Sure, Lewis, there are probably half a dozen, but only two that sound likely. North of Boston is the Fells, and south of Boston is the Blue Hills. They're both about half an hour from town, although the Fells may be a little closer. Why — are you planning on shooting someone?"

Instead of following his first instinct, which was to say, "No, but I may have shot someone a long time ago," he said, "Of course not — it's for a fiction piece I'm writing."

They went through the good-bye dance once again, then Lewis pushed the button on the phone that he fervently hoped would send Judy's call to the Front Desk. He would stop by later, or tomorrow, to pick up the fax.

The faxed photo would be pretty grainy, and maybe useless, but he hoped it would be just clear enough to allow him to hang names on all of those faces. He needed a suspect list longer than merely "Doc," as he was pretty damn sure that Doc was on the island, with him, and could not, therefore, have been in Massachusetts breaking into Judy's place. The same logic argued that if Doc was alive, somewhere, then neither Lewis nor anyone else had shot him dead. If Doc was behind all of the bad stuff that had lately invaded his life, he almost certainly had an accomplice, maybe more than one, and that accomplice could well be someone that they both knew. The picture that had been taken in front of the bar on that late August day, so many years ago showed almost all of the folks that Lewis and Doc both knew, many of whom were crazy enough and skilled enough to break into Judy's place in a town that had, in Lewis's opinion, way too many cops.

And, why would they leave the picture at all? It was hard to figure. It had been taken only days before he and Chrissie had left the Island- was that significant? Lewis really had to see the picture himself to be certain.

For a day that had begun so wonderfully, staying that way right through early afternoon, things had taken a decidedly ugly turn. Far too ugly to chance going out now. He wasn't particularly hungry, and had water, bread, a bit of cheese, and some coffee, should he get desperate. Now was the time to take a triple-dose of Valium, and turn in for the night. Tomorrow would be along soon enough.

Day 9 – Flashbacks, Memories, and Tails?

The night passed like a century of doubt and discontent for Lewis. If he truly slept at all, it was for the first twenty minutes, when the Valium had, very briefly, walloped his consciousness into submission.

He lay there in bed in a state of suspended agitation, with each nerve and muscle fiber fidgeting independently. Not awake enough to just say "Fuck it!" to himself, to get up and smoke cigarettes, to take more drugs that might let him sleep…and not asleep enough to find any small bit of ease, of rest. Not frightened enough by his waking dreams to try to scream himself back to the real world.

The following day, looking back on his ordeal, he hypothesized that he may have had something like the DTs, something that he had read about. This syndrome, the article had stated, can affect those who took benzodiazepines — like Valium — for too long, or those who sometimes took too much. But whatever he hypothesized, what it felt like was an acid trip — not good, not bad, really — but very real, and retrospectively, very necessary.

At almost exactly ten-thirty by the vaguely glowing hands of his wristwatch, he surfaced from his chemical tranquility to find himself observing an almost forty years younger Lewis, sitting in a booth of dark wood, in a dark bar that he remembered as being just off Huntington Avenue in Boston. There were two full draft ale glasses in front of him, and a glass in his right hand that was almost empty. The ashtray on the table was half full, so it was likely that Lewis, and the guy across the table who he was drinking with, had been here for a while.

For a long moment, Lewis could not attach a name to the lean, dark-haired and bearded man across the table from the young Lewis. Then, when he spoke, the man's singular accent told all — it was a criminally bastardized mélange of the Dorchester section of Boston, Down East Maine, and Harvard Yard accents, sounding, finally, like the accent that movie actors end up with when a lousy voice-coach helps to learn "the Boston Accent," as if there were just one. The accent said that the other drinker must be Doc.

Older, real-time Lewis couldn't hear Doc well enough to catch all of the words, nor could he hear his younger version completely clearly. With intense concentration, he was able to get the gist of the desultory exchange.

Both men had been drinking steadily the day before, and well into the night, and had been waiting, shakily, at the door of this particular bar at seven in the morning, when it opened. Other bars didn't open for a while, and the liquor stores even later. And, this bar had a particular drawing card — ten cent drafts of Pickwick Dark Ale. With their pooled resources of less than ten dollars, they could afford, at this joint, a pack of Luckies, a few pickled eggs for sustenance, and thirty-five glasses of ale, apiece.

So, they were, quite logically, talking about money. They were almost flat-broke, unemployed students, with regrettably expensive habits — eating, drinking, paying rent.

As their original kitty of ten bucks shrank throughout the day, their plans to acquire wealth grew increasingly more desperate. Lewis and Doc had not been close friends forty years ago, but they were alike in many ways, and had a certain respect for each other. They had similar tastes in drugs, a prodigious (and growing) appetite for alcohol, were both highly intelligent, and both displayed increasingly poor judgment and sometimes faulty moral compasses. Consequently, what real-time Lewis heard, as the conversation progressed, didn't surprise him terribly.

They had worked their way through all of the low-end cash cows known to the more creative students — selling blood, figure modeling at the art schools, even a day or two of backbreaking day-labor, which last week had consisted of unloading freight cars of 40-pound sacks of Low Industrial Locust Bean Gum, whatever the hell that was. The problem with these methods — most of them: they couldn't sell blood again for a week — were the low return and the high time-investment. So, they kept talking, kept scheming.

Real-time Lewis heard, very clearly, the next idea. Doc ground out his cigarette, as it was now too short to smoke without setting fire to his moustache, then drank off the last half-glass of amber brew in front of him. He sighed theatrically loudly, and said, "I guess we'll just have to move some grass. The harvest must be done, and the college students have been back for a month — they must be out of whatever they brought from home."

"Sure," the young Lewis responded, "but that's a hell of a lot of work for a thousand bucks....and a hell of a lot of risk, whether we move pounds or ounces. If we get popped, we'll get twenty years each, easy. It just doesn't make sense...we could rob a fucking bank, get more money, and get less time, if we get caught."

Real-time Lewis watched the two young men sit, silent, smoking. He was beginning to feel the first tingle, in his gut, of a very bad recalled feeling. He thought he knew what would be said next, and who would say it.

"Well," said Doc, in his most put-on laconic drawl, "we could rip ourselves off, so to speak…"

That was the instant when the Valium, or some force, came back for another round, starting with a punch that took Lewis to the mat, and took from him his God's-eye view of a conversation that may have taken place forty-odd years ago. He sank slowly down, back into dream-free, hypnotic sleep of the kind that is mostly enjoyed by alkies and downer-addicts. It seemed to last only seconds, and then, he was awake, and he had a headache that began at his shoulders and ran up the back of his skull with a vise-like, pounding grip. He felt queasy, perhaps due to the headache.

Within moments of awakening, Lewis was more alert than he ever cared to be. If he were to accept that which he had…seen?…recalled?…the night before, it would perhaps mean a lot about what and who he had been since then, and might explain this business of Doc looking for him. It could mean that Lewis was not who he thought he was at all.

Of course, he rejoindered to himself, it was just a dream, no more than that — some bits and pieces, clasping together as they fell from a high crag of his unconscious, not related, necessarily, to him, or to anything. The best thing to do about it was the most comfortable thing. For now, that meant doing what he had to get rid of this horrid fucking headache. And, for now, forget about the dream, which was already fading from his memory.

The morning routine went as it had yesterday, and as Lewis hoped it would go tomorrow. He shaved today, though, not such an easy task with three days of stubble and an old razor. He always re-stocked his shaving kit with meds, but rarely with shaving gear. Soon, as presentable as he was going to get on this day, he set about making the coffee, smoking more cigarettes, gathering his beach gear, chewing up half-a-dozen pills, and swallowing another few whole (they tasted vile). Then the screen door slammed behind him, and he was on his way, the dream left behind.

Still early enough that the heat was bearable, Lewis turned left when he got to the shore so he could walk north, along the water's edge, where the sand was wet and cool. He had done nothing in the way of exercise since arriving, and knew he had to work his muscles a bit to avoid the fidgety horrors later in the day. If he walked all the way up the beach to the big hotel favored by the Spaniards and Italians, and then all the way back down, South, to the Club, he could feel a sense of accomplishment, and get the last of the sour taste out of his mind.

He saw many younger couples with children, the children 5 or 6 years old, as he neared the halfway point. The young mothers were thin, pretty and topless to show off their small but perfect breasts, dark-nippled and tanned. They played with their kids at the edge of the gentle surf, and seemed oblivious to all else. Their men, heavier and hairier, sat further back, reading or napping in their lounge chairs, glancing proudly and possessively at their chattel.

It was as he was looking west, toward the lounging fathers, that Lewis noticed the two men — neither in beach-wear or lack thereof — who had stopped about fifty feet behind him, near the top edge of the beach where the row of hotel patios, restaurants, beach bars, and shops was strung out, just off the sand. He was fairly sure that he had seen them before, half a mile back, strolling north in a manner that just didn't look right. As an anxiety-ridden man, a child of the sixties, a paranoid of the first order, Lewis had constant if low-level radar for things that *just didn't look right.* These guys didn't look right at all. No one on a beach stroll would walk in the most congested area of the beach — one would have to zigzag around clusters of people, shops, hawkers selling sunscreen, and countess other obstacles.

He was doubly sure that he had seen them before, as they were dressed as no one else on the beach, very noticeable in dark trousers and shoes, and white short-sleeved dress shirts, of the sort worn only by dentists, engineers, unrepentant geeks, and Mormon missionaries. In fact, if they had bothered to add ugly, too-short neckties and backpacks, they would have looked exactly like missionaries, and would have thereby rendered themselves invisible.

The only glaring inconsistency in the behavior of the two suspected tails was that they were so terribly unskilled at following Lewis, that he could reason that they were not doing so. They were doing such a poor job of it that almost any quarry would catch them at it. He decided to challenge his mutually-negating assessments, or his anxiety would firmly take control.

There were only two simple ways to challenge his theories. The most logical, and the one he was most hesitant to do, was to walk up to them and ask them. He doubted that he could do that while sober. The other way, the way he settled on instantly, was to walk another half-mile, the remainder of the beach, as evasively as possible, and see if they tried to stay on his tail. The next half-mile, fortunately, was rich with opportunities for evasion. He could duck in and out of little shops, detour through hotels, and generally mimic an ADHD comparison-shopper who was badly off his meds. And this he did.

Within ten minutes, Lewis was sweating profusely, and desperately thirsty. He recalled a hotel pool with a bar not far away, and was able to home in on it and occupy a stool in short order. He cheerfully paid six dollars, U.S., for a good beer, drank it down thirstily, and ordered a second. He hadn't glimpsed either suspected tail since beginning his crazed trek and was starting to feel safe, and a bit foolish. Safe enough to relax a bit, safe enough to extract a damp cigarette from the flattened pack in the back right pocket of his sweat-soaked shorts, and light it with his ancient and battered Zippo.

Either alcohol or relief began to flood his brain, anesthetizing the spastic nerves that jitterbugged inside his skull. This wonderful relaxation prevented Lewis from noticing that a man in shorts and a moderately dreadful Hawaiian shirt who was, at that moment, walking up to the bar. To an alert observer, he would have looked an awful lot like one of the men who had, perhaps, been following Lewis earlier, but with a change of clothing. Of course, Lewis was looking, both consciously and unconsciously, for two men, not one, so could not be faulted for what might prove to be a dangerous mistake.

The second beer lasted almost five minutes, and brought with its completion a badly stifled belch, a calm mind, and a trip to the Men's. When he emerged from the toilet, he was ready to resume his journey He was halfway through with this leg, and anxious to complete the task.

He wound his way back to the beach, down to the wet sand, and fell into a slow, steady pace, his wet moccasins making a faint sucking sound with each step. He silently called cadence, blocking out most of what went on around him. Once or twice, he came close to running down a small child playing at the water's edge, a child as oblivious to reality as Lewis was.

As he approached the huge and final hotel on this beach, he became aware of bad, loud Italian rock music blaring from the pool area. More in the moment now, Lewis looked around. He noticed that almost every swimmer and sunbather had at least their genitals covered up, and many of the women wore relatively conservative bathing suits, were a bit older, and far less attractive than the women further south on the beach. This must be, literally and figuratively, the end of the line.

And then, on the periphery of his vision, he thought he saw two men, both fully clothed, walking slowly and purposefully along the beach. They were coming north, toward him, and even at a distance, the way that they moved looked familiar.

Looking about for nearby shelter, Lewis spotted one final shop just before the land attached to the large hotel. It fronted on the beach, tucked in behind an open-air kayak/chair/cabana rental emporium, and backed onto the parking lot that one entered from the road that ran the length of the beach, giving access to all of the hotels, bars, and restaurants. The shop was overflowing with any and all possible items that a nude-beachgoer might possibly want or need. Presiding over the narrow shop, which displayed most of its wares on a counter that ran down the center of the canvas-walled structure, was a French woman of indeterminate age. She was short, just over five feet tall, and had graying blonde (or maybe blonding gray) hair, a very deep tan, impressively wrinkled skin and was almost naked except for a sort of beaded loincloth. The loincloth was suspended from a very thin beaded belt, and hung to just hide her pudendum unless, of course, she moved, causing it to swing aside. There were many dozens more of these little beaded accessories for sale on the counter, and the few other customers seemed interested enough to paw through the collection. There were, of course, some additional abbreviated articles for sale, but whether they were clothing, jewelry, or merely decorations, Lewis did not know.

The Proprietress- overly friendly, overly chatty (but only in French) did not seem to be doing very much business, or at least, not many sales. Lewis was grateful for the number of gawkers in the shop, who at least provided some cover. He, too, gawked and poked about, as if he were carefully choosing exactly the right outlandish gift for that lady-friend back home in Council Bluffs.

He couldn't help stealing the odd glance at the store owner. She probably looked fairly attractive when clothed, but just wasn't the best advertisement for the nude lifestyle. Everything that could sag, had. It seemed beyond question that she scared away a fair bit of business. Lewis fervently hoped that she'd scare away the two heavies who seemed to be tailing him.

Sidling through the shop to the rear entrance, he was able to peer out and look for signs of his followers. He slipped out quickly, into the busy sandy parking lot, and then walked purposefully to the other side, where the sand verged on the stunted grass at the edge of the tennis courts that the big hotel maintained, despite their infrequent use. From there, it was an easy jaunt up to the elevated area surrounding the hotel pool, already loud from fifty feet away with voices, bad music, shrieks, and splashing. The over-amplified voice of some DJ type, punctuated with the warbling scream of feedback, called out barely comprehensible directions, rules, and progress to a pool game that had, clearly, been going on for some time. It was, if not Bedlam, close enough for Lewis's purposes. He made a bee-line for the pool, proposing to cut right through the insanity. *Let's see them follow me unobtrusively now,* he thought.

Except for quizzical, and sometime hostile, looks, he passed through the area with no problems at all, entering the lower lobby of the hotel. Before any of the unusually alert staff behind the registration desk could ask him what he was doing, he was up the stairs, out the main door, and right into the back seat of a waiting taxi. The driver may have been waiting for another party, but he wasn't going to argue with a large, red-faced, rather insane looking white guy — and, after all, a fare was a fare. To Lewis, it was more than that: it was salvation, it was information, and it was winning. He handed the driver the least-sweaty of his twenty-dollar bills, and asked him, in bad French and very good English, to please wait for a few moments. He wanted to see if his tails were any good, and he wanted them to see him escape.

In three or four minutes, both tails — one still in the missionary costume, the other dressed as a tourist — came through the same door that Lewis had burst out of, stopped short, and carefully, looked around. Before they got too curious about the taxi that was idling half-way around the circular drive, Lewis said "Okay, let's go!" to his driver, and the cab took off briskly, out of the drive and onto the beach road. They kept it to a sane, by island standards, 50 miles per hour on the one and a half lane road, careening past the hotels, shops and restaurants that cluttered the eastern beach. In less than ten minutes, Lewis was delivered to the back parking lot of the Club.

He walked down the narrow path to his cottage, locked the door behind him when he got in, and shakily swallowed a half-dozen pills with some cold and gritty coffee, left from that morning.

There no longer being any question that, first, the craziness that had prompted his trip to the island had followed him here, and, second, that he was being actively watched, and followed, at least some of the time. The only important question left was: why? Who was less critical, and merely a prompt to "why." If he knew who — and how many — were behind this B-movie bullshit that had taken over his life for the past days, that could help him to find out why these things were happening, and what the expected result was. But, how much did he really want to know "why"? As a question, it could be ignored for periods of time. The answer might not be so easy to dismiss. As skilled as Lewis had become at making problems disappear through focused neglect, he had a nasty feeling that the "why" of this issue was not just going to go away if he didn't deal with it.

He looked down at his right hand, still clutching the dirty glass that held the dregs of his strong and gritty coffee. The hand was trembling. The phone shrilled. Rather than crushing the glass in his hand, he released his grip, letting the glass drop to the table. Before it fell back to earth from its first bounce, he was picking up the telephone handset.

"Hello!" said his voice, angry and scared sounding, "Hello, who is this?"

"Lewis? My, what a greeting….it's Judy. Are you alright?" She sounded hurt and angry, or maybe, angry and concerned.

Lewis, a little shocked at his hostile greeting, backed off quickly.

"Oh, Judy, I'm really sorry. I didn't mean to sound so brusque. I've had a pretty fucked-up day, so far. How are you?"

"I'm okay, I guess — although you just scared the hell out of me. Are you drunk, or something? I called to see if you're okay. I've been having bad feelings about you, worried feelings. You know how I get. I've been looking at that old picture a lot. You know, I had never seen it before, and I didn't know all the people. But the ones that I did know, Lew, they're all dead. And you, and a couple other faces, are circled: I didn't notice it before, it's pretty faint, but in good light, you can see that they're sort of circled."

It was a full minute before Lewis realized that Judy had stopped talking: she could go on for quite a while, and he had learned to shut it off on his end. He sort of drifted into other thoughts, or none at all, alert for the tell-tale change in cadence that let him know she was wrapping up. Either she didn't do that this time, or, more likely, he missed it. Whatever had happened, she was through, and was waiting for some rational response from the crazy old man on the other end of the line. He didn't quite know what to say, so opted for making reassuring noises.

"Judy, I haven't had a chance to pick up the fax yet — did you fax it yesterday, or today? — but, anyway, I'll bet most of the folks you didn't know are dead, too. Lots of them were older than I was then, and would be in their late sixties, or in their seventies, by now — and lots of men are dead by then, as you know. And this was a high-risk group!"

Only silence from Judy's end of the line. Figuring that he hadn't fixed it yet, Lewis went on. "Those guys were pretty nuts, in some ways. Some of them had bikes, some shot dope, and most of them had guns around the house. Not a .22, Judy, more likely an M-16. This crew would give an Actuary a panic attack. I was different, in a lot of ways, and I changed the way I live, as you also know. I'm not going to die anytime real soon, if that's what has you worried."

No sound except for silence from the Arlington end of the connection, until he heard, very softly, the sound of Judy catching her breath. It occurred to him, then, that she had been crying, quietly, very quietly. "Judy, are you okay? Have you been crying? …I think you're getting yourself upset, needlessly; maybe making too much of this. It's only a photo. I'm not worried (he lied), why should you be?"

Her voice came back not with tears, but with an angry, defensive edge. "Lewis, you are worried, I can tell that you are, and you've been worried for days. Worried about some person, who says that he's Doc, who seems to be, according to you, trying to track you down. When you talk about it, you don't just sound worried — you sound scared. Your panic attacks aren't getting any better, they're getting worse. You're taking more meds than you used to, you're starting to drink like you used to — as if you need to. So, don't tell me to not be worried. I'm very worried, about you!"

Lewis heard the echo of his own fear in her voice. He knew, now, that he should never have told her anything about the Doc business. Or about anything else, for that matter. Just as was true with their divorce, this was all his fault. He knew better, had known better since he was twelve years old, to tell anyone at all anything at all regarding what he actually thought, or felt, yet he seemed destined to do it again and again. So, he said the only thing that he could, at this point.

"Judy, I don't want, or need you to be worried about me. You're not my wife, not anymore. If I have a problem, it's my problem, not yours. I truly do care about you — a lot. You're my best friend. But, butt out, okay? Goodbye."

He placed the receiver gently back into its cradle, then went directly to his shaving kit, intent on rustling up a little something for the awful pain of awareness. At a loss as to what to do next, other than sitting around, smoking cigarettes, and waiting for the pills to kick in, Lewis decided to walk down to the lobby, and claim what he expected to be a terribly grainy, indecipherably dark tele-facsimile reproduction of an old, black and white photo, faded by time, of twelve or fourteen people who he used to know well, better than anyone he had known before that time, or since.

Judy had, perhaps, exaggerated their odds of mortality: most of them, probably, weren't entirely dead quite yet, although he'd wager it was a real horse race for some of them. And if some were circled? Some people mark up photos. So what? But many were dead. And of the ones who weren't, the odds were good that at least one of them, maybe more than one, had been, and still was involved in spending time, trouble, and money to make Lewis life, already depressing and scary, significantly worse.

He washed up a little — very little — and donned a clean polo shirt that had been Navy Blue at one time. The shirt that he peeled off had been so soaked with fear-sweat that he didn't think that any amount of cologne would wash it clean of sin. He tossed it toward the kitchen wastebasket, so he would think about discarding it. His shorts were reasonably clean and, oddly, not soaked with sweat, or anything else. Apparently, he only sweated above his waist. So, the shorts stayed. His moccasins, not built for long hikes in the sand, hurt his feet badly. He dug his "old man sneakers" out of his carry-on. They were canvas-like nylon and leather-like leather, had extra padding and extra arch support, and were extra-ugly, extra-comfortable, and extra-expensive. Lewis loved them, although he was usually too embarrassed to wear them, as no one younger than 60 ever wore them. Wearing those sneakers (the manufacturer designated them "walking shoes") was not unlike wearing an AARP T-shirt.

He wondered, absent-mindedly, if he had enough medication aboard, then remembered that he had just taken an extra-large dose. And, if he needed more pills than the multiple of the therapeutic dose that he had already taken, he planned to be back in ten or fifteen minutes, and could take more then. So, out the door he went.

A few minutes of walking at a very moderate pace brought him to the small, but airy, lobby area. A few new guests were checking in, some of them half-naked already. They must, Lewis thought, have begun to disrobe in the taxi-van that had brought them. Lewis ignored them, and walked to the Concierge desk, which was very small, more of a lectern than a desk, and off to the left of the Registration desk. The presumed Concierge was, like his desk, very small, and was almost hidden as he stood directly behind it. He looked cheerfully stern as he regarded the large, vaguely disheveled man who was approaching him.

Lewis was not so easily put off, even by small, possibly fierce functionaries.

"Hello, my name is Lewis Melton — Doctor Melton, actually — I have asked that a document be faxed to me here: has it come in, yet?" As he was speaking, he was removing his money clip from his right hip pocket, and was peeling a U.S. five dollar bill from the unimpressive sheaf. The action wasn't wasted on the Concierge, who, somehow, was able to appear to be looking down at Lewis, with a combination of disappointment and disapproval.

"Well, of course, Mr. Melton...I'm sorry, Doctor Melton...we have been waiting all day for you to come by and pick it up. Although, I must tell you, I don't know how in the world you will decipher it. If it is a picture — some of us thought that it might be — it looks very much like one of those paintings done by chimpanzees, and then sold by Zoos for ridiculous amounts of money. Except, of course, it is in black and gray."

Lewis had expected a display of disapproval and rudeness if the Concierge turned out to be French, which he appeared to be. But, he was not to be cowed by one small Frog. He responded, therefore, in kind.

"I am so sorry to have kept you waiting....I hope it hasn't been too much trouble. And, no, it wasn't done by a chimpanzee. It is a photograph. Still, I need it. Will you please get it for me?"

"But, of course, Sir, of course. It is with your mail, there at the Registration desk," the Concierge said, gesturing vaguely and dismissively toward the desk that, now, had a short line of new arrivals. Lewis looked at the line, shook his head to indicate surprise and disappointment, simultaneously changing the five dollar note in his hand for a ten.

"I'm afraid that I am unable to wait in crowded spaces, or in lines...I have a very bad, almost disabling form of agoraphobia. Will you be able to retrieve it for me?" As he spoke, Lewis slid the somewhat ratty-looking ten dollar bill halfway across the desk. The Concierge looked at it, and sighed.

"As you wish, Mr. Melton. *Doc*tor Melton. The clerks are so slow today — they should never have a line like that. Let us see what can be done, if anything..." the Concierge sighed.

He strode importantly across the roughly twenty feet to the Registration area, and ducked through an entrance cut into the façade of the counter. Lewis lost sight of him for a moment, but then, like a cheesy magic show, the little man re-appeared with a manila envelope tucked under his arm, and re-traced his steps back to his own turf, not speaking until he was safely behind his own desk, again.

"Doctor, we are fortunate, in that those morons" he pointed toward he Registration desk with his chin, "had not yet had an opportunity to lose this, or to shred it by mistake. I'm sorry, but I must notify you that there is a Convenience Charge, which, with tax, will be twenty-four dollars, U.S. Would you like to pay that now?"

Lewis did not want to pay the ridiculous charge — twenty four bucks! — now, or ever, but asked that it be added to his bill. He thanked the Concierge, a bit frostily, he hoped, and headed back to his cottage.

His curiosity, always stronger than his ability to remember, allowed him only to get as far as the bar in the Club's clothing-extremely-optional restaurant. He mounted a stool between two scrawny, nude barflies (who, he observed, looked exactly the same as scrawny, clothed barflies) and, with some difficulty, opened the small, sharp metal clasp that held the very expensive manila envelope closed. With two large, arthritic fingers, he weaseled out the fax coversheet, and the page stapled to it.

The coversheet had written on it the same words that all fax coversheets have written on them, the only difference being the badly-drawn heart with which Judy invariably signed personal correspondence of any kind. He had no idea why she did this, which may have been a big part of the difficulty in their relationship.

The second page, despite the disparagement of the Concierge, was a damn fine reproduction of a very well photographed black and white shot, a 9 x 11 of a group of mostly cheerful-looking hippies, drunks, and other undesirables standing in front of a bar right after it was made public that September 30 would be the last day the bar would be open – only a month or so from then. It was an important picture, in that the bar was one of the more important epicenters of the already-dying Freak culture on the Right Coast. About which the Town Fathers were less-than-pleased, causing an unbroken sequence of secret events, deals, threats, agreements, and emoluments to, by, and for various important people — none of them Freaks — which had resulted, finally, in the closing of this bar, and the opening, soon, of its replacement, miles out of town, in a spot where the tourists who came to the Island to first, spend money, and second, be in no way made to feel uncomfortable, would be allowed to spend their money, and not be horrified by drooling stoned Freaks, oddly dressed, evil-smelling, badgering them, or even just existing, in plain sight. Gibbering acid-casualties depicted in *Life* and *Time* magazines were okay. Gibbering acid-casualties on Main Street, not okay.

The subjects in the photo, then, should have looked less cheerful than they did, as the bar, soon to close its doors, was where they spent most of their time. The dogs, who all sat in the front row, being shorter than most of the patrons, looked very sad. They loved the bar, and for good reason. The bar had a primitive microwave oven, which was used to heat up a brief menu of inedible treats: burgers, franks, meatball sandwiches. They all looked different, but smelled, and tasted, the same: foul. The bar's patrons all knew that the sandwiches were inedible, but, sometimes, a hunger-maddened dipso or pothead who simply could not tolerate one more pickled egg or Polish sausage would order one of the deadly sandwiches, hoping against hope that they'd get the first edible item that the microwave had ever birthed.

And every time, the poor salivating, ravenous drunkard, after suffering serious burns peeling away the 350 degree cellophane packaging, would see and smell the hot, gray, and reeking snack, then, with tears of hunger and disappointment in their red and yellow eyes, flip it to the hounds who lay in wait under the tables. The dogs would bark, snap and growl at the poisonous gift until it had cooled a bit, then, six or seven of the meanest curs would fight for a mouthful of the warmed, reconstituted offal. The loved this food above all other.

So, as Lewis studied the picture, did all of these details flood back into his consciousness. He could smell the bar. He could smell his old bar-mates.

He saw that four small faces that had been — not circled, but outlined — with some sort of broad-tipped pen, or a grease-crayon, of the sort used to mark raw lumber. There was no mistaking 3 of the 4 faces marked: there was him, Lewis, then Chrissie, next to him, looking ineffably cute, then Janey, looking beautiful, and maybe dangerous, not even trying to smile. And then, Terry, of course, next to Janey. Or maybe not Terry, maybe it was Doc...they really did look alike, in retrospect. Together, they probably wouldn't. He had never seen them together. But he was sure it was Terry, from the blue wool watchcap pulled down tight, and the full, black beard. And the dark glasses: lots of the guys had beards, lots had shades, even on a pretty and dark and dying Autumnal day, the sun long gone.

Lewis continued to stare, mesmerized, at the photograph through the bartender's progressively more pointed inquiries as to Lewis's need for a drink, for a sandwich, for something. Finally, the voice cut through his reverie. He ordered a lager, lit a cigarette, and returned his gaze to the picture, with eyes that, if anyone saw them, they might describe as "haunted."

What haunted Lewis, if anything, wasn't the picture, but his overwhelming desire to be in the picture, in that stopped time, that captured space. Not only because it was a very safe space for him, but because it was the crux, the point in time when everything that was, now, had begun. Where, and how, that path might end was less predictable than the time-path where it began. It was beginning to appear to Lewis that his contentment, his miserable and boring life — year piled upon year of it — was coming toward an end, that the time-path was running out. That he, among others, was outlined in the photo seemed to him as the notation on some limited direction-finding maps: "You Are Here." Except it was, really, "You *Were* Here." A photograph of Lewis at that very instant, about to take a swig of his already-warm beer, could be notated, "Now You Are *Here*." But where were all of the interim photos, where was he then — and what happened to draw at least some of the people from the first photo into his present?

When he did pick up his bottle of beer, not only was it warm, but the condensation had formed a pool on the bar. The little paper napkin under the bottle was sodden and falling apart. Lewis had been lost in his thoughts and in his space for some time now.

Cold or warm, beer was beer. He drank it down in just a few minutes. He looked down at his watch, turning it, in the uncertain bar light, so that he could see the face through the scratched, abraded crystal. Four-thirty: early, but for him, the day felt as if it was mostly beat. No beach-time for him today, although he didn't see that as a problem — one day off from the deadly rays wouldn't hurt him.

He swept the change, except for a single, off the bar, and folded the bills, messily, into his money clip. He had a colleague, when he had taught enough to maintain a regular office in the English Department, who was compelled to keep the currency in his money clip — and in his wallet, for he kept cash in both places — folded precisely in half, with the denominations in order, and each bill folded separately. Ones, fives, tens, twenties. His wallet held fifties, and sometimes, hundreds. Lewis suggested to him on one occasion, when he was feeling a bit mean-spirited toward those possibly crazier than he, that the currency-arranging really wasn't done properly unless the serial numbers were ordered lowest to highest, *and* alphabetically, so the letters that preceded the numbers began at A, or whatever letter was first in the bills that he had at any given time. This would require a re-ordering of the bills each time he tendered or received new bills. His colleague was stunned: why had he not seen that need years ago? But rather than re-ordering the bills each time he spent or acquired notes, he settled on keeping a third repository for currency that had not yet been appropriately placed. He reasoned that if too many people witnessed his re-ordering ritual, they might think that he was eccentric, or even neurotic. Lewis agreed, with some reservations. He felt as if he had done a good and valuable piece of work. And he chuckled, inwardly, each time he stuffed wrinkled bills, haphazardly, into his clip.

Deciding that he could study the picture further at his cottage if the need arose, he turned 180 degrees in his seat and slid from bar-stool to feet in a motion so artful, so seemingly effortless, that the bar's other patrons should have held up scoring placards, Olympics-style — he could take at least a Silver on the Men's Bar-Stool Slither-Drop (or so he liked to imagine).

Trudging toward the exit, he felt his mind go blank — this happened more and more of late — and could not recall if he had tipped, or even paid for the beer. Bu, no one yelled , "Sir!..." at him, so he kept on trudging, the envelope containing the fax folded in half, and wedged into his right, rear pocket. The short walk back to his cottage seemed like a five-mile hike. The stress of the day was exacting a price…Hell, he thought, this whole Goddamn trip was exacting a price. He had come down to the island for a couple weeks of R&R, and had, thus far, gotten not much of either. He knew that he was pushing sixty years of age. And now, the sixty years was pushing back.

He stopped at the small store, only minutes out of his most direct route "home." He bought a container of yogurt, some farmer's cheese, a baguette, and two liters of still mineral water. When he was almost to the counter to pay whatever the outrageously high bill would be, he stopped short, executed a sloppy U-turn, and peered about until he found a small tin of aspirin, and two packs of cigarettes — Chesterfield regulars, a cigarette that had been quite common when he was a boy, but that he had not seen — or heard of — in the States in thirty years. As he recalled, his father had referred to them as "lung-busters." That sounded promising. He bought them.

Back, then, to the cashier's counter, not without some cheerful ogling of the clerk's unfettered, uncovered, and pretty damn fine boobs, which she accepted graciously. Out the door then, clutching those purchases that he couldn't jam into one or another of his pockets. Lewis was tired enough that the final dozen steps to his door were made one at a time: no *faux-* youthful, put-on final burst of speed, no taking of the few steps two at a time, there was no one to impress, and even if there had been, he could not have done it for anything short of preserving his increasingly shitty existence. He concentrated only on gaining the safety and succor of his rooms.

He planned to have a bite to eat, at least the yogurt and a few bites of bread to cushion the three aspirin he wanted to take, and to then settle into a nap, and if he woke, to read the evening away. Not a churchly man, he planned, nonetheless, to pray for an absence of phone calls, interlopers, and dreams.

Day 10 – Every Picture Tells A Story?

The lamp on the table next to Lewis' bed was on when he opened his eyes the next morning. It was early enough so that, without the dim circle of light cast by the lamp, he wouldn't have been able to see very much at all. He experienced a moment of panic when unable to focus his eyes, due, he found, to his having fallen asleep with his reading glasses on. The glasses did allow him to easily read his watch, determining that it was just past four-thirty.

He had fallen asleep studying the photograph that Judy had faxed to him. If he had gleaned anything of import last night, he certainly didn't remember it now. It was the same self-identified gang of Freaks, Fisherman, Faggots and their dogs that had been in the picture yesterday. The very same faces were outlined as were outlined yesterday. No invisible ink had darkened to tell him the story of what all of this really meant. What the Hell did the outlined faces mean?

Lewis was a slave to panic, to assumptions of disaster, to the casting of the most negative light on any problem, real or imagined. His ex, Judy, had liked to say that some saw the glass half-full, some saw it half empty, and Lewis — Lewis saw it full — of poison. He hoped that he could avoid that this time.

To proceed logically, he needed to understand better why *those* faces were outlined, and perhaps by *whom*. He knew that all of the marked people were, if not friends, at least close acquaintances. Chrissie had been Lewis' girlfriend and POOSSLQ; Terry and Lewis certainly knew each other both here and to a lesser extent, in Boston. Janey was Terry's sometimes-girlfriend, Doc's sometime-girlfriend, and an old friend of Lewis. It looked as if Lewis was the pivotal character in the group.

What else, if anything, did they all have in common? They weren't all from Boston, or even Massachusetts. They didn't all work together, and only Lewis and Chrissie lived together, although Janey and Chrissie had shared an apartment for a time. They all drank at the same bar, but so did half the Island. They all used drugs, but, again, so did half the Island. They were, as were so many other Freaks, roughly the same age. And, as far as Lewis could determine, that was the extent of their commonalities.

It was, finally, a poor instrument, this comparative exercise, for solving the mystery of the circled faces, as those faces not circled met as many benchmarks of likeness as did those who were marked-up. So, perhaps the circled faces didn't share something in the past — perhaps they would share something in the future. Or maybe it was a warning code that he had really better figure out: "these people are all going to die," or, "these people are all involved in what is happening to you right now — so watch out!" Most likely, it meant nothing at all. A scare-crow. A Red Herring.

The panic and paranoia were leaking into Lewis' thinking, again. If he let them get established, it wouldn't be too long before the questions to himself became less nebulous, became more like "what are these people going to do to me — and what can I do to them, first?"

Rather than crawl further out on this branch of inquiry, with all the attendant paranoia that led nowhere at all, and had, on the previous night, not even been interesting enough to keep him awake, he made a decision to take advantage of this day by going to the beach, which was, really, the reason he was here. Hell, he could be paranoid anywhere. He set the photocopied photo aside, and busied himself with making coffee, smoking cigarettes, showering, and taking his morning dose of all the drugs he supposed that he needed to get through the day.

Lewis was sad, sometimes, and sorry, that he had to take all the medications that he took. He took them for high blood-pressure, stomach problems, sinus problems, anxiety, arthritis, and a few other maladies. He was having some trouble keeping them all straight. Ten years ago, or maybe eleven years, he was happy and proud to say that, except for the odd aspirin, he never took drugs except for recreational purposes. Now, he thought he might be only weeks away from having to purchase one of those dreadful fucking pill organizers, the really huge blue or yellow plastic contraptions, just to ensure that he took the right amount of the right med at the right time. This could not be a good sign.

He didn't like taking all the meds, not one bit, he thought. But, he was a realist, and if this was the price he needed to pay to be out and about, to be functioning, to control, or at least to minimize the symptoms of all of these fucking maladies that had been visited upon him by some cranky deity, well, then that was the price he gladly paid. Because, the alternative could well be spending the last 10 or 20 or, if unlucky, even more years of his miserable waning life in a rocking chair on the porch, or by the wood stove, or "minimally restrained" in a plastic and metal chair, slick with urine, at the County Home.

So he took the pills, and learned to really enjoy some of them, especially the morning dose. It only took a few minutes, it wasn't really any trouble. Kind of a nice little ritual, almost religious in nature, and might get him a bit stoned, and afforded him hours of functionality.

Some things the pills didn't help at all, such as his depression. He tried all sorts of anti-depressants, until a clever shrink told him that his depression was appropriate, reality-based depression. So, Lewis figured it was just part of the package deal that featured his earlier successes, and ended with his fall from grace to his current status, that of a barely tolerated, captive Curmudgeon Emeritus, paid what amounted to a stipend, a pittance really, to grace the masthead of what was supposed to be an iconically hip periodical, and to contribute a pithy column, one granted great latitude, as long as the dinosaur submitted his work on time.

His writing, his readings and lectures, all of his tasks combined, didn't eat up all that much time: if he was "busy" twenty hours a week, it was a great exception. He knew, they all knew, that he had been put out to pasture. He was oddly, infinitely sad that he was not going to be one of those guys who died with his boots on. He would not be found two days dead, slumped, stiff now, over his Selectric — which he had never given up for a Mac, because he was just one of those guys: a Living Fucking Legend, now dead, of course. He wasn't a Legend of any sort. Lewis considered himself more of a footnote to a Legend.

These thoughts and others like them, all pretty goddamn depressing, really went through his brain and his mind at lightning-speed almost every morning, as he was having his coffee and his cigarettes and his pills, and then dismissed, with a scarily loud internal "Fuck That Shit!" so that he could finish his coffee and cigarettes and pills, and do something with the day other than killing himself, which was, of course, the only other reasonable course of action.

As Lewis was having this Morning Review of Horribly Depressing Thoughts, a bright and blessed ray of light came burning through his mental cloud-cover, and began to spread an unbelievably positive glow of optimism throughout his awareness. He was stunned at the level of stupidity he must have been wallowing in for the past week or more, to have missed this obvious, possibly achievable boondoggle: this whole paranoid adventure, from the earliest inklings of the Doc-wraith hunting him, Lewis, down to all of the possible and of course fictionalized back-stories that could have led to the current situation, why, the whole goddamn thing was a Best-Seller and The Film Adaptation to Follow that was writing itself right in front of him. If he could avoid the obvious Post-Modernista Posse's revenge, he could still make it to Living Legend-hood.

One of Lewis's favorite throw-away lines was "Depression is its own reward": now he could have the chance to make it a battle-cry. He now, more than ever, had to get the whole story straight, so that the hard work of writing the Best-Seller was already done.

Despite his strong and lingering fears that he was in real danger, somehow — that someone (or more) wanted to do him at least psychological harm, he was also feeling at least a degree of hope. What the hell, he had to play it out, he had no choice — and he really had to see what happened. If he didn't get himself killed, he would end up with a hell of a story. And it may not have been his doing — he may have been put in the spot he was in entirely through the machinations of others, success found at the end of a paranoid fantasy.

As the wool-gathering had proceeded from suicidal thoughts to visions of glory, Lewis had absentmindedly emptied his coffee cup down to the last chewy mouthful of grounds and soggy bits of yesterday's baguette. He spat it back into the cup, and walked to the sink to rinse the out cup. As he knew he couldn't survive long in clutter, he had used only one cup, one plate, one knife, and one spoon since arriving, all of which sat sparkling on the countertop. Room service would be a damn sight easier, but wasn't available, for some reason. There was beach service, but no room service.

Time was wasting, the sun was up, and beginning to shoot tendrils of stupefying heat trough gaps in the breaking cloud-cover. The beach called, luring a barely dressed, fully medicated and coffeed-up Lewis out the door while there was still some dew on the sparse grass and the painted surfaces of the fence that ran alongside the path he must take.

The heat built fast: faster than Lewis remembered from days past, faster than he liked. One of the major draws of the Caribbean for him was the minimal variance in temperature. Most of the time, 72 to 82 degrees Fahrenheit — but there were the odd days when the heat rose too far, too fast, and the afternoon showers failed to appear to cool things down. Today could be a day when the high end would be reached by midmorning, and then exceeded, and the beach would be half empty by one o'clock, only the fools and the exceedingly tough sun-freaks remaining. A good day to stay under the umbrella, Lewis thought — or maybe retire to the bar, put pen to paper, and begin to rough-out the incredible book that life was giving him.

He had to wonder — if he wrote the story as he found it, with some changes, of course — would the changes, the fictionalization — change the reality? He wasn't sure how it would really end for him — perhaps not well — but if he wrote the ending that he wanted, is that how it would then end in "real life"? Was there some Barthian bear-trap built in, some killing-pit that would discourage the fucking-with of reality by the Mad Author? Or, was it only a very risky literary device that would, finally, kill the book, but not the writer? He guessed he might find out.

He settled into his beach chair, set up with umbrella in his favorite spot, paid for with a ten-buck tip to the chair guy. His Composition Book and pen came out of his beach bag, and Lewis stared out at nothing in the Bay. Should he begin the outline with another look at his dream — or memory — prompted musings that suggested he had been a player in the evil that had taken over the Pot Deal Gone Wrong, so many years ago, or, more reasonably, simply outline the story? The protagonist had to be different enough — certainly better looking than Lewis — in this fiction…it had to be more than reportage, it had to have the whiff of terror, the slapstick stupidity, and the believable portrayal of people and places that make a story real for the reader.

Lewis had never written fiction, except for the required, and not very good short-stories back in school. He knew that he wasn't good at dialogue. Damn few were. He should abandon the idea right now, he thought, when the shadow of a huge creature fell across him, blotting out the sun and half of the Bay. He looked up. The creature wore a security guard uniform, almost certainly from the Club. He was a tall and solid black man, handsome, except for his eyes which bulged a bit, and were red and tan as if there was something basically very unhealthy going on in his body. The rest of him appeared good, strong and well.

"You are Melton, staying with us at the Club?" he carefully pronounced, in a voice that held echoes of half-a-dozen different accents, half-a-dozen places he had lived and worked.

"That's me — Lewis Melton. What is it?" Lewis didn't hide the annoyance in his voice — he didn't care for uniforms, and cared less for interruptions of his beach-time. He assumed he had a phone call from someone who wouldn't accept an unanswered phone, and didn't want to leave a message. Or maybe a wire, or another fax. Or — hell, he bet they wanted to move him to a different cottage — they had done that once, and he had been so infuriated he almost didn't go back there. The security guard was looking very much like he had more to say, so, Lewis tried to look interested.

"I have come to find you here on the advice of my boss, the Security Manager. He had received a telephone call from the Police Commander in the capitol. They just picked up a guy, a criminal, who is wanted other places, not here. When they searched him, they found a piece of paper folded in with his money. The paper had on it our name, your address here at the Club. He won't say why. The Commander thought, maybe Mr. Melton would know why…."

LEWIS

Lewis, dumbfounded, needed a few beats to come up with a response. It wasn't a very good one. "Well, what's this guy's name, what does he look like? I don't know who the hell it could be — lots of planes fly in and out of here every day!"

The security guard with the bulging and colorful eyeballs did not change his expression, and retained his looming stance. A stance that was probably helpful with thieves, perverts, and other assorted low-lifes who might wander onto the Club's turf with nefarious intent, but, as he would soon find out, not helpful in dealing with a respectable paying guest who, first, had a deep and ingrained distaste for anyone in uniform that most survivors of the Sixties had, and, second, who had a deep and broad reserve of fear, anger and paranoia that pretty generally governed his reaction to things he saw as a threat. Lewis let the large and looming security guard, who he knew was only a blameless intermediary, have both barrels.

"Listen, pal, if you're here just to let me know about this guy who was busted for something or other, and had my name and address on him, thanks — you may go, now.

If you're here to request that I help the Island police ID this guy, that's not my job. I'm here on vacation. But, if you can ask the Security Manager to ask the Police Commander to send over a photograph of this guy — and any name he may be using — I'm willing to do my part as a grateful visitor to your lovely island. You may still go, now. If one of your superiors would like to come back with photo I've requested, I plan to be right here, or nearby, for at least two hours. Now, if you'll excuse me, I'm on vacation."

Growling a polite and indistinct, and, Lewis hoped, insubordinate "Yes, Sir...." the very big man backed away a few feet, then turned, and walked away at a faster clip. Now, thought Lewis, now I can finally get some sun, uninterrupted, and feel the heat permeate my ancient goddamn bones.

He manipulated the lounge chair to the flattest of positions, completing the task without the usual crushing of the odd finger, or the pinching, often bloody, of skin on his hands. He could now roll over onto his increasingly obvious belly and work on tanning his back, and the back of his legs. He often — because he tended to sit or lay face-up — ended his vacation with a two-tone tan. Resting his head on his right arm, he segued from disconnected thoughts to a fully relaxed beach sleep.

When he awakened, roughly an hour later, about one o'clock by his almost un-readable wristwatch, he heard the sound of a petty bureaucrat nervously, quietly, clearing his throat, an awful prompt to pull him all the way up to consciousness.

Lewis looked up, sideways, from his fully reclined state. The sleep or the heat, or the spirit of the beach, perhaps, had given him an erection of sorts, so, he couldn't really roll over. What he could see, from his skewed perspective, was a fully-attired (*sans* jacket and necktie) minor governmental hack: a bureaucrat on the beach, sweating profusely, clutching a briefcase. He kept his eyes on Lewis's head, as if it were the prize pumpkin at the County Fair.

Ambushed by a fleeting attack of empathy, Lewis inquired as to whether he might be of assistance in some way. The immediate look of almost fawning gratitude on the face of the overdressed government (police, perhaps?) official almost made Lewis regret his moment of empathy…he could easily have put it off for a bit. But, he had done it, and now he must follow through.

The fawning functionary spoke: Lewis was enthralled with the little man's ability to retain the overtones of obsequious servility, while pumping up the undertones of inherent threat from the Police, a word he seemed to never use.

"Oh, Mr. Melton, we at the Central Office are so pleased with your generous offer to help us out, perhaps to help us establish who, exactly, this colorful, cranky, no longer young man, who we are keeping with us, is…we need to know his real name, of course, before he may be extradited, if, in fact, anyone actually wants him. His fingerprints, you see, rang some bells in the States, and that is where we think he's from, anyway. But his passport doesn't jibe at all with the info they have on him — in the States, that is — so, we don't really know who he is."

The man from the Police reached into his attaché case, and extracted a manila envelope, from which he slid out two photos. He handed them both to Lewis. "The top picture was just taken this morning, and the other is his passport photo. As you can see, they don't look exactly the same. Our hope is that you'll be willing to come to our offices, take a look at this man — through one-way glass, of course — and put a name to him. Because, Mr. Melton, he did have your name and address with him — so we have to guess that he knew you. Do you know him?"

Lewis didn't need more than a fraction of a second to determine, without any doubt, that the man in the photos was Billy. He had known Billy, on and off, many years ago — on the Island, and maybe in Boston or Cambridge. His expression didn't change as he continued to study the pictures. After about twenty seconds, he allowed his face to reflect puzzlement. He turned to face the man who had brought him the pictures.

"I don't know, for sure.…the passport photo looks kind of familiar — the other one, not so much. I sure don't have a name for you, I'm afraid. The guy looks sort of like a lot of people I've known over the years, but not *exactly* like any of them. I'm sorry. What did you say his name is?"

The smaller man, the police investigator, looked pained, as if he had a toothache making itself known. He forced a smile, and responded.

"His name on the Passport is William Lancaster. He says his name is Billy, and, he says that he knows you quite well, Mr. Melton, and that you know him but would never say so, at least until you know more. He says he is here to give you a message, which he will not tell us."

Lewis wasn't surprised to hear that Billy was acting like Billy. Still, he had to see the prisoner himself, privately, if possible. He didn't know what Billy had to tell him, but was pretty certain that Billy — unless he had hit the lottery, or gotten hitched to one of the horse-faced heiresses who lurked about on the Island — would never have enough money at one time to afford a plane ticket anywhere. He had made very good wages when Lewis had known him, and was borrowing money 3 days after payday each week. So, Lewis reasoned, someone else had arranged for Billy to come down here: the only question was, was it a friend, or an enemy? As the so-far imagined plot unfolded, where did Billy fit?

"I'll tell you what, Inspector, or whatever your title may be, I'll come by the Police Station, or wherever you have this man, and see him in person — but I'd like to do it so that he doesn't see me, at least initially. Is this something that could happen late this afternoon? I'm engaged otherwise until then (like lying here in the sun, he thought)."

"Perhaps, Mr. Melton, we can send a car by at four o'clock, if that's convenient? We'll set up the viewing room with one-way glass. Then, after you've made your identification — or confirmed otherwise — we will drive you right back here to your hotel. Will that suit you?"

As he couldn't find anything to object to in the offered plan, Lewis acquiesced, and bade the little man good day, after promising more than once to be waiting in the lobby of the club at four that afternoon.

Lewis was starting to feel exceptionally hungry, and figured that it must be at least lunchtime. He wasn't a big eater, generally, despite his growing girth suggesting otherwise, but salt-air, whether in Maine or the Caribbean or the Elizabeth Islands, seemed to set off his hunger. He had sufficient motivation to leave the comfort of his chair and walk the fifty hot-sand paces to the Club's restaurant. He ordered a ham and gruyere sandwich on a roll, with spicy mustard to offset the bland cheese. It was an excellent choice, and even better washed down with a cool bottle of local beer.

He looked around the place as he slowly consumed his lunch — the crowd was pretty thin, with only a third of the tables occupied. It was not yet noon, and maybe a bit early for lunch for most folks. The only diners Lewis recognized were the couple who had witnessed his meltdown the other day, the ones who had diagnosed it as a seizure. Despite his looking directly at them, they didn't meet his gaze, but kept their eyes down, and whispered to each other. Lewis was delighted to see that they both had nasty sunburn — almost ER-level — and seemed, as a bonus, to be horribly hung over. They were treating that malady with Bloody Marys, which would not make the hangovers go away, but would launch them both into a whole new drunk.

The soon-to-be-drunk-again couple might not be watching him, but Lewis would bet dollars to doughnuts that *someone, or more than one someone*, was watching him. Doc, and/or his allies, and/or someone else had already gone to lots of trouble and expense to track his whereabouts, trash his car, invade his home, invade his ex-wife's home, and various other actions, ploys, and plots…they were unlikely to let him wander freely, unobserved, now. This was no longer just one of his paranoid fantasies. But, what did they want, and why?

As he finished up his lunch, gnawed at the pickle that was supposed to be a Kosher Dill, but was not, and sucked down the dregs of his flat, piss-warm beer, his mind went off on a new excursion, another trip back to the Pot Deal Gone Very Wrong. He had been flaying his ancient memory for details, details, details — for everything he could recall about the deal, before, during, and after…except that he kept drawing a blank on the week before the transaction. He was pretty sure that he, and probably Doc, had set up the buy, but recalled none of it. He had no memory of who the seller was, and that is not something one forgets about a deal of that magnitude. And he was missing a week or ten days… perhaps just a temporary fog, part of the Old Guy Package.

At least the fog wasn't current: it didn't interfere with his paying the check for lunch, or with his finding the way back to his chair on the scorching beach. He didn't get lost, or sidetracked. He didn't exchange words with anyone at all during the walk to his chair, or when, just after two o'clock, he left his spot, and cruised back to his cottage for a shower and a brief nap, and then at four, on to the lobby, to meet whatever vague pensioner the police would send to drive him to Headquarters to (not) identify the prisoner.

Lewis Melton was not an introspective man, not given to navel-gazing, not prone to self-examination of any sort, beyond the most superficial. But, he knew with absolute certainty all of the truly important things about himself, the foremost being that he was anxious, capital-A, and all of the time.

He had always been anxious, and occasionally fearful, but not generally for very long. He could, and did, deal with these personality defects every day, sometimes every hour, and knew, pretty well, how to treat his fear, and how to keep the awful anxiety under control. The anxiety and sometimes the fear were as much a part of him as his nose, or his left-handedness, or his annoyingly proper manner of speaking. Therefore, when he awakened briefly from his nap on the very comfortable but slightly-too-short Love Seat on the screened porch of his cottage, he felt the absence of his anxiety as dramatically as he'd noticed, once, the absence of his trousers and his boxers upon awakening in a snow bank without them. Feeling the absence of his anxiety freaked him out completely, and as he was casting wildly about for something to feel, he grabbed some serious depression (it was the closest) and slipped it right on like a favorite, if smelly, wool sweater. He felt so much better, although horribly depressed, that he moved from the too-short Love Seat to his bed, and fell immediately asleep, and slept until the Desk rang his room to tell him that his driver was on his way to pick Mr. Melton up, and Mr. Melton might wish to come down to the lobby fairly soon. As he listened to the caller, and grunted his agreement, he noticed that his anxiety was coming back, stronger than ever, and the depression had all but evaporated. And he felt like a new old man.

The call from the Desk had come fifteen minutes later than it should have, in true island fashion. Lewis had never been able to adopt "Island Time" into his actual practice, and had, therefore, to rush through his ablutions, and to be late in his arrival at the lobby. The driver that the police had sent was even later, arriving, finally at almost four-thirty, to find an impatient man pacing, smoking, and sweating heavily.

The Driver was an older, overweight, and tired-looking man with a very strong accent, probably German, possibly Dutch. Despite his somewhat foreboding look, he turned out to be a cheerful, garrulous comedian, who regaled Lewis with stories of his days as a cop in Holland, his retirement at 50, and his move to the Caribbean after his wife, who simply couldn't tolerate him being at home all day, every day, left him. He had joined the local police on the French side of the island, so that he wouldn't compromise his pension by joining the Dutch force. The downside, he said, was that the French hated him, and gave him progressively less responsible jobs. He said, "I'm only 67 now….if I live to be 70, and I'm still working for those bastards, they'll take away my gun, and have me cleaning the shitters!" He laughed loud and long at his own hopeless humor.

The Driver, whose business card identified him as Special Officer Augustus Erhard, may have actually been 67, but drove as if he was 87. If he exceeded 30 kph, it was by mistake. As he was in a marked police car, a growing line of traffic dawdled along behind him, fuming silently. They couldn't even sound their horns!

Their arrival at headquarters was in no way remarkable. Special Officer Erhard parked behind the station, so, when the two men stepped out of the air-conditioned cruiser, it was into the stifling trapped heat of a concrete courtyard. They were drenched with sweat by the time they stepped through the door and into the very cold headquarters building, whereupon the sweat began to freeze. Lewis had no idea how to convert Fahrenheit to Celsius, but pegged the temp at "really fucking cold" when he complained to his driver/ minder, who laughed about it. He seemed to laugh a lot, maybe too much. Perhaps, thought Lewis, he is senile, or deranged. Not that it would matter.

Erhard led them to a lift, the door of which had to be unlocked with a key. They stepped in, buttons were pressed, and within a few seconds, they were stepping out into a wide hallway with beige walls and an industrial-level dirty-elephant-gray carpet. Signs said that they were on the 7th floor. The doors that lined both sides of the hallway were painted a low-gloss industrial-gray enamel: there seemed to be one every 10 or 12 feet. The doors were numbered, but otherwise devoid of signage. Erhard stopped short at door number 9, rapped on the door with three short, sharp knocks, and ushered his "captive" in. There stood the little bureaucrat from the beach, smiling almost imperceptibly. Lewis turned to say good-bye to his amusing driver, but Erhard was gone. He turned back to the bureaucrat, who seemed more comfortable — and more powerful — in his element, and not surrounded by thousands of naked hedonists. He spoke, authoritatively.

"Mr. Melton, glad you made it. You may take a seat, right in that chair, facing the viewing window. We'll bring the prisoner in question out in just a moment. I'll be sitting next to you. Remember, the prisoner can't see us, it's a one-way mirror."

Lewis tried to appear marginally reassured, although, in fact, he hadn't been concerned. He didn't give a rat's ass who saw him if it would in any way help him figure out exactly what the hell was going on, in and around his life.

The bureaucrat, whose name Lewis didn't know, sat next to him, and spoke casually into his lapel.

"Bring the prisoner out, please."

A uniformed younger cop led another man, dressed, apparently, in street clothes — ancient-looking Levi's and a black T-shirt with some indecipherable script trailing across the back — to the center of a small stage, where he turned the prisoner so that he faced the one-way mirror. Lewis knew instantly that the Billy in question was the Billy he knew. He couldn't remember Billy's last name, but knew, without a doubt, that it wasn't the one that Billy had given the cops.

"Take your time, Mr. Melton — actually, it's Dr. Melton, isn't it — or do you prefer Professor? Either way, we'd rather be correct than hasty, after all the trouble you've taken to come down and assist us..." the bureaucrat cautioned. He sounded, to Lewis, more threatening than cautioning. And, he was, inwardly, dismissing the advice. He gave it another 90 seconds. Then, he announced in his most absolutely sincere and truthful voice, just barely tinged with regret, his findings.

"I can tell you, Sir, with no reservations, that I have never seen this man before. I do not recognize him."

The bureaucrat looked disappointed, but not surprised.

"Well, Dr. Melton, I can tell you, I am very disappointed. But not shocked, not shocked. I do thank you for taking the time. I'll send for your driver."

"Excuse me," Lewis interjected, "do you think it would make any sense to have me meet with this person anyway? He may have some valuable information that he'll tell me, but not you, if he thinks that he knows me. And, as much as I hate to admit it, he may well have met me, although I don't recall him. In some circles — mostly academic — I have something of a 'name' — consequently, people who I barely know are often introducing me to people who I don't know, and don't ever plan to know."

The bureaucrat — what the hell was this guy's name? — put on his poker face just a millisecond too late: Lewis had seen, just a flash, just the merest fleeting flash, of confusion and suspicion passing over his normally noncommittal mask.

Lewis could have been more careful — it was pretty certain that a big part of this guy's job was "reading" people — looking for out-of-character behaviors, flimsy rationales, all the indicators of prevarication, because, after all, who told cops the truth? He was feeling exposed, so, did an illegal U-turn.

"Nah — never mind — crazy idea. Besides, I don't really have the time. I'll bet you a dollar to a donut that he really doesn't have anything to tell me. Let's just forget it!"

The bureaucrat, of course, instantly recognized what Lewis was doing, and did the same.

"I do not know — I think maybe there would be potential gain for us.... if you are still even willing, I think you must go speak to him, we might even get his real name, which would be a start. Otherwise, we will probably have to let him go....we can't keep him forever just because other departments may want him. So, will you go in, see what he will say?"

"Fine! Okay! I'm sorry; I seem to have forgotten your name, Mr. ..."

"Inspector Eduard Pelletier, but I don't think I told you that before. Forgive my manners. It has been a singularly frustrating day."

"Thanks — I'm happy to assist, if I can, Inspector...how do you want to play it? Or, have I watched too many cop shows on TV?"

Lewis looked completely relaxed, and lit a cigarette, as he could neither go another five minutes without one, nor could he make sense of the well-used ashtray on a counter directly below a 'No Smoking' sign.

"Perhaps you have, Mr. Melton — or Dr. Melton, I suppose — but so don't we all. I wish the real thing were more like the TV shows, some days. But, forget that, for now. Why don't you simply walk in there, say hello, and see if he recognizes you — we know already that you don't recognize him, yes? — and ask him what it is that he must tell you that caused him to fly all the way down here from New York City?"

Lewis wondered if it would be better to continue this absurd dialogue, as the willing target of yet more ill-disguised snide comments, or just go see what the fuck it was that Billy wanted, relying on Bill's good street-sense to assume the room was wired for sound and picture, and to keep mum about anything true or important. The choice was obvious, so, he headed toward what looked like the correct door. He dropped his walk-away line over his left shoulder.

"I'm going in. I'm certain you'll be able to hear us clearly. If he jumps me, I hope you'll get some help in there, quickly."

"Of course, Dr. Melton. We would get you help. We may actually need you again, some day."

Lewis spent another several-dozen seconds examining the man in the glass cage. It must certainly be Billy, the exact Billy he knew, and the Billy who had called him, drunk, late at night. He began the long walk to the door that would let him into the past, but might not let Billy out of it. The problem that Lewis had with the past, he knew for sure, was that it just wouldn't stay where it belonged.

He grasped the doorknob and turned it clockwise. Nothing happened. Maybe it was a French doorknob. He turned it counter-clockwise. Nothing. He heard a loud buzz — at first, he thought he *felt* a loud buzz, thought that, somehow, he was being electrocuted by the doorknob — and the door opened. He stepped through. Billy was facing away from him, staring intently at the door on the other side of the cage. He seemed to think the buzzing sound had come from there, and had no idea that Lewis had entered the room. That, thought Lewis, is pretty much what forty years of smoking pot all day does to you. This could be touchy.

When he was eight feet away from Billy, Lewis spoke, but not too loudly.

"Who the hell are you, and why are you telling the cops you need to speak to me? You don't even know who I am, do you?"

He had to hope that Billy had sufficient brain cells left to pick up the prompts, so blatantly obvious that he presumed the police would ignore them, and prayed that Billy wouldn't ignore them. And, he had laid the "Boston Accent" on so thick that it almost rendered the two sentences incomprehensible to anyone, let alone a Frenchman who only spoke English when it was absolutely necessary.

Billy turned around very slowly, and looked at Lewis, first blankly, and then uncomprehendingly. He said nothing.

Lewis thought: this is going pretty good, so far — now, if neither of them blew it, he might find something out. He again addressed Billy, who was either doing a hell of a good acting job, or had finally tripped one time too many.

"Look, Pal, the cops here on the island came to me, and told me that you — and they say that you report your name as Billy — that you told them that you're only here to see me, to give me a message. But you don't even know who the hell I am, do you? 'Cause, I sure as hell don't recognize you!"

Billy picked up on the riff as if he had devised it himself.

"You're half-right, man....I sure don't know you, and you don't look at all like the pictures they showed me of 'you' — the people who sent me here wanted me to be *sure* that if was you. But it isn't you, so, I can't tell you anything at all. Therefore, Fuck Off!!!"

Lewis watched Billy's face — it was at odds with his speech. He was winking so violently and frequently that, if he hadn't stopped from time to time to make other gestures and bizarre twitches of his facial muscles to indicate that he was playing the Game, Lewis might have presumed that the man suffered from some dreadful neurological disorder.

Billy paused, from time to time, to lay his right forefinger alongside his lumpy, previously broken nose — apparently some signal that he thought Lewis would recognize. Lewis had to give the man credit — Billy could act! But, could he act skillfully enough to fool the cops, who were, without a doubt, observing them both most closely through closed-circuit television, and listening and recording each word, grunt and squeak with the microphones hidden throughout the room? And now, how to reciprocate, more subtly, how to send the message: Got it! Let's find a time, a way, and a place to talk....

The charade had to end soon, in a way that would wipe away any suspicion of collaboration, something that would change the atmosphere from suspicion to...anything, anything at all. Lewis looked at Billy, just a hint of question in his eyes. Billy made some incomprehensible signal, his forefingers, flat on his face, pointing up at his eyes, then, instantly launched himself from his chair onto Lewis, shrieking like a demented, rabid baboon — and knocked Lewis to the floor, Lewis shrieking now, too: he could get into this, whatever it was. When he felt a hand in his pocket, he thought, wow, this is an odd time for Billy to rob me...but Billy wasn't removing anything, he was leaving something, pushing something into the pocket.

Forty or fifty more seconds passed before they heard the doors slam open, heard the tattoo of boots running across the floor, then the softer percussions of batons on Billy's head, back, legs, arms, and they were dragging Billy off of Lewis, re-cuffing him, and shackling his feet. Lewis rolled over and raised his head to look around just in time to see Billy being hustled out the door by six burly cops — and off to the side, the little bureaucrat observing, wringing his hands, worried, advancing, now, on Lewis.

"Mr. Melton, we are so sorry. We had no suspicion that this man would become violent....you perhaps should not have insisted on speaking to him, I fear. I see that you are unhurt, thank Heaven. We will drive you back to your hotel."

Lewis acted upset, affronted, possibly injured. He held the back of his neck with his right hand, massaging it gently, turning his head, gingerly, and just half an inch at a time. He spoke, without looking directly at the Inspector.

"Okay, my own fucking fault, I suppose I just hope my neck isn't all screwed up again. I'll take that ride, as soon as possible."

The Inspector, now looking only vaguely worried, told his lapel to find a car and a driver immediately, as Mr. Melton must be driven back to his lodgings. Lewis was up, now, walking toward the door — the correct one, he hoped — and left the Inspector the job of catching up to him, stopping him, whatever he might do.

As he got closer to the door, Lewis half-turned to the Inspector, who did not appear to have moved. Putting one of his amusedly sincere voices on, he took a chance and posed a question that could either tip the police to some apparent double-dealing — and they truly hated that, unless they were the ones initiating it — or convince them that Lewis was even crazier than they had suspected.

"After you folks quiet that character down a bit, what do you plan to do with him? From what you told me earlier, you don't really want him — and I doubt that you'll want to feed him, and put up with his shenanigans, until whoever really wants him gets around to all of the extradition paperwork, if they do it at all. And then, they need to get around to coming down picking him up. You could be looking at months."

The little cop laughed. He had a particularly annoying laugh, thought Lewis.

"We've already done all we plan to do with him — you may see him outside, limping away. He'll find a way to get off our island now, you can bet.

But we most assuredly don't want him here, you are correct. If we have to, we'll put him on a plane ourselves."

"Clever…" said Lewis, meaning Billy, although the Inspector smiled at the confusing compliment he thought he had been given. Lewis followed his nose back out, the way he had come in, and was just stepping into the balmy air when his driver rounded the corner and screeched to a halt at the curb. Lewis slowly walked to the driver's window, and waited while he rolled it open.

"You know, I think I'll walk, at least into town. I could use a cold beer, and a sandwich. Thanks anyway."

The driver — not the grizzled old bastard he'd had earlier, but a younger man, whose expression hinted at his belief that the task was beneath him, anyway, and now….an insult (!) too (!)…said, "Okay, Sir" — and, with enormous control surrounding him like an aura, slowly drove away, back behind the headquarters building.

Lewis had walked for only a few minutes, fewer than five, and was only broaching the outskirts of the horribly touristy territory when a surprisingly un-bloodied and unbowed Billy fell perfectly into step — they both limped — beside him. Lewis had to ask, "So, how the hell did you manage to get yourself arrested so quickly? I want to ask, 'Why', too, but I am forced to assume that you really did want to speak to me, and you chose the fastest, easiest way to find me and to guarantee that I'd actually show up."

Billy grinned a snaggle-toothed grin at Lewis, and then dissembled, genuinely.

"Hey, Lew, long-time, no-see! And you, you're as friendly as ever! The answers are, in order: no fucking idea; don't know — it's a gift; and yes, and you should thank whatever morose god you honor that I do want to speak to you. Let's get some beers, and talk."

"Billy, if we stop now for a beer, we'll be busted in minutes. I'm too old to get busted…as are you, if you'd admit it. We need to find a private place, somewhere where we'll blend in. Meet me at 'Lucky's': it's a little hole-in-the-wall casino about ten minutes down this street. Let me go first — I'll be playing two slot machines, and stop playing one when you show up. You grab that one. We're just a couple of low-stakes Slot Zombies, talking to themselves…A sad and common sight, I'm afraid — happens all the time."

Billy gave Lewis an admiring look.

"Not bad…not bad at all! I'll need some money, to feed the slots. I'm almost broke. You got a C-note?"

"Sure…here…" responded Lewis, knowing that neither was Billy almost broke, nor did he need one hundred dollars to play a quarter slot machine for ten minutes. He peeled five twenties from the folded sheaf in his money clip, and put them in Billy's hand. In one smooth motion, the money disappeared from sight, from Lewis' fingers to Billy's palm, from Billy's palm to the right hip pocket of his Levi's.

Billy had looked quite respectable a few hours ago: clean, intact jeans, a newer sea-green and Navy blue, horizontally-striped, short-sleeved polo shirt, and worn, but not worn-out, boat shoes. His face, though, was starting to swell alarmingly from the nightsticks that had connected with it, and soon he would look very much like a middle-aged man who had recently been thoroughly beaten. A dark casino was going to be the best place for him, and a hundred dollars, if used wisely, would keep him there, free drinks and all, for several hours. After that, as far as Lewis was concerned, Billy would need to rely on his wits and the return-trip ticket he most certainly had, to get the hell out of town.

Within a few minutes, Lewis was happily planted on a seat with vacant seats on each side, a quarter-bet slot machine in front of him, and a tub of quarters in his lap. He fed the machine coins and yanked the handle in a placid, relaxed rhythm, and was shortly hypnotized, oblivious to all except the machine, the movements and sounds it produced, and the warm glow of perfect relaxation that suffused his brain and body.

He was startled by a sharp pain in his right ankle — then again, and again. He pulled himself back to reality, and saw Billy, sitting to his right, industriously kicking Lewis' right ankle, not at all gently, while looking straight ahead at his machine, and feeding quarters to the beast even faster than Lewis had been. His face and head were really quite swollen by now, but he could still talk out of the corner of his mouth, and proceeded to do just that.

"So, you stupid motherfucker, I don't know what you did to get this unholy mess stirred up again, but a lot of the people who got taken in that massive rip-off all those years ago...they're pretty convinced, now, that it was you and Doc — or maybe you *or* Doc — who were the assholes behind it all. A lot of what's going on is unclear, at least to me.

"What is definitely NOT unclear is that some of those people — who, by the way, are no longer stupid, overly trusting freshmen from Oconomawok, Wisconsin — some of them who have money now, and power — they think that some payback is due. They started to think this some years ago, but had some trouble finding Doc. You were too easy to find, after you came back from the Island. If you'd had any sense, you would have stayed on the Island. But of course, you didn't. Doc was much harder to find, and every time they'd get a line on him, *poof*, he was invisible again. But now, they know where you both are. If they needed any more proof of guilt, you guys provided it by showing up in the same place, at the same time.

"So, the very bottom line is, they want to be paid back. With interest. Suppose they only want five percent — a year. You can do the math. And they really think you idiots can pay them, somehow, but they've gotten themselves sufficiently worked up about his that they might even settle for the old pound of flesh — although I suppose it would be a pound of *old* flesh, har-har. Even if none of that happens, because, as we know, very few people have the ambition to go after old, nebulous, illegal debts, they could still make your lives even shittier than they might be. They think that there was very likely a murder involved. They have no details, as far as I know, but that doesn't guarantee that they won't do something with it — like drop it on the Suffolk County D.A.'s office."

Lewis listened, took it all in, and when he had, nothing remained except questions. He figured he'd start with the big one.

"Why did you call me from the Coast in the middle of the night — when was it, last week? — and why did you come all the way down here to tell me this? We were buddies, I guess, back on the Island…but not that close."

Billy kept pulling the lever on his slot machine as he spoke. He seemed to be winning pretty consistently, but paid no overt attention to the periodic vomiting of quarters into the coin tray in front of him. His attention was focused on his speech, which seemed, to Lewis, to be tightly controlled, to be practiced, and memorized. Billy's monotone rendition belied the desperate pain in his eyes.

"The ex's house I called you from? That was Chrissie's house. You must remember Chrissie…you abandoned her in Boston, just when she really needed you. She almost died, but only ended up in the State Hospital for a year or so — but you wouldn't know that, 'cause you never checked on her. She didn't forget about you, though….she made me call you, and she made me come down here to fill you in on the real level of danger you could be facing.

"She wouldn't call you; she believes that you hate her, still. She loves you. I love her. She dumped me because I started using again after years of being clean. You dumped her because you're an asshole who couldn't be bothered to help the woman you said you loved. And now, Chrissie's been clean and sober forever, I guess. And I'm shit, because I relapsed.

"Oh, and one other thing: do you know how surprised everyone was to find Doc alive? They were surprised because, word was, you killed him, so you could get all the money from the ripoff…so, you and Doc should have an interesting conversation. *Shit*! I was up better than four-hundred bucks, and gave it all back! Fucking slot machines…"

Billy turned to say one more thing to Lewis, after sixty or eighty seconds had passed. He wasn't above enjoying the effect that the Soap Opera called "life" had on people, himself included, to be fair. Now, he guessed that he had delivered his lines pretty well — Lewis' stool was occupied only by the air that had rushed in to take his place.

1965 – Back to Boston

The ferry wallowed into the proper slip at the terminal just after ten in the morning. Lewis had managed to suck down a six-pack of ale on the trip, so with Chrissie behind the wheel, they drove off the boat and through the small town as quickly as traffic would allow, anxious to get to the State highway that would take them to Boston. By unspoken agreement, they did not stop until they were well into the suburban hell that stretched south from Boston, almost one third of the way to Cape Cod. By then, they both had to pee so desperately that there was no choice but to stop at the first place that looked promising, and would not require venturing off the main highway — Route 3, now, soon to feed into Route 93.

It was through the small parking lot of an orange-roofed chain restaurant that they walked with the stiff-legged, pain-in-the-side, please let me last just another ninety seconds, God, walk that is more fun to watch others do, than to do one's self. They made it to their respective Rest Rooms without further embarrassment, and, after pissing almost to orgasm, settled in to a booth with orange pleather bench seats, and a beige plastic table that seemed forever imbued with the smells of fried clams, tartar sauce, cheeseburgers, and CocaCola. The table was still a bit sticky from the family that had just vacated the spot. All of this seemed right, and natural, and comforting, especially with an emptied bladder. The food smells were enticing; the day was full of the promise of good things. When the middle-aged but gray-haired waitress arrived, Chrissie smiled and joked with her, and dazzled her with her cutest smile.

They ordered without looking at the menu, as they had both grown up with the restaurant chain, and knew exactly what to expect — which would be exactly the same at any of the orange-roofed eateries from Hartford to Bangor. Chrissie had a BLT, toasted white bread, please, and Lewis had two cheeseburgers, rare, and two cups of famously average coffee, loaded up with cream and sugar to mask the absence of flavor. He couldn't convince Chrissie to have the coffee. She had a large fountain Coke, the kind that either hasn't enough syrup, or way too much. Hers had not enough, but killed her thirst admirably. She joked that she didn't need coffee, as she, of course, hadn't gotten drunk on the boat. She was a little too perky for Lewis, and had to ask him why he had started to look so glum. He said he was feeling a little sad, maybe, but wasn't sure why.

"I guess the air just doesn't feel right. Or maybe it doesn't smell right. Ever since we left the boat, incrementally, the car has been losing the strong, cold sea-smell that I've been breathing since I hit the Island. I guess I'm just really sorry to leave there, even though I know I have to — and, in lots of ways, I'm glad to leave. But, still sad."

Chrissie smiled, too fondly perhaps, across the sticky table. Sort of the way she might smile at a child who had said something ridiculous, but cute. She didn't stop there.

"Oh, honey, were probably less than five miles from the ocean right now....and Boston is right on the ocean, as you know, better than I. Have you considered that maybe it's pretty much a head-trip, just due to such an enormous change?"

Lewis fought the rising tide of resentment toward Chrissie that he could feel welling, expanding, in his gut. He couldn't allow it to grow stronger, to burst out in the evil, hurtful words that one must not say to one's girlfriend, or, really, to anyone at all…because that would be the end of that relationship: they would not be words that could be called-back or explained away.

He knew, he understood that this trip was neither her fault nor her idea… it was his stupid fucking idea, just one more echo of the lame expectations secretly implanted in is brain by the aliens, who may or may not have been his parents. So, of *course* he would leave a place and a life that he loved and, strangely, was good at — so. that he could go to Boston — likely not a safe place for him just yet — to finish school, to score his Master's and probably then his Doctorate, so that he would be equipped to do that which he did not want, but would need to do, if only to pay the debt accumulated in the pursuit, So, of *course* he was homicidally furious, realizing yet again that the Catch-22s of the Heroically Lame Lifestyle were many, varied, and inescapable. So, he shut his mouth so firmly that all of his teeth hurt, and backed off, mentally, to the best of his ability.

"You're probably right," Lewis stated, "it's just the change. I hate change. And the smell — I know this may sound insane, but the smell not being the same, it's really getting to me. Let's just eat, and get to the new apartment, I want to be settled in to the new place before midnight — or at least arrange something to sleep on other than the floor. I want this change to be done, to be over, so we can start to get used to it. If we don't do that very soon, I'm very likely to start trying to talk you into driving back to the coast in time to catch the last boat. I'll bet our place hasn't been rented out yet."

Chrissie looked at him closely — nothing in his eyes indicated that he was kidding (although, she admitted to herself, she couldn't ever really tell if he was serious), so she looked around for their waitress hoping that their order would arrive soon. It was possible that without food, they would be driving south again this afternoon.

The Female Gods won this round, demonstrating their power with the almost immediate arrival of their orders. They both ate ravenously, and Chrissie could see Lewis' attitude change, brighten, and calm down. He took the wheel now to pilot them to, and into, Boston, a sport best left to the experts. He picked his way through a baffling hodgepodge of one-way streets, alleys, avenues, and rotaries, ending up on Commonwealth Avenue. He hung a seemingly random right between two bars, then after two blocks, another right into an alley, at no time dropping his speed below 35 miles an hour, despite the load on the car's roof yawing more perceptibly with each turn, as the ropes stretched incrementally longer with each tug of the weight they had been asked to hold in place. The alley was a marvel of dumpsters, trash cans, rotting mattresses, possibly abandoned cars, and wooden back porches attached, somehow, to the backs of the brick and stone apartment buildings. Most of them looked as if they might give up and let go of the buildings at any time, although they almost never did.

Each building had at least one basement door, while some had two: they were all, roughly, the same color, which would be no color in particular, just the faded remains of the last paint job, ending up a nondescript, dirty "mouse gray." Chrissie was about to ask Lewis how the hell they would ever identify theirs, when he jerked the over-laden sedan to a shuddering halt at one unidentified door, threw himself out of the car, and, gesturing toward the door with an outstretched arm, announced, "This is it — I think. Let's go look! I'll bet it's a tiny, cramped little dump…and, we'll love it, 'because the price is right'!"

They found the "Super," who preferred to be known as the Property Manager, in his dark and spacious basement warren. Lewis had brought a brown paper bag in from the car: he pulled out a six-pack of Schaefer beer, and presented it to the Super, verbalizing his hopes that it would be alright. The Super protested the gift, briefly, while swearing that it was his favorite beer — truthfully, as they all were his favorites.

He led them up the two flights of stairs — three, counting the basement stairs — to their apartment, so freshly painted that the smell of cheap white latex hit them in the face yards from the door. They loved the smell, and loved what they saw when the door was opened to disclose, in exceptionally bright and pure white, a single bedroom, a living room/kitchenette with a tiny under-counter fridge that seemed to work, and completely insufficient cabinet and counter space. And, finally, a spacious bathroom with an old claw-foot tub, and black and white ceramic tile, on the floor, and three feet up each wall.

They loved it, on sight, as they knew they would, and they moved their possessions in from the car immediately. Seeing just how little they had, upon moving it in, they drove Chrissie's car to a store on Commonwealth Avenue — not the good end — and bought a decent futon, no frame, a cheap bookcase made from the lowest grade pine, with a masonite back stapled on, and an equally cheesy bureau that needed to be assembled. Lewis did this, but with glue and screws, not the brads supplied, hoping for a better outcome.

Within a week or two, both of them were immersed in their new and separate projects: Lewis back in school, crafting his plan for the dreaded thesis, Chrissie taking three courses, after negotiating transfer requirements for a BA program — and working in a boutique just outside of Harvard Square in her "spare time." She rarely saw Lewis, he rarely saw her, and neither of them recognized the growing problems until they had gotten too far along for much of anything to be done.

As close as Lewis could come to understanding the genesis and growth of the problem — and he wasn't very motivated to understand it, he was far too angry to care about the whys and the wherefores — was this: Chrissie got lonely, bouncing back and forth between school and work, work and school, rarely seeing Lewis awake except when he was buried in reading and writing that must be done, drinking coffee and chain-smoking cigarettes, not really having the time to spend, he thought, talking to Chrissie, or taking her out for a beer or six, or anything else…and on those rare occasions when he did have time, she did not.

Chrissie found a friend at work, at the boutique — Donna, a painfully thin, startlingly beautiful, scarily crazy speed-freak. They'd go out for a drink, and maybe to hear some music, after the store closed. Chrissie would be tired, exhausted, but initially, she turned down the meth crystal Donna offered. She finally gave in one night, and found it easier to give in every night thereafter. She snorted it, at first: the buzz was even better than she remembered, and she felt happy, and in control, and it was easy to rationalize doing a little meth. Hell, she was going to school, and working, too, all for Lewis, the bastard, who paid no attention to her now. She had to have some fun. And the extra pound or two that seemed to have attached itself to her hips was disappearing, not a bad thing at all.

Chrissie wasn't sleeping much, and was getting pretty tense, but nothing a few glasses of wine wouldn't cure. It wasn't until a month after she began shooting the meth — she was buying it, now, and couldn't afford wasting the buzz by snorting it, plus, the rush she got from shooting it was better than sex, and she wasn't getting much sex these days — that she began to notice the bugs. She'd see them in almost any place she looked, but the infestation seemed to be coming from between the tiles in the bathroom floor. She could scrub them out, but they always came back.

Lewis, not being entirely self-absorbed, began to notice odd things going on with this girl, this wonderful girl who he loved so much. He knew that he wasn't spending much time with her, wasn't paying the kind of attention to her that he knew he should, could still see the changes in her, the weight loss, the dark shadows beneath her beautiful blue eyes, the Goddamn *twitchiness* that was diving him crazy. But he had to try to ignore it, as much as possible. His coursework was much more demanding than he had expected, and, after all, he was doing this for both of them. They were both pretty stressed.

His initial response was far from guilt, or empathy, or sympathy when, coming home quite late from an afternoon and an evening spent at the library, he found Chrissie, sweaty and naked, scrubbing doggedly at the grout between the beautiful black and white tiles in the bathroom floor. The needle marks on her left arm stood out very red on her white skin. Arrayed around her were cotton swabs, bleach, ammonia, and paper towels, to supplement the worn toothbrush she was using as her primary weapon. She looked up at Lewis with pupils so dilated that almost none of the lovely arctic blue of her eyes was visible. She was trying to smile her sexiest smile, while grinding her teeth with diligence.

As Lewis stared at her, saying her name again and again, she was trying to think of something nice and loving and reasonable to say to explain what she was doing, naked and insane on her hands and knees on the bathroom floor at ten o'clock at night. When she realized that the looks passing over his face were not affection or amusement, but shock and disgust, she didn't really understand. As he turned and left, slamming the bathroom door behind him, she began to realize that things probably looked odd, as Lewis, of course, might not have noticed the bugs.

If she hadn't had so fucking many tiles still to do, that just had to be done (or the bugs that she kept seeing might come back, and once they burrowed under her skin, they were much harder to get rid of), she would have pulled some clothes on and gone to talk to Lewis, because, honestly, she was starting to feel like things were really slipping out of her control, and if she were honest, Lewis would certainly help her. But, she didn't, not that day, not for several days.

When she finally did speak to him, he didn't seem at all as if he wanted to help her. Of course, she couldn't get him to understand about the bugs, not really. Nor did he really understand why she pretty much had to shoot the speed. He looked sad, in a pissed-off way, and explained to her, slowly, that this was grad student housing that they were living in, and he was the grad student, and responsible — financially and legally — for what went on in the housing. It seemed to him — and he said he imagined that she'd probably agree — that inappropriate things were going on, and that she was a big part of the problem. So, he told her gently, she would have to leave — right now — and did she have a place she could go? He handed her an envelope with two hundred dollars in it, he said, so that if she needed to, she could stay in a hotel for a few nights, or she could go right to the airport, and perhaps go stay at her mother's place for a while. He told her he really cared about her, and really wanted her to get better, but she had to go somewhere else to do that. He helped her pack — mostly to make certain that she did pack, rather than getting sidetracked, and deciding to brush the lint out of her sweaters — and she was out the door within 15 or 20 minutes.

Lewis felt awful and rotten and devastatingly sad about the whole thing, but the Super had taken him aside weeks ago, and spoken to him about the strange people — drug addicts, he thought — going in and out of the apartment when Lewis wasn't home. And as Lewis hadn't done anything about it — what could he do? — his Advisor, and then the Dean of his department had spoken to him, and being, for academics, straight-shooters, told him that the problem could go away, or he could go away, and they'd prefer the former solution, but would settle for either. Lewis had not really been left a choice.

It was in February — gray and raw, but not bitterly cold — when Chrissie left. Lewis didn't check up on her: he was afraid he'd crumble, and throw away his life to try to help someone who wasn't ready to change. He had a good idea where she was, and it wasn't home with her mother, as her mother called Lewis every few days, seeking information, looking for support, hoping for words of hope. Chrissie called Lewis, too, a few times, to try to explain things, to ask for non-specific help, to tell him that she was sorry, that she loved him, that if he'd let her come back, she'd change. Lewis knew that she wouldn't change because she couldn't change, not yet. He knew that she wasn't telling him the truth. He hung up the receiver each time, with tears in his eyes, and what felt like a hole in his heart.

It looked to Lewis as if the late winter would be even more depressing than usual, despite his progress with school. He was looking forward to wrapping up his Masters, and was leaning toward going on for his Doctorate. The academic world was easier to fall into than to get out of, but it seemed like a good and reasonable and safe place to be, for now. The Draft Board would be more than happy to send him a cheery postcard that required him to report at some place he didn't want to be, to prepare him for a place he wanted to be even less, if he was stupid enough to let his student deferment lapse.

On the second Saturday of March, not spring, but almost spring-like, the temperature was in the 50's, the wind still bit, but the sun was very strong. If you found a place out of the wind, and in the full sun, it almost gave you reason to live. A good and high mood had begun to spread all through the student ghetto, which was all of Boston and Cambridge, except for the very good or very bad parts. It infected Lewis as he lay in bed, reading and making notes. He made an executive decision to trade a twelve hour library drudgery-day, making the final, final, final changes to his thesis, for a brave search for breakfast, beer, companionship, and good feelings.

Some minimal grooming might be needed: the line between student and wino could be thin in the eyes of a cop in a bad mood. Lewis went to the not-so-clean bathroom sink, and splashed cold water on his face and head, then combed his shoulder-length hair back and peered at himself. The stubble on his chin was hardly noticeable, so he passed up the chance to shave, and brushed his teeth. A fairly clean shirt, a pair of less-clean Levi's, a light wool crewneck sweater, and a ratty tweed sport coat seemed enough for such a fine day. He slipped his loafers on his sockless feet, in deference to the season, and to a lack of socks, and went out the door and down the stairs to the street, bare of snow and ice, but covered with sand, salt, small bits of wind-borne trash, and the broken green glass indicative of someone's good taste in beer or ale.

Half a block, then a left. Another block, and around the corner to the sunny side of Comm Ave, smack in the middle of the student section of the Avenue — everything, really, from Kenmore Square to Chestnut Hill. The Avenue below the square to the park was beautiful, but was not for students. They couldn't afford to live there, and it was too far from the schools, the bars, the bookstores, the greasy spoons. Where Lewis walked now, half a dozen diners and the like offered two eggs, bacon or sausage, home fries, toast and coffee, all for less than two bucks — with tip! There seemed to be a constant price-war, so the toll could dip as low as a buck-nineteen. One desperate rebel put up a sign offering the standard greasy breakfast for ninety-nine cents — the sign was down an hour later, possibly after his brother restaurateurs spoke to him regarding the gentleman's agreement that governed all their prices, and the unpleasantness that could be visited upon those who strayed.

Lewis ducked into his usual place, a clean and wholesome joint, run by a violent but never profane Greek who looked to be about sixty years old, and had, as long as anyone remembered, looked exactly the same. He seemed to like the students and took good care of them, as long as it didn't involve extending credit, and as long as they watched their language in front of the waitresses, all of whom were his daughters, or wives, or nieces.

The place was packed with sorrowfully hung-over undergrads, a few winos (of the better-behaved sort), and a few cops (of the corpulent and hungry sort, none of whom would pay one cent for the vast meals that they consumed). Lewis walked past them all, headed for his usual seat, a dark and tiny booth across from the far end of the counter. After the booth, there was the cigarette machine, the phone booth, and, finally, the restrooms. Proximity to the toilet could be critical when eating food as greasy as the breakfasts that were served here. Until the customer developed some tolerance, the food could prompt sudden, violent, bowel spasms, the sort that gives a ten-second warning. Not everyone made it within the allotted time.

In that almost no one — other than Lewis and his inner circle — ever sat in the tiny booth, probably because they didn't know it was there, he swung around the corner without looking, and emitted a faint, startled scream when his ass encountered not the suspiciously sticky red vinyl bench cushion, but the lap of a petite young woman, who then screamed, too, but not at all faintly. Lewis, lapsing toward panic, was about to scream even louder when it came to him, suddenly, that he knew the girl he had sat upon and scared witless. He turned the emerging scream into a query, and hoped that would forestall her next scream, which he could see building.

"Judy…? Is that you I'm sitting on?"

"Lew — I should have known — get the fuck *off* me!" she squeaked, as short of breath as any small person being sat upon might be, but not in a truly unkind squeak.

He grabbed the table, and pulled himself up and forward, while the girl extricated herself from under his not small carcass. She slid a foot or two down the bench, letting Lewis have room to sit next to her. They spent a moment regarding each other in silence, then began to talk at the same instant, which quickly devolved into laughter, and many verbal replays of the incident, and finally, breakfast and small-talk. They had gone out a few years back, when he was a sophomore and she a freshman. They had even slept together once, they thought, but apparently both had other things going on, and just didn't get interested enough for an encore.

An hour or so later, they left the restaurant together, and found opportunities to see each other quite a bit, and then exclusively. They turned out to be a good solid couple until they weren't any longer, but that was years away. Lewis not only loved Judy: he loved it that he didn't have to think about Chrissie anymore. When he had thought of Chrissie, he was almost overcome with feelings of guilt, so he made an effort to not think of her at all. He had always been good at forgetting people, places, and things, and got better at it every day.

Day 14

As Lewis came to life on the day he had, with fear and misgiving, promised to go and meet with Doc at Doc's motel/inn on the other side of the island (and technically, in another country — did that matter?) he felt suddenly unstoned, unstrung, unready. He was sweating freely, but not in a healthy way. He could hear and feel that his heartbeat was too fast, and maybe a bit off cadence.

He wasn't so clear on lots of things, such as the day of the week, the time. His wristwatch could have told him, if he had his glasses on, and if he had the right light, and held the watch just so, so that the liberally scratched and clouded crystal let him peer through. Anyone who could afford one would have bought a new watch, or at least a new crystal, except the man who owned the watch. He wasn't often desperate to know the day, the time, as he got older: it was just a fucking countdown to slow rot, or fast explosion. This all ran through his unstoned, unstrung brain at once, and life was looking all fucked up and hopeless. Then, he noticed his painful, swollen, bandaged arm, and it all came back to him, with the hopelessness edging away.

Despite a scary appointment pending with a man who had been thought dead, Lewis, was the new and proud owner of a respectable collection of narcotic analgesics and the nasty and addictive benzodiazepines to make it all hum pleasantly. The relative importance of day and time began to fade. He could now get out of bed — carefully, not abusing his bad arm — make some coffee, take some pills, smoke a few cigarettes, and then and only then, devote some energy to figuring out what he would do, if anything, to prepare for his upcoming meeting with Doc.

The island was small. It would take less than half an hour to get to the planned meet. Not to his liking. Lewis was not the sort of man who jumped into things, especially scary things, or things that had no knowable agenda. Maybe Doc would kill him, he speculated. That might not be too bad, if it was fast. And, really, how many years was he losing? But Lewis thought it unlikely that Doc would kill him, much more likely — and perhaps more unpleasant — was that Lewis would be brought to task for some past sin that Lewis had, seemingly, forgotten so effectively that he had, truly, no inkling of what had transpired.

Had he, Lewis, tried to kill Doc? Had he and Doc tried to kill each other, or, perhaps, someone else? It almost had to be at that level of seriousness: after all, this crazed motherfucker, Doc, had been trailing him, sabotaging him, frightening him for days and days, maybe longer, and all over the place: Vermont, Boston, Arlington, the Caribbean. This was going to be impossible to prepare for. Lewis didn't have a gun with him, of course, and didn't imagine that it would be easy for a foreigner — him — to buy one on a resort island owned by two countries that seemed to have very un-American ideas about guns, that is, they didn't think that they should be simple to obtain, and didn't think that folks generally, should be walking around with guns. And he wouldn't have time to get one, anyway: he had promised Doc that he'd show up around noon. Island time, which would be between late morning and mid-afternoon. He might have time to buy a machete, as they appeared to be common. But then there were the etiquette issues incumbent in walking into a meeting with a machete.

After setting a pot of water to boil for his coffee, Lewis weaseled his brand new stash out of the pocket of the shorts he seemed to have been wearing since the afternoon of the previous day. He carefully deciphered the dosage instructions that the Doctor had written on each string of packets, and then quadrupled the dose, and lined the packets up on the small square of countertop next to the gas rings.

His arthritic fingers weren't up to the tearing open of small foil packets, so he tenderly slit the packets open with a dangerously dull paring knife from the flatware-and-everything-else drawer. He opened four of each, exactly four times the recommended dose, which was probably a laughably small amount. Probably, he hoped. After a moment of silent staring at the naked little tablets, he revised his guess, and put two of the Xanax tabs into the small plastic pill case he carried. He wanted to be super-calm, not comatose, and could always take the second two, if needed. The coffee was ready, so he poured some and took a sip to wet his mouth, then chewed up four Demerol and two Xanax with another steaming sip, and swallowed them with the third sip...

Lewis got dressed while finishing the small pot of coffee. Not much sense in a shave and a shower for him today — life was too uncertain, and he always felt less vulnerable if he wasn't excessively clean. The khakis he had worn on the flight down met the requirement, not dirty, yet, not clean, and slightly wrinkled — just as the wearer was. He found a short sleeved linen shirt with a collar, and pulled that on, too. A few brief ablutions, some moccasins, and he'd be ready.

This was going too fast. There weren't enough preparatory tasks to distract him from his concerns about this visit with his old *compadre*, who might not be his friend at all. He had so much time left. He could have a leisurely breakfast, read all of yesterday's New York Times, and allow the fear to totally paralyze him. He had to stop projecting the various disaster scenarios that flipped through his skull, a new one every minute, each at least as bad as the last, and even less likely to be true. Where was the Xanax when he needed it? He had taken it twenty minutes ago, and it should be kicking in by now.

The Gods in Charge of Anxiolytics had heard his doubt, his fear, and took a moment away from playing bridge to activate the drugs in Lewis's bloodstream. He started to feel the muffling pad of calm fall over his wildly misfiring synapses. He was relaxing, even feeling sleepy, as he brought his cigarettes and ashtray and a cold half-cup of coffee to the loveseat on the porch, it was already hot outside, but the porch caught every breeze. By the time he had smoked a few more cigarettes, and had finished his coffee, he was dead calm. He let his head, too heavy now, sink back on to the cushioned couch-back, and traveled not far, just from a warm nod to a cool light constant sleep.

The slam of the porch door at the cottage nearest his caused his eyes to snap open, startled. He looked at his watch, moving his wrist in the bright daylight now falling on him, until, behind the scratches and abrasions on the glass, he could just make out the time. He had slept too long, more than an hour, and left himself just enough time to get from the Club to the Coral Inn, where Doc was holed up. No time to waste, just time to get a cab. Perfect.

Rather than call the desk and ask them to get him a cab, a risky proposition, he pulled from his wallet the business card given to him by the driver that he and Marian, or whatever her name was, had used to go out the other night. The driver picked up his cell phone right away, and vowed to be in the Club's back parking lot in five minutes.

Lewis cursorily buffed his old tusks, took a leak, filled his pockets with the things he always carried, and walked out his door without giving a second thought to his pending meeting, He was thinking about his drug supply, which he had hidden far too cleverly. Would he be able to find it again?

More than any other feeling, he was now awash with excited curiosity. He was going to sit down with an old acquaintance, business partner, sometime friend, and perhaps have the opportunity to fill in some blanks, of which his past life was, mostly, comprised. This seemed more important to him now, as he was realizing, more each day, that the machine which had animated him all of these years was beginning to wear out, was slowing down.

He knew he had forgotten too well, and perhaps, perhaps, too much, as his trick to get through this life. Each man and woman, he knew, if they lived in the world at all, had a way to get to the end of the day without excessive discomfort. Some drank or shot dope, some fell in love and then fell in love again, some fought, and some surrendered. Lewis forgot.

From what he could guess, he was now being taken to task somehow, although why and how, he didn't know. He was being called on, he feared, to justify, to explain, past occurrences in which he had perhaps been involved. This was all great and reasonable in a metaphysical sense, he agreed, but the world he lived in was not that one. And, he had no ideas at all about what he might have done. He was increasingly hopeful that Doc, who was not a metaphysical guy either, or at least hadn't been, could fill in some of the blanks.

With these good thoughts, and a head full of good drugs and strong coffee, and the good and deadly majestic Caribbean sun almost at zenith, Lew was, and looked, happy and friendly when the talkative cheerful Rastafarian taxi man pulled into the dry dirt lot in a cloud of dust. The van's mellifluous horn played the opening bars of a famous Bob Marley song, as the taxi skidded to a stop a few inches from Lewis's feet. The driver jumped out gracefully, and slid the rear passenger door open, bidding Lewis to hop in, all of this done smiling and wordlessly on both of their parts.

Lewis swung up into the van with his good arm and accurately catapulted his bulk on to a seat on the other side. He then greeted the driver, gave his destination, and settled back to enjoy the ride, if he could, and the warm Demerol glow that now suffused his body — with the exception of his arm, which still hurt like hell. A downside of habitual narcotic use was its resulting lack of effectiveness on real pain — unless the dose was ratcheted up to a level that terrified most doctors.

The driver remained silent, listening to music at a low volume, and watched the road. The roads on the island were narrow, perhaps one and a half lanes, and could be occupied by almost anything, from a truck coming from the opposite direction, to a goat, or a child or a mob of the ubiquitous fowl that looked like chickens , but were not. Lewis was quite content to stare out of the windows at the dry and hilly landscape. He wondered again if Doc had plans to kill him, and decided that he probably didn't. There had been plenty of opportunities already, and not entailing the complications inherent in icing someone in a foreign country. And, what the hell — better to die at the end of a vacation than at the start of one. Plus, he'd had a pretty good run, as far as he could recall. He was ready to meet Doc, or if things went badly, Mamie Eisenhower. He couldn't imagine any kind of heaven without Mamie.

They had just crossed to the Dutch side of the island when Lewis noticed a massive, towering bank of dark clouds creeping toward them from behind, from the southeast. They didn't resemble the usual afternoon clouds, the ones that appeared almost every day this time of year. Those clouds caused a five or ten minute temperature drop and a gusty four-minute rainstorm. The clouds today seemed to have more serious intent.

The driver had noticed Lewis peering at the clouds, and glanced at them himself, turning his left-hand side view mirror up to reflect the sky behind them. He made a quick assessment of the obviously threatening cloudbank, and half-turned in his seat to fill Lewis in on the weather situation.

"It looks like we going to get a little bit of a blow — kind of unusual, this time of the year. We might get an hour, maybe more, of rain and wind, so, looks like a better day for shopping than the beach."

Lewis was grateful for the information, and let the driver know that… as well as taking the opportunity offered to set up as much of a getaway plan as he could.

"I'm going to visit for a bit with an old friend who's here, so, I don't mind the weather. Can I arrange to have you come and pick me up from right where you let me off? About one-fifteen would be perfect."

"Sure, Mon, I'll be right where you want me at one-fifteen."

Lewis slid two twenties from his thinning money clip, and handed them to the driver for the thirty-dollar fare that he owed. Then, he slipped two more twenties out, and held them out to the driver.

"Here's my return fare — I know I can trust you. I'm going into that room," he said, as he pointed out the door to the room Doc had said he would be waiting in. "…and, if I don't come out of that room when you come back, and knock on the door, I want you to go to the police — or call them, and tell them that something bad may have happened to me. Here's a card with my name on it, so they'll get it right: you need to give them the card. Will you do those things for me?"

The driver looked at Lewis searchingly, as if trying to figure out what sort of a game he might be playing. Was this something that might get him in trouble, or was it okay, the right thing to do, and a chance worth taking — especially for forty dollars U.S.? And after all, no one would be there to make him involve the police. It was never, ever a good idea to involve the police. He took the bills, thanked Lewis, and wished him good luck.

Pleasantly stoned now, almost pain-free in his bad arm, Lewis felt absolutely calm, absolutely ready to keep his appointment with the past-made-new, no matter what. He moved at his usual rolling gait up to the door, and knocked the same knock that he had used with friends or peers all of his life. Not very hard, but hard enough to produce more of a boom than a bang: "Boom — boom boom boom — boom boom."

Although he had expected the door to open slowly before he had finished knocking, it hadn't, nor had anything else happened. He heard no noise from inside. Lewis was raising his hand, about to knock again, when he thought he heard a toilet flush, and the sound of water running, and water splashing in a sink. No sound of footsteps, but the distinct sense of someone coming toward him. The door latch clicked, and the door swung open wide.

There stood Doc. Thinner, if possible, than Lewis remembered him, but otherwise, unchanged except for the paleness starkly visible under the tan on his face and neck and arms. And that resigned look in his eyes, announcing to all who could recognize it, "Yes — you're right, I have a real and evil sickness percolating away inside me, and nothing, not a fucking thing, can be done about it. It's slow, but it's thorough. Please, don't ask me how I feel — unless you want to hear that I feel like I'm dying."

"Lew, you old whore-dog! I didn't really think you'd show. You rarely do, you know. Come in, come in, and have a cold beer — you're still a drunkard, aren't you?"

"I take a drink, on occasion, Doc...and I see that you are not dead. And I wonder why you have, alive, been haunting me, about something or other. I showed up only to find out what it is that is causing this epidemic of stalking a poor, defenseless old writer."

He followed Doc into the small, motel-like room, Doc walking backwards, and talking. Doc backed up to a chair he could not see, and sat down at the small table in the kitchenette area. He reached under the counter, into a small fridge, and pulled out a cool bottle of Jamaican beer. His talking on the way into the room had amounted to snide pleasantries, which Lewis ignored, and he launched back into his suppressed soliloquy.

"This is driving me bug-fuck, you know...I don't know how much you have to do with it, but your re-emergence into my life, my world, at the same time that all of this other shit is happening, well, it can't all be coincidence, can it?"

Lew signaled that he was through talking by looking around for a bottle-opener. He found one securely screwed to the side of the countertop, as it should be, so, Lewis pried the cap off, up-ended the bottle, and reduced the volume of beer by a third. He looked at Doc, expectantly.

"Fair enough, Lew. I need to start back a bit earlier, though — about thirty years earlier. So, settle back, drink your beer — there are five more, if you need them and you will — have a smoke, and I'll try to give you all I know about this oddness...and why I've been looking for you — to talk to, just to talk to — for a few weeks now."

Lewis, through the usually sufficient muffler of the narcotics, the tranquilizers, the other things, and, mostly, his necessary indifference, felt the poisonous worm of fear take a first bite. Left alone, it would kill him, he believed. He had to retort.

"So, you're telling me it isn't coincidence. Okay. Then tell me: why me?"

Doc stretched his skinny bones, as if they all hurt, and stretching might, at least, rearrange the pain. His face said "Oh! Pain!" too, as clearly as if he had voiced it.

"Let's save time — short on the general, longer on specifics. I don't know just how much time I have, by the way, as I seem to have picked up 57 varieties of cancer, none of them good. And that has a lot to do with why this isn't, as you said, coincidental.

"You probably really haven't noticed, but everyone else — almost everyone who knows you — has noticed, this: you walk away from too many train wrecks, and you don't pull anyone else out. You get a nasty scratch on your forehead, enough for a good scar. They burn to death, they end up paraplegic, and they get *damaged*. You get *a story*. I could name all of the damaged people, and you probably couldn't, because you remember the story, but forget the casualties. And, most of the damaged ones — they don't even see this! They still love you, or at least don't hate you. So, that's the general argument for why I needed to talk to you. You look blank — do you have any fucking idea what I'm talking about?"

The fear worm may have understood, because the fear worm was working slowly up Lewis's spine, stopping only to bite, again. Lewis was less clear, and had to ask.

"So, what do you mean? Do you mean that I'm the cause of bad things happening? Because no one wants to blame God, or bad luck, or stupidity, or chance…so Doc says 'Let's blame Lewis!' For Christ's sake, Doc, I'm not God — or the Devil. Shit happens. You think I should try to remember ugly events, work up a nice case of PTSD? People should hate me because I'm a survivor?"

Doc stared at Lewis. Lewis didn't mistake the look for one of empathy, or of agreement. Doc stared for a full two minutes before he said, "Lew, you're not a survivor. The people who got slammed are survivors. You are an avoider, a forgetter, a deserter. Anyway, enough Big Picture talk — we could go on all day, except that I'd probably beat you to death before two o'clock.

"There is one more thing, I guess, though, on the macro side. All your old friends I guess they were friends — as far as I know, they're not doing great. I guess, maybe, Janey is doing okay, materially, but she picked up some virus from some take-home dick she snagged at a bar, and she's been dying by degrees for years, now. But, she has money, a couple of houses. Like you, Lew, like you. You've done alright for a half-assed drunken carpenter. Name, fame, nice kid, and enough money to come down here and hang around, nekkid, with the better sort. Why is that, do you suppose? Luck of the draw? God likes you better? Or, maybe, you're really quite good at taking advantage, at playing people, at coming out on the bright side? Opinions vary, but, not much."

Lewis was listening, and watching a couple of lizards that were loitering, twitching, on the screen of a skylight above and behind Doc's head. The lizards appeared not at all alert, and focused, if at all, upon each other. Lewis doubted that was true: he guessed that they were looking for flies by not looking.

Lewis's face was getting red, as it did when he drifted toward fury. He could not hold his tongue, and wasn't sure he should if he could. He ignited a cigarette, and said, "Excuse me, my old *compadre*, but what the fuck is going on? I'm in the market more for some explanation, from you, concerning you — and probably others — and your new hobby, to wit, stalking and harassing me. And my charming Ex. But, gee, I'm starting to think that I've walked into a fucking amateur theatre workshop presentation of an unknown Existential play by a deservedly unknown Existential playwright, possibly a play about a trial. Or, maybe you had just a little too much acid the last time you tripped, and this really *is* a trial you've cooked up to entertain and amaze your friends. Or simply lost your fucking mind because you have cancer, and you're dying, and you want to settle some scores. Which is pretty much what I think I'd do, in that situation, so, I don't really blame you, but this is getting pretty fucking boring? Why don't you hand me another beer, and allow me to say a word or two — in my defense, of course, as this is a trial, the how and why of it, for now, not clear to me...let me say a word, or two, about my charmed life.

"Let's see: old, fat, lonely, in constant pain for which I am over-medicated, so let's add 'addicted' to my meds, and on and off with alcohol. Ex-wife who wants to run my life, daughter who doesn't know I have a life, and an Editor who actually does run my life, but would rather not. One friend, who runs the general store, and probably doesn't know he's my only friend, because then I'd be his. Name and fame? Twenty years ago, yeah. Now I just wait for the day that I get the call: my writing is just not connecting with the magazines demographic, so they'd like to find a way to honor me right off the semi-glossy pages of a barely read magazine.

"Depressed when I'm not too anxious, and anxious about getting too depressed. When will I finally wake up dead, alone, cold on the floor of my luxurious house in the country? Because I'm waiting, and it is the reward I wait for. I don't think I'm a survivor, or a deserter. I'm just sitting here in the waiting room with everybody else...the difference being, I guess (literally) being that I can't fucking remember. Not friends, not enemies, not books I've read or girls, women that I've slept with. Not what I've done and not done. Am I guilty? I can't remember. If being guilty means that I consciously did wrong, don't I have to remember it, too? All life's left me is these fucking bits and pieces. If this is a trial, I'm hoping it will be informing for me. I'll plead guilty, if I get my life fed back to me, even just the few parts worth remembering.

"I posit that you aren't even charging me with being a coward, but with not caring enough to be frightened, sad, glad, mad or bad. You're charging me with, I think, with appearing to succeed by choosing another reality. If that is accurate, can I get a change of venue to the reality I inhabit?

"Oh — and I need another beer."

Before responding, Doc dredged a beer out of the fridge and handed it over, unopened, then extracted a plastic bag from the fridge, and began to roll a joint with some of the pot the bag held. He was fast, and as Lew was sitting down again after opening the beer, Doc was passing him a smoldering joint of impressive, if not Rasta-impressive, size.

"Have a toke — after that desperate tearjerker, you may need a refresher course on reality versus a different reality, and this *ganj* will do it quicker than most. And, we both could stand to relax…after all, this isn't about life and death, it's about blame, punishment, and maybe even redemption, although I kind of doubt the redemption part. I think I may have told you, years ago, and surely drunk, that my father was an Episcopal priest, leaving me with a high-end version of PK syndrome. I do remember his bit on redemption, though. He often said that only Green Stamps are truly redeemed, and that everything else was politics…I still don't know what it means, but it worked well at cocktail parties. And no change of venue. And you need to shut up and listen: I must bring some specific incidents to light. I'm sure you don't recall them: this is why.

"You think that your expertise in forgetting is a skill, a talent, a parlor trick. I think that's mostly true. I know you make a point of putting things out of your mind…everyone does it, to some extent, as a defense — and you do it a lot more than that. I say, great, whatever works. What you have failed to take into account is that, when you got whupped upside the head with the barrel of a Savage-Stevens double-barrel 12 gauge scattergun by a large, stupid, strong Italian guy, you undoubtedly suffered a concussion, certainly a little brain damage, and likely entered a period of several weeks to several months during which your swollen brain didn't work so well, and your recall suffered badly. It is a really good bet that for at least a couple of weeks after your injury, you have huge gaps in memory. Your mind made up stuff for 'filler,' but none of the filler ever happened.

"What did happen you can't remember — almost as if you were in a booze-induced blackout. So stuff happened — and you don't know about it.

For instance, when you tried to kill me. Or, actually, when someone, reputed to be you, took a couple of shots at someone they thought was me, tried to 'kill me.' That happened the day the deal went bad, just after sunup. Guy's name was Tommy, I think — looks a lot like me. Might have been shot: might have just been shot at. Do you remember how hard it is to hit anything with a pistol? As it happened, I took advantage of the story, got out of town with my cut of the money, and left behind all suspicion of me being the guy who set up the rip-off. And, I'm not sure you pulled the trigger, but lots of folks were, and are. Just one more thing to hate you for.

"You also don't recall, I bet, that you and I set up the rip-off. After it went down, I was supposed to be taken as a 'hostage' to keep the other guys quiet. You were supposed to get knocked out with a gun barrel — a pistol barrel is what we had in mind, and just hard enough to raise a lump. The idiots we hired to rip us off hit you so hard it almost killed you, maybe because they used a shotgun barrel. We ended up having to take you, too, so you didn't bleed to death there on the floor. You were in and out for a day: we got the bleeding to slow down, made sure you'd live, and dropped you back at the scene the next. You tried to kill 'me' a few days later, when you decided I was double-crossing you. But I was on the Coast already: the guy the goons picked up, at your request, was someone else.

"Didn't you think it a little strange when, on a day that you thought was only a few hours after the rip-off, people were treating you as a pariah? How would they get the news, or figure things out, so quickly? Easy answer: they didn't. You compressed several days into one, and got the sequence of events all fucked up. Nevertheless, you did intend to kill me, and may have killed someone else. You need to carry that, remember that. I do hold it against you, as you're the only person who has actually tried to kill me. I'm choosing to spend some of my time, before I check out, in paying some debts, collecting others. I've talked to some of the old crew, those who are alive and on the loose. They all agree. You stoned, yet?"

Lewis hadn't smoked pot much in recent years; the buzz wasn't what he wanted. The stuff that was around now was just too strong, all of it hide-under-the-bed level, Afghani buds. So, yes, he was stoned…and having heart palpitations, distorted vision, and in abject fear.

He was afraid to ask himself if it was going to get worse, when the door crashed open. Three guys, two of them younger guys and the third older, a short, round and powerfully built man with a deep tan. He was carrying the shotgun, and as he moved toward Lewis, swinging the long gun by the grip in an accelerating arc that would connect, almost perfectly, with the left side of Lewis's head, he grinned. Lewis saw the grin, and heard Doc say, quietly, "Motherfucker," and saw finally, and only now at full day and with sufficient light — for an instant — where he had been all this time — for an instant. Then all went red.

He thought he heard noises from time to time: a powerful engine, a surge and a lift. He knew nothing else for what seemed an eternity. It took years before he was able to write the story, and have it come out with him alive, and remembering every single second.